One Bronze Knuckle

by

Kenneth Hunter Gordon

LANTERNFISH PRESS

PHILADELPHIA

LANTERNFISH PRESS
399 Market St, Suite 360
Philadelphia, PA 19106
lantermfishpress.com

COVER ART
Design by TK

Printed in the United States of America.
Library of Congress Control Number: 2018958104
ISBN: 978-1-941360-25-5
Digital ISBN: 978-1-941360-24-8

TK Dedication

One Bronze Knuckle

or

The Exquisite Catastrophe of Love

being

A Novel
in fifteen parts
detailing the lives and adventures of
various disparate—not to say desperate—characters
making their way through a world no less topsy-turvy
than our own,
derived whenever possible from original and authentic sources,
here compiled and accompanied by such
explanatory notes and digressions
as are necessary for
complete understanding,
and presented
with all humility and gratitude

by

Kenneth Hunter Gordon

DON'T LOOK BACK, MY DARLINGS. The past rages at our heels even as the future rushes in like the tide. In a world as wide and strange as this, what are we poor wanderers to do but seek such shelter as we can find, with such companions as are willing to share our way? What recourse have we when confronted with such a vast tapestry but to pick out one thread to call our own and follow it through warp and woof as best we can?

That's Donatello, I think, or maybe Smith. I could be mistaken. But the point is the same, either way.

That is, every journey starts out meaning well enough but in no time winds up in a terrible snarl. It loops along happily for a time, making perfect sense, and then—just when you're feeling easy and breezy—you end up right back where you started. Or even further back, before anything has even begun. It's perfectly understandable that we might end up a little rattled before it's all over; no one in his right mind could begrudge us that. I mean, great heaven, just look at what we've been given to work with! Thimbles and turnips, bootstraps and boomerangs—all manner of falderal and nothing more than our wits to bind it all together.

And among all that—the yarns spun and the nuts cracked, the storms weathered and the afternoons dozed away—among it all, what should we hope to find? Something beautiful? Something true? We should be so lucky. The beech rattles her tales in the breeze and the swallow weaves her stories in the sky. What they mean is secret, secret even from me. But every word—my darlings, you may rely upon it—every word is true.

Part I

The Burgermeister's Nephews

→ ONE ←

ONCE UPON A TIME there was a city with seven bridges. The city was built on an island in the middle of a convenient river, and the bridges connected it with the mainland on either side: three on the west and four on the east. Roads unspooled from the bridges across the countryside in all directions, and the river itself stretched from the distant mountains to the distant sea, so from a certain point of view the city on the island was in the middle of everything.

On maps, it was shaped like a teardrop or a misshapen fig. The people who lived there called it simply "the island," and the city "the City." The City was very old and had had many names through the generations, all of which meant *island* or *city* in one language or another. You may call it "the City" in whatever language suits you, and you will be part of a proud and longstanding tradition.

All the bridges had names as well, and the citizens defined their neighborhoods by the nearest bridges. Old Bridge led directly to the Old Fort, the oldest building in the city, which had been converted to a dismal prison. The neighborhood surrounding the fort was a nondescript jumble of homes belonging to the usual sort of persons and the assortment of shops that served them. The rich people of the city, who of course were not usual in the slightest, lived on the north end of the island, the point of the teardrop or the stem of the fig, near New Bridge, High Bridge, and North Bridge. The poor who worked lived on the south end, in the Low Quarter, between Wood Bridge and Second Bridge. The poor who were artists lived around East Bridge, and the rich visited their cafes to hear their music and watch their antics.

The poorest of the poor, though, those who couldn't—or wouldn't—find work, lived under the bridges, both on the island and on the river's outer banks: seven bridges with fourteen little villages underneath, hidden from the rest of the city.

A rocky hill rose in the middle of the island, and on top of the hill was New House, the home of the mayor, who had been elected for life from the ranks of the most prosperous citizens. The mayor oversaw all the official business of the City, and his officers were always present in the streets, attentive to the discharge of their duties. Each bridge had a mayor as well, of course, beyond the reach of the officers, whose task it was to settle disputes among the ragged families and tramps who made their homes among the piles.

Now. I have told you all of that so I may tell you this: Outside the city, at a distance of three days' travel, was a town of considerable size, ruled by a man who had elected himself to office and who called himself the Burgermeister. Despite the Germanic ring, this was not in the vicinity of the Rhinescholtz, and the Burgermeister didn't know a strudel from a knockwurst. He simply liked the sound of the title, thinking it had a certain grandness to it, and that was, as they say in certain circles, that.

His name was Jonathan Berger, and the town was called Bergerton after his great-grandfather, who had caused the town to be founded at that particular crossroads by capsizing his donkey while on a journey and refusing to move another mile for the rest of his life. His wife and children built a house around him, and in time a town grew up around the house.

Eighty years later, another Jonathan Berger—his great-grand-father's namesake—proclaimed himself Burgermeister Berger and proceeded to lead the town to greatness. Bergerton was surrounded by farms and villages and hamlets, which sent their produce and wares to the town and then on to the City. The City thus got what it needed in the way of apples and turnips, and the Burgermeister grew rich from his place in the middle of that endless stream of merchandise, just as the City grew rich from its place in the middle of the river.

At the frayed edges of the district, two days' travel or more past Bergerton, where the poorest farms faded into the wooded wilderness that surrounds us all, was a tiny hamlet called Wat's Hump. Beyond that was the last farm, and at the edge of the last farm's last field was a haystack where two boys sat huddled in the late afternoon, trying to figure out what to do. One was soaking wet. The other was dry and dusty, with horse dung in his hair. The wet one shivered, and the one with dirty hair spoke.

"We gone the wrong way. Nothing past here but trees and rocks. We gone the wrong way."

You will need to know that these boys were the nephews of the Burgermeister, one the son of his brother and one the son of his sister, and that they had run away from Bergerton. Later on you will need to know why, but for now it is sufficient that you know the older (by four months), dry, dirty boy was named Cordage Broome, and that the younger, wet, shivering boy was called simply Robert, having left his last name behind in the town. It was the same last name as the Burgermeister's, and Cordage thought it prudent, for reasons that will later become clear, that Robert release it to its own destiny.

Cordage was so named by his father, who had married the Burgermeister's sister. Mr. Broome was a dealer in rope and string, a good-natured tippler who thought when his wife became great with child that her expanding stomach resembled nothing so much as a giant ball of twine under her dress.

"Cordage, by thunder!" he had declared, rubbing her belly enthusiastically. "We'll name the little lump Cordage!"

The sign for his shop read "Nicolas Broome, Cordage," and before long he had painted "& Son" so the sign would read "Nicolas Broome and Son, Cordage." He was so delighted by his joke that he began laughing, was unable to stop, and after some months had to be sent to a lunatic asylum in the City. So Mrs. Broome and little Cordage moved into Uncle Burgermeister's house and things went uneventfully for Cordage until he was, oh, nine or ten years old and decided (for reasons that, again, will become clear later) to run away with his cousin Robert, leaving Robert's last name in the dust and winding up lost, grimy and pungent, in a haystack at the edge of civilization.

Robert was wet because he had fallen in the duck pond, just as Cordage had landed in the mule paddock, having been thrown out of the inn at Wat's Hump when the innkeeper discovered they had no money to pay for their porridge.

"Rascals!" he cried, and he tossed them out windows at opposite ends of the tiny hut that passed for an inn in those parts at that time.

This was immediately after the witch had foretold their doom: that one of them would end up living in New House in the City and the other would end up living under a bridge in the same City. They sat in the haystack considering this fate. They didn't know which was which, because the witch didn't know, and she had been silenced before she could complete her dark prognostications. Neither do we know at this time which will live in New House and which will live under a bridge. That it will become clear in time we can only hope.

I should explain that I know about the episode at the inn, the window out-throwing and the business with the witch, because I was there. In fact, the witch who was able to get only halfway through the prophecy before being summarily silenced was none other than me, myself. It may surprise you, but it should not. I have been and done many things—at that time I was a witch and that is all you need to know about it.

In any event, sitting at the inn, enjoying a cider of my own, I saw these two road-weary boys eating bowls of porridge. Bedraggled as they were, they were better dressed than the rest of the clientele, and I was taken with the sudden, familiar feeling of prophecy. I approached the boys and offered to reveal their future—both their futures, in fact—for a single bronze knuckle, half the going rate. (A bronze knuckle, you will remember, is a small coin which at the time was worth a round bun in the City, or two apples in the town, or two bowls of porridge at an inn in the country. Or a mug of cider, coincidentally.) In any event, the boys were intrigued by my offer and after some childish bickering produced a knuckle, an old and dingy and badly scratched one, but sufficient to the purpose.

I told them what I have already told you, that one would live here and the other there, and was about to continue when the older boy (only by four months, but older nonetheless) said, "Balderdash!" and shut me up like a clam.

He no doubt thought, as most do, that the word was a simple expression of disbelief. But it is in fact a powerful magic word that will stop any prognosticator in her—in this case my—tracks. So, none of us learned the rest of the prophecy, and neither will you, at this time. I kept the knuckle, of course. I couldn't have known it was the poor boys' last coin, but being shut up like a clam is an uncomfortable circumstance at the best of times. The knuckle was little enough payment for my troubles. As it was, I would be unable to speak another word of prophecy to either of them until what I had already said came to pass.

Balderdash: a powerful word with far-reaching and mysterious effects. You would do well to remember this word and use it sparingly, if at all.

⇀ TwO ↽

"I AIN'T GONNA LIVE under no bridge," Cordage muttered. He brushed horse manure out of his hair.

"What are you worried about?" Robert shivered. "Was she even a real witch?"

"I *ain't*," Cordage said, "gonna *live* under no *bridge*!" He paused. "Get rid of that stupid duck."

Robert shook his head. "No, he's mine. He followed me out of the pond." He tightened his arms around the plump, white bird and shivered again.

"That don't mean nothing," said Cordage. "Ducks will follow anybody. Like a sheep does. Ducks are the sheep of the bird world." He scowled and flopped backwards into the haystack. "Besides, that's a girl duck, anyway. The white ones are girls and the brown ones are the boys."

Robert shook his head again and then shivered as a fresh trickle of water ran from his hair down his spine. "I fell on him and he followed me out of the pond and he's mine and I'm gonna keep him."

"Fine," said Cordage.

"Fine," said Robert.

"*Fine*," said Cordage.

"I don't think she was a real witch."

"That duck smells."

"*You* smell. Like horse poo."

Both points were apparently irrefutable, and the boys were silent for a time.

"So now what?" said Robert.

"I'm gonna find that witch and get our knuckle back."

"It was *my* knuckle."

"I'm gonna get it back."

"I'm not going back. If we go back, that innkeeper will take my duck."

"Stupid duck," Cordage snorted. "Stupid witch."

The duck quacked softly as the light began to fade.

→ Three ←

I F I HAVE NEGLECTED until now to tell you about the duck, it is only because, in my experience, ducks are easily overlooked. And in truth, I didn't learn about it myself until later. After the boys were thrown out their respective windows, I sat in the half-light of the inn and kept my thoughts to myself. The *balderdash* episode had put a damper on my mood, so I finished my cider in silence, paid my fare with a knuckle I happened to have handy, and headed home. It would soon grow dark and the cabbages needed hoeing.

I was thusly engaged when the two of them happened along the lane that leads past my little home. The taller one—they were both rather short—called out to me, interrupting my solitary, cabbage-hoeing reverie.

"You! Witch! You owe us a knuckle."

I confess it was a moment before I recognized them. Such is the power of The Balderdash that the encounter had been nearly erased from my memory. They were, on the whole, an unremarkable pair of boys. The duck, moreover, confused the matter.

"Do I look like a witch?" I said. "Do I have a witch's hat on my head? In fact, I do not. I am not your witch."

"You *are* our witch! Go get your hat and put it back on and give us our knuckle!"

At the mention of the knuckle, the whole unfortunate event came rushing back. If I had known—if I'd had even the tiniest inkling—what the ensuing exchange would cost me in time and worry, I would have stopped it right there and sent the boys on their way with a short word and a swift boot. But alas, I let my argumentative nature get the better of me—not for the first time, mind you, nor the last—and set my hoe aside in order to address them more directly.

"First. It is not your knuckle, it's mine. You traded it to me fair and square for a genuine glimpse into your futures. Second, it's not mine anymore, either. I paid it to the innkeeper for a passable mug of cider. So the knuckle is gone, on its way, fulfilling its destiny as an agent of commerce. Good day." I picked up my hoe and returned my attention to the cabbages.

"But you didn't give us the whole thing! You stopped in the middle!" I think the damp one with the duck said that, but the light was dim and made the details tricky.

"No, *you* stopped me in the middle with your cursed curse. Besides, I was giving you two prophecies, one for each of you, so you really got two halves, which is the same as one whole one, so we're even." I turned and headed toward my little hut. Clearly, the cabbages would have to wait.

They straggled along behind me, variously whining and quacking and complaining.

"No, we're not even," said the dry boy. "Tell us the rest or give us half a knuckle."

Alas, I could do neither. It is common knowledge that one can't continue with a truncated prophecy until the parts already revealed have come to pass. Besides, as I have already explained, the knuckle was out of my hands. Yet they pestered me all the way back to my humble home, completely unwilling to accept the plain truth of the matter. Finally, to get them to be quiet, I offered them some cabbage stew and a place by the fire for the night.

The dry, smelly one was disinclined, but the damp one seemed eager for the opportunity to stop shivering. So in the end we had a wholesome, if somewhat bland, supper, and they fell asleep straightaway, curled up like puppies by the fire. They were so endearing it was almost painful for me to go through their pockets as they slept.

I might have saved myself the trouble. Between the two of them they had nothing but a rusty knife and some bits of string. So, rather than light my last candle, I decided to retire myself. It's a wonder I got any sleep at all, though, what with the boys snoring on the floor and that duck quacking outside the door.

* * *

→ FOUR ←

THE BURGERMEISTER RULED the little town of Bergerton benevolently for many uneventful years, happily oblivious to impending catastrophe. Upon the eve of this story, he was an old man, even by my standards, and to many in the town it seemed as if he would preside forever from the big house on the north side of the square. Indeed, he had been entrenched there for so long that most residents scarcely gave him a thought. As long as they didn't engage in any unauthorized business or cause any trouble they could live their lives quietly and securely in the tidy stone cottages that lined the narrow streets, tending their private fires without any idea how diligently their Burgermeister cared for the order of their lives.

He managed the affairs of the town like an invisible puppeteer, twitching the strings so subtly that for the most part his puppets thought they did everything they did by their own design. He sat at his desk and reviewed the papers brought to him by the councilmen. Some he signed; some he edited and then signed; some he refused. By these strokes of his pen the town thrived, balanced on the road between the farmland and the City. It was, he admitted to himself, an entirely satisfactory life.

In all those years he had managed to assemble, in addition to a town, a family that the house, big though it was, could hardly contain. The members of his household were, he sometimes complained, less inclined than the rest of the town to see the wisdom behind his managerial impulses. That is, they did what they pleased whether he signed their papers or not. His daughter, in fact, was the acting mistress of the house and he was himself cautious about crossing her purposes. He also had sons, two large, handsome ones, who spent money as fast as they could get it from him, along with two nephews (yes, *those* nephews) and a granddaughter who, as far as he could tell, did nothing but run up and down the stairs and slam doors all day. Add to that the nephews' mothers and an assortment of household staff—and perhaps others he couldn't bring to mind at the moment—and, well, one could perhaps forgive him for preferring management of the town over trying to make heads or tails of his own house. "A man's life is his work," he might have said, if he had come across the sentiment in a book of platitudes. He had, you might as well know, no gift for coming up with platitudes of his own.

So the town, which he had inherited from his father, occupied all his occupation. He managed the managers and handled the handlers and dealt with the dealers and was prepared to do so forever. He seldom stopped to think about it—in fact, he made a point of not thinking about it—but back in one of the dark pigeon-holes of his mind was the thought that eventually the day would come when no more days would come, and then the town would fall to his sons, and *then* what? They meant well enough, he supposed, but they could barely match their own stockings, let alone manage a whole town. No doubt inertia and equilibrium would keep things going for a time. No doubt the councilmen would attempt to keep signing and editing and refusing papers in the same manner as he himself had done. But eventually, probably sooner rather than later, things would become unbalanced and spin out of control. Life in the town would become chaotic and uncomfortable, and what would become of his puppets then? They would be lost and confused, and they would likely blame him in his grave for not providing for them in his absence. The thought that he would be remembered after his demise with anything other than unreserved gratitude was unbearable.

So, tentatively, almost cringingly, he prepared to begin molding his sons into the leaders of men that surely lay just beneath their slovenly surfaces.

They responded by taking up arms and marching off to war. (Quite literally. That is not a metaphor. Then as now, there was always a war somewhere, and they were not the first to disappear into that wild adventure, nor will they be the last.)

The disquiet he felt at their departure was partly offset by the relief to his pocketbook, and it was with this ambivalent perspective that he began casting about for another candidate—a successive successor, if you will.

He was left with one of his own children at home: his daughter, Margarita—also called Maggie. She was older and considerably more competent than the boys, with the added bonus that she already believed herself to be in charge of the whole town. But, fond and frightened of her though he was, the Burgermeister suspected there was little chance she would accept his instruction on the finer points of paper-refusal.

He briefly considered his nephews, whom you have already met—but they were only children and difficult to locate when one really needed them.

Which left the Princess, whom you will meet by and by, who was his only grandchild (to date) and the apple of his eye. She was thirteen years old, give or take, but in her the Burgermeister saw the sapling he could train into the tree that would support his legacy. She was intelligent but without cunning or guile, pretty enough but no great beauty, and thrifty (within reason) She would in all likelihood grow out of the rambunctiousness that currently engulfed the house. Well, all right, not really so thrifty as all that—but such things could be learned, could they not?

So pleased with this decision was he that he immediately made a note to remind himself to draft a list of items to discuss with his granddaughter at the nearest opportunity.

What strange lines are drawn for us by fate! A manifold calamity lurked in the wings at the end of that summer, but the Burgermeister, lulled into complacency by decades of self satisfaction, proceeded to pass over the note in favor of more urgent matters on a daily basis.

Some months later, though, he had finally very nearly decided to start the actual list and had even selected a piece of paper. But too late! A swirl of events unfolded that knocked the entire town on its ear. This general disruption was felt by all and resulted in many curious things. First: his nephews sleeping, damp and smelly, on my hearth. Second: wild fluctuations in the prices of certain agricultural products. And third: himself, the Burgermeister, immobile at his desk while a stack of papers grew past the top of his brandy glass, stricken to his core by terrible news—there would be no list, for there was no longer a granddaughter.

⇥ FIVE ↤

THEY SLEPT LIKE STONES, the boys did, scarcely moving until dawn broke and I rose to make breakfast. I looked through the cupboard, finding only the stale heel of yesterday's loaf. The boy with the dirty hair, who'd been dry the night before, woke up and noticed the knife and string and whatnot lying on the floor next to him.

"Why is all my stuff here?"

"You tossed and turned all night. It fell out of your pockets. You should learn to sleep more soundly—and you need to wash your hair. Go outside and dunk your head in the goat trough, and make your duck be quiet while you're at it."

He stood up, scratching and yawning. "Ain't my duck," he said. The other boy was still asleep. The scratching boy nudged him with his foot. "Hey! Go shut up your duck!"

The younger boy moaned and rolled over onto his stomach.

"It's his duck," said the scratching one, shoving his belongings back into his pockets. He opened the door and went out into the early light. "Shut *up*, you duck!"

The sound of splashing and gurgling came from outside. I poked the sleeping boy, whose dampness seemed to have resolved itself, with my stick until he rolled over and sat up blinking.

"Good morning," I said.

"Hullo," he said, rubbing his eyes.

The other boy stuck his head in the door and pushed his dripping hair out of his eyes.

"Hey," he said. "You should come take a look at this."

Outside, we saw the duck standing in the yard, staring at a white object lying on a tuft of grass.

"Look!" said the still sleepy, formerly damp boy. "Clarence found an egg."

The duck quacked, but whether it was addressing us or the egg I couldn't tell.

The formerly dirty, newly damp boy addressed the duck. "It's an egg, stupid. You're supposed to sit on it."

"No, only girl ducks sit on eggs," said the other. "Clarence is a boy."

The duck quacked, perhaps in agreement. The early hour made it hard to tell.

"Well, you sit on it then."

More quacking from the duck. What do ducks mean by quacking all the time? Do they not understand that every sound they make sounds exactly the same? That they could say all they have to say by quacking once and then remaining silent for the rest of their lives?

The conversation was clearly going nowhere, so I picked up the egg and took it inside, followed by the boys and the duck. I put it in a bowl on the table.

"It will be safe there," I said. "No one will sit on it in here."

"Then how will it turn into a baby duck?"

How indeed?

The duck settled down on the hearth and tucked its beak under its wing.

"Boys," I said. "Boys, boys, boys. It's clear we will not get far until some things are firmly established. For example, how shall I tell you apart? When you showed up last night, one of you was wet and the other one smelled. Now the one who was dry is wet and the one who was wet is smelly. I'm an old woman. I can't be expected to manage this way. I must have names for you if we are expected to accomplish anything at all."

The newly wet one eyed me cynically, but the younger, pudgier, smelly, formerly damp one piped up.

"I'm Robert," he said. "And this is Cordage. We're cousins." He pointed at the duck. "And this is Clarence."

"Yes, the duck I've met," I said.

"What about you?" said Cordage. "What do we call you?"

I sat back in my chair and considered carefully. "I've been called many things in my years. In the village they have taken to calling me Mrs. Bones. I'm not sure I'm very fond of that, but I suppose it will do for now. You may call me Mrs. Bones."

19

"That seems pretty formal," said Cordage, "for a witch."

"As it should," I replied. "'Formality is the soul of civility.' That's Groosemann." I lit my pipe. "Now, tell me about yourselves. Where you're from, where you're going. Last names, if you have them."

"No last names," said Cordage. "We left them behind."

"Fair enough," I said. "No last names for you, no first name for me."

"We're from Bergerton and we're going to the City," said Robert brightly. "We ran away!"

Cordage elbowed him. "We didn't run away," he said. "We're just traveling."

"You went the wrong way," I said.

"Can you help us?" Robert asked.

"We don't need no help," said Cordage. "We got everything we need."

"We don't have anything except some string and Uncle's knife. We already lost my lucky knuckle. We don't have anything."

Robert sat down heavily on the floor. He picked up the duck and held it in his lap.

"Interesting," I said, regarding them carefully. "So what I know about you is that you have run away, leaving your names behind in Bergerton—no doubt to avoid some trouble about which I hope never to learn—and you have gone exactly the wrong way trying to get to the City, now winding up here on my little farm, wet and smelly and probably hungry as well."

Robert nodded morosely. Cordage glared at me.

"What you need to know about me," I continued, "is that this is my farm, and onions and cabbages don't weed themselves."

"But can you help us?" Robert asked again. His voice had a

slight whining quality. And Cordage's sneer was most unbecoming. Neither of the boys was very appealing, to be honest.

"Go out and weed the onion patch and let me think about it." I broke the heel of stale bread in half and handed it to them. "The tools are behind the house."

They left, followed by the duck.

I watched them leave, then looked at the egg, still sitting in the bowl on the table. I contemplated its fate briefly before stoking the fire and fetching my favorite skillet.

⇥ Six ↤

THE BOYS CAME BACK two hours later, grimy and sweating.

"I'm telling you," said Cordage to Robert, "you don't know the difference between a onion and a weed."

"They all look the same to me," said Robert. He came over to where I sat at the table, hunched over the cards.

"Where's the egg?" he asked.

"Resting comfortably," I said.

"What are you doing?"

"I tried the dice. I tried the bones. I tried the crystal. The cards are my last resort."

"For what?"

"I'm trying to read my future, but it's no use." I pointed the stem of my pipe at Cordage. "Your cursed curse has blinded me to your fates, no matter what I try."

"Oh, balderdash!"

"Stop saying that!" I said. "You have no idea the power that word holds!"

He rolled his eyes and sat down heavily on the corner of the wood box.

"And since I can also not see my own future, that can only mean our fates are somehow entwined," I continued. "Most uncomfortable."

"How do these cards work?" Robert looked over my shoulder, holding his duck. "The Vagabond fortune tellers use cards with pictures, but these are just regular cards, like when our uncle loses money to the butcher."

I continued gazing at the cards while I answered. "Any card can mean something, if one is lucky, and if one has the sight." I put a red six on a black seven. It said nothing to me. "*And*, if the inner voice has not been silenced." I gave Cordage my best fierce glance.

He shrugged. "All right, that's fine, or terrible, or whatever," he said, "but can you help us now? We weeded the whole onion patch. Robert pulled some onions up, but we might have put them back."

I considered the two of them. Managing children is not what you might call my greatest talent, so the matter demanded careful attention. How much would they eat? How much work were they prepared to do? How much would they complain in the meantime? I prefer not to be rushed through decisions with potentially disastrous financial implications, but in this case the solution was obvious.

"Boys," I said, "I have decided to help you on your way." I fetched a burlap sack and handed it to Cordage. "You can take two cabbages and a few onions. There is a path through the woods that will lead you around Bergerton and on to the City, if that is where your fates take you and if you don't get lost or eaten by bears." I led them outside and around to the side of the house, where I pointed to the trees at the edge of the fields. "There's a little path back there that leads into the woods, used only by goats and by those that wish to travel quietly. The other path, the main path, goes back to the village, so—"

Gazing back up the more well-traveled path, I saw our mutual friend the innkeeper, perhaps a quarter mile away, at the head of a dozen or so stern-looking villagers. They were working at fording a stream, which was doing little to lighten their mood. Some of them had sticks.

I have led a long and complicated life. I have seen many places and dealt with a multitude of circumstances. Oh, yes, I have seen many things in my time, and one of the things I have seen more than once is a crowd of people stomping toward my house. Experience has shown that, unless it is my birthday, the intent of the crowd is not to wish me good day and inquire about the health of my cabbages. The secret to my success in this tumultuous existence has been flexibility. Why stick doggedly to a plan once circumstances have changed? In fact, that day was not my birthday, and I suddenly felt that a change of scenery would be just the thing to liven up my autumn.

"Boys," I said, "I have decided to show you the way myself. Back in! Back in the house! Back, back, back, back, back."

I herded them in and bolted the door, quickly bundled some things in a blanket, and handed it to Cordage. I gave the other blanket to Robert and put the stewpot on his head, then grabbed my stick and my traveling hat and climbed out the back window.

"Fine morning," I said brightly. "Perfect for a brisk walk through the fields."

One of them blinked at me stupidly and the other squinted.

"Well, come on, then," I urged them. "Let's not dilly dally!"

"The window? Really?"

23

Another time I might have congratulated Cordage on his cynicism, which would obviously take him far. But at the moment, time was of the essence, as they say.

"It's the most direct route," I informed him. "Why waste time going out the front door and all the way around the whole house when you can go straight out the back, cut through the fields, grab a few cabbages, and be safe in the forest in two shakes? Or even one shake. A shake and a half, at most."

"That's dumb," said Cordage. "The house is so small it don't matter. I ain't going out the window."

"And you call yourself a runaway," I said. "Every good adventure starts by jumping out a window. You should know that from experience."

"It's dumb."

"The front door's locked," said Robert from inside. "We're trapped!"

"You see?" I said. "It's the window or nothing at this point."

"But we've already spent more time talking about it than—"

Robert came to the window, tried to climb out, and fell on his head, which was fortuitously protected by the stewpot.

"Wise boy," I said. I dragged him to his feet and headed off through the field, followed by the scrambling and tumbling and grumbling and snorting of Cordage.

"I still say it's dumb."

"Well, you can thank me when we're safe among the shadows of the trees."

"Safe from what?" Robert asked. "From those people coming up the path?"

"Them?" I said. "Oh, that's nothing. They probably just want to talk about the goats. I'll settle that later."

"Settle what?" asked Robert. "Did you do something to their goats?"

"I did nothing to their goats!" I said. "Nothing that they wouldn't have done themselves eventually, anyway."

"No, really," said Cordage. "What did you do, turn them into sheep or something?"

"They can't prove anything!" I said. "Sheep, goats, what's the difference, really? Zoologically speaking they're practically the same animal. They'll get used to it. Give me that!" I grabbed the burlap sack from him. "Here we are, some lovely cabbages, perfect for a journey. And look! Some onions, already pulled! What great foresight on your part!"

"Told you," said Robert to Cordage. "I told you it was okay."

The duck quacked in an affectedly offhand way, as if to remind us it was there.

"Be quiet, Clarence," said Robert. "You'll give us away!"

"They prolly already seen us anyway," said Cordage.

"You, maybe," I said. "Not me. No one ever sees me unless I want them to. It's a trick of the trade."

"*I* can see you," said Robert.

"Or *can* you?" I said.

We had almost reached the trees when a muffled chorus of shouts rose up behind us. Across the cabbage fields we could see the villagers surrounding my house, peering in the windows and trying to force open the door. They had yet to see us, but they were already fanning out over the yard as if they were looking for something.

Looking for what, we may never know. Our fates had placed us on a different path, and we were mere yards, then feet, then inches from it, at the end of the last field of the last farm in the last hamlet at the very edge of the country, with nothing but a low stone wall separating us from the vast wilderness of forest and mountain beyond.

"Over you go, boys. You can't get lost if you don't know where you're going!"

"I thought we were going to the City," Robert protested.

"Time will tell," I said.

We scrambled over the stones and disappeared into the trees, dropping out of the villagers' sight and, for the foreseeable future, out of the history of Wat's Hump.

Part II

Lexi And The Princess

→ Oпε ←

THE STORY OF LEXI and the Princess really begins with the day Lexi appeared on the Burgermeister's doorstep, so dazzling his granddaughter that she was immediately taken into the household. But for reasons of my own I will begin sometime before that.

On a bright, early summer's day filled with portent, many years ago—at about eleven in the morning, if the clock in the tower was to be believed—a young woman appeared on the doorstep of the Burgermeister's house and stood before Tall Butler with a bundle in her arms that she'd wrapped in a shawl. She was dressed in her best clothes, which were rather threadbare, and her hair was pulled back and piled on her head in a peculiar fashion. In fact, everything about her—her clothes, her face, her speech—had a vaguely foreign quality.

"I wish," she said, in response to the butler's query, "to see the son of this house."

The butler wondered what he should do. The girl's tone was so clear and her eyes so fierce that his immediate impulse was to obey. But the Burgermeister had admonished him in the past Not to Open the Door to Wastrels. Tall Butler was not a quick thinker at the best of times, and when faced with any uncertainty the wheels of his mental oxcart ground nearly to a halt. On the question of wastrels he was not entirely clear, so he blinked solemnly at the girl while he tried to work through his thoughts. She, for her part, took his pause for an invitation and stepped over the stone sill into the spacious entry hall.

Relieved that the situation had been so neatly resolved, Tall Butler excused himself—"One moment, please"—and went to inform the Burgermeister.

"Pardon, Master, but a young woman has asked to see your son."

"Which one?"

"She doesn't say, Master."

"Well, fetch them both, then. And show her in as well."

The butler did so, and it happened that two coltish, lumbering young men entered the Burgermeister's study through one door at the same moment the young woman entered from the other.

When her eyes fell upon them she stopped in her tracks.

"Mother of heaven!" she gasped, clutching the bundle to her chest. "There are two of you!"

⇾ two ⇽

THE BURGERMEISTER'S TWIN SONS were notorious throughout the town and surrounding countryside: alternately cursed and celebrated, universally loved and reviled, and generally tolerated like a pair of big, ridiculous dogs.

"Those boys!" said the farmers, discovering their orchards had been pilfered.

"Ha! Those scoundrels!" said the townspeople when apples fell about their cars from the clock tower.

As boys they were full of good-natured mischief. As young men they were handsome and brawny, lads with friends aplenty and a moderate allowance from their father, who was confident the boys would soon "find themselves" and fall into a trade. In the meantime they knocked about the town every day of the week, merry as you please, and as alike as my two thumbs.

Which is just how the girl with the bundle saw them that morning in their father's study, coming in from a late breakfast and still in their nightshirts.

"Two of you," she said again. "Mother of heaven! I am doubly curst."

She is perhaps to be forgiven her surprise. Although the boys were well known in the town, she was, as has already been intimated, from parts far off. And although the boys as a general rule were as inseparable as they were indistinguishable, there were times when one would have a hankering for the ale at a certain tavern, while the other would prefer the wine at another. Also, as their interest in libation was hardly more than their interest in the girls that served it, and as their interests in that regard tended more to overlap than to diverge, and as their convergent interests invariably led to heated words and worse, they did on occasion find it in their mutual interest to partake of their refreshments independently of one another.

That is to say, if they went out drinking together, they fought over the serving girls at the taverns and wound up crawling home bloodied through the muddy streets. So, after spending their rollicking days together in the town, and after dinner at home with their father and starchy sister Maggie, they went their separate ways, thereby saving the girls in the taverns from the discomfort of their simultaneous attentions.

And so it was that the girl with the bundle had met one or the other or both of them on one or more occasions and had never known that the charming young man with the winning smile and a steady stream of cash was but one half of a matched set.

"Mother of heaven," she said again, feebly. No one else had spoken. The boys stood barefoot picking breakfast out of their teeth, and the Burgermeister sat at his desk with a look of amused alarm. Tall Butler was trying to think of an excuse to leave the room.

Finally, the Burgermeister spoke, not unkindly and with an air of great patience. "Well, what is it? What is your name, child, and what is your business here?"

"Please, pardon," the girl said, with an awkward curtsy. "I am Lily, a serving girl at the Yellow Beetle." Her nervousness disappeared as quickly as it had come. "Something I have for your son."

"For which one?"

The Burgermeister had begun to guess what was in the bundle. He cast his sons a wry, sorrowful look.

"I can't know," said the girl, darkly. "After this year all men look the same."

The boys looked dully confused.

The Burgermeister sighed deeply. "Well, let me see it," he said. "Bring the baggage over here."

The girl handed him the warm bundle and he took it carefully. The movement startled the bundle, so that it squirmed and cried an unmistakably frightened cry.

The Burgermeister glanced over his spectacles at his sons. For their part, they had only begun to understand what was happening when the bundle cried.

"What do you say? Do you know this girl?"

The sons of the Burgermeister made a great show of shaking their heads, shrugging, flapping their mouths, grunting denial, and pointing at one another.

"As I feared."

The Burgermeister lifted the corner of the shawl to look at the baby. She was tiny, with wispy, darkish hair, and the Burgermeister's heart melted in an instant, melted in a way he had forgotten was possible.

"Well, little one," he said, his voice cracking slightly, "what shall we do with you?" He looked up at the girl. "What do you wish?"

"The child, she is a curse to me," said the girl, staring at the squirming sons. "This town is a curse to me."

The Burgermeister thought quickly whether this short, sturdy girl would have a place in his home. She was accustomed to work, clearly, but she seemed sullen and unpredictable. So, despite the fact that she made his sons most amusingly uncomfortable, his decision was made.

"Would you like to return to your own country?"

"But the child?"

"The child can stay with me. And if you wish it, I can give you something toward passage to your homeland. Unless you wish to stay in the town?"

"No. No more of this town."

"Very well. Go and gather your things and return this afternoon. I will have my secretary prepare letters for your travel. Lily—is that short for . . . ?"

"Yes, gentleman, it is short for something."

"Lill—" halted one son.

"Lillimonde," stammered the other.

She fixed them both with a glance of smoldering rage to which they both silently professed bewildered innocence.

"Lillimonde, very well," said the Burgermeister, oblivious to the exchange of looks. He made a note on his desk. "For your traveling papers. And what is the child's name?"

He looked down again at the baby in his arms, into those pale, sea-colored eyes that would many years hence bewitch the Duke of Marbolo. The baby grabbed the long whiskers of his chin and held on gently.

"She was not named," said Lily. "Evil luck to name a girl with no father."

"Remarkable," said the Burgermeister, freeing his beard from the tiny, tenacious grasp. "Quite remarkable. Dear, dear, dear." He looked up. "Go now, Miss Lillimonde, and bring your things this afternoon. You boys, get dressed for mercy's sake, then find your sister and tell her we must engage a nurse for this little creature."

The young people filed out their respective doors, leaving Tall Butler to wonder whether he was dismissed or not. He had just started to edge toward the door when the Burgermeister addressed him.

"Henders," he said, without looking up from the baby. "I must ask you again not to open the door to wastrels."

"Yes, Master. Of course."

He returned to the entry hall to find the girl looking confused about which door led to the street. He guided her out and opened the door for her.

"This afternoon, Miss," he said, kindly. Kindness was his best thing. He was most happy when he could be kind. He closed the door softly so the clicking of the bolt in the lock wouldn't alarm her. Then he took a worn notebook from his pocket and leafed through it until he found the right page, with the word *wastrel* followed by a question mark. With great satisfaction he crossed out the question mark and wrote in careful, awkward letters, "a girl with a bundle."

→ THREE ←

WHEREAS THE CHILD, for all practical purposes, had no mother; and whereas in the absence of a mother she could hardly have a father, much less two fathers; and whereas it would never do for the most respectable house in town to harbor such a scandal; and whereas, however, the Burgermeister was irretrievably smitten with the child; therefore it was tacitly decreed that the child was the Burgermeister's granddaughter. All the other adults in the house, including the butlers and chambermaids, were her aunts and uncles, and all the children were her cousins. A more satisfactory solution could no doubt be devised at some later date.

Of course they intended to give her a name. After all, every respectable person has a name. The Burgermeister set himself immediately to the task of waiting for the proper name to occur to him. In the meantime, he called her "the baggage" or "the creature" or other such things, always with tremendous affection. He doted on her so much, in fact, that the rest of the household grew somewhat resentful and took to calling her the Princess. In time, you may know, she outlasted their resentment and was simply a little girl living in the house with all the rest. But by that time it was too late for any name to stick, and the Princess she remained, within the house and throughout the town.

"There she goes," people would say when they saw her walking through the town with her nurse, or her aunt (the Burgermeister's daughter), or her other aunt (the Burgermeister's sister), or her third and final aunt (the Burgermeister's brother's wife). "There she goes: The Princess of High Street." The child bore the title nonchalantly. Whenever anyone asked, "Princess what?" her inevitable response was "Princess *me!*"

She didn't act like a princess, or look like one, for that matter: a fairly plain little girl, given to dirty knees, something of a tomboy, and even at four years old possessing a most unruly shock of wavy, mouse-brown hair. Some thought her aloof, others merely dull. She laughed rarely and tended to stare at certain people, which caused them no small discomfort. In truth—though she would never have said this herself, because she was only four, and besides had a very clear sense of what was and what wasn't other people's business— she was often bored and felt incomplete, as though she were only part of a larger person who had become fragmented and scattered. It was as if, whenever something interesting was going on, the part of her that should have been interested was missing, and the rest of her was left behind, puzzled.

This was the state of things, then, when the Vagabonds passed through town at the end of summer, bearing in their party a little girl of five or six who was dazzling to behold, who danced like a field of wildflowers, and who was introduced to the crowd as "Lexi, former handmaiden to Princess Jessamine of the Wallakhai."

Alas, the Vagabond King told the rapt crowd, alas, alas, the poor little thing had been thrown out of the tribe when Jessamine became ill and died. Little Lexi was the first to find the deceased princess and the first to touch the cool suede of her cheek. Princess Jessamine's nurse found them in this attitude, and so Jessamine's mother, in accordance with Wallakhai custom and a mother's grief and rage, declared the child a harbinger of evil and banished her to the winter snows. It was only by purest good luck that the Vagabonds had happened by to retrieve her from that mountain of ice, and further good luck still that they had now come to this fair town, where surely such a child could find a suitable station.

"Handmaiden to a princess?" the townspeople said. "We know exactly where she belongs."

A little parade of Vagabonds and townspeople marched from the vacant fields at the edge of town, between the rival churches, through the oddly shaped plaza that passed for a town square, and along High Street right up to the big house, where they gathered at the Burgermeister's wide, oak door. Old Butler—Uncle Butler, to the Princess—blinked at the gathering.

"What do you want?" he shrilled. "Never mind. I'll go get the master."

The crowd voiced its approval of his efficiency but remained quiet enough to hear him shouting at the Burgermeister inside the house.

"A band of Vagabonds and wastrels at the door, sir."

An unintelligible mutter.

"No, Master, I didn't let them in."

Another mutter.

"Yes you did, sir."

Mutter, mutter.

"Indeed, sir."

. . . mutter . . .

"I don't know, sir, they didn't say."

A silence.

"Not grim, no, I wouldn't call it grim. But not festive, either, if you catch my meaning."

A pained mutter.

"I suppose so."

Resignation.

"Yes, I'll go and tell them."

Back at the door, Old Uncle Butler apparently took Filias Bunster, the carpenter, to be the leader of the assembled riffraff, for he grasped him by the sleeve and shouted, "The master will be here shortly. You can't come in." He then closed the door, leaving the crowd to murmur on its own and the little girl Lexi to gaze calmly at the enormous rosebush that grew beside the door.

Through the curtains of his study, the Burgermeister sized up the crowd and steeled himself for the encounter. He had a low opinion of Vagabonds, although like everyone else in the town he visited their camp every time they came to town to haggle over strange wares and hear wild tales. He mistrusted them in business dealings, perhaps because he found their methods too similar to his own. Besides, it was well known they were purveyors of stolen children and all other manner of dark commerce. Heaven only knew what business they had here with him!

⇥ FOUR ⇤

THEY SAY THAT IF YOU ASK ten Vagabonds the same question you will get ten different answers—and if you ask one Vagabond the same question ten times, you will also get ten different answers. This was doubly true of Slogoyban, who claimed to be "King of all the Vagabonds of the Eslich tribe between the mountains and the sea." That is, if you asked him the same question ten times you would get twenty answers, all of them true. Even among his own people his formidable duplicity was the stuff of legend. His work was so perfectly balanced between stalwart devotion to his people's well-being on one hand and his own insatiable lust for power on the other that it was impossible to tell where his heart really lay.

His origins, at least, were well known. Little Slogoyban was the son of a cobbler who had never made a pair of shoes in his life but could repair any shoe or boot better than new. Or he was raised by a maiden aunt who taught him to dance and paraded him at weddings as her own son. Or he was abandoned as an infant and lived with a family of bears until his seventh year, never speaking a word of human language until his first taste of whiskey.

He was a master of disguise who could pass unnoticed at a stranger's funeral or become a towering volcano of a man, visible from a mile away, with thunder in his voice and lightning leaping from the ends of his hair. He led his band through the wilderness, mooring their little fleet of donkey carts on the shore of every town for a hundred miles around, with a different name and a different story for every crowd.

For years after his death the saying persisted, "As Slogoyban speaks it must be true, and so the opposite must also be true."

Such was the man who greeted the Burgermeister's eye as he peered out his study window. The notoriously deceitful and instantly recognizable Vagabond King was a drab little man dressed in an odd but plain suit of clothes, somewhat shorter and less portly than the Burgermeister himself, with a patch over one eye (because with two eyes open he had too much of the Sight, or because he had lost an eye fighting sailors in Mantuna, or because he had the Evil Eye and needed to protect the community from its accidental wrath). He clenched an unlit pipe under a bushy black moustache.

"Well," grunted the Burgermeister, nodding to the butler. "No use putting it off, I suppose."

Despite all the Vagabonds' visits to Bergerton over the years, the Burgermeister and Slogoyban had never met face-to-face. The Burgermeister might have thought he was about to engage with a devious swindler, and the Vagabond King was likely preparing to address a ponderous bureaucrat. But whatever their preconceived notions, those who were there—and alert enough to notice, which was precious few—reported that the moment the two men's eyes met there was a spark of recognition, as though across the gulfs of language and custom and livelihood and the accidents of birth, each one glanced into a glass and saw his counterpart, an inexact but unmistakable reflection of himself, the biggest frogs in their respective ponds. There was no welcome and no greeting, for none was needed. They already knew everything they needed to know about one another and proceeded to be gleeful adversaries to the ends of their days.

"Well," said the Burgermeister, claiming, as owner of the doorstep, the right of first speech. "What do you want from me?"

"Nothing from you, Meister," said the other man, returning the serve smoothly. "*For* you, something we have." He gestured at the girl.

"*What?*" Any casual onlooker would have believed the Burgermeister's outrage to be genuine. "How dare you bring a stolen child to my house?"

The Vagabond recognized the maneuver and countered deftly. "No, Meister." He cowered slightly. "Do not misunderstand me. The girl—a tragedy. Her stepmother, so jealous of her beauty, drove her from the home and we found her, alone in the wilderness, without even shoes or hat. Now the woman, her stepmother, she follows us, intent to disfigure the child or slay her." His moustache began to quiver and his eyes grew moist, while the girl continued to gaze solemnly at the roses. "Please, Meister, she cannot stay with us. She will surely perish."

"Curious," said the Burgermeister, clearing his throat. "A curious child. Has she any skill? Will she work?"

"Oh, yes," said the crowd. "Handmaiden to a princess!"

"Like an ox she works." The Vagabond King nodded earnestly. "And, look. She dances."

Slogoyban clapped his hands and began singing one of his native songs in a high, hoarse, wavering voice. The girl began to sway and twist, writhing her arms and cocking her head in a characteristic Vagabond dance. The effect was especially entrancing because even at that young age, she had the striking features that would unsettle so many who met her in later years. She had arrow-straight raven hair and wide, dark eyes set in a heart-shaped, milk-white face. She pursed her lips slightly and stared intently at nothing as she turned and wove fluidly on the Burgermeister's doorstep.

It was at this moment that the Princess appeared in the doorway behind her grandfather and caught her first glimpse of the strange girl, who was a little older than herself but hardly taller, and dazzling in the late morning sun. The Princess stood stock-still with her mouth agape, not bothering to push her wild hair back from her eyes.

The Vagabond King stopped his song in the middle of a verse. The girl stopped dancing and resumed gazing at the rosebush. The Burgermeister puffed up his chest and put his hands in his waistcoat pockets while he considered the situation.

The Princess rubbed her nose, still staring raptly at the little dancer. She went right up to Lexi, while the Burgermeister and the Vagabond King muttered to one another.

"At's my grampa's roses," she said.

43

The other girl nodded. "It's nice," she said.

"It's bloo," said the Princess, which was true. That summer the roses were almost white, but with a pale cast of blue in certain light. "I'm show you." She started pulling flowers off the bush, not whole blossoms but chubby handfuls of loose petals. She handed them to the little dancer, then pulled more and more, too many to hold, until they spilled all over the porch. She went into a frenzy, pulling more and more flowers apart and flinging the petals into the air, spinning around in the sunlight, surrounded by laughter.

"It's raining flowers!" she cried. She stopped spinning and clutched the other girl by the sleeves, nose to nose, staring straight into her eyes. "It's raining flowers," she said, most seriously.

The dancer smiled and nodded, blue-white rose petals falling from her hair and shoulders.

The Burgermeister looked down at them. If he had been harboring any intent to send the new girl packing it was dispelled forthwith. He conceded defeat by way of smiling wryly at the Vagabond King.

"Very well," he said. "What is it you want?"

"Nothing, Meister, nothing. A pittance, a sparrow song. Enough it is to know the child she is cared for."

The Burgermeister cocked an eyebrow at the Vagabond King. "Come in and sing your sparrow song over a drop of brandy."

They emerged half an hour later, steadily enough for midday, with the girl employed at the Burgermeister's house until her majority and the Burgermeister's formal blessing on the Vagabonds' use of three vacant fields, twice yearly, until then.

* * *

→ Five ←

HER NAME WAS LEXI. It was short for something, but they were never able to learn what. It might have been Alexis or Alexandra. In his lighter moments, the Burgermeister proposed "Solarplexus" or "Perplexity" but was unable to elicit a laugh from anyone except Old Butler.

The girl herself claimed not to know, or to remember. She had no memory of any life before the Vagabond caravan, she said, where she was one of a dozen children and not the only one without family. She seemed to have been cared for as a community project by the tribe, with a place always found for her at one fireside or another. She would not admit that she had ever known any other way of life. She would only say, "My name is Lexi. It's short for something."

So she came to be part of the Burgermeister's household, nominally a handmaiden for the Princess but in reality just another child underfoot. In fact, it was her arrival which brought the population of the house to its peak. Shortly after the Princess had been brought to the house, the Burgermeister's older brother had appeared at the door to explain that his latest business venture—a scheme to weave woolen blankets that would keep newly shorn sheep from getting chilled—had failed for no reason whatsoever. He asked if everyone remembered his very young wife and wondered if his old room at the back of the house was still made up. Soon after that, the Burgermeister's sister moved back in with little Cordage, taking an upstairs room next to Maggie's.

After Little Robert was born to the Burgermeister's brother, it seemed as if there were children everywhere. Add in the two butlers, Old and Tall, and Cook, and Tansey the crooked old housemaid, and the big house on High Street was feeling positively crowded. Many a night supper was delayed as a screaming parade of children tore through the house: Lexi, the Princess, Cordage, and plump little three-year-old Robert struggling gamely at the rear. More than once the voice of the Burgermeister was heard to thunder from his study.

"Dash and double dash! Can a man not get a moment's peace in this house?"

He was deliriously happy with the situation.

It occurred to him to wonder when he had lost the knack for happiness. The scampering ruckus and the shrill outbursts from this new batch of children brought back memories of years past, when his own small children had brought the house to a similar state of chaos.

Of course, he'd been a different, much younger man then. Now, he was the stalwart anchor of the whole town, with all the puffed-up wisdom that the years had granted. Back then, he'd been a brand-new Burgermeister and full of all the puffed-up wisdom of youth. He'd been interested in the novelty of children but also terrified by his ignorance and ineptitude in that area. He had never felt inept before becoming a father, not in his whole life. To be sure, he'd had to work at many things, and some things had never come easily, but he'd been able to achieve at least basic competence in everything, even marriage. Nothing, however, had prepared him for the tiny, fragile, impossible advent of Baby Maggie. He had never felt so large and coarse, so lumbering and useless, as when he was confronted with that double handful of gently squirming pink magic. And his wife, Bonita, his Bonny, was suddenly transformed into an even more perfect creature than she had been before, a kind of maternal angel that knew exactly what the baby needed at every moment.

After trying and failing a time or two to care properly for the child, he'd taken Henders's advice and left the baby's care to the female folk of the house. He'd then turned his attention back to the business of the town, with the added motivation of providing for his little family. He could at the very least ensure she had an adequate environment in which to grow.

He threw himself into this project with grim vigor. The town prospered, the house prospered, and everyone had new clothes each season. He signed papers and approved projects in a frenzy. The school was expanded. The marketplace was paved. His sons were born. Wells were dug. All in all, he thought, things were going rather well. Then one day, when the boys had transmogrified into maniacal two-year-olds and his daughter was a stately seven, Tall Butler appeared in the study to inform him that Mistress Bonita had ordered a carriage and left for the City, or perhaps the sea.

Upon confirmation of this dark event, the Burgermeister—after a moment of catatonia—straightened his cravat, then held his breath for a minute while he gazed out the window.

"Very well," he said. "See to it a nanny is engaged at once. Tell Cook the children will dine in the kitchen tonight." He then approved half the papers on his desk, threw the other half in the fire, and retired to his room.

A week later, the earth having failed to open and swallow him whole, he emerged, pale and unshaven, and resumed his work. Nothing was ever mentioned of it again.

Now, so many years later, with children once more popping out of all corners of the house and dolls and toys again strewn across the floor of his study, he remembered with a kind of distant surprise the times when—even during those first black, suffocating months after his Bonny left—his own children had brought him moments of real joy. He would become wistful, particularly in the evenings, lamenting his lost chances to appreciate his own children while he had them. If he had only known—but how could he have known? And what could he have changed? In the end he always resolved to make a better campaign with this new batch, his nephews and granddaughter and Lexi.

"Thank Heaven!" he exclaimed when Old Butler brought coffee. "How fortunate to be an old man with a second chance!"

"I suppose," the butler shouted. "But the vegetables didn't agree with me."

→ Six ←

THE BURGERMEISTER WAS PLEASED that Lexi understood her place in the household and in the world. As handmaiden to his granddaughter, she performed her every act in service of the Princess; if she was sometimes imperious and demanding, it was only in pursuit of fulfilling that office.

Or so the Burgermeister was generally able to persuade himself. If she sometimes startled one by drifting from room to room like a silent wraith, or was occasionally nowhere to be found for hours on end, well, that was due to her questionable background, poor thing. If she was variously found in the back garden, or up in a tree, or on the roof of the stable, gazing at a horizon only she could see, well, honestly, she caused so little trouble compared with the other children that such peculiarities could be easily dismissed.

One day, when the Princess was ten, Lexi—who was eleven or twelve, as nearly as anyone could tell—strode into the Burgermeister's study and announced that Princess Bluebell did not wish to remain in the garden, she wished to go into the town to buy chocolate. (Lexi was the only person who ever succeeded in attaching names to the Princess, but they changed with such dizzying frequency that the rest of the house had long since stopped trying to keep track of them.)

"Very well," the Burgermeister said, "you may inform her Highness of my assent. Ask Booles for a knuckle."

Lexi curtseyed dismissively and swept off to find Old Butler. Princess Mayflower, she told him, required two knuckles for the purchase of provisions for a lengthy journey.

"Who?" shouted the man. "Which pumpkins? Never mind…"

Five minutes later, with one knuckle in her hand and one in her shoe, Lexi led the Princess out into the town in search of adventure and bonbons.

Through the rest of that summer, and through the next year and the next, they were a common sight throughout the town, sometimes with the boys in tow, or one or more of the aunts, or one of the long-suffering butlers (someone had to hold the parasol), but always the two of them, inseparable and inscrutable, and always with a knuckle or two to spend on dainties or sweets or other frivolous nonsense.

(I happened to learn—years later, purely by chance—that the girls rarely spent all they had on hand during their excursions, and that Lexi prudently collected the spare coins in an assortment of little boxes and parcels tucked into odd corners of her room. A motley collection of loose coin, ten dixit to the knuckle, six knuckles to the grip, four grips to the fillette [a fillette being half the value of a Caspian scruple, as is well known throughout the civilized world] until the whole sum came to more than seventeen kornig [a kornig being thrice the value of a fillette, as you no doubt know]. I doubt even she knew the true amount she had squirrelled away, and what she thought to do with such a sum I'm sure I have no idea.)

Curiously, for all her early fame as a master of exotic Vagabond dances, and for all that Slogoyban had touted that mastery as her chief value, Lexi was never seen to dance again outside the confines of her little room behind the kitchen. There, almost from the beginning, and through her whole stay in the house, she taught the Princess all the songs and dances she knew, to the Princess's great delight. Many an hour, the sound of clapping and singing and soft footfalls came from behind the closed door, punctuated by shrill bursts of little-girl laughter.

When the Burgermeister, or anyone else, asked to know what was going on or to see the dances the Princess was learning, the answer was always the same: Princesses do not dance on command.

So they made their way through the years and through the town, as little girls, then as gawky adolescents, and then one day the Burgermeister was astonished to discover two remarkable young ladies scampering into the entry hall to escape a late summer rain, their faces flushed and their arms full of parcels.

"Where have you been?" he asked, alarmed. "Not the Vagabond camp? Young ladies such as you have evidently become shouldn't frequent such circles."

They always went to the camp, they countered. Everyone goes to the camp.

"You should be accompanied," the Burgermeister grumbled. "Young ladies, after all."

Lexi stood straight as a stalk of corn, although not a very tall one, and fixed him with a look. "Princess Ambrosia intends to visit the camp every day until the feast of Sullivan."

As always, the Burgermeister was powerless before those calm, dark eyes (eyes that never seemed to be quite the same color as they were a moment ago), and before the flashing, sea-colored eyes of his granddaughter.

"Very well," he said. "But see if Booles won't accompany you, please."

The only response was a slight nod of triumph from Lexi.

The Burgermeister wondered if he had lost control of his household—if, indeed, there had been any control to begin with. His sons had gone off to war against his wishes, his little nephews would not stop climbing the trellises, and now he was confronted with two charming young ladies with whom he was entirely unequipped to deal. He felt suddenly flimsy and meager in a way that had only one remedy, so he shuffled into his study to pour a drop in a glass and consider his situation while the light faded in the windows.

→ Seven ←

LEXI'S ARRIVAL HAD had a profound influence on the Princess, so much so that in her later years the Princess would report remembering nothing of the time before, nothing except a wash of gray noise like cold porridge of the soul. Where she had been a somber little girl—even prone to sullenness at times—in Lexi's company she became excitable, at times frantic, and given to fits of giggling. Every morning she thundered down the stairs to drag Lexi to breakfast (there was nothing slight or waifish about the Princess). Through all their years together as children, she never appeared to notice that the only time Lexi's natural poise and calm demeanor could be ruffled was in the morning. Lexi blinked weakly while the Princess chattered through mouthfuls of toast and egg, recounting past adventures and planning the next.

On more than one occasion, in fact, Lexi nearly raised her voice. "Great heaven! Princess Mulberry!" Then, more evenly, "Will you take more sugar in your tea?"

They took lessons together in the morning and then spent their afternoons whirling about the house and the gardens, always together. When the Princess's cousins- arrived—Robert, born soon after Lexi's arrival, and then Cordage, who arrived in the house with his frazzled mother when he was two—she at first resented their intrusion on her time with Lexi.

"Don' wanna play with them babies," she announced, frequently.

"*Those* babies are your cousins," Aunt Maggie informed her, just as frequently, at which the Princess pouted.

But soon enough she annexed their territory into her empire, and by age eight she considered herself the undisputed ruler of the house. The only threats to her power were the Aunts: Aunt Sylvia, the very young wife of the Burgermeister's older brother, whose son was Robert; Aunt Lucy, the Burgermeister's sister, who wished she would be called Mrs. Broome at least once in a while, and whose son was little Cordage Broome; and in between them, Aunt Maggie, the Burgermeister's starchy daughter, who was as stiff and upright as a dumpling-shaped person could be, and who dragged the children every Sunday like a string of reluctant ducklings to whichever of the churches suited her current designs. (You might have noticed that Aunt Sylvia and Aunt Lucy were, technically, the Princess's great-aunts; but who's counting?)

It was on just such a Sunday morning, when the Princess was perhaps ten years old, that she sat with the other children at the little table in the kitchen—the dining room being still a-tumble from last night's dinner—and wove her machinatious web.

"And a dragon came and *whoosh* with fire and the whole house burned up!" she said.

"Yeah!" said Cordage. "And the people all burned up, too!"

"An a ammls too?" whimpered Robert through a mouthful of bread and jam.

"Yeah, the animals all cooked up like sausages and the dragon ate em up!" said Cordage.

"No!"

"With mustard!"

Lexi stared dazedly into the middle distance over a bowl of congealing porridge. Aunt Maggie bustled in.

"Finish up, children. Services at Saint Feldspar start in an hour and you're not even dressed."

Lexi blinked twice and picked up her spoon.

"Princess Aubergine does not wish to go to Saint Feldspar. This morning she much prefers Our Lady."

"All the animals ran away to the barn," said the Princess.

"And the dragon ate em raw!" said Cordage.

"No, they made *friends* with the dragon and started their own country," said the Princess.

"Yeah," said Robert. "Their own country."

Maggie Berger compressed her eyes and lips for the count of three. "Inform her Highness that Our Lady of Liberum Nummoram can wait until next week. This week Deacon Philbert is leading the choir at Saint Feldspar."

Lexi cocked a skeptical eye.

"Deacon Philbert," said Aunt Maggie, "is most enthusiastic."

"You can't make friends with no dragons," said Cordage. "They just eat you!"

"And remind the Princess that Saint Feldspar often has hot cider in the vestry afterward."

"Yay! Cider!" hooted Robert.

Lexi considered a moment. "Very well," she said, turning to the Princess. "More cream in your porridge, Mistress? We must haste to dress."

"Indeed, yes!" said Cook, beginning to clear dishes. "Clear out and stop cluttering up my kitchen with your falderal and balderdash!" (I should point out that Cook was also unaware of the powerful magic that underlay those words, although she should have known better, after the unfortunate business with her great-grandmother's chickens.)

Aunt Sylvia came in, poured a second cup of coffee, and tried to smooth Robert's hair.

"Good morning," she said. "Eat all that up, so we can get you ready."

Aunt Lucy snuck in close behind, looking as if she was already late.

"I don' wanna go to no church," said Cordage.

"*Any* church," said his mother. "You don't wanna go to *any* church."

"But indeed we are going," said Aunt Maggie. "Listen to your mothers and pull yourselves together, won't you please!"

The general pandemonium at the table continued until Lexi put down her spoon.

"Bergers," she announced. "The party will depart momentarily. Kindly make yourselves fit to accompany Princess Abalone on this venture."

Tansey the housemaid floated in last like the swaying of Grandmother's lace curtains. She was the oldest person in the household, having originally been engaged as a girl to look after the Burgermeister's older brother. She held a box in her hands.

"Cook! Someone's eating breakfast all over our dominoes table!"

And so it went from then on—the Princess, with Lexi at the helm, cut a deep channel and cast a wide wake through the house and the town every waking hour of every day. True, the Princess didn't always know what she wanted, but as soon as Lexi reminded her she wanted to plant daisies in the garden, or to dress in armor and stage battles in the hallway, or run up credit at the millinery, she wanted it with irresistible vigor.

The Princess will have cake on Wednesday. The Princess will read LeFeau rather than Schweinhumpf today. And the Princess will go to the Vagabond camp every evening until the Feast of Sullivan, while the Burgermeister considers the bottom of his brandy glass and wonders when he mislaid whatever it was that once enabled him to hold the household together.

An Expository Interlude

WHERE AND WHEN, you may ask, does all this take place? And who are all these people?

I can only speak for myself and say that I can keep track of this story no better than I keep track of my money. I am only, as you know, a simple cabbage farmer and sometime witch. I have a certain gift for seeing the future, but when it comes to dealing with the past I am worse than useless. So I propose to outline some related events in the hope that we may make it to the end without anyone falling overboard. If I get the time, I may draw up some sort of diagram, but for the time being we'll have to make do with my notes and a few reasonable assumptions.

So.

My understanding of the location is somewhat limited, as I have never traveled beyond the borders of this country. I can tell you that the capital is many days' journey from the City, and that it is many more days' journey from there to "the coast," which I have never seen. The river that contains the island that contains the City also leads to "the coast," but it may not be the same coast. I will have to investigate that more deeply at some point.

Beyond these simple facts, I can only offer my personal suppositions, describing the shell from within the egg, so to speak.

We are clearly in Europe, some time after the last of the plagues and some time before the widespread adoption of the cuckoo clock. The country was certainly at the frontiers of the Roman empire at some point. The agricultural details suggest a certain middle-northern, temperate latitude. And of course, there are the mountains. But there are mountains everywhere, so perhaps that detail can be disregarded. I suppose we shouldn't overlook the possibility that the City on its island floats in a river that flows through a larger island that itself floats in a larger sea. A larger sea within an even larger island in the largest sea of all.

And perhaps, as the Vagabonds will tell you, it is all enclosed within a clamshell held between the palms of She Who Is Both Creator and Destroyer.

Jonathan Berger was born into this clamshell more or less eighty years after his great-grandfather, Jonathan Berger the Elder, founded Bergerton by upsetting his donkey cart at a remote crossroads then called Sullivan's Bend. His universe was bounded by the fields around the town. He had a brother, Robert, who was twelve years older but early on showed his general lack of usefulness, so it was understood from Jonathan's boyhood that he, and not his brother, would inherit the rule of the town (from their father, who was called the Chief).

There is a theory in natural history studies—its formal name escapes me—which holds that systems churn along quietly, maintaining a kind of equilibrium, until their steady state is punctured by one or more abrupt and extraordinary events. Although he was unaware of this theory, the Burgermeister nevertheless recognized in his later years that his own life had been punctuated by three such swarms of events, or, as he charmingly termed them, *"tempestas stercores,"* which he claimed was Latin for "troubled times."

The first series of calamities began when young Jonathan was nineteen and the Chief was widowed. It is not clear how the loss of the wife and mother of the house affected the father and sons. Records are scarce. What is known is that the Chief took a new, young wife, who bore him a daughter and then vanished from the record. The father retired and then died six months later, leaving Jonathan Berger, at twenty-one, lord of the house, warder of both his brother, then thirty-three, and his infant half-sister, and master of a town which, although a hundred years had passed, was still little more than a hamlet, with a muddy market square, a handful of crafters' cottages, a little inn, perhaps a blacksmith, things of that nature.

The young man was sufficiently bewildered that he failed to notice two other extraordinary events happening that same year. In the summer, the Vagabonds visited Bergerton for the first time, setting up camp just outside the common pasturage. And it was that same summer that he first saw the future Mrs. Berger, a girl of seventeen, carrying bread in the afternoon. He didn't remember that sighting at all and would believe to the end of his days that he first saw her two years later, serving cider and ale at the Spotted Dog. They proceeded to meet and woo and what have you, to marry, to produce a daughter two years later, twin sons five years after that, and to build an apparently solid and satisfactory household. Then, as you know, when the boys were not quite three years old, Mrs. Berger herself vanished.

(I am aware that far too many women disappear in the service of this story, but what can I do? The records, or lack thereof, do not lie. It is a sign of the turbulent times, I suppose, with little to count on except one's fingers. And sometimes not all of those. Take it as a rule of life, as I do, to be grateful for everyone in your life who has not disappeared, and count as a blessing each of your remaining digits.)

There followed a period of ten years or so of steady, unremarkable growth of both the children and the town. The Burgermeister established a postal service and provided funding for Marshals to patrol the highways and ensure the safety of the produce that traveled along them. He acquired a magistrate and two lawyers to ensure the legality of whatever was convenient or necessary. There was a protracted controversy over whether market day should move to Thursday or remain on Wednesday.

But it all seems to have happened under the dark cloud that settled over him when Mrs. Burger vanished. He described it years later with painful clichés that don't bear repeating. His notes of the time are filled with dull gloom and flimsy pessimism, set down in spidery handwriting that becomes smaller and more desolate with each passing entry.

But fear not! *Tempesta stercore* the second is about to alleviate the Burgermeister of his melancholy and us of our boredom.

(Again, a diagram would be most helpful here. There is a family tree in the Berger family Bible, but there are no guarantees as to its accuracy. You may wish to draw one yourself. I will be happy to look it over and check your work.) Over the course of the next several months, the Burgermeister acquired two new in-laws and three additional children for the house. This agglomeration of extended family proceeded thus:

Lucinda Berger, the Burgermeister's sister, then twenty-eight and believing herself to be on the threshold of spinsterhood, suddenly announced at dinner that she would marry Nicolas Broome, the stringer, and wouldn't Jonathan like to help set him up in a shop of his own? The young man was only twenty and very energetic.

The Burgermeister's brother, Robert, then sixty-two, countered the next week by coming to Sunday luncheon with a turnip farmer's daughter named Sylvia, who explained she would be marrying old Robert before the harvest—so firmly that not even the Burgermeister's daughter Maggie, then a forthright woman of thirty, had the nerve to question it.

Lucinda and Nicolas produced Cordage. Sylvia and Uncle Robert responded with little Robert. Nicolas Broome's incipient lunacy blossomed beautifully, Robert the Elder began wandering the happy halls of dementia, Lily appeared from out of nowhere to deliver the Princess, the scoundrel Slogoyban foisted that peculiar enigma of a girl Lexi upon them, and at the end of it all the Burgermeister found himself living in the largest and yet most crowded house in town. He described it as having woken from a long black sleep into the sunlit pandemonium of a circus. The house was presided over by the Harpies (his word: meaning his sister, his sister-in-law, and his daughter, who had assumed control of the house only to bicker continually thereafter). It was filled absolutely to the brim with children, two of whom were enormous.

Things eventually settled into a more stable sort of chaos. If life was never calm, at least there were no more earth-shattering surprises to interrupt the flow of papers across the desk or the stream of apples and turnips through the town. After enough time passes, whether measured in moments or decades, even the most tumultuous maelstrom can come to feel ordinary.

The state of things, then, on the cusp of that fateful summer in which our story unfolds (as nearly as can be reconstructed from living memory and from the available documents [including the

Burgermeister's own papers as well as parish records at both churches and the ledger at the Yellow Beetle (the books at the Spotted Dog having been sadly lost in the fire)]), was thus:

Maggie, the Burgermeister's daughter, currently in command of the house, with the other harpies Sylvia Berger and Lucy Broome jockeying for position in the parlor; Robert the Elder no doubt upstairs somewhere; Cordage and Little Robert climbing the trellis or pestering Cook; Lexi and the Princess off to the Vagabond camp every night until the Feast of Sullivan; and he himself, the Burgermeister, lulled into complacency, having a drink by the fire in his stocking feet.

Oh, yes, he was ripe and ready for the third great disruption of his long life, a flurry of mishaps and mayhem that would leave him and the whole family and the whole town and even the surrounding countryside reverberating like a gong. The strange events you see unfolding before you now, which brought two bedraggled young boys and a rather handsome duck to my doorstep, began—as much as anything can be said to begin—that very evening, or one just like it. That is, it began when the Burgermeister's sons appeared before him in uniform and notified him that their regiment was heading north to the wars without delay.

Without delay!

Farewell!

Part iii

The Burgermeister's Boys

→ One ←

I T HAS BEEN SAID THAT the arrival of the Princess had some subtle yet profound effect on the Burgermeister's sons. I don't know when or by whom, and whether in jest or not, but it is reported to have been said.

For his part, the Burgermeister certainly watched them for signs of such an effect, as he also watched them for signs that they might begin to care about the state of their hair or take an interest in work of some kind. At first, he noted, they viewed the baby with a kind of alarmed fascination, which he hoped would be the seed of some sturdier affection or perhaps the spark of inspiration that would lead them to gainful employment. Later on, when they learned to actually play with the child, he was sure he saw them beginning to settle into family life and all the productive exploits that would surely follow. But in reality, the only measurable effect, the only definite change that anyone could with any confidence describe, was that after their usual days of ramshackle loitering, they no longer parted ways in the evening but sat down together at the Beetle, or at Sullivan's, or wherever their credit was still good, with nothing but a bottle and their silent thoughts between them.

Some in the town theorized that they were keeping an eye on one another. When one would wink at a serving girl, the other would nudge him reproachfully. Others supposed, as the Burgermeister hoped, that they were taking new stock of their lives and using the evenings to plan their joint future. In fact, one of them was sometimes heard to say something in favor of the idea of employment, to which the other would grunt affirmatively before pouring another glass.

But the truth is, hardly anyone in town paid them any attention whatever. When they weren't fighting over girls or spending their father's money, they were uncommonly tiresome. They muttered unintelligibly to one another, and whatever one said, the other would invariably agree. The young men who had sometime been their companions could neither follow their conversations nor cover their tab, so in a short while the boys became mere shadows, favoring the quieter establishments, loitering in dark corners until the proprietors swept them out into the street.

Things might have been different if the boys had been entrusted with any of the baby's care, but—times being what they were, and the boys being who they were—it was out of the question. Nurses and nannies were engaged as needed, and the Princess rarely crossed paths with her youngest uncles, she being asleep when they were awake and vice versa. For their part, the boys were more comfortable with their young cousins. The Princess never really gained an appreciation for the finer points of parlor combat.

One might even say that the Deluge of Children, as Tansey called it, allowed the Burgermeister's sons to postpone their maturity indefinitely. With such a ruckus going on underfoot, is it any wonder they should join in? Could they be blamed for encouraging the wilder aspects of the children's behavior? After all, there were more than enough responsible adults in the house to mold these young minds—the Burgermeister's boys were simply ensuring a balance of influences. Robert and Cordage deserved to learn how to swordfight up and down the stairs, and who else was there to teach them? The butlers? Who would help them dig for treasure in the herb garden? The Burgermeister? Certainly not; he had too much on his hands already. So the boys leapt into the breach and undertook to instruct their cousins in all the necessary skills of childhood.

Of course, not all was smooth sailing. The Burgermeister was sensitive to the sound of trellises collapsing, and Cook made it clear at least twice a week that preemptive raids against the pantry would no longer be tolerated. More than once an artillery battle in the dining room had be to suspended at a command from Lexi.

"Desist! for Princess Anomaly requires passage!"

Then spoons were lowered and crabapples ceased to fly as Lexi and her charge walked serenely through the room.

→ two ←

THEN ONE DAY THE BURGERMEISTER turned sixty. Where does the time go? When his own father was sixty, he, Jonathan Berger, then barely twenty, had begun taking over management of the town's affairs. Now, forty-odd years later, he sat at the dining room table, with all the household gathered around a lovely, celebratory flaming pudding, and discovered he felt ill at ease. He knew enough about numbers to know that "significant birthdays" were fictions foisted upon the unwilling by people who should know better. What difference could one day or one year more or less make? He was still the same man, wasn't he, that he had been the night before and would be tomorrow? These past years with all the new children and the bursting house had been full of energy and promise, had they not? Why should anything change now that he had three times the number of years as he had fingers and toes? And yet, and yet, and yet.

It proved to be impossible not to speculate on his own mortality, what with the entire household and probably the whole town congratulating him on looking so fit despite being one year closer to the grave. An birthday wish scrawled by the children only added poignancy to his mood. He told himself he was foolish to wish for more, that he was the benevolent ruler of as fine a town as any on the map and lord of the most delightfully unruly household between the mountains and the sea. His secret hope to begin sliding toward retirement was a tired man's folly. His hopeful expectations of his sons were unduly lofty. Surely they would find their path in time. Didn't everyone? Hadn't he? Why, only yesterday, hadn't they admired the brocade on some young lady's frock? Perhaps this nascent interest could be nurtured into a career as fabric merchants? Heaven knew he had done what he could for his boys, poor motherless things. And they didn't seem bright enough to be affected one way or another by the presence or absence of maternal influence. There was no way they could manage a whole town, the Burgermeister knew, when at twenty-seven they could barely manage their own accounts at the taverns.

He tried to appear cheerful as the pudding was served and to take the prickling banter of the Harpies in stride. But, upon seeing one of his sons returning from the cellar with yet another bottle of one of the rarer reds, he was at last overcome. Brushing the children from around his knees and standing up he addressed the boys directly and bluntly for the first time in years, perhaps the first time ever. He was surprised to find his voice somewhat choked.

"For the love of heaven, boys, why can't you find some sort of work?"

There followed the sort of strained silence that accompanies an unfortunate effluvium at a delicate time. A wedding, say, or one's sentencing at court. The family looked up from their plates, each frozen in some attitude of dessert consumption. Some paused with fork halfway to mouth, others stopped stabbing their pudding mid-thrust. One or two stopped in the midst of chewing, uncertain whether it was permissible to swallow or if the urge should be forborne. The offending son set down the bottle having poured not a drop.

All gazed at the Burgermeister with scornful perplexity. How dare he interrupt the dessert? What did he mean by bringing his own troubles to bear on the happy occasion of a flaming pudding? What were his anxieties and such to them? Would he please be good enough to have a sixtieth birthday and provide them excuse for celebration without muddying up the event with uncomfortable falderal? Only the youngest—lumpy little Robert—and Tansey, oldest of the old, continued eating.

"This pudding is too dry," said Tansey. "Put some more brandy on it."

The silence thus broken, Tall Butler rose from his seat.

"I'll fetch it, then, shall I?"

The Affair of the Pudding, as it came to be known, marked a turning point in the boys' approach to life. Outwardly, little changed. The daytime malingering and morose nocturnal drifting continued as before—they simply kept out of their father's sight as much as possible. By sleeping late, snatching a hasty lunch in the kitchen, wandering the town past suppertime and sneaking in past midnight, they sometimes managed to avoid his baleful looks for weeks at a time.

For his part, the Burgermeister took to thinking of them as lodgers and even established a secret account book for them so that, in case of a final reckoning, he could at least present them with a bill. Beyond that, he dealt with the issue by neglecting to consider it. They showed their obedience to family custom by doing the same, and so months and even years passed, if not happily then at least with the comfortable glow of willful ignorance.

→⟩ Three ⟨←

BUT ALL THIS CHANGED—how could it remain the same?—with the arrival of the Lieutenant-Major. Lieutenant-Major Alastair Hardly arrived in town with a clap of cannon fire and landed in the middle of the square like a forty-pound shot with a short fuse.

He was a dark, wiry little man with a knife in his boot and a purple plume in his three-cornered hat. He claimed to be on loan from a highland regiment and only just returned from the wars in Bolvania. He affected a kilt, which (despite his claims to the contrary) did not improve his dancing. He also had a document with ribbons and seals on it and informed the crowd that he had arrived to establish an official militia for the protection of the local habitants against all threats domestic and foreign. All perfectly on the up and up. Official, don't you know—orders right from the capital.

He took up lodgings at the Yellow Beetle and informed anyone who would listen that he was in the market for strong young men, on the one hand, and local patrons, on the other, so that the enterprise might be both manned and funded with a sense of community engagement. The merchants and craftsmen of the town, he insisted, should be willing to contribute to the cause without hesitation. War in the north was all but assured by the political climate of the day, don't you know, and should the trouble move south, well, *then* where would you be? With no militia?

Young men of the town, he cajoled, should see it as their civic duty to sign up as volunteers or irregulars or even full-blown infantry if you like. The finest young men in towns across the countryside had signed up without a thought of remuneration. Without a thought! Nevertheless, the Lieutenant-Major was able to offer a modest enlistment bonus, payable upon delivery of the young men's eager selves upon the town square Saturday next. Oh, yes, there would certainly be talk of uniforms and opportunities and even weapons and all sorts of military whatnot. Saturday next. Tell your friends.

That Saturday evening at the Beetle, about the hour that it becomes too late to call supper "a late supper," the Lieutenant-Major sat at a plate of sausages and red beans and contemplated his empty glass and slimming purse. He asked the proprietor about the two young men huddled at the corner table, identical in aspect and gloomy mood. He listened with interest to the answer and responded by picking up his plate and joining the boys without waiting for an invitation.

He didn't mind telling them, no, he didn't mind at all—as he filled his glass from their bottle—he didn't mind telling them he was disappointed with the town in general and with its young men in particular. Barely a half dozen had shown up for drills that morning, not even enough to patrol a chicken farm. And a sluggardly, vacuous lot they were, too. What sort of town was this, might he ask, that bred such lads? No, sir, it doesn't seem right, there must be more to it. Someone needed to light a fire under the collective heels of the town's youth. Leadership, by thunder! what was lacking was leadership. If he could only find two well-connected and ambitious young men to sign up as officers, well, then, things would be different. He didn't mind telling them, no sir, he didn't mind telling them at all.

Whereupon the boys, swept away by the torrent of words and left stunned in the sudden silence that followed, arrived at the obvious conclusion and asked him when they could start. There was just enough left in the bottle to toast the arrangement three ways. Before the last watch of the night sounded the boys stood before their father with the happy news and a list of necessary expenditures.

The Burgermeister was startled. He hadn't heard about the militia before this, but after meeting with Lieutenant-Major Hardly and very nearly inspecting the documents, he assented. The boys were clearly intent on making a go of it, and the financial requirements were modest, considering the benefits. So, with a half a dozen papers signed and a sum withdrawn from the storehouse, the Bergerton militia gained a corporal and a captain at a stroke. Their ranks were determined by the toss of a coin and by the available uniform coats in the Lieutenant-Major's trunk.

Lieutenant-Major Hardly was sorry they couldn't both be captains. But not to worry, boys, not to worry. Additional uniforms and supplies should be arriving from the capital any day, and then there will be all the promotions one could wish for. Sergeants and majors and lieutenants and all that, don't you know.

But the Lieutenant-Major needn't have been concerned. The boys found the situation wholly satisfactory. Captain Berger proved to be an able and fair commander, and Corporal Berger was friendly with the infantry and kept their spirits up. Also, they found that for the first time in their lives, they could actually be distinguished from one another. The novelty of individuality was exhilarating and they leaped into their military careers with all the gusto of the newly converted. They spent their weeks planning and devising and recruiting, and their weekends driving their growing band of infantrymen over the countryside and through the streets of the town. They marched, they drilled, they patrolled, they campaigned. They frightened the sheep in the pasture and impressed the young ladies in the marketplace.

True, only a few of the soldiers had yet acquired a uniform coat, and their weapons were brought from home, but the sight of them caused a wave of excitement in the town that even surpassed that caused by the visits of the Vagabonds. Lined up in tidy rows in the square or marching smartly through the streets, two dozen young men—mostly with shovels or adzes, but some with actual muskets—gave the townsfolk an unaccustomed sense of pride.

In the early weeks most of the enlistees were drawn from the ranks of those who owed money to the Burgermeister's boys, but soon the militia became a required activity for any man between the age of sixteen and thirty who wished to catch a young lady's eye or quiet his family's upbraiding.

The Bergers, Corporal and Captain, proved to be such capable military leaders that Lieutenant-Major Hardly was free to seek additional financial support from the worthy and notable in town. The Burgermeister himself was the anchor, but everyone—the magistrate, both lawyers, the innkeepers, the blacksmith and the wheelwright, the thatcher and the potters—helped to make sure the Bergerton militia was the sparkling pride of the whole district.

To be sure, the Lieutenant-Major assured them, to be sure, the boys will soon have the finest uniforms and the best arms available, and even ammunition, by thunder. Artillery could hardly be far behind, could it? The thought of a cannon resting in the town square galvanized the town. Donations poured in.

A cannon! Those upstarts in Feasley-on-Lobbe could say whatever they liked in the meantime. Once the cannon arrived, well, *then* they'd see who said what to whom!

→ FOUR ←

YOU MAY RECALL THAT, early in his career, the Burgermeister established a company of Marshals to patrol the surrounding roads and keep those who traveled safe from Hooligans. Well, in the intervening years, the Marshals and the Hooligans had achieved a kind of ecological balance, with just enough Hooligans lurking in the woods to keep things interesting and just enough Marshals to keep most of the people safe most of the time. The Hooligans eked out a living harassing travelers and relieving farmers of a share of their produce; the Marshals kept them at bay just enough to warrant the small levies they charged at bridges and stiles.

All in all, it was a satisfactory arrangement for everyone, and anyone who traveled the roads simply needed to plan ahead with a few spare coins or an extra bushel of turnips. It could truly be said that travel was much less convenient in other districts, not to mention more dangerous. The Marshals and the Hooligans both took pride in the glowing reputation their byways enjoyed.

However, this happy equanimity was disrupted by the advent of the Civil Defense Regimental Force of Bergerton and Neighboring Hamlets, as it was officially known, although in practice they simply called themselves the Bergerton Boys. Now numbering at least three dozen, their forays along the lanes and wagon tracks of the district caused no little discomfiture among the established authorities.

Those were the words of the captain of the Marshals, in a letter to the Burgermeister. The chief of the Hooligans had been to see the captain of the Marshals and complained mightily about the Bergerton Boys. It seemed the militia had found a small avenue of profit in overturning Hooligans' camps in the forest, which the Marshals had heretofore ignored by tacit agreement. The captain of the Marshals was incensed. Not only was his authority to police the byways as he saw fit being challenged and usurped, dear Burgermeister, but the militia's actions threatened to goad the Hooligans into a level of hooliganism not seen since his father's father's day.

Upon receiving the letter, the Burgermeister considered whether he wasn't somewhat discomfited himself and considered looking the word up to be certain. For one thing, he was sure he hadn't authorized the militia to police the highways or perform official actions of any kind. They were only to march in straight lines and pretend to shoot foreign invaders. And secondly, this was the first he had heard of anyone sanctioning the Hooligans' existence, let alone the miscreant activities that were their livelihood. He wished to speak with the captain of the Marshals and the chief of the Hooligans to learn more about these goings-on at the periphery of his universe. Perhaps he could work out a similar arrangement with certain merchants of questionable merchandise in the shabbier corners of the town. If the Marshals and Hooligans could forge such an unlikely peace, surely he could find a way for Bergerton to profit from *all* commerce—legitimate or otherwise?

He was in the middle of drafting a letter to this effect when he was distracted by the arrival of an emissary—from the capital no less, leagues and miles and furlongs away, much further than the City—an emissary, what is more, from His Eminence himself, with everything that that implied.

→ Five ←

THE EMISSARY, LEAN AND SALLOW and riding on a lackadaisical mule, appeared in the lopsided square late in the afternoon of a market day and inquired about lodging. His countenance fell as a crowd grew around him, intent on ensuring he had all the necessary details to make an informed choice.

One provincial town was the same as another to him. All he wanted was a bowl of something filling, a pint of something fortifying, and a bed away from the drafts. And the same for his mule, if that could be arranged. He didn't care that the Yellow Beetle had better ale but poorer pottage, or that the Spotted Dog had better rooms and on a normal day better bread, but alas, the baker there had taken fits and was resting at his sister's home. It mattered even less to him that the Beetle had been the better house in its day but that the Dog was now thriving under the sons of the former proprietor, who retired, you know, because of the gout.

Neither establishment had a stable, of course. No, of course not. Travelers usually park their wagons in the common pasture, they do. And gentlemen, when they come through, which is seldom enough, but when they do, why they puts up their mounts at the livery barn on the other side of town—that is, they did until it burned down last year, and then—

The emissary removed his spectacles and pinched the bridge of his nose. At length he gave a boy a knuckle to carry his bundle to the Beetle and promised him another if his mule was fed and watered and delivered to him in the morning. The crowd murmured its approval of his priorities, the ale being evidently the deciding factor, and at long last the emissary found himself seated at the long board at the Beetle with a pint and a bowl, fending off the Lieutenant-Major—all the while longing for his own fire in his own home, and his own sallow wife, and the fat little baby that rolled all over the floor like a cantaloupe.

Through all this, of course, there had been no mention of Sullivan's, the townspeople wisely preferring to keep that establishment to themselves.

The next morning the Burgermeister was just sitting down with a mug of coffee to work on his letter when Old Butler informed him of a visitor from the cabbages and something about elephants.

But no, the emissary explained. He was from the *capital*, representing His *Eminence*.

"Pity," shouted Old Butler from the next room. "The elephants have been such a nuisance since the cabbages ran out."

The emissary twisted his mouth in a hopeful attempt at good-natured humor. He gazed at the man before him in the shabby study and told himself it was just one more week. The Burgermeister presented what may once have been an imposing figure but was now simply large and rather worn out, like an old sofa. He was both puffy and slightly deflated, in clothes that must already have been out of fashion when they were tailored a decade or more ago.

Just a week, the emissary told himself again, a week, or ten days at the most. Four or five more towns and hamlets along the road to the City. That was two days. Then three more days, or at most four, in the City itself, and his circuit was done. From there it was a few days' ride back to the capital—or perhaps he could sell the mule and buy passage on a barge. Would the baby even remember him? Would he recognize the baby? Babies grew and changed so fast. The little mite had probably started walking and talking already—was perhaps grown and gone since that long-ago day two weeks earlier when his journey began. A full-grown man, probably, with children of his own, whom he regaled with the sad story of their grandfather who went off into the countryside in the service of His Eminence and never returned, being trapped forever in a ridiculous muddy town explaining patiently again and again that the service of all trained military men was shortly to be required in the stormy north, as war was all but certain.

The Burgermeister had a curiously frog-like aspect when confronted with this information. The emissary explained, again. Any veterans or militiamen. In the north. Ten days, no more. Really, the eye-popping and mouth-gulping was too much. It was all in the document—what was so hard to understand? That absurd Lieutenant-Whatever at the inn had certainly understood it well enough and had spoken at length about his own exploits before directing him to the big house on High Street. The innkeeper and the other locals had understood as well, although they responded somewhat less enthusiastically to the prospect. Well, things are difficult all over, aren't they. Young men everywhere get called from their homes for greater follies than this every day of the year. Did they think these wars would fight themselves? Didn't they care about him, out on the road these long days?

He extracted something like a promise from the Burgermeister, then took his leave and fairly bolted from the town, his thoughts reaching far ahead to his wife and child, who were almost certainly dead by now, victims of famine or disease or crime or accident in his absence.

He cursed himself for not leaving enough in the coffer for decent burials. The thought of them lying accusingly in unmarked graves moved him almost to tears and he goaded the mule into a lumpy trot with the town at his heels.

⇥ Six ⇤

BEFORE THE EMISSARY'S DUST had settled, word of the mobilization had flown through the town. The Burgermeister summoned the officers of the militia and was soon faced in his study by two magnificent young soldiers whom he recognized with a little shock of pride as his own sons, Captain and Corporal Berger, respectively. And indeed, the weeks of military exercise and the smart fit of the uniforms brought out the best in the boys. It could truly be said that, depending on the light, each was more handsome than the other. But where was the Lieutenant-Major?

Ah, yes, unfortunately the Lieutenant-Major had been called south to organize additional militias in the neighboring towns. But he left a letter, don't you know, a detailed letter, placing the town's unit in Captain Berger's most capable hands, and with the sturdy assistance of Corporal Berger he was certain of their shining success and foreign glory. And not to worry about the collected donations for uniforms and equipment, for he the Lieutenant-Major himself had arranged to have all such goods diverted north to intercept the Bergerton Boys en route to the front lines, a missive to that effect having been carried to the Lieutenant-Major's contacts in the City by His Eminence's recently departed emissary.

The Burgermeister was somewhat unsettled and would have liked to look into the matter further, but the boys were firm in their resolve. They would lead the militia north to glory and put Bergerton on the map. The exploits of the Bergerton Boys would put those upstarts from Feasley-on-Lobbe to shame.

So it was that barely a week later they struck out for the stormy north: nearly sixty men from all walks of the town, including a number of Marshals and Hooligans enticed by His Eminence's enlistment bonus. They gathered in the square, each with a weapon of some kind—farm tools figuring heavily in the total—and bundles of food and clothes lovingly prepared by their mothers and sisters and sweethearts, who lined the plaza, teary-eyed and waving kerchiefs.

At the head of the company, resplendent in their long coats and gold braids, Captain and Corporal Berger showed just what sort of men they had become. What was once an unruly knot of boys had changed under their leadership into as lean and organized a regiment of warriors as anyone in the town had ever seen. It stirred the heart and misted the eye to see them so alert and resolute.

The people of the town had never seen such a send-off before, mostly because there had never been anyone to send off, nor much reason for anyone to be sent. The town lacked a band, but the choir from Our Lady offered an impromptu rendition of "Farther than the Troubled Sea" that helped to set a solemn mood. When someone called for speeches, the councilmen took it in turns to launch wild flights of hyperbole over the heads of the crowd. The Burgermeister was too overcome with pride and dismay to do much more than admonish the troops to take care of their shoes. Tall Butler, who'd imagined himself the only real veteran in town, was not permitted to make a speech and so contented himself with wandering through the crowd muttering about the "dearth of grit" and "in *his* day."

Maggie was flushed and radiant, seeing her brothers turned out so magnificently. She had pinned a purple rose from the rosebush to each of their lapels before they set out from the house. After that she struggled to see them through the crowd, which didn't go unnoticed by Mr. Stoodler the pastry baker. He gallantly offered to help her up onto one of the chairs in front of his shop and equally gallantly remained close by lest she should topple.

The children of the town were swept up in the martial fervor of the day and began staging battles of their own all around the square. Several boys, Cordage among them, tried to infiltrate the ranks to sneak away for a little glory of their own. Several mothers then infiltrated the ranks to retrieve their charges. At that signal, all the other mothers and sweethearts swarmed into the ranks for one last bit of advice or one last lingering goodbye. The regiment now resembled a country dance more than a well-tuned fighting machine. It took the officers no few minutes to restore the men to their orderly rows.

In the end, it was only the threat of more speeches that persuaded to crowd to release its hold on the Bergerton Boys and allow them to step smartly out of the square. A few more tears, a few more songs and waving kerchiefs, and then down the street they went, across the pastures and out onto the road toward whatever adventure the Lieutenant-Major had bamboozled them into.

→⟩ Seven ⟨←

AFTER THE DEPARTURE of the company, the town immediately set about the business of returning to normal. The remaining Hooligans found an equitable balance with the remaining Marshals. The remaining sweethearts pined for a while and then became distracted. The turnip harvest came and went with no news.

Then summer, this troublesome summer, trailed on toward autumn, and with the apple harvest suddenly in the offing all attention turned to preparations for the Feast of Sullivan.

In the Berger house, as in every house in town, special dishes were prepared to share and compare with the neighbors. Cook had a secret recipe for chicken filigree, which she was sure out-filigreed any other chicken in town. (She had inherited it from her maiden aunt.) As in every house, rooms were swept for out-of-town guests, the parlor was decorated for surprise visitors, the children were admonished to remember their manners, Grandmother's dishes were unpacked, and everyone tried to worry as little as possible about the boys, the Bergerton Boys, off carrying the good name of the town on their worthy shoulders.

With their splendid cousins gone, Cordage and Robert became the men of the house, except no one would listen to them. When they tried to convince Lexi and the Princess to set things on fire with a candle, they were soundly rebuffed. Princesses do not engage in conflagration. When they suggested that cake be served for every meal, Cook explained that she didn't hear well and reminded them they were banished for life from the kitchen. Even the butlers and Tansey were united against them. Not only were they not allowed to live in the fortress they erected in the garden, they were forced to dismantle it and return the boards they had borrowed from Mr. Bunster before he even asked for them back.

What fun, they wanted to know—mostly, Cordage wanted to know—what fun was a festival if you couldn't even festivate? Surely they were not the first young men to ask that, nor will they be the last.

In any event, as always, against all odds, preparations were completed just in time, and as always the whole town turned out. As with most celebrations, the original reasons for this one had been lost in the mists of time, and the festival had become its own reason for being. Crowds of people milled through the streets and across the square, festivating for all they were worth, shouting "Bono Sullivan!" at one another and trying not to lose the children.

Was the merriment of the day dampened by the fact that so many young men were absent? Did a more-than-usual number of young ladies remain at home or gather in little groups at the edges to share their private woes? Did mothers shop for woolens and wish for an address to which to send them, and did fathers make time among the many toasts of the day to toast their valiant boys—off making Bergerton proud, putting Bergerton on the map, showing those foreign cads what the Bergerton Boys were all about?

Yes, all of it. All of it and more.

Part IV

The Harpies

→ ONE ←

THE WEEKS LEADING UP TO the Feast of Sullivan had been
filled with a flurry of activity that exhausted the Harpies and
tested their fragile triumvirate to its limits.

I should explain that, although the Burgermeister believed his
pet name for the three women of his household was his special
secret, they were in fact known as the Harpies all up and down High
Street and throughout the Square.

For my part, I think "the Fates" would have been more
appropriate, but there's no accounting for public taste. The
manner in which they attempted to direct the lives of the children
and everyone else in the house, not to mention the way they could
cut one's life short with merely a glance of their evil eyes, clearly
suggests the Fates to me. I can see them in my mind's eye now,
lurking in the kitchen with grim shears poised, waiting to sever
the thread of some innocent life—perhaps mine, perhaps even
yours.

To my way of thinking, they bore little resemblance to the
fearsome, bewitching winged creatures that torment travelers and

lure the careless to a terrible death, but there you have it. In this matter I am outvoted. The Harpies they remain.

And lo! here they come now. It is not market day, so the square is largely free of carts and stalls when the three women appear. They are taking the children to the shops to acquire smart new outfits for the Feast of Sullivan. They emerge into the space—a fluttering flotilla of skirts and bonnets—and pause to regroup and forge a plan.

Consider them for a moment *en tableau*. Aunt Lucy—Mrs. Nicolas Broome, neé Lucinda Berger—commanding the left flank, attempts to steer her son Cordage with a tentative hand on his shoulder, which he brushes away with a sullen shrug. Sylvia Berger, the still-young wife of the Burgermeister's aging brother, has drawn up on the right, a slight impatience already brewing upon her forehead. She is shadowed by her little Robert, whose face will not remain unsmudged. At the fore, drawn up to her very short full height, holding the purse and peering as well as she can across the square, is Maggie Berger, the Burgermeister's daughter, clenching the sleeve of her niece the Princess—who will not stop jumping about—while assuming an attitude of deliberation. And bringing up the rear there is Lexi, who is only Lexi: hands clasped behind her, radiating an air of calm. There is only a slight smoldering in her eyes to suggest anything other than infinite patience.

They are a formidable group, and the shopkeepers might look to their descent with some trepidation, were it not for the fact that theirs is the best money in town. From across the square we can see—but wait! They are about to speak. Let us move closer, just within earshot, and see what we can learn about their intended exploits.

"I think Rupert's is the place to start," Aunt Maggie decreed.

"Aw, I don' wanna go there," said Cordage. "All's they got there is girl stuff."

"Ladies first," said Aunt Maggie. "We'll start there for the girls and then try Mr. Amos for the boys."

"I don' wanna."

"Oh, of course you do," said Aunt Lucy. "Don't you want to look smart for the feast?"

"Don' care."

"For mercy's sake," said Aunt Maggie, "you're all a-tatter, both you boys. It's new jackets for the both of you at the very least, and trousers too if the money will stretch."

"We've plenty of money," muttered Sylvia.

"Prudence," said Maggie with a prim expression. "I'm only advocating prudence."

"I like *this* jacket," said little Robert. "It's got all the pockets."

"It *is* a little frayed," said Sylvia. "And it's getting too small, now you've grown so big."

"I should say so," said Maggie. "You look like little Vagabond boys."

Lucy tittered a little too abruptly. "A Vagabond!" She tried to smooth Cordage's collar. "What would your father say?"

"I *wish* I was a Vagabond."

"Of course you two could take the boys to Mr. Amos while I go with the girls," said Maggie. Then she became thoughtful. "But you would have to come find me for the money. Or I could give you some now, but I don't know how much you would spend. No, we should stick together after all. Oh, for the love of heaven!" She tugged at the Princess's sleeve. "Won't you settle down!"

She headed toward the shops, dragging the girl through a mad hop from one cobblestone to another.

"It's a game," said the Princess.

"You can only step on one stone at a time," said Robert.

"That's a stupid game," said Cordage.

"You're an excellent rock-hopper," said Sylvia. "Maybe you'll grow up to be a frog."

"I *am* a frog!" said Robert.

"Me too," said the Princess. "I'm a magic frog that turns into a bird when it rains." She hopped and flapped her wings and knocked Aunt Maggie nearly off course.

"Mercy," said Maggie. "Can't you please contain yourselves?"

"Yes," Lucy chimed in. "Please do contain yourselves."

But there was to be no containing at that time. Maggie managed to lead the little party to the shop, where the game switched to squirrels hiding in the forest among the bolts of cloth. Lucy and Sylvia drifted among the stacks, fingering first one fabric then another. Maggie attempted to get the proprietor's attention while Lexi leafed through a rack of knitted shawls with a look of distant half-interest. The Princess ran up to her breathlessly.

"Lexi! Hide me!"

"I shall not hide you. Hiding is unladylike."

"That's right," said Maggie, coming up with Mr. Rupert trailing in her wake. "We must be serene young ladies if we're to make the proper impression at the feast."

"But Robert will *find* me!"

"Of course he'll find you," said Lexi. "You're standing right here."

Maggie turned to explain to Mr. Rupert that they needed new frocks for the young ladies—comely but not too comely, if you know what I mean. Meanwhile, Lexi swiftly and stealthily secreted the Princess between two bolts of Turgistani velvet. Maggie turned back, slightly flushed, and asked wherever in the world the Princess had gone.

"Princess Saffron has other matters to which she must attend but will return shortly," said Lexi. "I think this emerald taffeta will be suitable for me."

At length the Princess emerged. Fabrics were chosen and styles determined, and all the minute details were given to the seam-stresses. Finally the children were herded outside, leaving the ladies in the sunlit quiet of the shop, "while we look at just a few little things."

"I certainly don't need a new frock," Maggie said, once some decorum had returned to the shop. "But I haven't a really *nice* bonnet, and some of these are quite well priced."

She moved from one table to another at a leisurely pace and cautiously watched the other women do the same. It was up to her to keep their spending moderate, and there were still the boys to think of. Best to consider carefully when it came to determining what was "necessary," especially for married ladies like Sylvia and Lucy. There was no need for either of *them* to be concerned with catching any eyes or turning any heads.

Oh! This bonnet was quite nice, and just the right pattern to go with Maggie's blue gown, which certainly still fit.

Sylvia was testing the drape of a lavender sateen over her arm. Lucy stood looking somewhat baffled by the variety of hats available. Both women were all right, Maggie supposed; they *had* after all managed to marry, to some degree. But really, anyone could get married, couldn't she? If one were in the market for dotards and madmen, that is. Maggie herself had much more discriminating tastes. She made her final choice and summoned Mr. Rupert with a smile.

→ TWO ←

EMERGING FROM THE SHOP—Lucy had finally chosen a tidy bonnet and Sylvia had selected two yards of the blue "to do something nice with"—they discovered the children all helter-skelter with a mob of other waifs in the spot the Burgermeister had promised would one day be the home of a public fountain. Years had gone by since that promise, and as yet no fountain had materialized. Instead the spot was a perpetual mud puddle and a magnet for children from as far away as the Outer Wemblys. And there were the Harpies' charges, in the thick of it, running and shouting and splashing away like mad puppies—even Lexi, who could generally be counted upon to maintain her own decorum if not that of the rest of the children. Excitement about the upcoming feast had gotten the better of them, no doubt.

"Oh, heavens," Maggie said aloud. "Lucy, go and get them before they're completely spoiled."

"What?" said Lucy. "Oh, yes, of course. Children! Children!"

She trotted unevenly over the paving stones and attempted to pick out her son and the others from the writhing mass. Maggie watched with some disdain as Lucy labored to attract any sort of attention from the children whatever. Finally, she could wait no longer.

"Lexi!" she called. "Help Aunt Lucy to collect the children!"

Lexi's face was flushed, her eyes bright with laughter and her hair wild from the uncharacteristic rambunctiousness.

"Of course," she said, coming to a stop. She pushed her hair back from her forehead with the back of her hand—a gesture Maggie thought somewhat affected and a little too coy—and shouted into the throng.

"Bergers! You are summoned!" She was again the calm pillar at which the children found anchor, but Maggie noted the fire that remained in her eyes. She determined to return to Mr. Rupert's to ensure that Lexi's new frock was not too fetching at all.

The boys were now much too untidy to present to Mr. Amos the angular tailor, but there was nothing else to do. There was, Maggie informed the rest, just enough left in the purse for the boys' outfits and perhaps something sweet after, so they were dusted off as well as could be and goaded by their mothers into the narrow hallway that served Mr. Amos as a shop. Lucy followed Maggie's guidance and selected a pleasant sturdy tweed for Cordage, jacket and trousers both, and put a deposit on a handsome waistcoat.

"And I'm sure your Uncle Jonathan has a nice scarf you can wear with it," Lucy said.

"I ain't wearing no scarf."

"You *aren't* wearing no scarf," corrected Lucy.

"Oh, of course you will," said Maggie. "You'll be so sharp—so handsome, the girls will be all aflutter!"

Sylvia might have rolled her eyes at this. Lucy certainly had nothing to add, having never imagined Cordage as half of a pair of anything, let alone sweethearts.

Cord snorted again about the scarf and sat down on the tailor's little stool while Sylvia tried various jackets on Robert. Against Maggie's advice, they chose a tan linen twill that would never stand up to the weather.

"It looks so crisp," said Sylvia. "With a clean shirt and a wash of that face, why, you could be mistaken for a lawyer!"

Lexi and the Princess, meanwhile, finding boys' clothing understandably dull, were loitering at the window, trying to catch glimpses of heaven knows what.

"Girls!" said Sylvia. "Doesn't your cousin look charming?"

"Does it fit him right?" asked the Princess, barely glancing at them. "His tummy pooches out."

Sylvia scowled and tugged the lapels of the jacket gently across Robert's middle. She thought his stoutness was charming, and anyway he would grow out of it. His older cousins, recall, had been lumpish boys, and look at them now. Officers in the militia and the pride of the whole town. Robert had the best of that line, it was plain to see. As opposed to Cordage, who was clearly taking on his mother's lanky gawkishness.

"It's perfect," she said. "Room to grow."

Maggie might have rolled her eyes. Lucy certainly had nothing to add, the perpetual growth of children still being something of a mystery to her.

→ THREE ←

BACK IN THE SQUARE—many years later Little Robert, after travels abroad, would take to calling it the *Plaza*, with a soft Andalusian lisp—and away from the musty gloom of the tailor's shop, Maggie found she did indeed have enough small money left for sweets, so she sent Lucy into her favorite pastry shop. She would have gone herself, you understand, but the heat, and her feet and whatnot, so she would find a bench for them in the shade and if Lucy would be a dear and just fetch a half dozen plus one of whatever looked freshest?

Lucy had no little anxiety over this task. The prospect of taking the wrong things back to the party at the table was frankly terrifying. Her Cordage would be dissatisfied regardless, but she could deal with that well enough. But the others presented pickles of quite different sorts. Robert and the Princess would gobble up whatever was presented and then complain that they wanted more. Lexi, that perplexing thing, would graciously accept whatever was presented, only to nibble vaguely at it until the remainder was divided between Robert and the Princess.

But Maggie, oh dear, Maggie, she was the real puzzle. Would she want the sticky buns with jam? Or the apple tarts? Who could fathom the mysteries of Margarita Berger's taste in baked goods? Should she just pick out seven different things and let them all fight it out amongst themselves?

"Miss Berger, how good to see you!" The proprietor popped in from the back room. "What can I get for you today?"

"It's *Mrs. Broome*," Lucy muttered.

"I beg your pardon? I didn't catch that."

"Nothing. Never mind. Just some pastries, please." She stared at the rows of pastries and deliberated herself into a complete standstill. But the pastry baker was a patient and kindly man, a full head shorter than herself, and seemed in no mood to rush her. He inquired politely about the family while she remained cemented in place.

How were her nephews? Doing well off at the war, it was to be hoped? And the Burgermeister? And all those children? Oh, and—he apologized; he could never keep straight if Miss Maggie was Lucy's sister or a niece. But in any case, it had been some time since she'd been in the shop. How was she?

Lucy told him fine, fine, Maggie's my niece, they're all fine, sitting outside if you like. In desperation she chose seven of the largest plum dumplings and hoped for the best.

The pastry man—whose name she could never remember, although she knew it wasn't Strudel—thanked her and followed her out of the shop. He hadn't any other customers at the moment, and there was certainly no harm in taking a little sun himself. He sat inconspicuously near the door and could just hear Miss Maggie tell Lucy she should have gotten something glazed or frosted. Quite right, too. If he'd known Miss Maggie was there he would have recommended the same.

The ladies were seated at the table and the children gathered around to commence the traditional bickering about who got which one. When do children learn, he wondered. There was no need to panic. The pastry of the moment is a fleeting thing, to be sure. But there will be more than enough pastries in the long run.

Once the dumplings were sorted out a relative calm came over the little party. The children focused on consumption, with the exception of that strange girl with the black hair, who pulled hers apart into crumbs and nibbled at them. The ladies chatted, as ladies with pastries do, their words blending with all the other sounds of the square in the afternoon. Maggie Berger held forth about something; Lucy Broome raptly agreed. Sylvia Berger—whom the pastry man still remembered as Sylvia Popper, who once sold turnips on Wednesdays—seemed attentive enough, but her face betrayed no opinion one way or another.

Their table was near the middle of the square, unfortunately close to the muddy future fountain, and as soon as the lure of pastries had faded, the children began edging toward it. They started up a seemingly harmless game that would take them steadily closer and closer to the mud—before the ladies knew it, they would be irretrievable. Sylvia nearly thwarted the beginnings of the game by reminding Robert to keep his shoes clean. But that proved only a minor setback, to which Robert responded by simply removing the shoes altogether. At last the children, achieving their end, entered the mud and were sullied beyond redemption.

Lucy called out, "Cord! Cord!" and waved her hands in a desperate attempt to stop him from throwing a large stone into the middle of the puddle.

"Heavens, Lucy, don't shout," said Maggie.

"Boys!" shouted Sylvia. "You've made Aunt Lucy shout!"

The game involved pirates or brigands or some such scoundrels, and before long it included a dozen or more desperate characters from across the square, divided into two teams. Lexi remained at the periphery, strolling with her hands clasped behind her and paying attention only when her services as arbiter of justice were required. Cordage was captain of one team and Beamish the cobbler's boy led the other. Cordage stood upon the pile of building stones that were not yet the base for the fountain and faced Beamish's team, taunting them with a stream of deprecation that was both ungentlemanly and unintelligible.

The game quickly devolved into mayhem, with mud and water flying in every direction and Cordage and Beamish wrestling in the middle. Maggie, who had been contemplating the purse and the possibility of another pastry, looked up in horror.

"Oh heavens! Oh heavens!" she said.

Lucy responded with, "Mercy! Boys! Mercy!"

The effect of their calls was negligible, so Maggie stood up for added emphasis.

"Good heavens! Boys!" Her voice was somewhat thin and gave way to a shrill squawk in times of pressure.

Lucy added, "Goodness! My goodness!" in her ineffectual, raspy voice.

Robert and one or two of the other children actually turned to look at this, but then they merely continued as before.

"Oh, for pity's sake," said Maggie finally. "Lexi!"

Lexi was standing just out of range of the spray with an inscrutably amused expression. She gave Maggie a quick sidelong glance, waited perhaps a trifle too long, then raised her clear, flute-like voice above the raucous shouts of childhood warfare.

"Bergers!"

All action ceased. Robert, sitting in a puddle, stopped stacking rocks, the Princess stopped mid-twirl, and Cordage reluctantly let go of a handful of Beamish Cobbler's hair, which he had so recently won at great personal cost.

"Follow," she said.

They obeyed, leaving the rest of the children to complete their engagement sans Bergers. Lexi turned on her heel and glided back to the table, leading the others like three bedraggled puppies.

"Princess Anemone and her party are ready to depart at your leisure, Aunt Maggie," she said.

⇥ FOUR ⥻

UPON RETURNING TO THE HOUSE, Maggie ordered all the children to the kitchen for a thorough scrubbing. But Sylvia took Robert up to their rooms separately, and Lexi had somehow vanished, so only Cordage and the Princess were available for the ministrations of Maggie and Lucy.

"Stop it," said Cordage. "I can wash my own face!"

"You're a fright," said Maggie. "Let your mother take care of those ears."

The Princess sat sullenly while Maggie sponged at her with a damp rag.

"I don't know why she won't bring that boy down here," said Maggie. "Their rooms will be in a state."

"I don't know," said Lucy. She wondered silently if she mightn't have better luck with Cordage in *their* rooms.

Maggie regained her grip on her charge. Well, after all, it wasn't she who would have to clean up little Robert's room, so why should it matter? She turned the Princess around and began working on the other ear.

"That girl keeps that boy too much to herself," she said.

That girl was only two years younger than Maggie herself and presented an unremarkable, not-quite-middle-aged aspect. She might have been pretty when she first appeared at the house, but in truth, she was so young at the time it would have been hard to know. Every woman is a beauty at twenty.

"I don't know," said Lucy, who often felt inclined to admire Sylvia's sense of style.

"She thinks your Cordage is a bad influence on Robert, you know," said Maggie.

"Really?"

Cordage scowled and squirmed under his mother's ineffectual daubing.

"Yes, isn't that ridiculous? Our Cord!" Maggie held the Princess at arm's length and scrutinized her work. "Scandalous to think our little gentleman here would lead that lump astray."

"I don't know." Lucy wondered what *she* would do if offered the chance to be led astray.

"I don't know if little Robert has enough imagination to be led astray, anyway." Maggie released the Princess and waved her away. "Oh, very well, that will do for now."

The Princess ran off. Cordage wriggled away and followed her without so much as a by-your-leave.

"But you'll bathe tonight before bed!" Lucy called after them. The ungentlemanly reply of Cordage doesn't bear repeating here.

"Mercy, that boy's a caution," said Maggie. "He'll be the death of us all."

→ FIVE ←

MARGARITA BERGER HAD ASSUMED CONTROL of the house at the fierce and tender age of seven when her mother handed her the reins by disappearing without a trace. Even at that age, Maggie exuded the impression of someone who knew her own mind but also knew her opinions would be thoughtlessly or even willfully disregarded unless she sternly enforced them. It wasn't that she always knew the right thing to do or say—the best dress for an occasion, the appropriate morsels to serve a visitor, or the proper way to raise a child, for instance. She simply knew the wrong way when she saw it and was diligent in pointing it out.

Her aunt, the future Lucy Broome, was at the time a storky girl of fourteen called Lucinda who wore an expression of perpetual alarm. At the time of The Departure That Was Never Again To Be Spoken

Of, Lucy was preoccupied with a litter of kittens in the stable, so it was a relatively simple matter for Maggie to proclaim herself Lady of the House. Even as a child, she could rarely bring herself to think of Lucy as her aunt. Instead she dealt with her sometimes as a sister, sometimes as a lieutenant, sometimes as an obstacle. If nothing else, she could count on Lucy to agree with her opinions, back her up in the face of any challenge, get out of her way with minimal prompting, and generally do whatever Maggie told her to do.

Then, sometime after the arrival of the Princess, Lucy—without any consideration for Maggie's convenience at all—disrupted this favorable arrangement by announcing in a terrified giggle that she would be marrying the stringer and moving into his shop.

Nicolas Broome was known to Maggie—they were the same age and had in fact danced together once at some gathering or another. But she found his attention span to be erratic, his prospects in the string and twine market moderate at best, and he had too high an opinion of his own sense of humor. She disapproved of him in general and of the marriage to Lucy in particular, but upon reflection there was no denying that getting Lucy out of the house would simplify the management of Maggie's dominions. The stringer was *much* too young for Lucy, but if she was willing to go and twist string with him in his little pauper's flat, well, let her be on her way, then.

But Lucy had been gone hardly a month when the Burgermeister's brother brought Sylvia to Sunday dinner (Robert Junior presumably *primum venire*) and announced that, ahem, his business had failed, but—well, you have heard the rest. Mrs. Broome, as Lucy had taken to calling herself—already showing, by the way—wondered whether Nicolas mightn't move his enterprise from its current location behind the blacksmith's to The Shop, to which the Burgermeister replied with some strain that he believed that's what the cursed place was there for, so why not? Mrs. Broome giggled. Mr. Broome looked startled and eyed the decanter for support.

Sylvia at first presented no obstacle to Maggie's authority, simple girl that she was, but as Little Robert drew closer and finally arrived, she proved herself to be most obstinate regarding the wisdom and advice available from the more experienced members of the household. This absurd country girl seemed to think she knew everything there was to know about babies. She refused all advice, no matter how well meaning or obviously appropriate. She did whatever she very well pleased, dressing the child however she liked, feeding it whatever she wanted, and all the while cooing over him in the most undignified manner.

Motherhood with this one was dishearteningly homey. Nothing at all like the stalwartness of Lucy, who followed Maggie's advice before and after the birth and wound up with Baby Cordage— who, despite his unconventional name, was as angelic a bundle of lightning bolts as one could ask for.

If Maggie Berger was glad of one thing, it was actually two things. One, that Nicolas Broome had gone so thoroughly batty so quickly that there was never really any question what to do with him. And two, that after gamely trying to manage the string shop for a few months, Lucy had returned to the house, providing Maggie with a solid ally against that rascal of a farm girl. If Mr. Broome had descended slowly into his happy delirium, why, it might have been months or years before Lucy could come home, and Sylvia here all that time stirring things up. What might have happened to the balance of the household then? What indeed?

Not that Maggie and Sylvia were constantly at odds. Of course not. The household had its share of strife, but by the same token no two people in it were constant adversaries, strictly speaking. Why, just the week before the feast of Sullivan, Maggie and Sylvia had the most pleasant talk over a pot of mint and lemon verbena tea in the little garden behind the house. The day was either a cool late summer's day or a warm day of early autumn. Maggie remarked how well little Robert was turning out, despite everything. And at least he was a quiet enough child, when his cousin wasn't leading him along. That Cordage was a scamp—charming enough, but mercy, what a terror that boy could be. And of course his mother could hardly expect to control him, a woman her age, you know. The raising of a child is nothing to take lightly, no indeed. She simply got started too late, which, well, it's a different game from starting too young, isn't it?

⇀ Six ↼

ASIDE: THE SHOP IS AT LEAST peripherally important to this story, so you may as well have the full picture.

It is a tiny place, quite old and right on the square, in a good location near Sullivan's, with which it shares a wall. Like all the oldest buildings in town, it is built from local, undressed stones stacked and balanced with a mortar of stubbornness and prayer. It has been replastered inside so many times that one could probably gain an extra foot of floor space all the way around if one took out the plaster and started over. In fact, the only thing that stopped the Bergers from doing that very thing was fear that without the plaster for support, the walls would collapse back into their natural state of disorderly slumber.

The Shop has a unique and unmistakable bouquet, made up in descending layers of every business and occupation that has inhabited the place. I invite you to stop by the next time you are in the neighborhood and to stand in the middle of the main floor with your eyes closed. Dried herbs and flowers, sour pine shavings, mulling spices, raw leather, glues and paints, the steam from dye pots, the faint metallic wisp of oak-gall ink—the whole history of the town is embedded in the crevices of those ancient walls. Don't linger too long, though. The current occupants are likely to call the constables.

The Shop proper consists of a small front room with a window on the square and a variety of shelves and counters for merchandise, and then a slightly larger space in the back that serves as a workroom. Upstairs, there is a small apartment with windows on three sides, lovely in the summer and drafty in the winter, with room enough for a single person, a couple, or (at most) a couple with a baby. Quite enough to house many an emerging enterprise, and all thatched with good Bergerton thatch. For details enquire at Morris & Son, thatchers, at Woodwell Street and Church Lane.

It was the first holding of the Bergers in Sullivan's Bend, acquired from the Sullivan himself by Jonathan the Elder after the episode with the donkey cart. Its early history is lost, but there are rumors that some primordial Sullivan had the place built as a fishmonger's shop to provide a front for some other unsavory business.

In any case, it was the Bergers' first home in town and has remained in the family, hosting a variety of tenants from both within the family and without, ending with Old Robert's sheep-blanket emporium and then the Broomes' enterprise. Since Nicolas Broome and his reason parted ways, the place has remained to all appearances vacant, with a sign on the door that reads "Closed due to lunacy." I have it on good authority, however, that it is used for winter shelter by a band of itinerant circus performers.

→ Seven ←

THAT SUMMER, despite the Burgermeister's sons being away at the wars, there was a great deal of hullabaloo in the house—be ye warned, *hullabaloo* is another powerful word: use it with caution—and on the day of the Feast of Sullivan it was centered in the kitchen.

Why is it that the kitchen is so often the intersection of all the various streams of activity that comprise a household? Does it benefit Cook to have mothers and children underfoot conversing earnestly about shoes? It does not. Is the tea better steeped or the biscuit better toasted by the presence of young ladies loafing at the table, building tiny houses with Tansey's dominoes? The paucity of evidence disallows a formal scientific analysis, but it was Cook's opinion—and my own, for what it's worth—that the formal business of the kitchen was not in any way assisted by the milling throng.

"Mother of heaven!" she sputtered. "Can't you all dress in your own chambers?"

"All the cloaks and shoes are down here by the fire," said Maggie. "The children must bundle up against the rain."

"Ain't gonna rain," said Cordage.

"*Isn't*, dear," said Lucy, working his hair gamely with a brush. "It *isn't* gonna rain."

"The sky looks clear to me," said Sylvia, frowning as she had a second go at the part in Robert's hair. "Stop squirming, sir. It will never do to have such a sturdy boy be seen with a crooked part."

"Well, whether it's *going* to rain or not," sniffed Maggie, "it's prudent to wear cloaks with the children so well turned out."

"Your house is too little," said the Princess. She pointed at the small pile of dominoes in front of Lexi on the table. "A mouse would never live in that."

"Yes, Miss," said Lexi. She stared pensively at the fire.

"Greetings, all!" boomed the Burgermeister, face aglow from his morning constitutional pint. "Fine day for the feast, yes? Not a cloud in sight!"

"We're wearing cloaks anyway," said Maggie, pulling the boys from their mothers and presenting them to their uncle.

"Of course, of course," said the Burgermeister. "Sharp as buttons you look, boys, and twice as tall! Wait a moment." He fished in one pocket and then another, finally handing a small pocketknife to Cordage. "Go out in the garden and see if you can't find a couple of late roses for those buttonholes."

The boys straggled out, happy to escape but chagrined at the errand.

"And bring in some more for your mothers and aunts and cousins and all these other lovely ladies."

"I want flowers!" shouted the Princess. She jumped up from the table, upsetting the mouse houses, and thundered after the boys.

"Mercy," said Maggie. "Lexi, follow her and make sure she doesn't destroy that frock before we even leave the house."

"Ma'am," said Lexi. She glided after the others with such grace that Maggie wondered if that new skirt wasn't perhaps just a trifle too flowing after all.

"What about some porridge, Cook?" the Burgermeister said, flumping down at the table.

"You're in a fine mood," said Maggie, pouring him a large mug of coffee.

"Finest day of the year," the Burgermeister said.

"You would well say so," said Maggie. "You and that fool Sullivan making such a to-do."

"The Tapping of the Keg is a solemn and hallowed tradition," said the Burgermeister. "The whole town looks forward to it."

"Perhaps," said Maggie. "All we have to look forward to is carrying you home after midnight and pouring you into your bed."

"I want to visit the Vagabond camp this year," said Sylvia. "They've been here nearly a week and I haven't managed to go yet."

"Oh, don't bother with that," said Maggie. "The best of the Vagabonds will set up booths in the market with all the locals. All that will be left at the camp are the worst of them, and that's saying something."

"I still like it," said Sylvia. "It feels more authentic."

"It certainly smells more authentic," said Maggie.

Lucy Broome stifled a brief burst of hysterical laughter.

"And I suppose you'll be making a speech again," said Cook, retrieving the Burgermeister's porridge bowl.

"But of course," he said. "It's another long-standing tradition, ever since my grandfather's day."

"At least after all these years you don't have to put much thought into what you'll say," said Maggie.

"*O, contrarium*," said the Burgermeister. "That's Latin. It's just possible I will have a surprising and delightful announcement this year."

"Are you going to allow an election for a mayor, like that young man on the council wants?"

"Of course not!" said the Burgermeister. "*If* there were to be an election, and *if* it were run properly, I would certainly be the winner, so why go to the trouble? No, this announcement may or may not have to do with the fountain in the marketplace—final plans for its design and whatnot."

"Wonderful!" said Lucy. "Although the children will miss the mud hole."

"I'm sure we can find a place for another mud hole," said the Burgermeister. "Never let it be said that the Burgermeister of Bergerton neglected the needs of even the smallest of his charges!"

A wail from the back garden drew Sylvia away in a rush. Maggie watched her with some disdain.

"If she rushes to that little lump's rescue every time he squalls, he'll never gain any fortitude."

"I don't know," said Lucy. "He's just a little boy, really."

"Hmph." Maggie fell back to regroup. "He's got some way to go to catch up with your Cordage, in any case. We just bought those trousers and he's already nearly too long for them."

"He takes after his father," said Lucy apologetically.

"Let's hope not!" said Maggie.

The Princess loped back into the kitchen with a handful of chrysanthemums and pranced from one person to the next, exhorting each to smell the flowers. Lexi slid in with a distracted expression and came to rest by the table.

"Here now, here now!" said Cook. "Lexi!"

Lexi blinked twice.

"Princess Eiderdown," she said. "I remind you that young ladies do not act like wild horses."

"All right," said the Princess. She galloped back outside for more flowers and Lexi resumed gazing at the fire.

Robert came in, sniffling and disheveled, guided by Sylvia and followed by a scowling Cordage.

"Mercy, look at the state of you!" said Maggie.

"Cord lost my lucky knuckle," Robert sniffed.

"It's just a stupid knuckle," said Cordage. "We got a thousand of 'em."

"It's my *lucky* knuckle," Robert said. "It's *mine*! I'm the wannat found it!"

"'One *that* found it,' dear," said Maggie.

"Yeah," sniffed Robert. "But Cord knocked it out of my hand an' lost it."

"It's just a stupid knuckle," said Cordage, "and besides we found it again anyway."

"It was under the grapevine," said Sylvia, not quite smiling. "In plain sight, right?"

"Yeah," said Robert. "But Cord's still a meanie!"

Lucy gave Cordage a look. He rolled his eyes.

"Well, all's well, then," said Maggie. "Get yourself tidied up. I'm sure Uncle Jonathan has enough knuckles for all of you."

"Why surely!" said the Burgermeister. He fished his purse out of a pocket and handed the coins around, three knuckles and two grips for each of them.

"Hold this for the Princess, won't you?" he said to Lexi. "She seems to be a little flighty today."

"Certainly," said Lexi with a quiet smile.

"I'm not spending my lucky knuckle, though," said Robert. "See, it's old and it's got a R on it."

"No one cares about your stupid knuckle," said Cordage, to which Mrs. Broome said, "Sss."

"It's too old, anyway," said Cordage. "Probably you can't use it because no one would take it."

"They would, too!" said Robert.

"Once a knuckle always a knuckle," said the Burgermeister.

"You keep it safe, then," said Sylvia. "Keep it in a different pocket or something."

"He's gonna lose it anyway," said Cordage. "He loses everything."

"I'm *not*!" said Robert. "It's lucky. You'll see!"

Part V

Bonita

→ Oᴨᴇ ←

Y OU WILL HAVE TO KNOW about the Burgermeister's sometime wife, I suppose.

If Jonathan Berger the Younger at twenty-one was not the
most handsome man in town, at least it could safely be said that
he was far from the ugliest. (The ugliest at that time was easily
Bertram Walgraff, the cooper's son: a stooped, popeyed little man,
pale and scrawny, with enormous feet and hands. Nevertheless,
he must have possessed some charms for he settled down quite
comfortably with Eliza Cotton, the milliner's assistant. They
proceeded to create additional Walgraffs until the town had as full
a complement of popeyed urchins as it could care to ask for. But
that is another story.) Anyway: being not the ugliest, Jon Berger
turned his share of heads as he tromped through the muddy
market square going about his father's business.

The exact number of heads he turned may never be known,
memory being what it is, but remember that Bergerton was still
a very small town at the time: barely more than a hamlet, with

only one clock and no lawyers whatsoever. You may make your estimations from there.

He was tall and his frame was broad, with just the fore-echoes of the imposing stoutness that would characterize his later years. His gaze was steady and his jaw was strong. Is it any wonder the young women at the flower stalls, or the girl carrying bread, or the farmer's wife behind the stacks of carrots and new onions gave more than a passing glance as he strode by? He was the heir apparent, if rumors about his older brother's—intellectual capacity, to be delicate—were to be believed. Handsome enough, energetic enough, and certainly rich enough, it should be no surprise he left no small amount of murmuring in his wake.

He nodded to this person and that as he went, perhaps setting a heart aflutter, perhaps not, and then arrived at his destination. He didn't look at the sign over the door, for he had painted it himself— "Robert Berger, Esq. Leather Goods"—nor did he wipe the mud from his boots when he entered. Robert emerged from the back room looking dazed.

"Jon?"

"Robert."

"It's good to—that is, what day—can I help you with something?"

"Yes, it's 'that day' again."

"Ah."

"The Chief wants the rent. And last month's, too, if you have it."

"Ah, you see, the thing is . . ."

The conversation had an air of being well practiced, but Robert's discomfort was obviously genuine, as was Jonathan's smirking pleasure.

"Father has told you often enough what will happen."

"Yes, but you see, business hasn't been—"

"Of course it hasn't. Have you had any sales at all? What have you to sell? What's this?"

"Oh, that—that's not ready. A work in progress, you might say. But once I work out the strapping it should bring a nice price, I think."

"And this? It's rather a nice satchel."

"Oh, that—that's not for sale. I've promised it to someone as a gift."

"I see. And all these here? They look quite good. Are they yours?"

"No, I buy them from Mr. Underway and then resell them here at a higher price. Just like you and Father said: sell goods at a profit."

"But does anyone buy them?"

"A little bit, they do."

"No, they don't, because they can walk up the lane and buy them from Mr. Underway just like you did."

"I don't know. Maybe."

"And the goods you make yourself are still . . . substandard, wouldn't you say?"

"I'm getting better."

"Have you anything at all to sell? That apron you're wearing?"

"No, I can't sell this. I'm still paying Mr. Underway for it."

"Well, then," said Jonathan, with infinite patience, "what shall I tell the Chief?"

Pauses in conversation may be measured by both length of time and level of discomfort. Time and discomfort act upon one another in a complex interrelationship for the duration of the pause. Most commentators agree that time and discomfort exacerbate one another until a certain imbalance is achieved which succeeds in compelling the end of the pause. Some argue that a theoretical limit exists where a pause of infinite time and maximum discomfort would result in the collapse of the cosmos. We will never know how close the Berger brothers came to this limit, because eventually Robert dropped his eyes and spoke.

"Tell Father I will be home Sunday for dinner and we can talk about it then."

"Very well. Bring him a new wallet or something."

"Thank you, Jon."

→ two ←

JONATHAN BERGER HAD HIS OWN designs for the shop, as you may have guessed. But even if you haven't guessed, he had designs all the same. What need was there for a second leather-goods merchant in town? What need was there for a second one of anything in so small a market? Robert's problem was a lack of imagination. He couldn't think of any business other than those he saw before him. The leather-goods shop would fail and Robert would move home again. Father would again fail to lease the shop to someone else. Then Robert would get it into his head to be a tin merchant (just like Duggle Fitzer) or a baker (just like that Fogleby chap), and the Chief would again bankroll a business destined for failure. Maddening!

What was required was imagination, and that he, Jon Berger the Younger, possessed in abundance. What the town needed in that shop, he was convinced, was a woodworker. And not just any woodworker, mind you—there was already a carpenter and a cabinet maker—but someone who turned objects on a lathe. A lather, or lathier, or some such word. The people would benefit from sturdy, cheap wooden dishes and bowls, and the nicer houses would benefit from intricate balustrades and finials. The potter should welcome the competition, which would push his wares into the realm of luxury goods. Yes, by heaven, that was just the thing.

Jon was so engaged in the appreciation of his own imagination that he stumbled against a girl and nearly upset her breadbasket without so much as a *beg your pardon*. She did her best to look bewitching, but his head was lost in the clouds of his own marvelousness. So she watched his retreating form, then squared her shoulders and made her mind up once and for all.

Nearly two years later, in the springtime of all things, her determination came to its fruition. Their paths had crossed in the meantime, of course. How could they not, in a town so small? But each time he had utterly failed to be smitten by her obvious charms. For all his business acumen, when it came to women he was dull as a lump of wax. Could he be forgiven for his oblivion during the summer and fall after their first collision? Perhaps. After all, his father the Chief had died suddenly just the next Sunday, choking on a bone in front of the whole family. So young Jon was suddenly thrust into being Head Man of the town, not to mention taking charge of his brother and infant sister. Considering all that, a few months of distraction could be excused.

But at the Yuletide caroling he neglected to notice either her fetching cloak or her sparkling eyes. At May Day he displayed complete ignorance of the flower she carelessly dropped on his plate. The next fall he was so engrossed in the Tapping of the Keg that he scarcely noticed anything at all, let alone her cunning new frock, which had lace all the way from Bortavia (famous also for its wines: deep-red and fruity, never too dry).

She spent the next Yule indoors with the sniffles, just to show him, and by that spring he was absolutely the furthest thing from her mind. She was no longer a mere courier of bread for the baker but a serving girl—the *senior* serving girl—at the Spotted Dog, the best and cleanest such establishment in town. There was no shortage of young men trying to win her affection, and she cultivated their attentions with supercilious grace, raising their spirits with her liquid smile and leaving their hopes to dry in the sun like mown hay.

When Jon Berger appeared at the door one day, a wave of surprise rolled through the room. The New Chief, for so they called him, was seldom seen at the Dog, preferring Sullivan's and the Beetle, in that order. No doubt word had spread of a particularly fine cask of stout that had just been tapped. Jon blustered jovially across the room, greeting one and all and no one in particular, and found a seat at the bar. He slapped a grip on the counter.

"A stout, if you please!" He spoke too loudly, with the artificial familiarity one reserves for a person one has never seen before in a place where one has rarely been.

She drew a mug and placed it in front of him with an air of cold inscrutability. Someone else called her name. She smiled a tiny smile, turned away from Jon, and left to join the conversation at the other end of the bar.

With that tiny smile, his doom was sealed. You might as well have cracked a thunderbolt over his head and opened the earth beneath his feet. Bonita. Her name was Bonita. What a delightful name. Just look at the way she holds her head, the angle of her jaw. Quite a tasty stout, as well, very good indeed. Her eyes sparkle green and gray, and she smiles when she talks. Why is she talking to them and not to me? Ruffians and scoundrels, no doubt. Except Mook the butcher there. He's a good sort but married already. Why is she talking to him? Good heavens, look at the way she tosses her hair back over her shoulder!

He ordered another mug and then another, determined to drink through the whole grip on the bar and every other coin in his purse if necessary, if only she would talk to him the way she talked to them, with the sparkling and the laughter and the rattling of mugs and the jingle of coins in the box.

Well past midnight he found himself at his own front door, thick-headed and dizzy, knocking and knocking until Tall Butler finally let him in and asked if he'd had a pleasant evening.

"I don't know, Henders. I don't know if I'll ever know."

→ Three ←

HE BECAME A REGULAR at the Spotted Dog, of course, just as she had planned. And, as she had also planned, she maintained in his presence an aloof restraint that bordered on indifference for nearly a week, until her affectation was shattered by the bowl of violets he left behind when he paid his bill. That such a naïve and clumsy gesture would scale the ramparts of her heart was a surprise even to her. Actually, it was a surprise only to her and to Jon. The other patrons of the Dog, and most of the rest of the town, already knew more about them than they knew themselves.

Ah, spring! What change in the air, what shift in the light could possibly account for the tumult of longing, the delicious fear, and the ecstatic sorrow of love? What swells from the ground to overcome the young? To convince every pair of lovers that every flower, every birdsong, is theirs and theirs alone? As for me, I say leave them to it. Who else has the patience to endure endless walks through the orchards? Who else could so enjoy the bitterness of solitude or the agony of separation? Why would anyone else subject himself willingly to the desperate thrill of uncertain reunion and soft kisses in the cool half-light that melt like butter on the tongue?

No doubt you, worldly as you are, have experienced your own lovelorn angst. I can tell you nothing about it that you don't already know. What's more, it would probably stir up uncomfortable memories. I propose to do us both a favor and avoid relating the more cloying details of the next few months. Agreed? Done.

→ FOUR ←

AS ALL LOVERS DO, they made it up as they went along. There is no recipe for the exquisite catastrophe that is every love affair. Once the initial storm had passed, they discovered that their chief joy lay in bantering about everything and nothing, playing a verbal game of battledore and shuttlecock as if their very lives were at stake. The chief wrinkle they encountered was Bonita's adamant determination not to be absorbed into someone else's household. She had set herself up quite nicely in a little room at the back of the Dog and found a serving girl's wages sufficient to her simple needs.

To be sure, she soon became a fixture at the big house on High Street. She was friendly with all the staff and could recognize Jon's baby sister Lucinda on sight. She took an interest in planning the meals and lent an able hand to redecorating the dining room and several of the bedrooms. But she put off giving up her post behind the bar. A girl needs her own income, she said. And when Jon suggested most respectfully that she might take one of the rooms in the house rather than her little garret at "that place," she demurred. How would *that* look, do you think? A girl needs a place of her own, after all.

After little more than a year of this, Jon formally proposed marriage and dared to suggest that, as his intended, she should think about how it looked to be living as she did. She heard his proposal with icy calm and informed him that she would retire to her home to give it the proper thought. Three weeks later, he was at her door with a bowl of violets. His proposal was accepted, she remained in her room, and nothing was ever spoken of it again.

More months passed. If the townsfolk whispered about the woman he was keeping, he gave no indication that he heard. He was well occupied with the management of the town, which was growing steadily. Day by day he worked at perfecting his system for denying and approving the papers that crossed his desk. On the evenings when he wasn't at the Spotted Dog, he pored over a list of possible titles he had chosen for himself. Now and then he would ask Bonita's opinion of one or another, and she would tell him he was a fool. He would agree and scratch it out or put a question mark after it.

A thorough search of the available records gives no indication that a formal wedding date was ever chosen. Nevertheless, there seems to have been some sort of alarming event which led to the hasty purchase of a new dress and impromptu nuptials at St. Feldspar the very next day. (Whatever that event was, it wasn't what you think. There are several competing theories, most having to do with Jon's well-known impulsive nature.) He began signing his name J. Berger, Burgermeister, and continued to do so for the rest of his life. She signed her name Mrs. Jon Berger just once, in the parish registry, and thereafter reverted to Bonita W, the name by which she was known across town and into the countryside.

"But why won't you be 'Mrs. Berger?'" the Burgermeister asked. "What kind of a name is 'W,' anyway? What happened to the rest of it?"

His Bonny replied that it was all the name her family had ever had, and it was entirely sufficient, thank you. More than enough in some cases.

She did finally give up her room at the Dog, although she still tended the bar every other Thursday night. It was her chance to hear the buzz around town and keep him informed, she said. She moved into the big house, rearranged all the furniture, and planted a rosebush beside the front door. For luck, she said. That summer, the blooms were a deep crimson. They pressed some of the petals between the leaves of a book in the Burgermeister's study. For the future, she said.

→ FIVE ←

THE BURGERMEISTER AND BONITA presided over a period of growth and expansion the likes of which had not been seen since the town was founded a century before.

(I know a humorous anecdote associated with the founding that may not be entirely out of place here. Jonathan Berger the Elder was a merchant or tinker of some sort, traveling with his family from one place to another, either toward the City or away from it, depending on which version you have heard. All their possessions were heaped in a donkey cart and Jon and his wife walked one on each side to keep the donkey on the road. Upon reaching Sullivan's Bend at dusk, his wife, a charmingly pragmatic woman named Sophia, and his children wanted to stop at the little inn, but Jon wanted to continue a mile further to a grove of trees he saw on the horizon and sleep out in the open for another night.

His wife and children pled the case for a roof and fire for a change, but he would not be moved.

The health of the open air, he insisted.

Whereupon his wife grabbed the lead and attempted to steer the donkey into the paddock in front of the little inn. Whereupon Jon grabbed it back. Whereupon the donkey added his opinion to the argument by spinning about in the middle of the road, upsetting the cart, knocking four Bergers over like ninepins and dragging the inverted cart a good while along the road bank, scattering their possessions as it went. Then it stopped to eat a thistle.

The donkey's name was Mort, which wasn't short for anything.

Very well, Jon conceded, they would stay here. His wife and children gained lodging in the small building adjoining the inn, but he himself stayed out on the roadside with their scattered goods, intent that not a thimble should be lost. All the next day and the day after, he combed through the grass and the weeds, looking for every last bit.

The saying in town is that his family built the house around him when he refused to move. Most take this as poetic license, but I know it to be factually true. They began by building a sort of awning on posts over the area to protect him and the lost items from the weather. Walls were added later, as winter set in.

The little building next to the inn they bought outright and established the first oddments store ever to be seen in that part of the country. They sold off their own belongings as John unearthed them, then began acquiring tatty old things from the townsfolk, cleaning them up, and selling them at a profit. The business prospered. Eventually the house was complete enough for them to move into—it had walls and a roof, in any case, and enough room for everyone, plus a large kitchen. In fact it was unquestionably the largest house with dirt floors anywhere in the district.

They had built along the full fifteen yards of roadside where the donkey had dragged the upturned cart, and to the end of his days Jon Berger the Elder believed that some of his property was still missing somewhere in the ground. He spent the rest of his life digging his way from room to room, sifting through every spade-full of soil, looking for that last lost coin or wayward thimble. The house became larger and finer with each passing year, but he permitted no floors to be installed on the ground level until after his death. So the house has the distinction of having been built from the top down, instead of the ground up. I leave you to sort out the relevance of this story for yourself, as I am running short of time.)

If the Burgermeister had had a throne, Bonita Berger née W would have been the power behind it. Sometimes she directly influenced his actions, as when she suggested a regular postal service to replace the system of leaving notes on fence posts with the hope that some passing farmer would deliver them. Sometimes her influence was more subtle, as when she suggested in passing a fondness for satin and found the next month that a merchant specializing in imported cloth had been established in the square. And sometimes, if the Burgermeister had had a horse, his Bonny was the cart he would have put before it, as when he had the back garden planted in willows and dogwood just because he thought she would like it. (She did not but said nothing at the time.)

Within the household she brought a note of focus and organization that had been lacking since the Burgermeister's mother passed away. Tansey in particular was overjoyed to once again have a woman in charge and was not shy about reminding the household at large of her feelings.

"It's about time," she would say. "The place would have fallen down around our ears if we'd left it to the men much longer."

If Bonita's family background had ill prepared her for the management of a large household, she lost no time in gaining the necessary education. It was not really so different from managing the tavern, after all. The occupants of the house were only slightly less well behaved than the clientele of the Spotted Dog and responded just as quickly to her rebukes. The butlers, when they could be found, were more responsive to her commands than the stableboys at the Dog, and Cook needed replacing only a bit more frequently than at the inn. A pantry and a cellar were a pantry and a cellar no matter what the establishment, and keeping them stocked was no mystery at all. The only real difference she could see was that she couldn't charge her new customers a fair rate, and the tips were not nearly as good. But room and board were included, and when you threw in that delightful oaf of a husband, well, the situation was quite satisfactory.

→ Six ←

THEN, A YEAR IN, something happened. Things began changing, swelling and whatnot, and before Bonita had been quite two years in the house there was suddenly a baby girl. She hardly knew what to make of it. Jon was baffled and thrilled and wanted to talk of nothing except what to name the child and how to set her up for a successful life. Bonita, on the other hand, was only concerned with keeping the little thing alive from moment to moment. Managing a household or a tavern was one thing, but this was completely different: a bundle of squirming, whimpering, squalling impulses, with slate-blue eyes and the tiniest, tiniest fingers she had ever seen.

Thank goodness Tansey was there.

"Finally, another baby!" she said. "What have I been waiting around here all these years for?"

She was as helpful as Jon was useless. She had managed every baby in the household since Robert was born. True, babies in the family proper were few and far between, but there was always an adventurous chambermaid with a surprise to share, or a gardener with a sudden complication. And always Tansey was there to teach and guide and scold and upbraid and admonish and generally keep mother and baby alive and well by sheer force of will.

And since it had been seven long years since the Burgermeister's little sister Lucy arrived—the chambermaids being unusually well behaved for the duration—she had been getting restless, even to the point of making veiled comments to the Burgermeister about his "prowess." So with the advent of Margarita—the name being taken from her mother's side of the family—Tansey became again the mother hen she was born to be.

The butlers drew the Burgermeister gently aside, as they had drawn his father aside before him. Old Butler had no children, so he had the benefit of years of unbiased observation. Tall Butler had two or three, perhaps, but long ago and in another town far away. (Their mother had kept them, he supposed. There was a war or something in between, and that changed everything.) They explained patiently what work was best left to whom and poured the Burgermeister a glass of something comforting, before returning as quickly as possible to their usual duties.

Their advice, he reflected, seemed dubious, but—lacking other sources of wisdom—he assented to their guidance. Thereafter, he limited his parental energy to totting up balance sheets and agreeing with everything anyone else said regarding babies and their mothers.

He concealed his lack of knowledge with an air of vacuous wisdom that Bonita found endearingly infuriating.

Mostly, he appeared quite taken with the baby, once he had gotten used to her, and rather enjoyed holding her so long as she didn't squirm or cry or do anything besides coo and clench his whiskers in her little hands. The moment she did anything else a look of panic came into his eyes and he froze, not daring to move a muscle. The rest of the household quickly learned to recognize this look and to respond by relieving him of the baby and depositing her in more capable hands.

This generally meant Tansey, who regarded babies as things to be kept in order, or with Bonita, who, it should be noted, was scarcely more practiced than the Burgermeister in the ways of infant husbandry. But, times being what they were, everyone assumed motherly instincts would be sufficient, so Bonny was left to work out motherhood largely on her own. It is possible that she felt judged, that she felt her every action was apprised and critiqued by the other women in the house, but if so, she kept those feelings to herself. She built a little island for herself and her baby and fortified it against intrusion with great subtlety.

The first line of defense was food. Baby Maggie was a good eater, and if nothing else, Bonita was uniquely qualified to address that need. She rejected every suggestion of engaging a nurse and spent many a long hour, day and night, with the baby, curled close in that endless circle of comfort that only a mother and infant can know.

The second line was sleep, for Maggie was a fitful sleeper and only Bonita seemed willing to wake and sleep at the little creature's whim. The nursery was quickly abandoned and the baby moved into her parents' room, since her tiny lungs were capable of sending bone-shivering wails through the furthest corners of the house. Shortly after that, the Burgermeister relocated to a pallet in his study. The lack of sleep was impacting his business dealings, he said. And if it was good for the baby's bed to be closer to her mother's, then, by the same token, the pallet in the study was closer to the liquor cabinet.

So the months and then the first year passed. With the introduction of porridge and other foods Maggie at last started sleeping through the night in the nursery. The Burgermeister forewent his pallet for the warmer comforts of the bedroom, and the household supposed a new equilibrium had been achieved.

Then the walking started.

Never having been much of a crawler, Maggie surprised everyone by becoming such a prodigious walker she was likely to turn up in any corner of the house at any moment. What was she doing in the pantry, up to her elbows in the flour bin? How did she get to the piano in the parlor? More importantly, how did she get on *top* of the piano and where did she expect to go from there? Couple that with her dogged fascination with her father and his work, and the real tumult of the house could be said to have begun. The child might toddle into her father's study at any moment and clamber up onto his lap, intent on denying and approving papers just as he did. The Burgermeister was good natured about it until an inkwell was toppled or a favorite quill was chewed up, and then he would call for her mother to come and fetch her. He couldn't very well maintain a household, let alone a whole town, with such—

He never finished the thought, because Bonita was never more than a few steps behind the baby and would come charging in like the cavalry to sweep Maggie away to the kitchen for some sweet distraction.

In this way another balance was reached, with Bonita attentively herding the child away from anyone engaged in any kind of activity and collapsing at the end of each day, too tired to remove her own shoes.

⇢ SEVEՈ ⇠

THEN THE BABY WAS THREE, then four, then five years old. The roses were a peachy orange and the Burgermeister had just begun to consider the question of schooling when there was another change and more swelling—really enormous swelling this time. Before anyone was quite ready, twin baby boys, the most beautifully matched pair of babies anyone had ever seen, appeared as if by magic. The household took this tripling of the children in stride. There was no thought to putting them in the nursery, which had become the sole domain of Maggie the Terrible. They went right to the bedroom, and the Burgermeister went right to the study to renew his acquaintance with the brandy cupboard.

The babies grew, as babies do. If anything, Bonita was even more delighted and more exhausted than with the first. The boys were dazzling to behold, as handsome as their father, as graceful as their mother, and with all the intelligence of both sides combined. If everyone else saw only ordinary, slightly mushy babies, well, they were shortsighted and misinformed.

There was talk of naming them after men on their father's side and using their mother's family name as a middle name.

"But what kind of a name is W?" the Burgermeister asked again.

Bonita was in *no mood*. "W," she said. "Take it or leave it."

So the boys were named after distant uncles and given the middle name W (pronounced "W"). Since it was impossible to tell the boys apart, however, they were simply referred to as, and would only respond to, "the boys," "Boys?" or "*Boys!*"

Maggie took to spending afternoons in her father's study, sitting in the big chair by the fireplace and playing with a doll or a cat or some such thing until her father suggested she go and play with her brothers.

"Don' wanna play with them babies."

"They're not babies anymore, really. They're more than two years old."

"They'll always be babies."

Maggie may be forgiven her assessment, considering her tender years. Others might have described the boys as a litter of rhinoceros puppies, or monkeys escaped from a zoo for insane animals, or a rampaging herd of wild horses ridden by ocelots. Or perhaps all three combined. Cook took to collecting all the broken crockery in a bag to show them once they were grown what terrors they had been but gave up the project after six months because it was too disheartening. The butlers would draw straws to see which of them would have to suffer with taking them on their afternoon outings. The loser was sure to return home having to explain torn clothing or bloodied knees to the mistress of the house.

"Oh, boys, you are in a state," she would say. "Henders, however did you let this happen?"

"It was the work of a moment, Madam."

Cook was particularly sensitive to their interest in her domain.

"Can't you keep those ruffians under control and out of my kitchen?"

"They're just boys, Cook. Rambunctiousness is a sign of intelligence."

The Burgermeister found them to be singularly, or perhaps doubly, obstinate and contrary, if not outright disobedient.

"They positively enjoy going against my desires!"

"They're only children, my darling dearest. They'll grow out of it."

"Still, it seems they should have a little more respect for their father's feelings. I know I did!"

"You're a fool to be butting heads with them at this age. Imagine how it will be when they're grown!"

Bonita considered the butlers to be lackadaisical and willfully ignorant of the boys' charms, Cook to be jealous of their obvious good looks (Cook's own son being buglike in many respects), and the Burgermeister to be threatened by the mere presence of other males in the house. Nevertheless, she too was heard to shout from time to time, "For mercy's sake, boys, can you not behave?" When she was not actively managing children or defending them from their detractors, she took to sitting quietly in her room with the shades drawn and a book lying open and unseen in her lap.

Living alongside all this, don't forget, is little lost Lucinda Berger, the Burgermeister's sister, who at the time presented no clues that she would one day become Mrs. Nicolas Broome. When Bonita came into the family, Lucinda understood immediately that she herself had moved one layer further into obscurity. She was a strange and gangly child who occupied her time with trying to keep out of the way. For several years she had been the only child in the house, and while she was maintained and more or less educated by the adults around her, for the most part she had discovered that the less noise she made, the better.

When Maggie was born, she was fascinated but was not allowed to play with the baby. Bonita had horrible visions of the clumsy girl dropping the baby on the hard stone floors or letting her slip down the well. No, Lucinda could play quietly alongside her and join outings and whatnot, but she mustn't touch the baby.

Of course Lucinda used every furtive skill she possessed to sneak into Maggie's room at every opportunity to steal a snuggle or stroke her silky hair. When she was caught, as she invariably was, she would giggle her hysterical giggle and say, "But she's so cute! I love her!"

The boys, when they came along, were not nearly so cute and she didn't love them nearly as much. She was twelve by then, and Maggie five, or nearly so, and for the first time in living memory there were enough children in the house to be considered a gaggle. Maggie, being Big Sister, was obviously meant to be in charge, and she made every effort to make the boys conform to her will. Lucy's role became to act as Maggie's enforcer when Maggie was around, and to be led by the boys into all manner of mischief when she was not.

As noted, she didn't love the boys nearly as much, but rampaging through the house with them was more fun than she had ever had in her life. A certain type of person, a person of charitable and sympathetic constitution who didn't have to live in the same house with them, would find her heart warmed by seeing this ungainly girl enjoying her lost childhood while on the awkward threshold of womanhood. As it happened, no one of such constitution was around to have a heart so warmed. Every rampage ended with hysterical giggles from Lucy, bewildered astonishment from the boys, and stern scolding from whichever adult happened to be present, seconded and affirmed by Maggie.

When the boys were old enough, they were moved to a new room built especially for them, across the hall from their sister.

Whereupon the Burgermeister again forsook his pallet in the study for the rediscovered comforts of a feather bed. He also found room on his bedside table for a small decanter, whereupon Bonita discovered his talent for snoring. Whereupon she moved the pallet to Maggie's room as a bulwark against sleepless nights. Whereupon Dame Maggie scolded her for taking up valuable floor space and suggested she go sleep with them babies. So it happened that Mrs. Berger could be found one morning snoozing on a chaise in the parlor, the next in a chair by the fire in the study, and the morning after that sitting in the kitchen, waiting blearily for Cook.

For a time, the Burgermeister began his days by searching her out and confirming that all was well. He received this confirmation so consistently that he soon chose to believe it and stopped asking. He then perceived that she became irritated when he sought her out, so he fell out of the habit and took to simply greeting her whenever their paths happened to cross. He was increasingly occupied with the management of the town but could always be found in the study if she needed him. He took pains to be cordial, no matter how trivial the interruption.

Then there came a day—it might have been at any time of year, but it happened to be in the middle of a rather dreary summer—when the children were even more disruptive than usual, galloping up and down the stairs and through the hallways engaged in a fierce territorial battle. The Burgermeister was engrossed in some particularly troubling correspondence but when his train of thought had been interrupted for the fourth time he was driven to act.

"Bonny!" he called from his seat. "Can you not get those children under some kind of control?"

At the sound of his voice the tumult subsided but soon rose again to an even more fevered pitch.

"Bonita!" he called again. There was no response. He summoned Tall Butler and told him to find Mrs. Berger. Upon finding her, he was to ask her, if it wasn't too much trouble and if she wasn't otherwise involved, to please find something to occupy the children other than tearing up the house by its roots. The man nodded and turned to leave, deftly avoiding a fusillade from the back stairs.

He returned twenty minutes later, bent close to the Burgermeister, and murmured in his ear, at which the Burgermeister sat bolt upright.

Great heavens! Had he seen her at all that day? Or the day before, for that matter? Great heavens!

He dashed up the stairs to see for himself, then wandered back to his desk to stare at the unfinished letter while the ink dried in his quill.

The sudden evaporation of Mrs. Jonathan Berger left several unexpected gaps in the workings of the household. Besides management of the children's behavior (which thereafter was largely ignored) there was the decorating to consider (also ignored), the purchase of foodstuffs (taken up by Tansey and Old Butler, with the help of mostly illegible written instructions by Cook), and planning the garden and caring for the rosebush, managed with marginal effect by the Burgermeister himself when he cared to step out of doors.

Most serious of all, however, was the vacancy in the role that comprises the moral center of power in that or any household, that of Mistress of the House. There were two viable candidates, of course. It could have been Lucinda's moment to come into her own. She was fourteen or so and still the three-year-old twins' favorite playmate. But around adults she was alternately shy and hysterical, and no one who noticed her was able to take her seriously.

Maggie, on the other hand, a poised and severe seven-year-old, early on demonstrated her willingness to take on the role of arbiter of all things proper. One night at dinner, only six weeks after The Event, she scolded her father for leaving his napkin on the table. He looked up at her with some surprise, then sheepishly moved the napkin to his lap. With that her ascension was assured, and her rule of the house remained largely uncontested until the arrival of Lexi nearly twenty years later.

Mrs. Berger's whereabouts remained a mystery. There were vague rumors, and the prevailing opinion was that she had run away to the City. Or perhaps the sea. But the Burgermeister soon forbade all discussion of the matter. If he cherished any hope of finding her in his infrequent travels, he kept that hope well hidden. To all appearances he had walled off that chamber of his heart and turned his back on such matters.

Permanently.

A Second Expository Interlude

I HAVE NO DOUBT THAT, clever as you are, you have long since deduced the importance of the rosebush outside the Burgermeister's front door. Well, of course it's important. Why would I include anything frivolous or inconsequential in this or any story? Especially a story of such scope and magnitude? You should note every detail, no matter how small, and examine it as a piece of a gigantic puzzle that will one day, through the fortune of heaven, make some kind of sense.

In any case, the rosebush, not being a character per se but a sort of mile marker along the path, will have little opportunity to relate its own provenance. Therefore, I propose this interlude, both to impart valuable information and to provide some relief from the slapdash action we have heretofore withstood. So fix yourself a cup of tea and a bit of something sweet and sit back for a moment. I will do the same and join you shortly.

Now. Within weeks of The Wedding, the new Mrs. Berger planted the rose. It was midsummer, a trifle late to be planting a new rose, but there was little to worry about if the following autumn was mild (which it was, mercifully). The plant came by special delivery—from a distant uncle, Bonny said. It was good luck, she said. Every W family had one to keep the wraiths away.

It had the extraordinary quality of changing its blossom color every year, sometimes even shifting from one color to another in a single year—if the moon was right, she said. The year she planted it, the blossoms were deep crimson. The following year saw a pale shell pink and the next, the year their daughter was born, lemon yellow with a violet heart. Bonny kept a collection of petals from each year that passed, pressed between the pages of a book of syrupy poetry. She was never able to explain how the colors happened, only that it had something to do with the grafting and that the bush must therefore never be pruned except to have dead canes cut away. You can cut fresh flowers for the table, she said—of course, don't be foolish—but take care not to attempt any pruning while you are at it. She was well aware that *some people* might take it into their heads to sneak some pruning in under the guise of cutting flowers, but it must not be done. The stems must be long enough to reach the bottom of the vase and *no longer.* No longer!

She instilled this rule so severely into every member of the household that there is to this day a statute in the town against pruning any rosebush at any time. I have since learned that Bonny's account was true in some respects and dubious in others. Many W families (and the related Uv families) do indeed keep a rosebush of this kind, but in many of these households the reason for the tradition is lost and the bushes are pruned regularly with no ill effect on the plant. The plants are made from cuttings of an existing, healthy bush in early spring (under a waning moon, by some traditions) with the cane grafted to rootstock from any wild rose. In some circles, practitioners claim that different wild rose roots will give different colors or that the time of year of the grafting will affect the fluctuations. However, I have found no evidence that the changes in the blooms are anything other than random. Two or more identically prepared and tended bushes grown side by side will never display the same blossoms with any kind of frequency. If the changes in the blooms are indicative of anything, it is the caprice of nature as she toys with our attempts to elicit a sense of order from the universe.

The secret of the rose was never shared in the town, so although the bushes are common in some districts, it remained the only one of its kind in Bergerton until recently. It became quite the conversation starter and a regular stop for the traveling merchants who visited year after year. The young mistress of the house was suspected of having some small magical skill, which suspicion she never took the trouble to deny.

Mrs. Burgermeister's Rose, as it was called, grew with varying degrees of enormity, depending on the skill of that season's gardener, until it spread three feet wide and taller than the imposing front door of the house, with a gnarled ball of matted canes at its base as big as your head. It didn't have a great many thorns, but those it did have were nearly an inch long and sharp as needles. After the boys' mother vanished into the east or maybe south, the bush developed a habit of growing one or two canes toward the door to snag the clothing of those who passed.

Typically, it was the Burgermeister who was so ensnared, being by far the broadest person to use the door. He responded by taking it entirely too personally.

"Curse this wretched thing," he would say, and threaten it with a drastic pruning at the next opportunity. However, in the end he always heeded his absent wife's admonition and simply bound the sprawling canes back against the rest of the plant. Year after year this happened, until the bush looked like a bundled-up briar thicketg, bound together with a hodgepodge of twine and string and whatever else had been handy at the moment, including a shoelace from the Burgermeister's second-favorite pair of shoes.

More years passed. Decades, even, and the rose persisted. Then, one spring, with Maggie in the kitchen scolding someone and his sons out patrolling with the regiment, the Burgermeister looked at the calendar and realized the day was the fortieth anniversary of his marriage. Several hours and several bottles later, he succumbed to the slow rage that sometimes consumed him in his darkest hours. These rages were as maudlin as they were infrequent, and hardly a piece of furniture in his study had escaped being upturned during one inept rampage or another.

On this occasion he left the furniture alone, however, and reeled outside to confront The Rose. It had yet to bloom that year. What cared he if it ever bloomed again? Heedless of admonitions, heedless of thorns, he grasped the plant by its knobby base and tore it from the earth, scattering soil and stones and whatnot across the pavement, flinging the plant down upon the front stoop.

He stood shaking and tremulous over the vanquished plant and wept aloud. He was a ridiculous sight, as all men in great passion are, and he said the most ridiculous, artless things, as only the greatest depths of sorrow and destruction of the self can wrench from the soul.

"Oh, my Bonny, where on earth, where under heaven can you be?"

He collapsed and sat like a clod where he was, shrugging off the butlers' assistance until long after dark. Then he made his way to the garden shed for a spade and replanted the rose carefully by the rising light of a waning moon.

Is it too much to say he watered it with his tears? He did just that. Would it sound too foolish if he cajoled it not to expire on his account? What else could he do?

He performed whatever clumsy rites his mind could conceive, tamped the earth down with his hands, and stumbled into bed, grimy and thorn-pricked and all tumbled about inside. Yes, tumbled about, but perfectly still, like the wreckage of a ship after a terrible storm.

To his surprise, he and the rose both survived until morning. The rose wilted drastically; he plied it with water and manure. It sulked; he misted it with nettle tea. Then, just before the feast of Sullivan, it began to show signs of revivification, with maroon sprigs of new leaves and even one small cluster of tiny buds. The Burgermeister was cautiously grateful and promised to look after the rose to the end of his days—no matter what color the blooms, no matter what color, even if they were no color at all.

Part VI

The Feast of Sullivan

⇴ One ⇷

I WAS ONCE TOLD NOT TO START a story with the weather—
that any necessary atmospheric information can be woven into
the action or the dialogue, thereby avoiding interruption of the
narrative flow. Instead, therefore, I will tell you that the Feast of
Sullivan takes place every autumn in Bergerton and is unique to
that community. The central event of the festival is the Tapping
of the Keg. Other than that, it is much like any harvest celebration
anywhere. Farmers bring their late crops to the marketplace; all
the craftsmen and merchants in the town set up stalls to hawk
their wares; the Vagabonds visit for the week surrounding the
festival and provide entertainment as well as their own eclectic
mix of merchandise. All in all, it is an unremarkable event, but one
observed rigorously by the entire town as a chance to get out and
mingle and eat too much before winter closes ins.

The Sullivan chooses the date each year, based on what he
determines to be the optimal time to tap the Keg. The Keg is the
first cask of schkoltsch to be opened after aging from the previous

season. Schkoltsch is a peculiar liquor—not to my taste at all, really—distilled only by the Sullivans, and subject of much local pride.

And now, the weather. The day dawned bright enough, but by midday the sky was threatening rain, as it always did for the Feast. The townspeople were not bothered, however, since it had never rained on the festivities until after midnight, at least in living memory. Some wizardry on the part of the Sullivan allowed him either to predict the weather fortuitously or to keep the rain at bay until the event was over, either of which seemed equally likely. After all, with the power to make schkoltsch in hand, what couldn't the Sullivan accomplish?

A little wind blustered through the square around noon and molested the merchants and crafters as they tried to set up their stalls, but by midafternoon things had settled down under a comfortable, soft gray sky. There was just a hint of autumn edge to the air. The leaves had fully turned but had not yet started to fall in great numbers, so the surrounding hillsides were properly bedecked in reds and yellows and a few dignified browns. The light breeze that remained sent handfuls of early-fallen leaves scudding across the square.

The Burgermeister's nephews shuffled and scuffed through the leaves. The Burgermeister himself stumped through them, while the ladies of the household variously minced, loped, waddled, or sashayed. The butlers paced dutifully behind, and Lexi of course seemed to glide without touching the ground at all. The walk to the square was short enough, barely a hundred yards, but at Aunt Maggie's insistence, they were all decked out with every manner of hat and muffler and cloak and parasol imaginable.

"Be prepared for both sun and rain," she said, "and you will never be disappointed."

(To "wear a sunhat with your overcoat" has since become a proverb in the town.)

At the square, the crowds had already started to gather.

"Not so many stalls as last year," Maggie sniffed.

"It will fill up soon enough," the Burgermeister said. "It's early yet."

"The market has been dismal all summer," said Maggie.

"Saving the best for the Feast," said the Burgermeister.

"Let us hope."

Now that I think of it, I don't know whether I have thoroughly explained the arrangement of the town. Pay close attention, or everything that follows may elude your understanding. You may wish to draw yourself some sort of map.

The town is still centered on the ancient crossroads that was previously known as Sullivan's Bend. The High Road (called High Street within the town) travels roughly from left to right, with the right way leading to the City and the left way leading (after some difficulty) back to Wat's Hump and environs.

From the crossroads, heading toward the bottom of the map and away right, is a road called the Forest Road, which leads to the wooded wilderness that borders the district on the south. In town, this road is called Church Street, where St. Feldspar faces off against Our Lady at perpetual loggerheads. Then, leading up from the crossroads toward the top of the map and veering left at an awkward angle, it is called simply The Way North and leads through farmland and pastures and hamlets and towns, then across a river or rivers to where the Wars are taking place.

The square—which is not square but an irregular space shaped something like a pork chop—sits squarely at the crossroads, with Sullivan's at the upper right corner, the big house just off the upper left corner, and shops all around the edges.

From the square, the town spreads out in all directions in a charming snarl of alleys and lanes. Just south of the square is a collection of workshops, and just beyond *that* is the large common pasturage used by all the goats and cows of the town when it isn't being used by the Vagabonds, as it was during the festival. Where the cows went at that time I don't know. Perhaps their owners moved them to one of the other pastures. Not being acquainted with the ways of animal husbandry I couldn't tell you. The goats, I know, were free to wander, and were even accorded special status during the festival, given honorary titles and whatnot.

On market days, the square is filled with an assortment of farmers' carts and itinerant craftsmen's wagons, while the shopkeepers set up stalls in front of their establishments. On the day of the feast, and indeed on the days leading up to it, the number of stalls seems to double and one can hardly move through the square for the number of wagons and carts.

The square is paved and drains well when it rains, all the water collecting in the middle at the site of the alleged future fountain. The pasture, by contrast, is a soggy place at the best of times and in rain becomes a veritable swamp. The Vagabonds park their carts on the higher patches, so visitors are obliged to hop from one hummock to another to avoid sinking to their ankles in the mire.

And while a collective of merchants pays Rinkart Hupperson and his sons to keep the square swept clean of any contributions by the farmers' horses—not to mention the Lord Goat and his court—no such accommodation is made in the pasture. Shoppers keen on perusing the Vagabonds' multifarious wares or watching their distinctive entertainments are well advised to keep one eye on their purses and the other on the ground. Whether that is the sort of authenticity to which Sylvia referred I really can't say.

It is into this milieu that the Burgermeister's household stepped that afternoon. Maggie had commanded that a strict phalanx be maintained, but her forces were unprepared for the onslaught with which they were met and they were soon scattered, leaving her with her officers to strategize from the safety of the pastry shop.

The boys had disappeared at first sight of the tinker's wagon and his collection of tin whistles.

"Can I buy one?" asked Robert.

The Burgermeister exhorted them to spend all their money on that and whatever else might catch their eye.

"It's good for the people to see us spending money," he explained to their mothers (as Maggie looked visibly pained). "It stimulates confidence in the working classes." He elbowed Old Butler with an air of conspiracy. "Off to Sullivan's then for a pre-tapping snootful? After all, it won't do to open the Keg on an empty stomach."

"No," answered Old Butler, "but I'd rather go to Sullivan's if it's all the same."

Lexi and the Princess wandered off in search of frivolity while Sylvia and Lucy went seeking a fortune teller.

"I always start by having my fortune told," said Sylvia.

"Well, for mercy's sake, stay out of that dreadful camp," said Maggie. "I'm sure there will be plenty such nonsense right here in the square."

Tall Butler took Tansey in search of a flannel nightshirt, after which she insisted she would head straight for bed after only one dram.

"Horrid stuff," she said, "but once a year I can make the sacrifice."

That left just Maggie and Cook and the young chambermaid whose name was—no, there she went, off with a group of young people and that boy who—what does he do? Helps the tailor or something? Well, no matter. Maggie and Cook settled themselves at a table and Mr. Stoodler the pastry baker came over beaming.

"It's so marvelous to see you," he gushed. "My two favorite customers!"

"And you must tell us this year," Maggie said coyly, "which of us is your *absolute* favorite."

"And as I tell you every year," he replied, "that I cannot do until you tell me which is *your* favorite of my pastries."

"Then we shall have to try them all, I suppose," said Maggie.

"Of course," he beamed.

"Peculiar man," said Cook as they watched him walk back to his shop.

"He fancies me, you know," said Maggie.

"No, it's me he wants," said Cook, "but he's afraid to compete with me in the kitchen."

⇀ two ↼

THE BURGERMEISTER STEPPED THROUGH the low door and into the smoky gloom that was Sullivan's perpetual atmosphere. The chimney drew poorly, and the majority of its patrons favored a pipe. But even when there was no fire and no one smoking, a faint haze filled the air. It was the same door through which the Burgermeister's great-grandmother had peered in hopes of assistance while her husband crawled along the road looking for lost property, and the Burgermeister felt sure that some of the haze in the room was a remnant of that which had greeted her over a century ago. He breathed as deeply as he dared. After a smoke it would be easier, but starting out it was always best to go cautiously. He went up to the bar to find the Sullivan himself serving.

"Brother Jon," the man said. "First to arrive, as always! Something to moisten yer throat? It's a long night ahead."

"Afternoon, Mog. Don't mind if I do."

The men had been childhood friends and remained close in their mature years but had never worked out which was the older. They had both simply always been around. Moggly Sullivan was the great-great-grandson of Harward Sullivan, who had presided over the little wayside inn when the fates of the Sullivans and the Bergers became so suddenly and inextricably intertwined.

"The stout's a little off, but I need to run the cask out, so I'll let you have it for half price."

"Make it two for one, and you've got a deal. And a short ale for Booles here."

"No, just a short ale for me," shrilled Old Butler.

In fact, the families' paths crossed each other so often it was a wonder that no Berger had ever married a Sullivan, or the other way 'round, for that matter. The right combination of man and maid and moonlight had apparently never occurred.

Sullivan set down the mugs.

"Somethin to eat with that?"

The Burgermeister shook his head.

"No, this is nutritious enough on its own."

The building was very old, built of native stone, shingled with slate, and lit within by sputtering lamps and narrow windows glazed with ancient, leaded glass. In legend, it had begun life as a military outpost on the frontier of some forgotten kingdom. Sullivan's had been the hold and the building that became The Shop had been the barracks, or so it was said. To me it seems more likely that The Shop was simply a farmhouse and Sullivan's was originally the cow barn, but people will tell their tales. So let it be a frontier garrison, and let the soil all around it be stained with the blood of hundreds of attackers, repelled by the fortitude of the dozen soldiers within. It costs us nothing to allow a town its fanciful history.

"I'm happy with the Keg this year, Jon. Got a good feelin about it."

"Good, good." The Burgermeister smacked his lips. "We're due for a good batch. Will it be brighter than last year's?"

Sullivan nodded, wiping the bar with a dingy rag. "Much brighter. Fiery, I should think."

"Well, hopefully the old men will start to straggle in soon and we can get things underway."

The "old men" were Sullivan's Dozen. That is, a baker's dozen plus the Sullivan. That is, fourteen men from the town. They were the chosen few permitted to be present at the Tapping and to have the first taste of the new batch. The group had its roots in the fourteen men who were present at the first Tapping, which at that time represented everyone of legal age in the hamlet of Sullivan's Bend. Jon Berger the Elder was there, and Harward Sullivan, and a dozen others. Schkoltsch, and the preparation thereof, was already ancient at that time, but Harward Sullivan had a flare for the dramatic, and the little ceremony he extemporized became enshrined in tradition, right down to the fourteen participants, the speeches they made, and the glasses they used.

"Patience," Sullivan advised. "They will come when they will come."

Many of the old men were direct descendants of the original fourteen. Others had been voted in by secret ballot when no
successor was available (or, in more than one case, when the only
candidate refused his succession, claiming the drink to be "vile
in the extreme"). Not all were old—the youngest was only twen-
ty-four—and not all were powerful men in town. A mason, a few
farmers, two carpenters, a rag picker, and others of similar standing.
All they shared were deep roots in the town. No one whose people
had arrived after Jon Berger capsized his donkey cart could ever
hope to be one of Sullivan's Dozen.

"Where's my second pint, you scoundrel?" said the Burgermeister.
"By heaven, I'll get my money's worth from you!"

(Drinks for Sullivan's Dozen were complimentary on the feast
day.)

Not that some latecomers hadn't tried to worm their way into
this exclusive club. Over the years, a number of would-be applicants
were turned away because their people had only been in the town for
sixty or seventy or eighty years. Only ten years ago, the magistrate
and one of the lawyers had made a case to join the affair based on
their standing in town and even threatened to make the event illegal
if they were excluded. They relented only when the Burgermeister
closed their accounts and billed them for all services past due.

Curiously, although it wasn't specifically chartered, there had
never been a woman among the celebrants. Not that there couldn't
be some rationale for it. Sylvia Berger, in fact, would have a claim if
Nathan Borscht remained childless, since she was the oldest child
of Nathan's half-brother Damanto Popper and was likely to receive
both estates, such as they were, if and when calamity befell the
brothers, heaven forbid.

Sullivan refilled the mug. "The stout's a bit off, as I say," he said.

The Burgermeister drank deeply. "Terrible," he said. "Hardly worth the price."

Not that Sylvia would be likely to press her claim, having been heard to describe schkoltsch as "burning like dragon piss."

→ THREE ←

SCHKOLTSCH (SPELL IT LIKE IT SOUNDS) is a pale brown liquor, distilled from local sources. The exact recipe is kept secret, handed down from one Sullivan to another, but is essentially a combination of apples and barley mash. Apples and barley have been staples in the region for centuries, and the community is congenially divided into aficionados of cider and those who are content to guzzle ale.

The story goes that, in time beyond memory, a traveling Dolomitian friar brought the secret of the distillation of spirits to the region. The ale drinkers clamored in favor of whisky, while the cider drinkers expressed their preference for a pleasant apple brandy. Unable to resolve the conflict, fearing for the peace of the neighborhood, and having, in any event, access to only one still, the Sullivan of the day hit upon a solution by combining apples and barley malt into one mash, thereby satisfying all, if delighting none.

The result is a brittle spirit with a sharp finish, earthy, smoky, and strangely sweet, not unlike muddy bacon. As I mentioned, not really to my taste. The tradition endures to the present day, with the Sullivan distilling a dozen or more barrels of the stuff each autumn. It is aged a year in used cider barrels, and the bulk is polished off during the following year. For the most part, it is reserved for special occasions: marriage toasts, holiday feasts, wakes, and the like. It is not cheap, and the town as a whole goes through only ten or so casks in a year. The remainder are kept at Sullivan's in reserve, where they continue to age and are indulged in at the Sullivan's discretion. Any evening, especially at the week end, you may find a few or several of the town's notables at the bar, happily paying a double grip or more for a dram of "the old stuff."

As I said, not cheap. At the Feast of Sullivan, however, the first keg is doled out at a knuckle a dram to all comers until the last dregs are drawn.

→ Four ←

CORDAGE AND LITTLE ROBERT, having escaped the adults, knocked about the marketplace with unaccustomed congeniality, at least until their money ran out. But as soon as Cordage had spent his money on two sticky dumplings, a mutton pie, a frothy sweet drink made from fresh cider and cream, and a tin whistle that promptly broke, he fell into a foul mood.

"You should buy me something, you still have money left," he said.

"I just have two knuckles, and I'm saving em for something later."

"You have three knuckles."

"Yeah, but that's my lucky knuckle. I can't spend it cuz it's for luck."

"You *could* spend it, like Uncle Jon said. A knuckle is always a knuckle."

"Yeah, but I *won't.*"

"That's stupid."

"*You're* stupid."

"I bought you a sticky dumpling, so you owe me," said Cordage.

"I didn't eat it, though. You did."

"That ain't my fault."

"They put nuts on it."

"Ain't my fault! You *owe* me!"

"Fine! I'll give you one and you can pay me back," said Robert.

"Yeah, I'll pay you back."

"No, you won't. You never do."

"Sure, I will."

Robert handed Cordage a coin and they wandered between the stalls.

"What do you wanna do now?"

"I'm going back to that tinker's and get him to fix my whistle," said Cordage.

"You shouldn't have poked me with it and broke it."

"I didn't poke you hard. This whistle is no good."

"Mine's fine. It didn't break. You broke yours cuz you're too rough."

"It's junk."

Little Robert tootled a tune on his whistle until Cordage made him stop.

"Well, what do we do now, then?" said Robert. "Should we get our fortunes told?"

"Nah, I don't wanna go to the Vagabond camp. It's dumb."

"There's an old Vagabond lady in the square. Over by the butcher. She tells fortunes. Our moms went there."

"Nah, that's a waste of money." Cordage rubbed his nose. "They just make stuff up and take your money and if it doesn't come true you can't ever find em to get your money back."

"How do you know?"

"That's what Old Butler says. He says he gave money to a fortune teller this one time and she told him he was going to be rich and good-looking and marry for love and all that, but instead he turned out to be a poor unmarried scarecrow."

"That's mean."

"That's what he said. He called himself a scarecrow, not me."

Note, if you please, Cordage's stated aversion to prognostication, and then consider the boys' engagement of Yours Truly as just such a functionary in the opening episode to this tale. Are you curious to know how this apparent discrepancy will be reconciled? I know I am.

"Look! Sausages!" said Cordage.

"How can you still be hungry?"

"I like sausage. Let's get some."

In front of the butcher shop, a brazier glowed with several plump sausages sizzling over the coals.

"No, they're too much money. It says they're two knuckles each."

"Or two for three knuckles. We have three knuckles."

"No, you have one knuckle and I have one. My lucky one doesn't count."

"That's stupid."

"We could get one to split."

"I ain't splittin no sausage with you. Just spend your stupid lucky knuckle and get us two sausages and we can each have one."

"No! Stop grabbing it! It's getting dark! You're gonna lose it again and I'll never find it!"

"You're the worst cousin I ever had!"

"Stop it! Cord!"

* * *

→ Five ←

LEXI AND THE PRINCESS QUICKLY ascertained that everything in the square was exactly the same as last year and made a beeline through the crowd to the Vagabond camp. They were already known there, of course, as they had been visiting every day for a week. And through the years Lexi had maintained some acquaintances among the tribe, just enough to ensure they were given the best of all possible bargains on every purchase.

They made their way through the camp, tracing a winding path through the various obstacles. The Princess dashed or loped or hopped over puddles, rushing to see this juggler or that dancer or to sample exotic foods prepared over dazzling fires. She had a coltish exuberance that the Vagabonds found charming (and profitable). Meanwhile, Lexi glided along in her customary attitude, hands clasped behind her back.

The camp, as always, was a magnet for the young people of the town. Children loved the novelty and adolescents reveled in the slight sense of danger. But even among all the bright young things Lexi stood apart and attracted a kind of alert notice. Striking though she was, she was not a particularly pretty girl, to my eye. But she was able to *act* pretty, if you catch my meaning. She was one of those girls who, at fourteen or fifteen years old, slide easily into the attitudes and expressions cynically affected by women twice their age to allure and entice—the parted lips, the jaded poise. So, not a pretty girl, as I said, but forcefully young, with a bright hard edge and the summer's freckles across the bridge of her nose.

She wafted through the camp. If she knew what malingering

was, she would have malingered, but as it was she wafted. From one end to the other and back, gracing the boys with her scorn, unwilling to be absorbed into any of the little groups of girls that sparkled at the margins and around the stalls. Only once or twice did some annoying urchin interrupt her languid progress or some rambunctiousness crack the young lady's decorum and reveal the furious child underneath. But only for an instant, only the briefest petty flash of fire, and then the calm returned. The eyes settled back into the dark smolder that terrified and fascinated everyone who caught her glance.

She looked like a girl with a secret, and for once, at least, it was true. Her purse was heavy not only with pocket money from the Burgermeister but with every coin she had managed to secret away during all the ten years she had lived at his house, attended to his granddaughter, eaten his food, and confounded everyone who tried to make sense of her. She smiled a tiny smile to herself. There was a letter in her purse as well, a letter that would remain unread until the proper time presented itself. It was the best letter she had ever written, she was sure of it.

The Princess tumbled up to her, breathless and glowing. "They have some candied nut lumpy cluster things! Do we have enough for that?"

Lexi considered. "Yes, Princess Huckleberry, we have enough for anything you want."

Just past sunset, black clouds began to gather against the distant mountains, held in check by the Sullivan's powers of prediction. Lexi wondered what it was like to be a cloud in the dark, to wait in the sky with a belly full of rain and feel the starlight on your back. It would be so easy, and such fun, to rush down the valley and sweep over the town, to tear through the trees and chase the people all indoors. While she watched the clouds they flashed and grumbled among themselves and waited for the spell to be broken.

→ Six ←

SULLIVAN'S WAS A SMALL PLACE, as wide as it was long, and as night fell no amount of lamp-, hearth-, or candlelight could completely dispel the cozy, smoky gloom of the place. The Burgermeister was already well into his cups when the last of Sullivan's Dozen—a man named Corkerley who had taken over the wood lathe shop and moved it to a new building at the edge of town some years ago—arrived and took his place at the bar. Normally, places at the bar were first come, first served, but on Tapping Day they were reserved for the Dozen. Attendants, protégées, entourages, and other invited guests and party crashers filled the benches that lined the walls, or stood about. A hundred people or more, crammed into a space that normally hosted two or three dozen at most.

"High time you got here, Cork'ley," the Burgermeister boomed. "We were about to vote a replacement for you."

"Nonsense," said Fillister, accepting a mug from Sullivan. "Without me to turn the stoppers there would be no keg to tap at all."

"We'd bung it with a rag, as my grandfather did," said Sullivan. "Drink up and gird yourself for the task, lads. There's an ugly mob outside fixin to riot."

Outside, Sullivan's corner of the square was crowded with people, knuckles in hand, eager to feel the warmth of the first dram of the new batch.

"Hear, hear!" The Burgermeister slapped the bar heavily. "As Burgermeister of Bergerton, son of the Chief, rep'sentative of the people of this fair town, I call this unhappy lot to order and entreat upon the Sullivan to bring forth the Keg without delay!" Cheers all around. "Who's the maiden this year?"

"That'd be Mook."

"Then make way, make way!" the Burgermeister said.

The crowd pressed back from the center of the room and pulled a man from the bar into the space. Mook the Butcher—a second cousin to the Sullivan, incidentally—was as jolly as they came, red-faced and bright-eyed and only a hair taller than he was wide. He made a show of protest but allowed the crowd to bedeck him with flowers and colorful rags. He then performed a mincing, twirling dance that all agreed to be the best by any sacrificial maiden in recent memory. Once he retired, puffing, to his place, the Sullivan came out from behind the bar.

"Order, order," called the Burgermeister. "Receive the Sullivan and crave his gen'rousness!"

"It's 'generosity,'" Mook whispered.

"Hush." The Burgermeister waved him away. "Sullivan, we wait upon your mercy."

"Are the Dozen assembled?"

"Yes, oh Sullivan," the crowd shouted.

"Has the sacred space been purified?"

"Yes, oh Sullivan!"

"Then bring forth"—here he paused for dramatic effect—"the Keg!"

Again, cheers all around, shouting, the stomping of feet and the banging of mugs. Two young men—sons or nephews of the Sullivan, I believe—rolled a wooden barrel out from the back room. The behavior of the assembly became even less civilized and threatened to get still worse.

I'll spare you the details of the whole tedious affair in favor of a short summary.

The Burgermeister started his traditional speech but was informed it wasn't time yet. The Sullivan introduced the Keg and gave an account of its provenance. The crowd sang an unsavory traditional song. The Dozen all carved their names in the sides of the barrel. The Burgermeister then had to be awakened to give his traditional speech. After the speech collapsed under the weight of its own non-sequiturs, the Sullivan called for cups, and his sons or nephews brought out a wooden box with an unlikely assortment of fourteen mismatched vessels made of wood and pewter and glass, the very glasses used at the first tapping over a century ago. Each of the Dozen took his cup and with much solemn ballyhoo the Keg was finally tapped. The riotous cheer that followed faded quickly to a reverent, pensive silence as the cups were filled and the Sullivan gave the formal toast.

They were words without meaning, learned by heart and passed from one Sullivan to the next. They said it was the ancient language of their forebears, an appeal to the gods for good fortune. But in my travels I have never heard any words remotely similar nor read of any such language in the ancient past.

Still, the world is wider and stranger than we can imagine, so who am I to say that the Sullivan's gobbledygook isn't what he says it is? I will reproduce it here, so you may judge for yourself.

Schlobonoft i fyrngin ys'galmt,
Ko ocht'ool ko tozhanalm yst'oalt.
Hamn ne ocht'hamna ko ahosq y'folsh
Schlazanog hakfilsh y'fta!

I can't vouch for the spelling, but to my eye it captures the sound of the original well enough. It may be out of form in this tale for me to insert such a long passage of nonsense. I only include it because in my research I happened to come across a transcription and thought you might find it diverting. I would include a proper citation, of course, but unfortunately my notes in that regard were lost, as so many things were, during the recent troublesome events with which we are all familiar, and which bear no repeating here. If it bothers you, you may take it up with the publishers.

After the toast, the Dozen knocked back their drams in unison. Silence prevailed as their reactions were noted. Some winced; some flinched; some coughed. At last the Burgermeister was able to speak.

"It passes muster," he croaked as his eyes watered. "Most definitely brighter than last year's!"

⇀ SEVEN ↽

S O. AFTER THE TAPPING and the Tasting and the Approval, and after those inside were served, the Keg was wheeled outside, where the Sullivan himself began doling out drams to any and all comers while the young men collected the people's knuckles in an ever-heavier burlap sack. Next to Sullivan's, the Shop was home to a temporary smokehouse operated by Mook the Butcher. It was hung inside with hams and sausages and sides of bacon. Outside, cuts of beef and whole chickens roasted over an open pit.

Throughout the square, the merriment and tumult of the festival was in full swing, none the worse for the the blustering wind, and the evening fires had just been lit. A dram of schkoltsch by an open fire is just the thing to ward off the autumn chill, to distract one's heart from its profitless yearnings, to toast the absent and the departed, to lend a veneer of adequacy to what had been a lackluster summer, and to steel oneself for the uncertainty of the coming winter. Or so they say.

On the opposite side from Sullivan's, a small band of vagrants appeared, looking haggard and dirty and bewildered. At first, they were known to none, but a little washing and dusting off revealed them to be none other than some of their own local boys—a mix of Marshals and Hooligans, with a few townsmen thrown in—returned at last from the wars. And what a sad story they had to tell, once a round of ale and a joint of beef had revived their spirits!

Alas, alas, they hadn't had a chance. Poor country boys as they were, they little knew what horrors awaited them on the fields of battle. They had traveled north for weeks, planning to join the other regiments and so continue to the front lines. But before they could do that, they were surprised by an encounter with a mighty, hostile force, and in this, their first campaign, they were sorely defeated. Desperately outnumbered, they were, out-manned and out-gunned—it was a wonder any survived at all. They turned from face to rapt face in the surrounding crowd.

Except for the few you see before you, all were killed, or lost, or captured. All except for we few.

What about this young man or that? people asked.

All gone. Lost or captured or killed, same as the rest. It was a brave fight, to be sure, and the boys gave it their best, but . . .

The tale stopped, silence or a draught of ale being the only suitable response.

It was then that the Burgermeister emerged, eyes streaming from his second dram of schkoltsch, to hear what he hoped he had not heard.

"But the officers," he said. "My boys?"

Shaking of heads; wide, shocked eyes.

"All gone, I tell you. All but we few." The little pool of silence around the tale-tellers began to seep through the square as the news spread. "All them boys is gone."

There was more said after that, but he didn't hear it. *Them boys is gone*, he heard, over and over again. He sat down suddenly and completely, without benefit of a chair or stool, plump on the ground like a sack of potatoes.

Them boys is gone echoed in the silence that surrounded him, a widening circle of stunned horror at the thought. The silence pushed against the competing revelry as word spread across the square.

Them boys is gone rolled past the Keg, past the tailor's shop and the Beetle, and past the farmers' carts, on toward the muddy place of the future fountain—where it met a wave of panic coming from the opposite direction.

A shower of sparks burst into the air on the far side of the square. A fire had broken out! The wind was kicking it up into the thatch of one shop and then another.

The stunned silence from one side and the panic from the other combined to goad the crowd into muddled flight. Half the crowd rushed to the center of the square to avoid the flames, while the other half rushed into town to try to save what could be saved. Fully half of each half forgot midway which half they belonged to and changed course in the middle. Horses and mules panicked, wagons were overturned and goats ate the contents, and the flames spread from roof to roof pursued by the wind until the square was nearly surrounded by flames. There was just as much screaming and pandemonium as you might expect.

The Burgermeister sat where he had collapsed, watching from a dazed distance as the Keg was knocked loose and rolled toward him. He thought for a wild moment that it was coming to his rescue, but it took a left turn at the last moment and rolled into the butcher's fire-pit, upsetting a rack of roasted chickens and exploding spectacularly, a geyser of blue-white flame reaching nearly to the sky.

"Good heavens," he said. "What in the name of mercy can have happened to my boys?"

→ EIGHT ←

PERHAPS YOU HAVE LIVED IN a village of half-timbered cottages and shops with thatched roofs, and so I needn't tell you how a fire behaves in such a neighborhood. Perhaps you have seen first-hand the ecstasy with which the flames leap from roof to roof, the intimate embrace they share with beam and rafter. If not, you must rely, as I do, on second- and third-hand sources, and the stories passed along among the families who survived.

Those who weren't attempting to fight the fire or save their belongings or flee the town altogether gathered in the center of the square and beseeched the sky for rain. But in vain. The clouds remained piled against the mountains, watching from a distance as if they had some other pressing matter to which to attend but would turn their thoughts to the town shortly, if they could spare the time.

The Burgermeister, to his credit, after overcoming the shock of the dual loss of his sons—not to mention witnessing the suicide of the Keg—had pulled himself together and rallied the town as best he could. Wells were plumbed dry and every pail in town was put to use while in one corner of his mind he was reworking his design for the fountain in the square. If only there had been something there besides a mud puddle, then more of the shops might have been saved. If only someone had braced the Keg, or if only the butcher had put a barrier around his firepit. If only his boys had listened to reason and gone into business. If only, if only.

By the next morning, a gray, smoky dawn, the fires had been beaten out or had run their courses. By nine in the morning, the clouds finally made up their mind to cover the town, and black sheets of rain snuffed out the last embers in the smoldering thatched roofs. If only the rain had come sooner—if only the Sullivan hadn't kept the rain away with his dreadful traditional efficiency! The Burgermeister trudged toward home to see about collecting his household and making some kind of plan for some kind of wretched future.

In the wake of the disaster, most of the shops on the square were damaged and some destroyed completely. Sullivan's and The Shop survived by virtue of their slate roofs. And fully half the houses in town had suffered at least some damage.

The big house, however, had been spared thanks to Tansey's insistence that no harm would come to it or there would be hell to pay. But the stable in back was lost, the horses had vanished into the hills, and the garden that Bonita had labored over so long ago was a wasteland of cinders and charred trellises. He arrived to find a half-empty house and an agitated panic among those who were there.

Robert and Cordage were gone! Lexi and the Princess were nowhere to be found!

A similar story was forming in many a house throughout the town. Had Father been consumed in the fire? Had Grandmother been driven into the countryside and lost? Had the children been swept away with the Vagabonds during their hasty retreat?

For a number of days it remained unclear how many people had succumbed to the flames versus how many were simply misplaced in the uproar. But when the smoke cleared, more than a hundred people were gone—almost two hundred, by some reckonings. Shopkeepers, tradesmen, wives and sons and daughters, one of the deacons, one of the town councilmen, two of the Dozen, and Tall Butler—all unaccounted for. (Tall Butler would later be found taking refuge in the attic of the Widow Baily, convinced that the wars had come and determined not to be taken alive.)

The town as a whole, and the big house in particular, at a stroke became bleak and dismal places. The Burgermeister held vigil on the front stoop beside the poor, scorched rose he has so recently brought back from the brink of death, prepared to settle down into a miserable winter after which there might well be no spring. How could there be, when all that was good and bright and young had been taken, and all that was left was old and tired and worn thin, worn to the very bone? What else was there to do but shut the doors and wait for night and the black release of sleep?

Part VII

Through Forest and Field

⇾ One ⇽

YOU MAY SUPPOSE THAT CLAMBERING over the wall at the far end of my cabbage patch was the most difficult part of our journey and that we proceeded quite easily and merrily after that. If that is your supposition, you may skip forward and save yourself the disappointment of learning that our troubles had barely begun. And by "our troubles," I mean "my troubles," because the boys themselves certainly took no actions nor made any great effort to keep us hale and hearty as we ventured forth.

In the first place, their lack of trust in me was deeply hurtful. What had I ever done to indicate I meant them any harm? Had I not safely delivered them into the welcoming arms of the wilderness when the tempests of civilization howled around my house? Was I not that very moment going decidedly far out of my own way to guide them and deliver them to the City, which was their stated destination? And, by their own admission, did they not wish to travel discreetly? Anyone could have found the way by the usual roads, but they did not know the lesser ways—the ways through forest and glen, visited but rarely by hunter or Hooligan or Vagabond. And

179

I did. So here was I, offering them the benefit of my knowledge, acquired over many seasons of surreptitious travel, but were they grateful? Quite the contrary!

"We don't need no help," the tall, scrawny one kept saying. "We can find our way fine by ourselves."

"Oh, can you?" I retorted. "Which way is it?"

"It's east."

"And which way is that?"

Silence.

"You see? You're already lost. And I should leave you that way and let you perish in the woods. Let the bears and whatnot eat you. The only thing that keeps me from simply walking away is a passing interest in the futures which you have so carelessly hidden from me. So, if only to put my own mind at rest, since I certainly feel no great obligation to you, I will lead you to the City by the safest route."

"Thank you," said the pudgy one.

"We don't need you," said the taller one.

"Hush. I already regret letting you tag along on my little jaunt. Don't make me have to take the trouble of choosing a hollow tree for you to curl up and expire in."

"Hang on," said the taller one. "We're the ones trying to get someplace. When did it become *your* trip?"

"Details," I said. "Syntax and semantics will be the death of you. The important thing is that the three of us together have a mathematically indefinable but philosophically better chance of getting to the City alive than each of us on our own."

"I'd be fine," said the taller one. "It's him that's a danger to both of us."

The pudgy one nodded good-naturedly. "I lose things," he said. "I lost my whistle."

He still had the stewpot on his head and wore the blanket like a cape. Holding a lumpy bag of cabbages and onions in his arms, he was unexpectedly beguiling. But I recovered quickly.

"Two miles," I said.

"Until what?"

"To where?"

"I give you two miles before you both collapse like little boys and ask to be taken home."

"We *are* little boys," said Pudgy.

"We already come twenty or thirty miles," said Gangly. "All the way from Bergerton."

I was unimpressed.

"That's because you were on a road. Any pair of fools can follow a road. People probably gave you food and you probably slept in haystacks like you were planning to sleep in mine."

Gangly remained defiant but Pudgy nodded.

"But our path is much more treacherous—" I looked at Gangly. "You are Cordage, correct?" I said, and turning to Pudgy, "And your name is Robert."

They nodded.

"Very well," I said. "Our path is much more treacherous, Cordage and Robert. The woods are full of bears and wolves and even things that pass for lions, if you don't look too closely. Not to mention the aforementioned Hooligans and Vagabonds. To get to the City, as you want, and to remain unnoticed, as I want, and to remain alive, as I presume we all want, traveling as a group is the only thing that makes sense."

"Cord says we don't wanna be noticed, either," said Robert.

"At least until we're on the other side of Bergerton," said Cordage.

"They're prob'ly looking for us."

That was no doubt true. News of the Great Fire had reached Wat's Hump the day before the boys themselves turned up. No doubt the search was on for the many who had fled the flames in terror and ended up wandering the fields in a daze. No doubt, no doubt. Why the boys wished to remain undiscovered, though, that question I chose to leave unasked until another day. Never pry more into the lives of your companions than you wish them to pry into yours, I say.

They gave me their two miles, then collapsed like little boys and asked to be taken home. I compromised by finding a very hospitable elm tree with a comforting pile of leaves at its base.

"Welcome home, boys."

→ Two ←

I N THE SECOND PLACE, these two young men—barely more than children, really—were entirely unequipped for such a journey, both in terms of mental and intestinal fortitude and in terms of actual equipment. A pocketknife and some string? What kind of traveling kit is that? A good start, perhaps, but hardly enough to get you through your own backyard, let alone the wide world before you. They had no money, no bags or packs, no blankets or food, just the clothes on their backs and the shoes on their feet.

The tall one, at least, had a sturdy tweed jacket and trousers— new, by the looks of them, although the sleeves and legs were already too short. Wrists and ankles all over the place. The other one only had a linen jacket, which might wear well enough but was nowhere near warm enough for an extended journey. I suppose they might be forgiven a certain lack of preparedness, having run with a panicked mob from a burning town and all, but to have come as far as they had, with as little as they had to sustain them, well, all I can say is it's a good thing they became acquainted with me when they did.

Or perhaps not.

That first night, despite having collapsed under the elm tree, they recovered remarkably as soon as I had started the fire. They simply would not stop throwing in leaves and pine cones, lighting twigs on fire and then waving them about, rushing about like mad things leaving trails of sparks, writing on stones with the charred ends, and then tumbling back to the fire to start it all over again.

"Mrs. Bones! Mrs. Bones! I found some acorns, can I put them in the fire?"

"I can write my name in the air with this glowing twig!"

"Can I put a rock in the fire?"

"This weed won't burn."

"Stop it, stop it! You're getting cinders in the cabbage!"

That last one was me. I was gamely trying to fix something for supper with ridiculous shenanigans going on all around me. They complained about the food yet gobbled it all up, and then we spent half an hour finding all the blankets.

"How can the blankets be lost?"

"I dunno, they were right here."

I found the blankets scattered in the undergrowth and then had to search for the cabbage bag, which I discovered in a hazel thicket.

"Boys," I said. "I understand that you may find it amusing to pick up objects for no reason and then drop them somewhere out of sight. Who knows, perhaps you're not even aware that you're doing it. Maybe it's some juvenile compulsion or animal instinct. In any case, if we are to survive our journey—and if I am to survive you—I must ask you to not touch anything at all unless I put it into your hands directly. Then, don't put it down until I tell you exactly when and where to do so. Are we clear?"

"What about sticks? Can we pick up sticks?"

"I can't find my knife."

Against all expectations, we survived that night and the next and eventually fell into a sort of routine. Each morning I woke at dawn and poked them until they arose, and we breakfasted on the remains of yesterday's supper. We located whatever had been misplaced the night before, gathered our baggage—it was really all my baggage, remember—and then set off. We trundled through the woods, I following my nose with practiced ease and they stumbling through the bushes like a pair of baby bears.

Even though we had a path to follow, they grumbled and groused and staggered into each other and into me until each mile started to feel like a hard-won battle against insurmountable forces of nature. They were too hot, they were too cold, they had to rest, they suddenly had to sprint ahead to see something and get lost while doubling back to me.

And for some inscrutable reason they felt a compulsion to inform me every time they must go into the woods to perform their gentlemanly offices.

I have heard that whole populations of people make such journeys as part of their daily life, whole tribes moving from one place to another, including the young boys. How that is ever managed is now a mystery to me. Were I in charge of such a tribe, we would leave a trail of young boys behind us as we went. That would speed up our progress and also allow us to find our way back by following the trail of sulking lumps sitting in the middle of the road poking the dirt with a stick. However, having only two boys with me on this journey—not nearly enough to mark my path homeward—I determined to make the best of things and keep them with me against some future need.

→ Three ←

IF I MAY DIGRESS, it could be said with some veracity that I am not the most maternal of creatures. Children have entered my world but rarely and have never stayed for very long. I wouldn't say their care and maintenance are a complete mystery to me, but there are many other things for the custody of which I am better suited.

Cabbages, for instance. Now, there's a well-behaved vegetable. A cabbage will stay right where you put it, in the garden or in the larder. A cabbage will not suddenly turn into a raving demon when it had been a sweet angel only an hour before. A cabbage will stay a cabbage to the end of its days, not grow and change and become something unrecognizable virtually overnight. Cabbages don't become jealous of the onions or resent being put together in the same soup. Give them a little manure, some water and some sunny days, hoe the weeds and pick off the slugs, and cabbages will reward you with tasty meals long into the winter. They don't complain that the manure is unsatisfactory or that those slugs was their fav'rites and they was playin with them.

No, having given the matter full thought and weighed one against the other most thoroughly, I have definitely come down in favor of cabbages. Narrow-minded and selfish of me, you may well say—but one can't hide from one's true nature, can one?

* * *

→ FOUR ←

AFTER THE FOURTH DAY the cabbages ran out and we were left to survive on what we could gather, along with the occasional duck egg. Yes, the duck was still with us, following at the tail end of our little procession and speaking its mind at every opportunity. Being a barnyard duck, it was capable of something that almost resembled flight, which it would employ whenever it got too far behind us.

Robert being not the swiftest hound in the pack, however, the duck's stuttering near-flight was seldom required. More often, Cordage and I were obliged to sit and wait until Robert had complained enough to catch up with us. I used the time to pass along bits of useful information and valuable traveling skills.

Nothing dark or dangerous, mind you—simple, practical things. How to gather nettle leaves without getting stung and then how to boil the leaves up for pottage. Which mushrooms were the right ones for eating and which were the right ones for becoming ill or deceased. How to start a fire against all odds in the rain. Things every wanderer ought to know.

He was an apt pupil, to my surprise, and his knife was useful more than once. I always intend to carry a knife myself but somehow I am unable to keep track of them. One of my few failings.

One afternoon, sitting by the side of an overgrown path, I was showing Cordage how to pull the fibers from milkweed stems, and he was showing me how to twist them into twine. It's a tricky thing, requiring more dexterity in the digits than a woman of my age should have to manage, so I told him to make the string and I'd pull the fibers. Robert stumped up to us carrying the duck. He plopped down next to me and handed me an egg.

"Clarence found another one," he said. Robert never ate the eggs himself but had become resigned to Cordage and I enjoying them on the promise of a whole flock of ducklings when we reached the City. The duck squirmed out of his arms and sat in the grass. Holding the egg in my hand, with Robert on one side, staring vacantly out of his pudgy, smudgy face, and Cordage on the other, jaw set and brows knitted as he twisted milkweed fibers back and forth, back and forth, I was moved by something that I can only characterize as feelings of genuine warmth for the boys. That, of course, would not do at all.

"Up, boys," I said. "Up, up, up, up, up."

"But, Mrs. Bones," Robert groaned.

Cordage said, "Hang on. 'Most done."

"Bring it with you," I said. "We must keep moving. If we're where I think we are—and I am always where I think I am—there's a place to stop just another mile or so ahead. Robert made a whining sound that cannot be reproduced using the standard alphabet, and Cordage grumbled and the duck quacked, but they all followed me between the trees.

As I had thought, within less than half a mile we came to a swift little brook with a hazel thicket on one side. One of the benefits of being a part-time witch is the ability to find shelter in any circumstance, and this was as pretty a place to camp as any. Cordage started a fire—just because he wanted to; there was no need yet. Robert and I gathered hazelnuts.

"Once you've got enough string, use your knife to cut a switch and I'll use an enchantment to turn this needle into a fish hook."

(Always carry a needle in your hatband. I give you that advice free of charge.)

"You don't need magic," said Cordage. "Just use a rock."

"Who says a rock isn't magic?"

That evening was almost pleasant, even by my exacting standards. We caught two small trout. After a supper of trout and duck egg with roasted hazelnuts and nettle tea, and with the little circle of warmth from the fire driving back the autumn chill, there seemed to be, on balance, more to be contented about than not.

"Tell me about yourselves, boys," I said. "Not like before, when it was just names and dates. What deep dark currents flow beneath those grimy surfaces?"

"We told you already," said Cordage before Robert could say anything. He needn't have bothered; Robert was nearly asleep. "We ran away from the fire. And the whole town burned down so we got nothing to go back to."

"We don't know for sure," Robert mumbled. "Maybe the house is still there."

"No, the whole thing burned down. We seen it, remember? The whole town ran away."

"Yeah," said Robert, suddenly excited. "We almost got trompled, but we ran with all the people down through the Vagabond camp. I dropped my whistle and I went back for it and then you grabbed me and dragged me down into this ditch and we stayed there until it got quiet, and—"

"And then we headed for the city, like everyone else, cuz the town was gone," said Cordage. "Only we gone the wrong way. And you know the rest."

"Yes, yes, I know all that." I wished, not for the first time (nor the last, alas), that I had remembered to collect my pipe during our hasty departure. "But what about your lives before that? You had mothers, I suppose? Cousins?"

"Everybody died," said Cordage.

"No they didn't," said Robert. "We don't know. Our moms are prob'ly fine and we'll go back—" He stopped at a look from Cordage.

"We gotta go to the City first," said Cordage. "Like we said. If we go back to Bergerton it's all burned down and everybody died."

"No they didn't."

"When we was running," Cordage told me, "all the people said they were going to the City 'cause the town was gonna burn down." He turned to Robert. "The City's got places we can go and get a job so we don't need to go back."

"I don't want my mom to be dead," Robert sniffed. "I think she went back to Grampa Popper's turnip farm, even though she said she'd never go back there in a million years. Grampa Popper would take care of us. Why can't we go there?"

"We don't know where it is."

I, of course, knew very well where Popper's Turnip Farm was, but for the moment my lips were sealed.

"Well, I don't want my mom to be dead, either, and I didn't want my dad to be a lunatic, and we had to give up the shop and move into Uncle Jon's house where everything smells old and weird. And stupid Lexi." He turned to me. "She thinks she's the most important because she's the oldest, but she's not even a real cousin, just this stolen Vagabond baby that Uncle Jon bought for the Princess." He stared into the fire and poked it with a stick. "Better off anyway, probably," he muttered. "All those old people were so old, and my mom just crying all the time."

"Mine, too," said Robert. "Why do moms cry all the time?"

"Do they?" I shrugged noncommittally. My mood was ruined.

Serves me right for wanting to plumb the depths of these waifs' souls. Will I never learn?

"Curl up, now, boys. There are still more miles ahead than behind."

Watching embers fade is the best kind of lullaby.

⇾ Five ⇽

O F COURSE, I WAS UNABLE to sleep. I dozed for a while, I suppose, but woke hours before dawn with that sudden, crystal-clear percipience from which there is no recovery. I tried, mind you—I tried to recover the thread of a dream and let it lead me back into slumber, but to no avail. The moon was high and bright in the sky, not quite full, and the clatter of the little brook was just slightly too loud to ignore. If I'd been bundled in something more than just my cloak, I might have drifted off, but the boys had absconded with both the blankets, leaving me wide awake in the chill. There was nothing to do but pull myself up and take an invigorating walk through my woods.

Yes, *my* woods. All wild places belong to those who travel them.

The world at night, particularly the woods, is different from the world in daylight. Or, rather, the world is the same, but darkness allows one to see it with truer eyes. The light of the moon pulls all the color from things, leaving their truest selves revealed. The bone-white beeches and black pines are the realest trees, and the shadows beneath them are the blackest, densest shadows ever to be found. Anythingg at all could be crouched or nestled in those shadows.

And the open spaces have a kind of broad clarity that is impossible in the daylight. Specific details are indistinct, perhaps, but look at the meadow, the whole meadow at once, with your whole eye, and you will see more of it than you could have known existed. Do you want to know the secret? What color is the sky? Empty and infinite cobalt. What color are the stars? All the colors, with all the air that shimmers between, and wispy clouds striated and segmented like the backbone and ribs of a colossal sky-whale, beached on the shore of the heavens. That is the secret. That and the silver trees and the black ferns, the ice-cold streams that come down from the mountain and the hard little trout that wait in the pools.

→ Six ←

IN THE THIRD PLACE, the boys quickly lost interest in traveling unnoticed. I lost count of the number of times I would be moving along in a quiet reverie only to hear "Mrs. Bones? Mrs. *Bo-ones!*" come sailing through the trees. They don't put boys in the cathedral choir at St. Breccia for nothing. You can hear them a league away.

A week into our journey we came to a clearing where our footpath crossed a road, the only real road that runs through the forest. The crossing of ways is marked by a huge stone, bigger than a house and carved all over with messages from untold centuries of travelers. The boys wanted to waste time climbing the rock, but I was more interested in leaving the clearing and plunging back into the dark, leafy safety of the trees.

"That road leads north from here to Bergerton, you know. If you want someone to recognize you and take you back, then by all means climb the rock and try to attract their attention. Sing and dance, if you want."

They wisely followed me back into the woods, but after that Cordage became dangerously insubordinate and Robert whinier than ever. I could put up with the whining—after a time it became a kind of monotonous background noise like the quacking of the duck. (Why do ducks quack and quack and quack as they walk along? It's the opposite of stealth. It's as if they're inviting the foxes to join them for supper at the earliest convenience.) In any case, Robert's complaints were a minor matter compared to the other one's surly obstinacy.

"Why do we gotta stay in the woods? We're way past the town by now. Why can't we go where the roads are? No one knows us outside the town."

I pointed out that just because no one would recognize *them* didn't mean no one would recognize *me*. I have, after all, a certain reputation.

"What, as a lousy cabbage farmer? Or half a witch?"

"I am an entire witch, thank you very much."

He shook his head. "Half a fortune telling, half a witch."

The nerve some people had! I sat them down on a log and prepared to deliver my finest lecture. Then I thought better of it and delivered my third-best lecture. There was a good deal of ground yet to cover. Why pull out all the stops now?

"Listen, you tadpoles. For better or worse, we're on this path together. And like it or not, I'm the more seasoned traveler. I have a set of skills that will save your miserable hides, and if you don't cooperate I'm at least enough of a witch to allow you to become dinner for the bears. Those are my blankets, too."

"Half a witch at best," said Cordage.

Robert nodded.

That was too much for my pride to withstand. I didn't come from a long line of teachers of the dark arts to have my honor impugned by two such bumps as these. You may well say that it was reckless and thoughtless of me to do what I then did—that I compromised my position by revealing my true powers. Well, what's done is done. I pulled an acorn out of Robert's ear and handed it to Cordage. I told him to put it under his hat, from where it disappeared. I told him what card he had chosen before he even looked at it himself. I juggled stones and turned them into flowers. Robert was immediately convinced, but Cordage remained skeptical until I pulled his knife from Robert's pocket and handed it to him.

"Can you teach me how to do that?"

Of course I could not! The dark secrets of the sorcerer are closely guarded and only shared with the most trusted acolytes.

"I'll carry your bundle for you and Robert will gather all the firewood."

Done.

"Wait," said Robert. "I'll do what?"

To my surprise, Cordage turned out to be mostly adequate as a pupil. For the next week, as we continued to make our way through the woods, he learned one technique after another, and barely a waking hour passed that he wasn't practicing this skill or that. After only one day he could pull all manner of objects from Robert's ear. (Of course I never allowed him to pull anything from *my* ears. Everything in these ears must remain inviolate.) Soon he was working with cards and dice and strings and rings and wooden balls. Sadly, we hadn't a single coin between us, or I could have taught him another whole branch of magic.

"Why don't you pull some coins out of my ears?"

"Robert, my boy, don't you think if there were any coins in your ears your cousin would have pulled them out by now?"

"That's right," said Cordage. "I've pulled so much out of your head that now there's nothing left but air."

Of course he wanted to learn fortune telling, but that's a different matter altogether. It requires a certain gift and a willingness to open one's inner eye to the fate of another. I didn't think Cordage had the right temperament—to be honest, I'm not entirely certain how I do it myself. A feeling comes over me, generally encouraged by a wide-eyed acceptance of everything I say as the truth, and the future just comes spilling out. It's a mystery, to be sure. I gave Cordage a few pointers and hoped he would forget about it.

After nearly three weeks we had at last come within two days' journey of the City. How is that possible, you say? Is not the City only five days from Wat's Hump by highway and byway?

True, but consult your map, if you'd be so kind. From the farm, my cabbage farm, that is, we headed south into the woods, and once there we headed east toward the City. Travel through the woods is slow going at best. We picked our way through the wilderness until we came to a point almost due south of the City, separated from it by twenty-odd miles of farmland and village. Considering the rough terrain we had to cross and the circuitous route by which we traveled, I'd say three weeks is an admirable time and I invite anyone who thinks he can do better to go ahead and try. Say hello to the bears for us.

The boys were happy to be walking proper footpaths and cart tracks again, and I was happy for the opportunity to eat something besides hazelnuts and duck eggs. I used our little cross-country jaunt to teach the boys—particularly Cordage, who under different circumstances might have made a fine protégé—some other of my many and varied skills. They learned how to liberate a chicken, determine which vegetables would hardly be missed, notice which loaf the baker would have discarded anyway, and so on. Robert was concerned at first because he thought we were stealing, but once

Cordage and I explained to him that travelers were all but entitled to supplies along their way, he calmed down.

"Don't worry," I told him. "One day, when you have your own house, some other traveler will need something of you, and then all will be in balance."

He seemed doubtful but at last acquiesced, which was fortunate, since—being the smallest, and somewhat less plump than when we had started—he was the one who could most easily get in and out of a hen house or root cellar unnoticed.

→ SEVEN ←

THE COUNTRY IN THAT DISTRICT is low and rolling, dotted with farms and convenient woodlots: a very pleasant landscape, with good roads between the villages and good secret places for avoiding notice. We made good time, all things considered, and had no trouble finding a cozy barn for shelter from the autumn rain.

I was actually in no great rush to get to the City, so the two days' journey stretched to four or five. Who was counting? Midway, we came to a large-ish town that I should have remembered was there but had in fact forgotten about. The town is called Wasserbrink and is, like Bergerton, the market town for its district. By great good fortune, we happened to arrive on the night of their harvest celebration. Their version of the Feast of Sullivan, if you will. The region specializes in stone fruits, especially sour cherries and apricots, and their fruit wines are justly celebrated. They have nothing on a good Bergerton cider, you understand. But when in Rome…

As I have noted, our purses were empty, and I felt it would never do to reach the city in such a state.

"Boys," I said, "the closer we come to this town, the more I feel my prognosticatory powers returning. I feel an irresistible urge to join the festival and give the good citizens here the benefit of my second sight. I can hardly withhold my services when so many are in desperate need, can I?"

"Can we come, too?" asked Robert.

The boys were a sight. I will assume you have never traveled on foot through fifty miles of forest with two young boys, but if you know anything at all about boys and forests, you can probably imagine what they looked like.

"No, boys, you stay outside town. Find a loose pie or something and wait in that barn over there. Your Auntie Bones will go attend to her business and return for you before dawn. With any luck we will be deep in the countryside by first light."

They grumbled but relented and I headed toward town. Of my experience there I will only say that it was moderately profitable, that the reputation the town enjoys for its produce is deserved, and that my departure had less to do with being pursued than it appeared at the time. I retrieved the boys and by the time the morning sun had driven the chill from our bones we were two miles away, standing on the crest of a hill looking down into the broad valley that contained the river that contained the island that contained the City.

The valley was thick with farms and manors. From where we stood, the road ran almost straight to the City: a distance of perhaps six or eight miles with a dozen inns along the way. The City itself fairly glittered in the sunlight, perched as it was on the hilltops of the island. Except for New House and the Old Fort, individual buildings were lost in the shimmering light. There was a slight haze from the smoke of a thousand chimneys. The clusters of houses on the opposite banks seemed not to have grown much since last I'd seen them.

How many years ago was that? I had once known the City well, but that was ages and miles ago. Some things are eternal; some things change before one's back is turned. Heaven only knew what we would find there. But the boys wanted to go the City. Fate had delivered them to me, and I would deliver them—to the gates, at least, if not beyond, and from there to wherever the fates might—

My reverie was interrupted by a cart of turnips—Bermdale turnips, by the look of them—and its driver, who admonished us to clear the way. Clearly, his turnips were more important than a weary band of travelers' moment of reflection. I was about to repay his kindness by turning him into a newt, but Robert suggested that instead we ask him for a ride to the City. The driver was reluctant at first but relented when Cordage promised to help unload his cargo.

Is jolting along the road in a cart full of turnips, behind a most unattractive man and the most unattractive parts of two horses, preferable to traveling the same road by the effort of one's own feet? It's hard to say. I'll have to give the matter some more thought. That some turnips found their way into my bundle is certainly a factor worth considering.

⇀ Eight ↼

THE TURNIP FARMER TOOK US as far as the informal market at the mainland foot of Second Bridge, where Robert almost made good on part of Cordage's promise to unload turnips. Then, by virtue of our superior skulking, we were able to mix with the crowd of citizens and thus avoid any complication with the officials at the bridge.

Second Bridge is very old, so narrow it will only allow foot traffic, and low enough to allow fishing, if one is so inclined. Robert wanted to throw sticks into the water. Cordage wanted to throw Robert in the water. I myself was tempted by that thought, but in the end we made it across, baggage and all. Crossing Second Bridge into the Low Quarter is not the most momentous way to enter the City, but as they say, from that point there is nowhere to go but up. And up we went, toward the hilly parts of the City, as nameless and aimless in the throng as we had been alone in the woods.

The boys had apparently set themselves the goal of reaching the City without having any idea what they would do once they got there. Cordage had a vague plan to "take care of things," while Robert was fixated on finding "someone to help us."

I parked them on a bench with a couple of pastries and let them stew in that muddle for half an hour while I made some inquiries of my own. Thankfully, some things had remained the same since my last visit. I collected the boys, and a short walk from New Bridge— around New House and past the garment district—brought us to the formidable twin edifices of The Sisters of Hope and Mercy and St. Jasper's Home for Wayward Boys.

These venerable institutions had operated in the city for as long as anyone could remember (and may continue to this day, for all I know). They loom side by side over a small courtyard in one of the less glamorous neighborhoods. The Sisters of Hope and Mercy are dedicated to the care and housing of all who are unable to care for themselves, while St. Jasper's has the noble task of taking in orphans and other un-homed boys and looking to their education and welfare.

The buildings are imposing, with high walls surrounding a jumble of dormitories, classrooms, workshops, and the like. Behind their iron gates, they share an inner courtyard that is divided down the middle by an iron fence. I led the boys across this courtyard to the front door of St. Jasper's.

As I expected, they would be happy to have the boys. Excellent. Delighted, of course. Plenty of room for even the smallest in need. Just wait out in the courtyard and the headmaster will be with you shortly.

I nudged the boys out into the sunlight while I finished up the last of the paperwork and then joined them. On St. Jasper's side, the courtyard was empty except for us. We sat on a bench near the door. Through the fence we could see several of the poor souls who were in the care of the Sisters. Sullen, ragged things, huddled in corners or pacing abstractly from place to place. Some of them mumbled; others spoke to the stones under their feet.

And then one laughed and called out.

"Cordage? My little lump?"

A man stood at the fence, tall and oddly jointed—and, except for the beard, the spitting image of Cordage, who responded by turning white.

"By heaven, it is you," the man said, giggling.

Cordage turned to me, his eyes dark with suspicion. "Where'd you bring us?" he asked.

The door opened and the headmaster emerged in a cloud of fragrant rosewater.

"Come along, then, boys, we're all set," he said.

"Where'd you bring us to?"

"Cordage, Cordage! Did your mother send you?"

"Come along, boys."

I am uncomfortable with such emotional exchanges and decided the most prudent course was to make a swift exit and leave the boys in St. Jasper's most capable hands, while I continued on a course of my own.

"But, Auntie Bones," Robert called out through the gate. (I had already come to regret having referred to myself that way in a moment of lightheartedness, but there was nothing to be done. Alas.) "Auntie Bones, I thought you were going to take care of us."

"I have taken care of you, boys, and now it's St. Jasper's turn. You'll be fine here, with schooling and food and beds with real roofs over them."

"Indeed, boys, come along and I'll show you the place."

"You're much better off here than wandering the wide world with me. The city's a fine place for a couple of clever boys such as you might possibly be. Why, in no time you'll be in charge of the place."

"I ain't stayin."

"Can I keep my duck?"

"Cordage, Cordage!"

"I ain't *stay*in! Hey, lemme go, you—"

The headmaster led them in and I made my way back out to the street, alone again, as I had so often been before. A wandering life is a weary and lonely one, but on the whole, it may surprise you to know, I prefer solitude. When others are with me I seem to find myself diluted. When one is alone, one is whole. Still, it would be unfair to say I had no regrets at parting ways with the boys, particularly where the carrying of baggage was concerned.

But fare thee well, boys!

I hoisted my bundle and headed off in the direction of the nearest mug of consolation, with only the weight of the finder's fee in my purse for company.

Part VIII

Through Village and Town

→ Oпe ←

I DON'T KNOW ABOUT THE VAGABONDS of your acquaintance—whether they share the reputation for sudden arrival and equally sudden departure. I can only speak for those I have encountered myself: Slogoyban's little band, and one or two others whose names escape me. I have heard that elsewhere and in more recent times the various Vagabond clans have settled in towns permanently, and that some have even built houses and planted gardens. Slogoyban, if he still lives—or his shade, if he has traveled beyond the last horizon—surely quakes at the very thought and casts a charm into the fire to ward off such a wretched fate.

In that place and at that time, Vagabonds were known to come and go as easily as a flock of birds, to sail across the land as effortlessly as a cloud sails through the sky. And among all the tribes in the land, Slogoyban's was known to be the stealthiest and most agile, often as not appearing in the pasture without having been seen along any road, then disappearing as if having soaked into the ground like a summer rain.

When fire broke out in the square, Lexi and the Princess discovered that the Vagabonds did not in fact sink into the earth, nor did they dissolve like smoke nor blow away in the wind like leaves. The girls were still in the camp, the Princess eating sweets and Lexi looking at shawls or scarves or some such nonsense, when the screams reached their ears. Without delay, and without any signal being given, the singing and dancing ceased. Stalls were collapsed and bundled into wagons, cooking fires doused, donkeys hitched, and within minutes the whole camp was uprooted and flowing south, away from the town amid a wave of scrambling, weeping refugees.

When the flight started, Lexi, seemingly without a thought, put the small bundle she carried in the nearest wagon, helped the scarf-and-shawl woman pack up her stall, and then calmly led the Princess by the hand as the tribe started away. If the Princess was frightened or confused, she was mollified by Lexi's composure. If she had ever had any doubts about who would watch over her and guide her steps, those doubts were forever allayed. Amid the disorganized panic of the townspeople, and amid the practiced and frantic flight of the Vagabonds, Lexi was an island of cool clarity.

"Keep with me, Princess Allium. It's only a fire. The tribe will protect us."

Could she have been remembering similar flights from her past adventures with them? She would have been so small at the time that it hardly seems likely. Had she had some premonition—was she somehow prepared? If you had asked her, perhaps she would have replied that, since she expected nothing, she was ready for everything at all times.

Whatever the case, Lexi and the Princess fled with the Vagabonds and remained with them a week until news reached them.

"The town is destroyed, Princess," Lexi told her. "All who remained have perished." The Princess sat in silence for a respectful moment and allowed a tear to flow through the week's worth of grime on her cheek.

"That is that, then," she said. "There is nothing for us but to travel the wide land as wanderers and make our way as best we can."

→ two ←

THE LOSS OF HER HOME and family seems to have put only a small damper on the Princess's enthusiasm for this new adventure. She would later say—in her memoir, which someone transcribed for her, the occupations of her later years not allowing time for such an indulgence as literary pursuits—that while it was very sad to be an orphan and without a home, things were happening so quickly and changing so fast that there was no time to grieve. And besides, she had always been half an orphan anyway, with no idea about mothers or fathers or any of that kind of thing. She missed her aunts and uncles, of course, but they were only aunts and uncles after all. She missed her grandfather's wrinkled, sad old sagging face and the amused annoyance in his eyes when she tugged on his whiskers. She missed her dresses, but the colorful garments Lexi procured for her during their travels were more than adequate substitutes. She missed Cook—or, more accurately, she missed roasts and bread baked in loaves.

But it was thrilling—thrilling!—absolutely thrilling to be out in the world with Lexi and with these strange and wonderful people. She loved everything about it: traveling the countryside in the wagons, dancing around the fire until all hours, sleeping nestled with Lexi like two spoons under scratchy homespun blankets.

And she loved Lexi most of all, Lexi who was everything she wanted to be, narrow and poised, funny and kind, Lexi who could talk to anybody about anything and always knew what to do. She didn't stop to think whether it was worth the trade-off, her whole town in exchange for this adventure with her best friend. She didn't have to. The adventure had swallowed her whole and she had gone most willingly down into the depths.

I cannot say with any certainty whether Lexi's long association with the Berger household increased or diminished her usefulness when she unexpectedly rejoined the Vagabonds. She could certainly read and write better than most members of the tribe. And at the very least, she had become acquainted with several dishes—exotic to the Vagabonds, if not completely unknown—which she was able to prepare for the Princess when she became homesick.

The dining customs of Vagabonds are less formal than those of more settled folk, and it took the Princess some time to feel comfortable with them. In brief, at eventide, each family that feels the inclination or happens to have some ingredients makes up a large pot of whatever comes to mind. The members of the whole tribe then wander from fireside to fireside with a bowl and a spoon, sampling whatever catches their fancy. It is by its very nature a cuisine that favors soups and stews and jumbles of meat and vegetables, curiously spiced and served with the ubiquitous flat bread of the Vagabonds, grilled over the coals in the classic fashion.

This method of cooking did not suit the roasts and baked breads that were the Princess's special favorites. Lexi did manage over time to create a beef stew with turnips and cabbage that approximated Cook's roast. It was flavored with rosemary and thyme, which were novelties to the Vagabonds, and the dish is called Princess Stew to this day.

But Lexi was never able to work out baking bread at an open fire. (To be truthful, she was never, before that time or since, able to bake any kind of bread under any circumstances. There were many incidents with varying degrees of failure, including one with particularly amusing consequences, but that is a story for another time.) Later in their travels, the Princess developed an annoying habit of sneaking off and being found later with no money in her purse and a half dozen buns in her bag.

They stayed with Slogoyban's tribe through the winter, traveling south to the slightly warmer climate of the next district. Sometimes they met and traveled for a time with another group of Vagabonds. Sometimes they would see another troupe across a valley and turn around to go the other way until they were out of sight. Vagabond politics were a mystery to the Princess, as they are a mystery to me, worldly though I am.

Lexi claimed she had lost the peculiar, gnarled language of the tribe, but she still understood enough to translate for the Princess as needed.

"We will camp on the far side of the river," she would say. "It's bad luck to camp on the inside of a bend in a river. It angers the river spirits." Or, "We mustn't wear any green between now and the solstice, or the winter will be too long." And, "Stay down in the wagon, Princess, until the Marshals have passed."

The Princess was subject to the tempests of emotion common to young ladies of a certain age, and she was often quite vocal in her displeasure with one thing or another, but in the main she seemed to enjoy the journeying and the sporadic visits to villages and towns that she had previously known only in name, if at all. She began remembering the dances Lexi had taught her as a child and joined the circles around the fire at every opportunity. Lexi, as you know, was never seen to dance, but she still remembered all the songs she had ever heard—some quite old, and not all of them Vagabond songs—and could be coaxed into singing from time to time.

That she could still sing in the Vagabond tongue but could not be persuaded to speak it was a mystery that remained unexplained. Slogoyban and a few others were proficient enough in the common languages of the countryside, and virtually everyone in the tribe had enough words to haggle in the marketplaces they passed through. In terms of book learning, the Princess was the most educated member of the party. Languages had not been emphasized in her schooling, but she had a passable mix of both literary and vernacular Vodlovian (courtesy of Tall Butler, who had a grandmother, you know) and had learned to conjugate a great many verbs of one sort or another. Enough of various languages, in short, to order dinner, if not to avoid giving offense.

So with this tenuous web of shared speech, they all got along quite nicely. In fact, by Yuletide, a half-dozen young men of the tribe had heard enough of Lexi's jewel-like voice that they were prepared to profess their undying love, despite sharing barely a dozen words with her.

The Princess, too, found her attachment to Lexi growing the longer they traveled together. She imagined them as two lost kittens on their way to a magical land of cream and fat mice. Or she pretended they were two wild ponies, roaming freely over the land, eating the sweet grasses and drinking the cold, clear water of secret springs. The disaster at the town drew further into the past and further from the center of her mind—from day to day, she was happy to jostle along whatever road Slogoyban chose for them.

Lexi, although she had never seemed discontented at the Burgermeister's house, was more cheerful than the Princess remembered. She laughed often and lightly, and spent less time observing the goings-on from the perimeter. She still scolded the Princess, but less pointedly, almost with a sense of fun.

"Princess Teakettle, how can you be a proper Vagabond with such unruly hair!" "Princess Parasol, please concentrate on the dance and leave the singing to others." "I must say, your royal and most esteemed highness, that one or two more layers of mud might definitely enhance your loveliness."

She still had a secret, Lexi did, although for the time being she no longer looked like a girl with a secret. She looked like a girl with a purpose, or perhaps a lingering intention. But in fact, she was still a girl with a secret, and she worked on sustaining it whenever it happened to cross her mind.

Where once it had been a straightforward and simple secret, the advent of the fire and the addition of the Princess had introduced some unexpected variables. She was obliged to adapt her secret accordingly and to bide her time with her well-known patience. She worked on the letter as well, and over time it became so much better than the best letter she had ever written that she was almost afraid of the day she would have to give it up.

She wasn't worried about the consequences, mind you—those would take care of themselves. No, she was simply so pleased with the letter and so enamored with her sparkling turns of phrase that she hated to give it up. At length, she resolved to acquire another sheet of paper and to make herself a copy.

She thought for a moment that perhaps the letter would lose some of its luster after it was all over—that the copy she kept wouldn't have the same delicious glamor of the original, taut and poised for flight like an arrow in the bow. But it would have to do. It would be something, anyway, and all the lovely phrases would be hers forever.

She turned the words over in her mind as the tribe struggled through the early spring mud, awaiting sporadic chances to pull it out and make changes in her careful, tiny, somewhat childish script.

→ THREE ←

I MAY AS WELL TAKE A MOMENT to tell you about the languages of the place. As with most languages at that time—if not all languages at all times—there was, despite the best efforts of scholar and professor, no hard-and-fast standard for grammar and pronunciation.

From the capital, to pick an arbitrary starting point, one might travel sixty miles to the next city of any consequence and find the speech there to hardly differ from one's own. Go another fifty miles to the City at the center of this tale and again, the differences are but slight. There is now a nasally tone, called "island twang" by the residents of the capital: found by some to be charmingly coarse and by others to be simply vulgar. Another eighty miles to the coast, and the change of accent is quite marked, with some interesting variations in vocabulary.

The same is true if one goes in the opposite direction, two hundred miles to the lakes beyond the mountains, the furthermost border of the country. The speech there is distinctive but easily understood by anyone from the capital. And yet, if someone selling timber from the lakes meets a seafarer from the southern coast, they are apt to stare at one another in the deepest perplexity until someone is found to translate for them.

The language of Bergerton is essentially the same as that of the City but has a more pronounced twang and adds some regional variations in vocabulary, particularly as regards the names of apples and other fruits.

Now, add to this a half-dozen Vagabond tribes, each with its own language, not to mention immigrants and refugees from other lands, and you may begin to understand the nature of the linguistic porridge Lexi and the Princess were attempting to navigate.

The Vagabond tongues are particularly troublesome for scholars, due partly to the unusual number of consonants they contain but mostly to the Vagabonds' reluctance to be studied. They are not especially secretive about their languages and speak them openly in any company, but neither are they eager to dilute their power by teaching them to people who are merely curious. For example, I once overheard the following exchange (in circumstances that have no relevance to the tale at hand) between a professor of languages from the capital and an old Vagabond woman selling beet greens.

"How would you ask me for a fish?"

"I would learn your words, and then I would say 'Give me a fish.'"

"But in your language?"

"In my language I don't want a fish."

So. Lexi had been fluent in the tongue as a child but professed to have lost the knack. There were some among the Vagabonds—Slogoyban included—who thought her ignorance of the language exaggerated. The Princess picked up a few of the less awkward words and delighted in trying to make herself understood, but Lexi was never heard to speak any of it at any time, apart from the songs she was persuaded to sing.

* * *

→ Four ←

THAT WINTER WAS NOT ESPECIALLY HARD, but it was hard enough that those who lived out of doors welcomed the first breath of spring with quiet gratitude. When the snow became slushy and the icicles began to drip in earnest, the Vagabonds turned north up the road that would lead them back to Bergerton and its environs. For forty-odd years they had entered this valley just in time to see the apple orchards in bloom and then spend two weeks or more at the town, their welcome being somewhat warmer there than elsewhere.

Over the winter they had acquired a sizable stock of useless items from the neighboring districts and beyond, and they were hopeful that enough of the town remained for them to find a ready market. In particular, Slogoyban had a peck of abalone shell fragments, which could be picked up for free at the coast or purchased for a song in the south and sold for a premium in Bergerton, where mother-of-pearl inlays were the height of cabinetry fashion. The profit on that commodity alone could carry his little band through the next summer, perhaps even to the extent of re-shoeing some of the donkeys, poor footsore things that they were.

As their course northward became more definite, Lexi began passing by Slogoyban's wagon from time to time to exchange a few words with him. When they were only days away from entering the forest she went twice a day to discuss one thing and another. On the very skirts of the woods, where the green buds strained to burst, she cornered him at his fireside and made the most pointed suggestions and recommendations.

The town was gone, she told him. They had all heard the news.

There was no point in going there except to mourn the loss of friends. And for her part she had no friends there to mourn.

But we have heard other news as well, he rejoined. The Burgermeister, he still lives, they say. They are building up the town again. They have money but no roofs. We can help them build their roofs and they will give us their money and more.

The town is gone, she insisted. Did Slogoyban not flee the town himself and feel the wall of fire at his back? There is nothing to visit but bones. Nothing to build but crypts.

But the Burgermeister, he lives.

The town is gone.

Around and around it went until Slogoyban reverted to his native snarl of language, knowing full well she understood every deprecation with which he laced his argument. She remained placid, blinking slowly as if to say she understood not a word, until his ire was spent and he reverted to their common tongue.

The Burgermeister, he lives.

The town is gone.

They are building roofs.

The town, it is a curse to us.

The impasse did not appear to be resolved, but at length Lexi withdrew with the excuse that she must prepare Princess Calliope for the journey.

The next morning, after ensuring that the party had enough food for the week it would take to traverse the forest, they set out. The way was not far—a person on foot can make the journey in two days, or one very long day on horseback. But the road is quite rough, and donkey carts and Vagabond caravans travel slowly on the best of roads. Best to take it slow and not risk breaking an axle or laming an animal.

Besides, they had made the trip twice a year for decades, if not longer, and their stopping places were well defined—even named, with secret names known only to the tribe. The first night they camped at Two Pools and replenished their water supplies. The next, they rested at The Walnuts, a remnant of an ancient orchard that provided them nuts on their fall journey and cabinetry lumber for trade in the spring.

After the third day, which marked the longest single stretch of travel through the woods, they stopped at The Stone, the same ancient marker the boys and I had crouched behind mere months before.

At one time, the stone had marked a true crossroads. Now, although the north-south road still saw some use, the east-west had long since been lost to the forest. The east-west road had originally skirted the northern edge of the forest and defined the boundary of a tiny kingdom that once called this land its own. But the kingdom had withered away, and the forest flowed north to engulf the border, and the road was lost to all but deer and squirrels and bears and witches and little lost boys and other such creatures.

Did you know that forests flow like a slow tide across valley and dale? That they wash up and down foothills, splashing the knees of the mountains like the green waves of a leafy sea? Well, now you do.

Being midway through the forest, The Stone was a popular stopping place for all travelers, and a broad meadow was kept cleared by the perennial search for firewood. The caravan arrived at dusk. The snow had mostly melted, so they spread out across the whole space to let the donkeys graze on the new grass and browse among the shrubs. Lexi and the Princess were still traveling with the scarf-and-shawl woman, a widow who was glad for the company.

Lexi led her donkey to a little patch near the edge of the clearing, where the grass was thin but the ground was level and drier. The Princess collapsed on a tussock and watched Lexi build a fire and help the scarf-and-shawl woman spread out the sleeping rugs. The woman chattered to both of them and seemed neither to notice nor to mind whether they understood her. Lexi, of course, never gave any indication of comprehension, but when the Princess said, "She wants you to put the rugs closer to the wagon," Lexi said, "Of course she does. What else would she want?"

In the morning, the Princess packed up all her belongings in a tidy bundle as Lexi had taught her over the past months. She might have been surprised when Lexi offered to put it in the wagon for her, but she overlooked the detail. Lexi was always doing something for somebody, after all. Once she had hitched the woman's donkey and secured the baggage, Lexi beckoned the Princess into the forest.

"Just for a moment, to gather fiddleheads."

The woman called after them and the Princess told her they would be just a moment. What she actually said, with her patchy command of the language, was "Be us waiting slowly time," but the woman nodded as if she understood. She clucked to the donkey and turned it toward the road, jostling for a position among the other wagons.

Compared to the hectic flight from Bergerton, this was a much more relaxed affair (if just as disorganized). It took a full three-quarters of an hour to get everyone underway, with much shouting and good-natured cursing and last-minute gathering of children. The woman barely noticed that the girls weren't with her— people frequently rode in whatever wagon was convenient, or chose to walk. Everyone always caught up eventually, so she gave it hardly a thought until the band reached the Four Oak Trees (which were then three, but would one day be five) and there was no one to help unhitch the donkey.

→ FIVE ←

LEXI AND THE PRINCESS EMERGED from the woods with a basket of fiddleheads and some mushrooms. The Princess surveyed the rutted, empty meadow with a look of dismay.

"I don't understand—where did they go?"

"South. To see the ruins of Bergerton, maybe to comb through the rubble for treasure."

"But I don't understand. Why did they leave?"

"They have their places to go, their things to sell."

"I don't understand."

"You understand perfectly well, *Princess*."

"But—"

"They are on the road to Bergerton. Do you want to go there and sift through the ashes of your home for the bones of your dead grandfather? There is nothing there for us but tears."

The Princess looked at her blankly.

"We are going somewhere else," said Lexi. She retrieved their bundles from under the bracken at the edge of the forest, along with two blankets and a waterskin, and began to deck out the Princess for travel. "We are taking a different road."

Her calm had returned. Had it ever left? She took the younger, taller girl's hand and met confused anxiety with kind amusement.

"Fear not, Princess Fiddlehead. I won't let the bears eat you. There are no bears in these woods, anyway."

Alas, I never had the opportunity to travel the wilds with Lexi and critique her performance. I could have offered many helpful bits of information, as well as point out some grave shortcomings. That matter with the bears, for instance. There *were* bears in those woods, as there are to this day, and they will eat a hapless traveler without a thought, especially in the spring. The business with the fiddleheads and mushrooms was very good, but she overlooked some other opportunities for fresh greens. She had collected a small cooking pot and a spoon but no knife, a flint and steel but no tinder. In all, not a bad turn for a first wilderness adventure, but it's only by the greatest good luck that things did not turn out much worse than they did.

Well, wind through the leaves, as they say.

Suffice it to say the first few uncomfortable nights were worth it in light of all the adventure that was to follow. After three days they emerged from the woods, looking for all the world like the two bedraggled wastrels they were. They slept in a hay barn, dined on pilfered eggs and new onions (very good traveling practice, that), and found their way the next day to a small hamlet with an inn.

The hamlet's name is lost to history, but it was practically indistinguishable from Wat's Hump. All hamlets are the same. You may call them whatever you like.

They approached the inn at midday and begged a room and a bath and a bowl of porridge. The landlord didn't trust Lexi's promise to pay, but as a father himself, with his own daughters grown and gone, he could hardly turn these two grimy waifs away. His surprise, then, was even greater than that of the other patrons of the inn when, that evening, two glorious creatures emerged from their room, bathed and coiffed and dressed in the very party frocks they had fled the fire in, Lexi having insisted on keeping them clean and packed away against just such an opportunity.

It gave her great pleasure to present, she said, the Princess Angelika, late of Vodlov and Zbedania, tragically orphaned by the wars and now thrown upon their mercy. She craved their indulgence, she said, while the Princess partook in the only joy left to her, the simple dances of her exotic homeland.

Lexi began to clap and sing, softly, while the Princess stepped to the center of the room. She stood there perfectly poised for a full half-minute, her clear, sea-colored eyes raised just above the heads of the farmers who were seated at the bar enjoying a well-earned ale.

Just when it seemed that perhaps she had forgotten why she was there, she dropped her eyes, turned her head to the side, stepped out, and raised one arm in a low arc. She twirled. She moved her hands in intricate, delicate patterns, while her feet flashed below the hem of her skirt.

The farmers were transfixed—ale, well-earned or no, neglected at their elbows. When the dance ended and the song trailed away, a burst of applause greeted the Princess, who curtseyed gracefully, just as Lexi had taught her. This was different from dancing with the Vagabonds or dancing all alone in Lexi's room all those years ago. This was frightening and exhilarating, and the uneven floor had presented an unexpected challenge. But when she saw Lexi's pleased expression, the Princess blushed and asked for a cup of water in the careful foreign accent they had contrived.

So it went on into the night, until Lexi told the crowd that it was time for Princess Angelika to retire, and that she appreciated immeasurably the small tokens of appreciation they had bestowed.

In fact, there was more than enough appreciation to pay for their room and board the next morning. The landlord asked if they wouldn't like to stay another night or two (as the bar had done very good business as well).

Sadly, no, Lexi said, they must continue on their way, pursued as they were by enemies of the Princess's late father. No one believed a word of it. It was the talk of the town for months to come.

* * *

→ Six ←

LEXI, YOU WILL NOT BE SURPRISED to learn, had retained all the money she had carried away from Bergerton and even added to it while living among the Vagabonds. Their engagement at the nameless hamlet had netted a small profit as well, so they could have hired passage to the next town, as the Princess suggested. But Lexi pretended not to hear. Then the Princess asked who it was that had done all the dancing last night and who, therefore, deserved to ride at least part of the way.

Lexi explained patiently that, back in their traveling rags, they were at most half an hour from securing charitable transportation of some sort. She had hardly finished speaking when a farmer with a cartload of peas and new carrots approached them in the lane. When he learned that they were half-sisters by marriage and had been summoned suddenly to their aunt's deathbed, he not only carried them to the next town but gave them a pound of vegetables for their supper.

And so they journeyed, through the spring and into the summer. Princess Floribunda of a minor branch of the Glotchburgh Horffstaads danced at the Green Willow in Hickettston, after which a cloth merchant carried two cousins to Aftford to attend a wedding.

The Princess Hazelrose—who was tragically mute and disowned by her mad stepmother—danced at the Dragonfly. Two orphans thrown together by fate rode with a tinsmith all the way to Leffer's Fork.

All through the summer they went in a great circle through the district, twice circumnavigating the City without ever coming within fifty miles of it. It seemed to the Princess that she had danced at every tumble-down inn and wayside market that could possibly exist. But by genius or pure luck, Lexi always led them over some unknown hill to a hamlet or village or full-fledged town which they had never seen, and which, more importantly, had never heard of them.

Sleeping in hedgerows or haylofts on some nights and at inns or even the townhouses of local barons on others, they wandered and thrived. The Princess fluttered after Lexi like a devoted bird until all the awkwardness was wrung from her and she became nearly— without knowing it, mind you—nearly equal to her muse in poise and grace and ineffable inscrutability.

Midsummer, late summer, early fall, mid-fall. The leaves changed in the countryside, and they found themselves walking along a wagon track toward some town or another. Lexi sang softly to herself, and the Princess trailed her fingers through the tall, dry grass.

"What shall we do for the winter, do you think?" Lexi asked.

"I don't know. Go stay with Slobbygan again?" The Princess's pronunciation of the Vagabond language remained atrocious.

"No, I think they mightn't welcome us back quite yet. Next year, perhaps—but that is too far off to consider."

"Well, I don't know, then. We could go to one of the bigger towns and find work at an inn or tavern or something. Something besides dancing for a while?" Lexi remained silent. "Or help some farmer with his harvest in exchange for a room for the winter?"

"Does Princess Traildust really suggest we demean ourselves by common labor?"

The Princess giggled.

"Cultured young ladies of good breeding need hardly stoop to such things."

Something in her tone silenced the Princess and they continued on their way, accompanied only by the sound of the breeze in the grass. One wonders, doesn't one, whether Lexi's aversion to actual work of any kind will ever be tempered by the necessity of survival. Time will tell, I suppose.

In any case, their joint reveries were interrupted by a beet farmer who came up behind them in his lopsided cart and asked if they were on their way to Upper Spratt for the festival.

Of course they were going to the festival. Where else would anybody want to go?

He was jolly and ancient and pumpkin-colored. He offered them a ride if they didn't mind sharing the space with bushels of beets. The graciously accepted and he gallantly tried to help them up, after which they were obliged to help him back up into the cart. They reminded him of his own granddaughters, who he ain't seen in heaven knows how long. Their mother keeps them from him, you know.

Once they arrived at the village, the Princess, out of long habit, began to scout a likely location for their operation. The chattering of Pumpkin Man had confounded their usual planning, so she didn't know whether to find a spot in the marketplace for the Traveling Orphans or a tavern for the Dancing Princess. Really, at a local festival, they could do either with equal success, so she wandered among the stalls and carts and gave the matter perhaps less attention than she should have.

It was just like the Feast of Sullivan, really, and like a hundred other events just like it that the Princess had seen in the past year. They seemed so important to the people of the towns, but they were all the same, with the same foolish traditions and the same tired crowds full of grubby exhausted children and excited shoppers. They all had the same bad local food, with occasional surprising delicacies, and endless rows of crafters and merchants selling the same indistinguishable trinkets.

Where had Lexi got to? Something had dampened her mood and she had wandered off. Well, no matter. The Princess would find a few likely spots and then Lexi could choose the best one for her purposes, whatever those purposes might be at the moment.

Finally she found Lexi on the far side of the marketplace, where a small band of Wayfarers had set up camp. (Wayfarers being, as you know, distantly related to Vagabonds, sharing certain cultural roots and traveling practices. In fact, there are some scholars who believe the two to be one and the same, with different names attached depending on which countries they traveled through to reach their current territories. But that is a question for more academic minds than mine.)

Lexi was prone to visit such camps whenever they encountered them, although the Princess had begun to find them dreary and only marginally profitable. Lexi liked hearing the news they brought, particularly anything regarding Slogoyban and his whereabouts. She occasionally learned new songs, as well, which helped relieve the monotony of their performances. The Princess found the camp by going downhill from the marketplace, and she found Lexi standing outside a particularly shabby tent with a distracted look in her eye and a small, covered pot in her hand. The Princess thought it was cheese, but Lexi stopped her.

"It's for your complexion. You have a spot. And we're going to the City for the winter."

"Did you go to a fortune teller again?"

"We'll take a carriage if we make enough money here."

"Fortune tellers are pretend. *You* know that better than anyone."

"Rub this on your face now and tonight and in the morning."

"Why the City? What can we do there?"

"We have to be there by the first snow."

"I don't have spots."

"I don't know how much a carriage costs. Maybe the beet farmer will take us."

"I think a carriage would be better. I don't want to ride on beets all the way to the City."

"You just have a little spot on your nose and a tiny one on your cheek. They're not bad."

"It smells like cheese. Are you sure?"

"We have to be there by the first snow."

In the end, the Princess did have a spot on her nose; they made enough to hire a carriage; and the Princess never learned what had made Lexi suddenly want to go to the City so urgently. She did, however, learn why the first snow was significant.

"Because who wants to travel after the snow has fallen? It's nothing but mud as far as you can see."

* * *

→ SEVEN ←

THE CARRIAGE DEPOSITED THEM at the waystation at the end of Old Bridge, opposite the City, where a handful of shacks and stalls surrounded a guardhouse. The carriage wasn't licensed for the city proper, so they were obliged to continue on foot.

Lexi was flummoxed by this development and by the snow-flakes that started to dance about them as they stood in front of the guardhouse.

"What do we do?" asked the Princess.

Lexi said nothing, only gazed across the bridge (which was lined with shops in the old style) at the heaped-up jumble of buildings beyond, topped by New House. The whole thing looked like a, she didn't know, like a big something on top of a huge pile of something jumbled. Why was it so crowded? Where did all these people have to go in such a hurry back and forth? What could possibly be the point? And this big oaf of a girl, this ridiculous child, what use was she at all? How had she been saddled with her all this time? A full year or more? And the man coming over from the guardhouse was clearly irritated with them, sterner and more richly uniformed than any village official she had ever confronted. She could barely hear the Princess hiss her name. They had obviously already done some-thing wrong in the guard's eyes and were to be turned away at best or thrown into the river at worst. The Princess hissed Lexi's name again, twice, and then the man stood before them and asked what they wanted.

What *did* they want? Whatever in the world could they possibly want? Lexi hesitated just a moment too long, and the next thing she knew the Princess was speaking.

"Thees ees the Princess Macadamia," the Princess said, "here to visit thees great city and enjoy the winter away from her native Grompagne." Her pronunciation of "Grompagne" was perfect, a detail that was not lost on Lexi.

Forgeeve their appearance, they had fallen among thieves, and all their papers and letters of introduction were taken. The guard softened somewhat and invited them into the guardhouse out of the weather to record their entry to the city.

"Macadamia," said the Princess. "M, A, C . . ."

And her name? Lexi, just Lexi. It was short for something. Lexi thought about giving the Princess's hand a little squeeze of gratitude but contented herself with flushing slightly and remaining perfectly still as the formalities were completed.

"Thank you, officer," said the Princess. "Come, Princess. We must find adequate and economical lodging so you may prepare for your audiences tomorrow."

If the guard caught the sly glance they exchanged, he gave no sign but merely helped them with their bundles and even saluted respectfully—with hardly any irony—as they stepped back out into the early winter twilight.

A Third Expository Interlude

THE CITY ON THE RIVER—which is not the city you probably think it is—has been the center of its district forever, since long before it became part of the larger nation and even before the first Roman centurions arrived, back when the name of the island was "the place where we keep our fishing boats." Some might say that even today the connection with the capital is tenuous at best: a matter of economic convenience, reinforced by the tired habit of forgotten treaties, rather than anything like a deep cultural sympathy.

But one could say the same about Bergerton in relation to the City, or about Wat's Hump relative to Bergerton, or about my cabbage farm in relation to that. The mysterious interplay of separation and connection between places makes the discussion almost pointless. I can tell you that cabbages grown on my farm and carried to Wat's Hump may be eaten there or carted to Bergerton. From there they may be pickled or they may be moved by the wagonload to the City on the island.

Perhaps someone there will eat them, or perhaps they will be fed to hogs, which will make the hams that will sail down the river to the sea and finally grace the tables of foreign lands. Farmer Popper's turnips may be toted on the backs of donkeys all the way to Feasley-on-Lobbe and from there to the City on barges. Hazelnuts from the forest may be gathered by Vagabond children and end up in the liqueurs brewed by the mysterious Brothers of the Little Caverns, far away over the mountains.

But do I care if my apples might brew the cider that fills the mug of the Prince of East Borscht? I do not. Does my indifference keep me from hauling them to that wretched inn each Wednesday in September to get every knuckle I can for them? It does not.

So the capital believes itself to be the center of a nation, and the City on the river pays its tribute (when it is reminded very nicely). Bergerton and Feasley-on-Lobbe keep the City fed without a second thought for its actual well-being. Wat's Hump rolls its cabbages down the lane to the town. My farm deposits them at the innkeeper's door, and my haystack, at the edge of it all, no doubt wonders when it shall be taken apart to be scattered over the remaining onions to help them over-winter.

That preys on my mind as well, to be frank. The onions can withstand a hard frost, but if the ground freezes deeper there will be nothing left in the spring but brown slime. I should have taken more time before leaving or left instructions with someone. Perhaps the man who thinks he is the rightful owner of my farm will come back to take care of it for me. Well, what's done, as they say. Who knows where one may be blown in this wide world? Thistledown may have a disagreement with the wind, but the wind's opinion will prevail in the end.

Part IX

The Glory of Battle

→ Oпe ←

IF YOU HAVE BEEN SUPPOSING that the Burgermeister's sons, Captain and Corporal Berger respectively, did not perish at the hands of hostile forces but were instead captured and held by their enemies in a foreign land, then you may congratulate yourself on your optimistic temperament, because you are not far wrong. More than that I cannot say at this time, but ease your mind and let your anxieties subside. They are not dead.

The climate of the country we have thus far seen is temperate, with winters that are just a bit too cold and summers that are not quite too hot, lovely long springs and wretched, muddy autumns. The inhabitants also have a generally equitable temperament, with little inclination to engage in any kind of collective violence. Oh, there is the occasional tumble-about at a tavern, or the infrequent group of malcontents who gather at the gate and insist on "being heard," but on the whole the people mind their own business, the government leaves them to it, and the surrounding countries barely know the place exists.

To the north, however, a different set of circumstances prevails. There, the climate is stormy and wet, with wild winter gales and summers soaked with rain. As a result, the people there are given to armed clashes over the most trivial matters and the organizations that pass for government are hard-pressed to contain the outbreaks. Indeed, the whole land—"up there" as it is called in Bergerton—is always on the verge of warfare, and every few years news reaches us that they, up there, are "at it again."

And wars, as you well know, are no respecters of borders. When sabers rattle and shields clash "up there," the country is obliged to mobilize its own troops and send out expeditionary forces to push the squabbles back over the border. A sort of geographical house-keeping, as it were.

It was just such an expedition to which the Bergerton Boys were called, and they set out in high spirits, fully expecting to nudge their neighbors back into their own country and be home in time for the autumn cider. The officers led them on an easy march each day, sometimes a shorter distance than any of their training excursions. One reason for this was that they only had a vague idea of their destination. They didn't have a compass, so they estimated north by the angle of the sun and double-checked by the pole star at night.

That suited them well enough for a time, since the only way to get "up there" was to go north. They fully expected to receive more detailed orders at any time, so it seemed prudent not to proceed too hastily. They rose and breakfasted when it suited them, ambled along country lanes until their stomachs moved them to picnic for lunch, dozed a while in the shade, then made another mile or two before finding a place to camp. Their fires burned late into the night, and they regaled one another with tales of their valiant future deeds or the winsome charms of the girls they had left behind.

They slept under the stars, the Captain having the only tent, and so long as the weather held out they were jovial and comfortable enough. The food ran out after the first week, and from that point things were slightly more haphazard. But not to the point of desperation. Although they were a motley-looking band, the Captain and the Corporal were resplendent enough to lend credibility to the outfit, and the farms and villages they passed were as likely as not to provide them some foodstuffs in exchange for a promise to depart the next morning. After all, what alderman doesn't want to appear supportive of the state's well-being? To what farmer is it not worth a brace of chickens to ensure these young men are removed from his daughters' presence at first light?

So the weeks wore on and the miles reeled off and the squad became hardened to the trail, so to speak. They were not so boisterous as before, but there was relatively little grumbling. The Captain had an uncanny knack for understanding the mood and desires of his company. Those who gave it any consideration attributed this to his nightly conference with the other officers. (The other "officers" were the Corporal and two of the privates whose families had made particularly substantial contributions to the enterprise.)

Each evening, when the Captain retired to his tent, the Corporal would follow soon after. The two privileged privates would then begin to feel neglected and join them. Often the conference amounted to a simple card game and the privates returned with nothing to report to the rest of the company. Occasionally there was some discussion of strategy or a sharing of perplexity regarding the lack of orders from headquarters, and once there was a heated hour's discussion on whether to turn left or right at a fork in the road. But for the most part, the conferences were congenial and fruitless.

Yet the Captain seemed to anticipate every whim of his army and almost without fail would lead them exactly where they wanted to go. They set out when they wished, stopped when they wished, ate when they wished, and were seeing the sights of a new country in the bargain. It would be lovely to say that the experience forged inviolable loyalty—that the company was prepared to go to the ends of the earth in support of their shared cause. It would be more accurate to say that their quarrels were few and petty, and that, to this point, no one had deserted for very long. (Reggie Mook, the butcher's son, disappeared for an afternoon once but came back in the evening, saying he'd rather be lost with the group than by himself.)

⇀ Two ↽

THEIR ROUTE HAS NEVER BEEN accurately reconstructed. There was an attempt in later years to compile information from the surviving personal accounts and plot it on a map, but there were too many gaps in the record and the effort was abandoned.

At some point they came to a river they could not cross, probably the Lobbe, and doubled back. Accounts vary, but it seems likely they passed by some villages more than once, Pottley two or three times, and Orbuckle no less than four. While they were not, strictly speaking, going in circles, their progress seems to have been singularly looped. Back and forth, to and fro, left and right, always drifting approximately northward, and then finally we come to that fateful late summer day when they found themselves trudging down a pair of wagon wheel ruts, miles from any farm or hamlet.

This "road" crossed a wide, hilly, tree-dotted plain. It ran east-west in as straight a line as possible, with no sign of ever turning the slightest bit north. Despite the love the soldiers held for their Captain, a simmering discontent had been growing among their ranks, and the sight of this dreary frontier road did nothing to improve morale. The privileged privates expressed an opinion on behalf of the entire regiment by flopping down in the shade of a grove of beech trees and refusing to go another step.

"We ain't gonna get there," said one.

"This ain't the right road," said the other.

The Captain suggested perhaps the road would *lead* to the right road.

"Nope. It's got mountains you can see in that direction, and we know there's that river in the other direction," said the second.

"And there's no food around here," said the first.

(Why is there no military rank between private and corporal for the station these two occupied? Everyone knows that among the infantry there are always those few privates who carry special prestige and influence, for whatever reason. Why is there no formal designation for them? I shall have to take it up with the General next time we meet.)

The Corporal whispered to the Captain, and the Captain expressed his certainty that there would be food around the next bend, or at most the bend after that.

"Ain't no bends in this road," said someone.

The Captain explained that he had been speaking figuratively and that *hill* could be substituted for *bend* if it made them happy.

"No, it don't make us happy," said the first private. "We say we goes overland. Either north until we get to something like what we set out for, or south until we get home."

The second private nodded his assent, as did the others (at least those that were paying any attention whatever). The Captain and the Corporal retired deeper within the grove and could be heard conferring in hushed, agitated tones. There were sounds like scuffling and thumping. There were strained deprecations and more than one barbed remark about imagined past offenses. The infantry exchanged nervous glances and began collecting beech nuts in the leaf litter for something to do.

At length the officers emerged, only slightly more disheveled than before, and announced that the regiment would head overland immediately: due north, perpendicular to the currently offending road, into an apparently trackless wilderness where they would test their collective mettle and no doubt meet their doom. This proclamation was greeted with some enthusiasm and some dismay. Then the Captain gave the order to make camp, it being midafternoon, and commanded the company to gather nuts in earnest, that and a little oatmeal being their whole stock of food for the foreseeable future.

→ THREE ←

BEECH WOOD MAKES A LOVELY FIRE. It burns clean and bright and not too fast, and has a pleasant aroma. Such a fire does much to soothe the spirit of a traveler, whether alone or in a party, and the Bergerton Boys were no exception. After a simple supper of porridge and beechnuts, with nothing to look forward to upon the morrow, they lay down by their bright fires and slipped into lassitude, thinking of home or dozing off.

The Captain retired shortly thereafter to the tent, followed by the Corporal, and they were heard to murmur, no doubt consulting maps and military things of that nature. One of the privileged privates snorted at the indignity of a hierarchical system of authority, flicked his last beechnut hull into the fire, and stomped off toward the tent. The other privileged private, weary of the burdens of leadership and on the verge of casting off his privilege, said nothing.

The voices from the tent became clearer as darkness fell and conversations around the fires trailed off. Someone asserted that there weren't nothing beyond them hills to the north but more hills, and they should head south until they found a town or something. This was answered by some rather stern murmuring. Then some high-pitched murmuring that grew into a reassertion that there weren't *nothing* at *all* beyond them hills. Then a confused muddle of both stern and high-pitched murmuring that was markedly indistinct.

The troops back at the fires had just begun to wish the party in the tent would be considerate enough to speak more clearly when a voice rang out with an admonition to go and check for yourself, then, for pity's sake—you call yourself a scout and the moon's bright enough, heaven knows, so stop pestering us and climb that blasted hill to see for yourself.

After a short silence—during which the other private definitively renounced any privilege he had ever claimed—the newly appointed scout emerged from the tent and slunk back to the fire. Retrieving his knife and squaring his hat, he set off into the dark.

"See you keep those fires bright," he said. "I don't aim to be lost in them hills all night."

He departed with a solemn and tragic air that did much to lighten the mood in the camp. The ranks speculated lightheartedly on what he would find, and a few members of the party garnered great appreciation for their efforts at imitating the scout's attitude and demeanor.

But this jollity had gone on barely a quarter of an hour when it was punctured by the scout's return. He rejoined the circle of firelight, his face white as a winding sheet, and decanted the most dreadful news. An army lay encamped just over the brow of the hill. Large and foreign they were, flying a strange flag. Fate had brought them to the very doorstep of the enemy! He lamented the lack of anything stronger than brook water to fortify himself and went to inform the officers.

⇾ FOUR ⇽

I DON'T KNOW IF WHAT HAPPENED next was a colloquium or a confabulation, but it was noisy and rather agitated, and resulted in the Captain emerging from the tent, flanked by the Corporal and Special Private Willitz, each with a look of anxious, determined resolve fitted to the individual contours of his respective face. Or perhaps they were looks of determinedly resolute anxiety. The dim light made it tricky.

In any case, the Captain announced with great aplomb that they had at last encountered the foe and the only possible course was a surprise attack at dawn. The men of the regiment took the news with stoic grace and dignity, considering most of them were half-asleep, and they listened almost attentively as the officers outlined and then detailed the battle plan.

They would amass on the crest of yonder hill, just out of sight of the enemy camp, and then, at first light, they would attack. The Captain, being the best charger, would lead the charge, while the Corporal and Special Private Willitz would each lead a flank around either side of the camp, the goal being to both divide and surround the enemy. In their pre-breakfast confusion, the enemy would likely capitulate at once and agree to be taken prisoner rather than suffer the ignominy of defeat in combat.

To the regiment, the training exercise that sounded most similar was the famous campaign at Ferd's Meadow, when they had valiantly separated Farmer Spoone's sheep from Dunk Wofford's goats. They wondered vaguely if there would be any dogs to contend with, that having been the chief difficulty of the previous engagement.

No, of course not, they were told. Dogs had no place in warfare. And what's more, the enemy over the hill wouldn't simply bleat and trot obediently into a bunch. They were armed, battle-hardened enemy troops and would put up a terrible resistance unless the Bergerton Boys really socked it to them from the first. The only chance was to surprise them at their morning coffee while they were away from their weapons.

The regiment wondered why the enemy had coffee when they themselves had to make do with wild mint tea.

They were reminded that the officers were speaking figuratively and not to concern themselves with trivial details. The important thing was to bed down and be well rested for the morning, and not to lay awake all night dwelling on the certain injury or death that awaited some of them.

The next morning, a trifle longer after first light than had been hoped, Special Private Willitz rousted the men, somewhat bleary-eyed from having lain awake all night dwelling on certain injury and death, and presented them to the Captain.

They wanted to know when Willitz became a Special Private.

They were admonished not to worry about that and to gather their weapons, and weren't there somewhat fewer men than there had been the previous evening?

No, really, they wanted to know, what makes him a Special Private and the rest of us just privates?

It was a new semi-official rank created in the field, if they must know, for distinguished service to the regiment, and they ought not to be distracted by such matters when glory and triumph were close at hand. They were all to earn copious medals during the coming months, and they could quibble about minor details of rank over foaming mugs back home at the Beetle when it was all over. Those who survived.

Without allowing time for further discussion, the officers moved the men out, led them silently to the crest of the hill, and arranged them in as discreet a line as possible. Crouched under bushes and behind trees, they peered down into a little valley with a pretty stream running through it.

Camped around the stream, not a quarter-mile away, fully a dozen tents were pitched, with men milling around them, going about the normal morning activities of a troop of soldiers on the move.

"Mercy," said Willitz, counting the tents. "Are there that many officers?"

No, he was informed, the enemy was simply better equipped than they were. But not to worry, they would all have tents when they were able to join the regular forces. In fact, after their victory today, they would have those very tents before them, and the coffee, too, and they would make their wretched prisoners sleep out on the hard ground.

So it was, then, when the Captain gave the signal, that the Bergerton Boys rushed out of the woods, descending upon the enemy camp for fame and glory and medals, yes, but mostly for the promise of tents and coffee. They fell upon their astonished foe with what can only be described as a wild fury of earnest desire for it all to be over as quickly as possible.

* * *

→ Five ←

NOW. GORMER POLTSCH WAS A BLACKSMITH and rough carpenter, and so the sole wheelwright in Lesser Spleen, a village of twenty-five hundred souls some three days' journey north of the capital. He was also the commander of the local village militia, a post he had inherited from his father and all their fathers before them, back to the founding of the village in the days of Habram the Lesser. He had no military training or title and commanded his band simply by virtue of being the most familiar with the weaponry, having fashioned most of it himself.

He was quiet and sturdy, not bad looking for a man in his middle years except for a mass of gray beard like Spanish moss that was his pleasant wife's sole complaint. He led his fifty-odd militiamen not so much with commands and drills as by unlocking the armory.

Being so far north, they were reasonably well practiced, having to go most every summer to poke at the foreigners with pikes and staves and pitchforks, encouraging them to take their troubles back to their own side of the border. Upon receiving this year's summons, they had gathered a mile from the village at Wensbrook Meadow, as they always did, to double-check their gear and drink ale for a couple of nights before setting off.

It was easy enough, as the regular army did all the real fighting. A chance to see the countryside and pick up a few trinkets for the children. That morning, the tents being all repaired and the cask having been polished off the night before, there was really nothing left to do but load the wagons and head out.

The men were lounging around the fires, doing their best to avoid that calamity, when the sound of a disturbance reached their ears.

Three hundred yards off, at the crest of a hill, something thrashed in the shrubbery. There was a kind of strangled cry, and then the most curious collection of ragtag bumpkins they had ever seen emerged to careen down the hill toward them, led by what Gormer Poltsch thought must be a clown in a theater costume from a production of "The General's Mistress."

Their flight was tinged with such panic that he thought at first they were pursued by bears. His men put down their coffee mugs and porridge bowls and joined him at the edge of the camp to watch. As the strangers drew closer, it became clear they were not running away from anything, but there was still no certainty as to their purpose. Then some of them slowed to a walk and one came to a full stop, putting his head between his knees. The apparent leader, however, and those around him continued at a run, or at least a weary trot, if you like.

"Are we under attack?" someone asked.

"I think we might be," said Gormer.

"What should we do?"

"Wait and see, I suppose."

The invaders stumbled out of the bushes and into the meadow. Their leader, encrusted in gold braid, was making straight for Gormer's band of militiamen. His sword was still sheathed at his side.

Normally, Gormer Poltsch's weapon of choice was a long pikestaff, in order to keep himself as far away as possible from his adversaries. But he also carried an old blacksmith's hammer. Like the hammer in the old joke—it may well have been the original source for the joke—the handle had been replaced innumerable times and the head re-forged at least thrice. It had been in the family for years. In fact, it was the very hammer with which his ancient forebear had threatened violence upon a certain distasteful person, thereby enabling the founding of Lesser Spleen and forever cementing the reputation of the Poltsch men as "none to be trifled with."

His pikestaff was stashed with all the other weapons in the wagons at the edge of camp, and out of reach, but the hammer hung at his belt, as always. He drew it out and held his hand up, fingers splayed, to encourage the approaching man to stop and explain what in heaven was going on. The man trotted up to him, puffing mightily, caught his foot on a root, and fell forward into Gormer's arms. His forehead struck the head of the hammer and he collapsed at the blacksmith's feet, as senseless as a sack of potatoes.

If anything could have induced greater confusion on the part of the invaders, the defeat of their leader was that thing. Some stopped dead in their tracks; some turned and ran. Then a virtual mirror image of the leader—but with less gold braid—rushed up to Gormer brandishing an un-cocked crossbow, stammering something about a father. Two or three of the invaders actually confronted Gormer's men with what he assumed were meant to be weapons but looked more like garden tools. These were easily disarmed and led into the camp, where they asked for coffee.

One singularly frantic-looking man armed with a length of fire-wood threw his weapon at the nearest tent, missed it completely, then turned on his heel and sprinted back up the hill.

"Follow the Special Private!" someone called, and within minutes, fully two-thirds of the strangers had disappeared back over the hill, never to be heard from again. The remainder—the leader, his less-braided twin, and a handful of others—were gathered together and placed under guard.

Gormer was inclined to simply relieve them of their weapons and let them go. Since he could think of no earthly reason for them to behave the way they had he felt it would be easier to send the problem packing and pretend it had never happened. But young Strommond Stovepipe—the magistrate's son and his own second cousin—insisted that these vagrant ne'er-do-wells be brought to justice in the village, in accordance with the well-defined anti-nuisance statutes put in place by his father.

Besides, someone suggested, who was to say this morning's scuffle wouldn't count as their required military engagement for the summer?

"Look here," said the baker's apprentice. "I got a scratch on me arm from that shambly devil there. Wounded, I am!"

So in the end, despite the braided leader's protestations, the rabble were bound by the hands and led a weary mile back to the village to face the solemn justice that surely awaited them.

→ Six ←

THAT VERY AFTERNOON THE REMAINING Bergerton Boys stood before the magistrate of Lesser Spleen and awaited his stern judgement. The case against them was made by Strommond with addenda and clarifications by Gormer Poltsch. To summarize, these rascals had attempted a bold ambush of the village's finest, with the clear intent of prosecuting a massacre, and nothing would do but that they be delivered to the darkest depths of someplace very deep and dark indeed.

The Captain, as spokesman for the whole party of the defense, made his case again, as he had made it on the journey back to the village: that they were fellow countrymen, and the whole thing had been a misunderstanding. The nuances of his argument were apparently lost on his audience, however—possibly because, still reeling from the knock to his head, he could barely string two words together, and his speech had an odd whuffing quality that the magistrate found off-putting.

In the end, the magistrate made two rulings anyone could have predicted. In the first case, the rogues from Burgerville or what-the-devil-ever were to be imprisoned until something could be found to do with them. And in the second case, the militia of Lesser Spleen was not allowed to remain at home but would return north with all haste, with the magistrate himself as second in command to ensure no further ridiculousness. However, they *were* allowed to procure another cask of ale for the road.

Gormer and company found the decision to be not altogether unsatisfactory and departed the following day to heaven knows what end.

The Captain, the Corporal, and their hangers-on were installed in the local jail. Deprived of their braids, the officers were once again indistinguishable from one another, and from the rest of their band, for that matter. From being the shining pride of Bergerton they had fallen to become mere vagrant ruffians, bewildered and discouraged, detained indefinitely in a dismal foreign land.

The jail itself was a curious affair, and worth some closer examination. It was just outside town, a row of inexplicable caves in a low cliff face. They were fenced with stout timbers and iron bars—a local farmer had once used them as stables until his goats refused to participate any longer.

When the goats had made their final exit, some visionary thinker had seen the obvious application of the cells to house criminals. In the absence of a body of law, however, the jail lay fallow until the town council was convinced to acquire a magistrate. Even then, despite the new magistrate's judicial enthusiasm and the subsequent proliferation of statutes and offences, he soon determined it was more profitable to levy fines than to impose incarceration.

So the lusty, trusty lads from Bergerton were to be the first official occupants of the cells since the goats had turned their tails on the place. And, by a happy chance, there were just enough caves, eleven in all, for each guilty scoundrel to have his own to himself, the better to reflect on his misdeeds and to prevent communication with his nefarious companions.

As the summer ended and autumn began to nestle its elbows into the corners, each sat in his own cell, not knowing what had happened to the others—if they were alive or dead, or if they would ever be released, the magistrate having been somewhat vague on that point. Their only contact with the world outside the bars was the daily visit by women from the village, charged with their maintenance, who brought bread in baskets and water in buckets and steadfastly refused to engage with them in any conversation whatever.

What a wretched turn of events! What dismal circumstances! The evening of the first frost, the former Captain Berger sat in his cell and watched the woman bring his basket, labeled "Berger" with a paper tag. The brown loaf was good enough, he supposed, and the water was fresh. But the woman wouldn't speak a word or even meet his glance. Probably no woman would ever meet his glance again. He felt the chill in the air and watched the light fade in the sky.

Did he sigh? Did he even weep silently to himself? It is not for us to say. Let us turn our eyes away discreetly and only note that an identical scene was played out that same night in each of ten other cells, with ten other loaves and ten other glances unmet.

That same evening, as chance would have it, Special Private Willitz downed his second mug of ale and said again, "All gone. All them boys is gone."

PART X

WinteR

→ Οne ←

NOW YOU KNOW AS WELL as I do that the Burgermeister's sons did not die in the epic battle of Wensbrook Meadow. What is more, you know that his nephews did not perish in the marketplace fire stampede, never to be found, nor were his granddaughter and Lexi kidnapped by Vagabonds and murdered that same night. But the Burgermeister himself knew no such things, and he clung to these facts as insurmountable truths: his sons, dead; his nephews, dead; the girls, spirited away and dead or worse.

He gazed from his half-empty house out onto a half-ruined town and despaired. The morning after the fire, the damage was discovered to be less than everyone had feared, but as the weeks wore on and winter set in, it turned out to be quite a bit worse than they might have hoped. Virtually every shop on the square was damaged and fully a third were destroyed completely—including, most lamentably, that of Mr. Stoodler the pastry baker, who was never seen again. More than half the houses in town had also suffered some damage, mostly to their thatched roofs. But most of the missing townsfolk eventually reappeared, having taken refuge in the countryside, so it turned out there had been mercifully few casualties, all in all.

(I do not mean to diminish anyone's loss. What does it matter if deaths in the town are ten or a thousand to a man who has lost his wife, or a mother her child? What care the newly orphaned brother and sister that their parents were among "mercifully few casualties"? There are many such stories born of what came to be called the Great Fire: small, intently focused, white-hot tragedies concerning one or two persons, or at most a small family, and these are enough to fill a volume, or scores of volumes. Each human life is a string of such tiny tragedies and equally tiny triumphs. They fill a person's world to the very brim and yet pass unnoticed by the rest. We will leave these stories where they belong, alone with those affected. We will not burden ourselves with the borrowed weight of their sorrows and will allow them the dignity of our careful ignorance.)

Of those that did return, many left again shortly, and more after that. Even if you have not experienced it yourself, I suppose you can imagine how many winter nights one would spend in a roofless stone cottage before deciding to seek shelter elsewhere. By the time the snows began in earnest, the population of the town was barely half what it had been just a month before. It seemed to the Burgermeister that he looked out upon a blasted wasteland where the wreckage of homes still smoldered and monstrous insects picked over the carcass of his beloved leviathan.

That was fanciful on his part. The smoldering embers of the fire had been extinguished by rain the following day. The vapors he saw after that were simple winter mists and smoke from the remaining chimneys. The insects were only the townsfolk, huddled against the cold, going about whatever business they had found with which to occupy themselves. But he is perhaps to be excused for the misconception. The mist on the windows, after all, or in his eyes, might have obscured his vision.

The winter days at that latitude are short and dull gray, the nights long and drearily dark. If you have never lived through such seasons, I invite you to do so at some point in your life. The long, bright days of summer, when evening lingers in the sky past ten o'clock, invite one to ramble over the hills at all hours, and light, easy adventure waits around every corner and behind every hedgerow. One needs hardly sleep at all, lest one miss something.

Contrast this with the short days of winter, when the sky barely brightens past a kind of twilight and the nights stretch interminably through hour after hour of bone-crushing cold. One must summon the strength to rise in the dark, do one's work in the dark, and stay awake through supper before succumbing gratefully to a sodden and dreamless sleep. Living through such variation is good for the constitution. A year in such a place strengthens the character. I recommend it to everyone.

→ two ←

WITH THE ONSET OF WINTER, the Burgermeister felt himself sinking into the familiar numbness that had been his companion for so many years after his children's mother had evaporated. It wasn't melancholy—no, he wouldn't characterize it as sadness. It was certainly joyless enough, but beyond sorrow, somehow, as if all the sorrow had been mopped up with a rag and then wrung out into the street, and he was left with just the damp rag by which to remember it.

This state was friendly and comfortable, in a morose, linty kind of way. As moods go, it required almost no effort to maintain. It settled into him like snowflakes into the black surface of the pond. It subtly altered his perspective and allowed him to say to himself such things as, "One day's clothes are much the same as another's," and "It hardly matters whether there is more brandy in the bottle or in me. Between the two of us, we contain all the brandy." When the fire burned out in his study, he wondered why it had ever been lit at all. When Tall Butler announced he would be marrying Widow Baily and would remain in the service of the house but would henceforth take up residence in her attic, all the Burgermeister said was, "Very well, Henders," and his only thought was that one empty room more or less hardy made a difference when the sky was falling.

And fall it did, all through the winter: agonizingly, imperceptibly slowly. He could sense it descending like a great blue-black glacier, could hear it grinding past the peaks of the distant mountains. He stopped going upstairs. He took to walking hunched over to avoid scraping his head on it when he was outdoors. He felt like getting on all fours and crawling away, but he knew there was no escape. It was coming. The sky was coming to crush him, to grind him out like the poor, spent match he was.

Tuesday afternoons were the worst, the days of his weekly meeting with the town councilmen, and he looked forward to them with grim resignation. Except for this meeting, he could remain safely enclosed in the house, watching the papers cross his desk, watching his hand approve or reject them, watching the sliver of light behind the closed curtain cool to darkness by middle afternoon to signal the end of the day. Except for this meeting, he barely needed to gain full consciousness at all, and indeed, many a paper was approved or denied while the Burgermeister remained in his dressing gown with a bowl of cold porridge at his elbow.

But Tuesday afternoon arrived, as it always did, immediately after

Monday night, and he was obliged to rise and dress and breakfast and remove himself to the large, formal dining room, which had assumed the auxiliary function of town council chambers after Town Hall was lost in the fire.

Town Hall was also known as Upstairs at the Beetle and had once boasted the longest table in town. The council had had a standing reservation since the early days of the Chief's long tenure. In those bygone, simpler days the business of the town had rarely consisted of anything more onerous than resolving questions of pasturage or trying to determine who had pilfered building stone from whom. It was in the Burgermeister's heyday that the meeting became concerned with the actual business of an actual town, and the council, after some initial objection, took to it with full vigor.

They devised an impenetrable system of permits and licenses for everything from building homes to tearing them down; births, marriages and deaths; buying and selling and giving away free; cats and dogs, goats and sheep, hens and chickens; traffic in and traffic out; water usage; quiet hours; and public holidays. They then esablished an equally intricate system of exceptions and exclusions, so that any snarl of contradictory statutes could easily be gotten around if one had the right connections. These systems were maintained at the meetings, and holding the meetings at the Beetle ensured that only a limited amount of actual work—and therefore only a limited amount of damage—could be accomplished before the townsmen began arriving for their evening constitutional.

While the town was growing and the Burgermeister was exercising his genius for inventing revenue streams, there was little else to discuss but what to build next and what to do with the extra money. The Burgermeister and the councilmen were prudent, good-hearted men, with only a moderate and sensible level of self-interest.

Therefore, they only became slightly wealthy, and any examination of the books would reveal that the great bulk of the town's income indeed went toward the good of the town.

After the fire, with the Beetle half burned away and so many genuine and grave problems facing the people, the councilmen showed their better sides and insisted on continuing the meetings in the Burgermeister's dining room so they could address the ongoing issues facing the town while availing themselves of his cellar.

Even with the reduced population, they were faced with a potential shortage of firewood if the winter turned bitter. Should we mount a collective wood-gathering expedition into the forest? The Burgermeister supposed it was preferable to dismantling the remaining vacant houses for kindling.

Fortunately, the wells had not yet frozen, but many of them were still befouled from the fire. The Burgermeister didn't know how to cleanse a well. Couldn't they all get by some way until the wells cleaned themselves?

There had been reports that the Marshals and the Hooligans had formed a confederation and were raising the price of safe travel beyond the means of the farmers and merchants who traveled the highways. The Burgermeister buried his head in his hands and lamented the woeful lack of sons that had befallen the town. A stalwart band of sons could surely ride out into the countryside and set things to rights. Alas, all the sons were gone and had taken the crossbow with them, and only the Marshals and Hooligans had returned.

Between the peril of the highways and the destruction of the marketplace, not to mention the halving of the population, commerce in the town had shrunk alarmingly, with a corresponding reduction in revenue from tariffs and fees.

On this point the Burgermeister was silent.

A great number of repairs were needed to restore the town, its needs being beyond the resources of the individual townspeople.

The Burgermeister folded and unfolded his hands, unable to find the right position for his fingers.

People were traveling overland to Feasley-on-Lobbe and sending their goods to the City by barge, rather than coming through Bergerton.

The Burgermeister closed his eyes against the red haze that threatened to occlude his vision.

And many of the people faced destitution or starvation, more than could be helped by the churches.

The Burgermeister fought the urge to crawl under the table and wait for them all to go away.

The last order of business was to note that the snow had started up again and the meeting was adjourned to allow the councilmen to be home before dark. After they had filed out silently into the gloom, Old Butler came in to remove the tea service.

"One more, sir, before I clear up?" he shrilled.

Without waiting for an answer he filled the Burgermeister's cup and placed it in the hand that reached out from under the table.

→ THREE ←

THE APPROACHING YULETIDE promised to be a particularly joyless one for the town, despite the lovely blanket of snow that hid the worst of the damage. Both churches, being built wholly of stone and standing, besides, on the downhill side of the square, had emerged largely unscathed from the flames. Both had provided emergency shelter as well as they could, and as winter settled in, both pastors worked to guide their little flocks through the sorrow to some kind of hope.

Joy itself still seemed out of reach, but what better time than the Yule to try to find the spark that would lead to hope? They admonished the people to be of good cheer and to spread the word that the Yule services would be uncommonly cheerful—at least, as cheerful as they could be within sight of so many fresh graves in the little cemetery.

Maggie Berger, of course, had been and remained a faithful attendee at both churches, favoring one over the other from week to week but carefully dividing her time equally over the longer term. Sylvia Berger and Lucy Broome had only ever been sporadic churchgoers in the past, but since the fire they had seemed to find a quiet solace in the regularity of the service. We can only speculate, of course, on the effect the shared loss of their sons had upon them. Better we keep a respectful distance from that facet of their lives and take comfort in the fact that we know what they do not: namely, that whatever peril their boys may be in, they are not dead.

We do know that the women attended services regularly, every Sunday morning and every Wednesday afternoon, and always together. They tended away from Our Lady, finding the dark, ancient chapel of St. Feldspar and the sonorous monotone of Father Umberly more suited to the tenor of that season of their lives.

One Sunday morning—dark, as all Sunday mornings in December are dark—Maggie bustled into the kitchen while Sylvia and Lucy were pouring tea.

"Won't you come with me to Our Lady this morning? Deacon Thistlethwaite is giving the readings."

Lucy looked into her cup as though she hadn't heard.

"I think Father Umberly is expecting us," said Sylvia.

"Well, of course," said Maggie, "and you must do what suits you. But Father Klieg always asks after you."

Lucy whispered something without looking up from her cup.

"That's very kind," said Sylvia. "Do give him our best."

→ FOUR ←

YOU MIGHT THINK IT UNUSUAL for such a small town to have two churches. If so, you're quite right—although I would also understand if so minute a detail has failed to capture your notice. Nevertheless, the circumstance is something of a curiosity and deserves explanation.

St. Feldspar's is, as you may have guessed, the older of the two by far, having stood at the crossroads called Sullivan's Bend since long before the first Sullivan ever saw the place, when it was still called Eichtcross and the stars had not yet found their current places. It was older than old, built in the ancient style with thick, solid walls and narrow slit windows. It had a steeply pitched roof and a stubby little steeple that housed a single bronze bell crusted green with centuries of neglect. St. Feldspar's served the people of the hamlet and the surrounding farms quite nicely and without incident for centuries, and the parish of Sullivan's Bend was noted in the records of the City's cathedral as having as equal a number of births and deaths in its registry as it is possible to have.

With the advent of the Bergers, however, and the creation of Bergerton, and the ensuing increase in population, the congregation began to outgrow the little chapel and people began to murmur. As people do, you know. Anytime things aren't going quite as well as they would like but not badly enough to warrant a ruckus or an outcry.

One of the murmurers was Mrs. Penelope Berger, the Chief's mother. She murmured so much that when the Chief took office his first act was to notify the keepers of the cathedral in the City that the liturgical needs of Bergerton were woefully underserved. The cathedral had never heard of Bergerton and had no record of any such parish. But indeed there is such a parish, insisted the Chief, with upwards of a thousand souls in need of shepherding. The number was an exaggeration, but he can perhaps be forgiven, the murmuring having risen to such a pitch.

When the cathedral heard this, the thought of so many lost sheep stirred a certain low-level functionary to action, and within the month a party was dispatched to Bergerton with funds and plans and an entire complement of builders, including a master mason, a master carpenter, a glazier, a blacksmith, a tinsmith, and a brand-new, sparkling pastor fresh from seminary. The pastor's name was Father Periwinkle, and he descended on the town in a burst of lilac and frankincense.

The townspeople had hoped for a simple expansion of St. Feldspar's, but what they ended up with five short years later was a completely new church, with real windows of colored glass and three new bells in its graceful belfry, faced off against the old stone chapel across Church Street. For a town that actually had barely six hundred people, it was a veritable glut of churches, and for a time the rivalry between them was openly acrimonious. Each struggled to fill the pews with any kind of regularity, and the respective pastors engaged in a contest of attendance the like of which has never been recorded elsewhere.

When, in order to appeal to the traditionalists in town, one stressed its adherence to the ancient liturgical rites, the other introduced celebrations with modern polyphony to appeal to those who fancied themselves forward thinkers. When one pastor's homilies became friendly and humorous, the other's became downright entertaining. I have been unable to confirm the rumor that either church actually implemented a Saturday night communion with schkoltsch and chips, but it is not beyond the realm of imagination.

As the town grew, of course, both churches found their pews full enough often enough to allay any fears of one or the other fading away. The rivalry then became friendlier and, of course, much more personal.

The chief difficulty, aside from choosing dates for each congregation's summer picnic, was interpreting conflicting instructions from the cathedral. St. Feldspar would receive instructions to decorate the vestry in white, only to discover that Our Lady was bedecked in yellow or green. One would receive one answer to a thorny ecclesiastical question and the other would receive an answer just different enough to divide the town for weeks.

But things came to a real head several years before the fire, when each church received a different date for the feast of St. Bernadette of Cloves. Resolving that something must be done, Father Umberly and the very young, newly installed Father Klieg traveled to the City to settle the matter once and for all. They found their way to a minor official who was able to locate some paperwork on both churches and gazed at them pleasantly while they described their troubles.

But the longer they talked the more confused he seemed. Was the problem with farmers in the country having to choose between the two parishes in the two towns? Was it a question of resources?

The Fathers tried again.

Were the wafers meant for one church being delivered to the other?

They tried yet again.

But the official was irretrievably perplexed. Why, it almost sounded as if they were describing a single town with two—it almost seemed laughable—two churches. That could certainly never be allowed to happen, and if it did, why then, one would certainly have to be closed, the congregations combined, and the pastor reassigned elsewhere. It would, after all, never do to have a multiplicity of liturgical authority in such a place as Bergerton. Or Sullivan's Bend, for that matter.

The Fathers exchanged a glance, each imagining how dreary life would be without their Thursday game of boules in the cemetery, and with one voice they agreed that there was indeed no problem they couldn't resolve themselves. They made sure to thank the official so *very* much for his time before beating a hasty retreat back home. Thereafter, the question was never brought up again, and the feast of St. Bernadette has been celebrated twice each year, which goes at least partway toward explaining her function as the patron saint of mixed messages.

→ FIVE ←

ON THE EVE OF THE YULE, as the gray sky was fading to black, three women made their way to Church Street. They took the long way around so as to avoid passing through the ruined square. Bundled against the chill, they were nevertheless easily recognizable among the little throngs making their way to the churches for the evening services. Tall, lanky Lucy Broome; short, plump Maggie Berger; and Sylvia somewhere in between.

But where are the men? Doesn't everyone, simply everyone, attend one evening Yule service or the other? The Burgermeister had promised to catch up with them as soon as he attended to some important business but in fact had fallen asleep in front of the big fire in the parlor. Old Butler had gone with Tall Butler to fetch his new bride and planned to head to the service from there. The Burgermeister's older brother, Robert the Elder, sat in a dressing gown beside the smaller fire in his chamber, wearing a pleasantly vacant expression and wondering about Tansey.

Tansey had been mistress of the nursery when he was a child in the house—when he was *the* child in the house. She was his Nanny. How strange and wonderful, he thought. He had always been here, and so had she. She didn't like the cold, and neither did he. Everyone else had gone, but she was still around somewhere. In her room, the same room as always, forever her room.

Where had they gone? To the churches. Was it a wedding? Or a funeral? No. Perhaps a blessing for a new child. What child? There had been a child, but he had gone, or perhaps he was at the church. And that girl, that lovely girl. She was his wife. How extraordinary. He had gone to the market for turnips and come back with a wife. And what a cozy little time they had had at The Shop, while it lasted. The Shop had come and gone. The child had come and gone. The girl—his wife, Mrs. Robert Berger, Sylvia the turnip farmer's daughter—she came and went and came and went like all the others.

Except Tansey. Except his Nanny. Always in the same room.

The fire guttered low and he thought there was something to do about it, and about the cold that began to creep in under the door. But the dim light was lovely. He had gone to the market for turnips. She was lovely. It was lovely indeed, the light on his face and reflected in his wide eyes and on the old, old hands resting just where he had left them on the gnarled arms of the chair.

* * *

Young Father Klieg was no longer as young as he had been when he journeyed to the city with Father Umberly, but he was still young enough to be called Young Father Klieg by all who knew him. He had a boyish air that he would have regarded, had he been aware of it, as both a blessing and a curse in his role as leader of a congregation. He was pleased that people found him approachable and were even eager to engage him in conversation after services or during the week at the square. But the topics of their discourses were always rather on the light side. He began to suspect that he was not seen as an authority in the more substantial matters of life. He had a wealth of good will and an earnest desire to guide and support people in their times of deepest need. But when illness struck or disaster loomed over a household, they sought out gruff old Father Umberly in the gloomy cottage that adjoined St. Feldspar.

The only exception seemed to be young people struggling with matters of the heart, the very matters which Father Klieg felt least able to assist with. Why didn't they come to him with sorrows or pains, that he might minister to them? Why did they come with their hearts full of flowers and make him blush uncomfortably? Why did he perform most of the weddings and Father Umberly most of the funerals? Would it become proverbial (aside: yes, in years to come it would!) to be "married at Our Lady and buried at St. Feldspar"?

As the Yule approached the town was still stunned from the events at the Feast of Sullivan, and Father Klieg began to feel anxious about the service he must perform. He desperately wanted to bring people hope but struggled to feel any himself. The cemetery was knee-deep in snow and there would be no boules until spring, so he invented a shortage of wafers in order to contrive a visit to Father Umberly. He failed to pour out his heart but managed to allude to his concerns enough that the older man finally understood some advice was in order.

"You can tell them what they want to hear," Father Umberly said, "or you can say what you think they need to hear, but you can't always do both. You sound like you feel you're failing them, somehow, but don't worry about that. They already like you, so at least you have that going for you. They don't like me. I don't know why they come. If you want to help people, keep the chapel well lighted so they don't stumble. Feldspar's is a cave. It's a wonder anyone gets out alive. Have some more tea. It's a cold one out there."

At Yuletide evening Father Klieg stood to the side watching the chapel fill and wondered whether Father Umberly's advice had helped at all. It had seemed sensible and comforting at the time, but back at his writing desk he had struggled to bring any of it into focus. Now, with the church filled to overflowing—as it always was just this one night each year—and the service starting he felt the familiar twinges of panic, enhanced with an extra pinch of inadequacy especially for this evening.

It was one thing to give a disorganized sermon to the usual small gathering on an average Sunday, but the people wanted and deserved something special on this night of all nights, in this year of all years. He barely heard the readings, and when he did pay attention he admonished himself for envying Deacon Thistlethwaite's sonorous, gravelly voice and the ease with which the man addressed the seated rows of rapt faces.

He cleared his throat quietly, knowing he would have to clear it again, noisily, as soon as he began speaking in his own reedy baritone. And indeed he did, as well as ruffling the papers in his hands, the sounds reverberating through the astonishing silence that met him every time he addressed the people. He wanted to conjure up a vision of a hopeful future, but really, what hope was there for the people? For any of us?

His words rang hollow in his own ears, and though he wanted very much to believe the things he said and spoke with a well-practiced, earnest tone, in truth he had seldom felt so meager, so inadequate to the task of nurturing his little flock. What right had he, after all, to ask them to hope for spring when clearly this was the last winter any of them would ever know—an eternal winter to carry them through old age and into the grave and beyond?

Whenever he dared to raise his eyes, the focused gaze of each upturned face quickly drove him back to his written notes. Was there scorn in the glance of the butcher? Disgust in the eyes of the children—or simply boredom? And what was the meaning of the inscrutable expression in the limpid eyes of Miss Berger? Or any of the rest, for that matter? If they were moved by his words, they were deceived. If they were not moved, he had failed to reach them. But thank heaven he was on the last page and soon the singing could start again.

Across the street Father Umberly addressed a smaller, quieter gathering in the dark little chapel. No matter how many candles were lit the place had the feel of a quiet room with a single light for a single person. As indeed we all are, he thought, each of us alone in this little room, with our own little light for comfort.

"Sorry for the cold," he said. "Personally, I've never understood the lack of a fireplace in the chapel. But there's a good one going in the parish hall, and we can all warm up afterwards. It's a curious thing at the Yuletide, strange to celebrate new life on the darkest night of the year, to rejoice in the birth of a child when we all know what it will lead to. We all know in our hearts that the birth of the child means a loss in the future, however much we hide from it, however much we wish for something different. The birth of a child, the death of a child. A life lived, long or short, when lived and done, is done and gone. You can warm your hands at the memories of loved ones passed. You can warm your toes at bright thoughts of the future. But don't forget the real hands of the real loved ones in your life right now, on this night, this darkest of all nights. These are the hands that will warm you down into your bones, these are the hands that guide us home, the hands, the very ones, that will see us through winter and, God willing, into spring."

→ Six ←

THE NIGHT SKY AFTER SERVICES was brilliantly cold and clear—moonless, with stars so close one could touch them, glittering stars made of the same stuff as the frost that glazed the windows and the icy particles that hung in the air.

Maggie met Sylvia and Lucy in the street among the milling townsfolk. The air around them was filled with the sound of bittersweet holiday wishes.

"Oh, my dears, the service was so wonderful." She pressed between them, linking arms with each and pulling them close. "Father Klieg's sermon was so moving, so beautiful." She twisted her head around to press one eye against Lucy's shoulder. "I wish you could have heard it."

The three headed off through the snowy street, still arm in arm.

"And how did you enjoy your service?" Maggie prompted.

"It was very nice," said Lucy.

"Very quiet," said Sylvia.

"Yes, Father Umberly has a quiet way about him," said Maggie. "Very dignified, but friendly, too, in an odd way." She was thoughtful for a moment. "Rather like that old cat we used to have. Do you remember Thumpkins?"

Lucy nodded.

"He was already gone when I came to the house," said Sylvia. "But Robert sometimes asks after that cat. I have to tell him Thumpkins is out chasing mice, or he won't sleep."

More thoughtful silence, stepping quietly and slowly through the careful snow.

"I'm thinking," Sylvia started.

After a pause Lucy said, "Cook says 'be careful about thinking.'"

"I'm thinking of taking Robert and going to the farm."

"But it's so cold," said Maggie.

"It's because of the cold," said Sylvia. "The big house is so drafty, and I can't trust him to keep a fire going in his room. The farmhouse is small, but it's tight and warm and I can look after him better there."

They turned the corner toward the big, dark house that waited in the shadows.

"Is it bright, the farmhouse?" asked Lucy.

"It's so long since I was there, but I remember it brightly." Quiet steps through the snow. "Warm and bright, and always something bubbling in a kettle on the fire."

"It sounds wonderful, Sylvia," said Lucy, squeezing Maggie's arm. "Take me with you?"

"Of course," Sylvia said. "You can all come. We can all sleep in the loft like when we were children."

"I'll pack tonight!" said Lucy.

"Oh, dear, I really couldn't," said Maggie. "My father will never leave this house, and I certainly can't leave him to Cook's mercy!"

As they entered the house, they woke the Burgermeister where he lay dozing in the parlor. But their high, girlish laughter was such an unfamiliar sound that he assumed he had dreamed it, and he lugged himself to bed without seeking them out to say goodnight.

→ SEVEN ←

THE NEXT DAY TANSEY began to fade, and two days later she lay in the narrow bed in the only room that had ever been her own: pale and gray, with barely enough strength in her frame to hold up the coverlets. Her skin was translucent and frail as crepe, with only the barest flickers of life at the corners of her eyes and around the creases of her lips. They sat with her in turns, singly or in twos or threes. Old Butler came to the room a dozen times a day asking if there wasn't anything he could bring her. Cook produced an endless stream of pies and cakes. Maggie was paralyzed, and the Burgermeister in desperation wished to scold Tansey for the inconvenience she was causing.

Her actual care fell to Lucy and Sylvia. Tansey had taught them both well, and with their own children gone, they attended to her with all the devotion of a religious office. They rubbed warmth back into the little hands and brushed the wisps of white hair back from the precious egg of her forehead.

On the last day, she called for the boy Robert. Sylvia choked on her words, so Lucy answered for her.

"The boys are gone, you know. The boys have gone on before you."

"No, you silly girl." Tansey opened one eye and fixed her with a look. It apparently took all her remaining strength to put up with such foolishness. "*My* Robert. Bring the boy to me."

Sylvia went to Robert's room and helped him up from his chair.

275

"Tansey wants to see you," she said. "You know Tansey?"

Robert looked perplexed but allowed himself to be guided down the hall to the old woman's room. When they entered, Tansey opened both eyes.

"You there," she said. Then she closed her eyes and breathed deeply.

"Yes, ma'am," said Robert.

Tansey paused, working to pull the words from deep in her ancient, fluttering heart. "Take care of Johnny," she said. "He thinks he's all grown up. You're a big boy now, you take care of him."

"Yes, ma'am." Robert blinked solemnly, like a tortoise.

"You take good care, Robert," she said. "Good care. You're the big boy now."

"Yes, ma'am."

Tansey closed her eyes and settled into something like sleep.

Sylvia took Robert back to his room and eased him into his chair.

"Where did we go?" he asked.

"That was Tansey, Robert. You know Tansey?"

"Yes, ma'am."

"She asked for you."

He gazed at the fire with his wide, blank-slate eyes.

"You look tired. Do you want to lie down?"

She helped him to bed, arranging the blankets around him and the pillows behind him. She said some things, none of consequence. Soothing sounds for a quiet time and nothing more. She kissed his forehead, smoothing back the slight worry that lined it.

"Thank you, Nanny," he said.

* * *

→ EiGHT ←

A FTER THE YULETIDE, after Tansey's passing, after the New
Year, the usual, unaccountable early thaw melted all the snow
and ice, leaving mud and soot and ashes in a damp, gray crust over
everything. Then the usual Arctic blast blew down from the north
and froze everything but brought no more snow, so the town was a
rigid clod of frozen mud with the burnt ends of former houses stuck
in it up to their knees.

Assailed by loss on all sides, the Burgermeister reached out
blindly for something to occupy his thoughts other than the immi-
nent demise of himself and his entire household. He took it into
his head that the rose, still recovering from the recent uprooting
and replanting, would freeze, although it was sheltered by the walls
of the house and had weathered forty-odd winters just as harsh or
harsher. He wrapped it in an old woolen blanket and piled stale straw
from the stables around its base. He would creep out of the house in
the morning and pinch a stem or finger a twig before wincing and
skulking back inside.

He worried that someone would meddle with the rose while
he was otherwise occupied, whether out of malice or carelessness.
Didn't townspeople surreptitiously snip flowers from it for their
own tables? Didn't he come out the door at least once a year to find
petals scattered every which way as if someone had pilfered whole
bouquets by night? He constructed a preposterous system of wires
and strings connected to triggering devices, all leading to a brass
shopkeeper's bell suspended above his desk in the study. That should
do it, he hoped feebly. That should keep the beggars away.

There was no sun to speak of, and no moon, and no discernable clouds for six weeks. Deep, saturated black nights lightened into murky, foggy mornings. Throughout each day the fog disspated until it was nearly invisible, but light and sound were still stifled, and the ceiling of the world was a uniform stone-white. Only someone who has experienced this kind of winter will know what I mean: when the air has lost its clarity in the bitter cold and the sun, when visible at all, is no bigger than a doorknob.

The rose responded, as always, by shrinking back and losing its brown leaves. The Burgermeister reacted as if he had never seen a sleeping plant before and had to be dissuaded from holding vigils and lighting fires next to it for warmth.

The winter lingered rather longer than usual, and the rose was rather slower than usual in rebounding. At the spring equinox the town was only just starting to thaw, with half the wells still frozen over. By April some green had at last returned to the hills and spring rains began to wash the ashes from the streets.

The rose begrudgingly offered the Burgermeister a little green about the bases of the canes, but nothing more, and for a time he despaired. But on May Day he discovered little tufts of new growth deep within the bush: soft green and burgundy leaves on tender, tentative stems. By June definite new canes had sprung up from the base of the plant, with a few small flower buds sprinkled at the ends, almost as an afterthought.

And then, one sunny morning in mid-June, when the town appeared nearly ready to get back on its feet, the Burgermeister stepped from his front door to be greeted with a full flush of blossoms, each perfectly formed, with a strangely musky scent and petals as black as the night is long.

The Burgermeister stared, then nodded to the plant, accepting the somber blooms as his due. He continued to minister to the plant—dutifully, if less than enthusiastically—and it continued to provide its sable blossoms all that month and through the next, and even after that, so far as we know. So far as we know.

Part XI

The Peculiarities of Fate

→ Oпе ←

EVERY WEDNESDAY AFTERNOON, Arthur Clewes, the headmaster of St. Jasper's Home for Wayward Boys, joined Emmaline Wortherly, imperatrix of the Sisters of Hope and Mercy, for a mug of something hot in the winter or a cup of something cool in the summer. Of course, they met often during the week in the course of their supervisorial duties, but Wednesdays were held apart as a private and purely social affair, with no business conducted and only casual reference to goings-on at their respective institutions.

Neither of them held or pretended to any holy office, but each adhered publicly to a rigorous celibacy befitting the professional tone required of charitable institutions at that time. Unwed, chaste, with all their youngest years behind them, they maintained a warm and cordial friendship as they piloted their little vessels of goodwill through the narrow straits of urban calamity that threatened them at every turn.

That awkward metaphor was the headmaster's, who thought of himself as captain of a ship, if not admiral of a fleet—as if he had always wanted to run away to sea but lacked the nerve. He called his office "the bridge," commanded his mates with equanimity, and loved to mingle with the seamen on the mess deck.

The Wednesday after our boys' arrival he waited for the imperatrix in the little attic parlor that was their accustomed meeting place.

An architectural note: The two institutions had been built separately, begun centuries ago in adjacent plots. Facing the street, they still had the outlines of individual buildings, but as they had expanded over the years, they had grown toward one another and finally converged along the property line where they leaned upon one another as additional levels were added. From behind, especially, where the dormitories and workshops stood, they seemed for all the world like a single edifice.

After the Great Storm during the reign of Lembert the Blameless the whole agglomeration was roofed over, and by some oversight, the attic space was never divided. It was used by both institutions for all those atticky purposes that seem so necessary at the time. Storage, mostly, with decades upon decades' worth of precious forgotten miscellany jamming every corner.

And amid that tumble-down maze of thimbles and bobbins, someone in forgotten days had caused a cozy little parlor to be built, with its back against the exposed stone of the exterior wall, a tiny fireplace for warmth, and a gabled window with an excellent view across the city as far as the docks on the south shore, the masts of ships just visible above the warehouses. It was reachable by narrow wooden stairs from either building and was an excellent place for the quiet contemplation of the peculiarities of fate, among other things.

Where in heaven was she? Attending to some business or other, no doubt.

Arthur had been alerted to the parlor's existence by the previous headmaster, a man named Plimt. He himself had furnished it with the comfortable chairs and the carpets. The imperatrix had provided the little drop-leaf table and the chaise lounge against the back wall. It being winter, and the afternoon chilly, Arthur had arrived early to start a fire and warm a kettle.

He had brought spiced cider for the kettle and a little something to flavor it with, should the occasion arise. He flavored himself, in the meantime, so that Imperatrix Wortherly arrived some time later with a plate of pastries to find him dozing sweetly by the fire, his ridiculous big feet propped up on her chair.

"Good heavens, Arthur, you're no better than those boys of yours."

He sat up languorously and blinked at her. "Fine boys, every one," he said. "Proud to be associated with them."

"Those two new ones were a sight when they came in."

"Apple bumpkins. Bergerton boys, though they won't admit it. You can tell by the twang."

"That Bones woman always brings in the most wretched creatures. It's a wonder you still pay her the fee."

He poured a mug of hot spiced cider for each of them. An intriguing ship appeared on the horizon, drawing nearer.

"Doing a good turn all around. Boys off the streets, school and workshop filled." He took a pastry from the platter. "What's in these lovelies?"

He approached the vessel, ran up flags of truce and goodwill.

"These are plum jam, and these are a cherry compote with gooseberries."

"Delightful."

He longed to draw up alongside her, grapple her broadside, form a boarding party, and engage in mutually beneficial commerce.

"Yes, it's my grandmother's recipe. I make them every Sunday for the Sisters."

Ah, yes; the Sisters. Alas. They were pastries of purity and devotion. There would be no commerce.

"Well, those boys cleaned up well enough in the end. The fat one's quiet, but it's the tall one that worries me. Something in his eyes."

⇀ two ↽

"APPLE BUMPKIN," INCIDENTALLY, in addition to being a City pejorative for anyone from Bergerton, is also quite an adequate pastry made in the capital. It's a kind of apple tart, spiced with cloves and cinnamon in a flakey crust. Peel and chop the apples and toss with the spices and a little flour. Roll the crust out into an approximate circle and place some of the apple mixture a trifle off center. Fold the dough over the apples into a lopsided half-moon shape, like a badly made turnover. The two layers don't come together evenly. The bottom layer sticks out like a pouting lower lip. It's difficult to describe, but if you stop by some time I'll be happy to demonstrate. Pinch the crust shut loosely and bake in a hot oven until golden brown. When this is done properly, the juices from the filling flow out onto the lower crust and form a sticky glaze. Delicious served warm with a trickle of sweet cream. When cooled, the tarts travel well and are a favorite element of picnics in the countryside.

* * *

→ THREE ←

MEANWHILE, the Burgermeister's nephews were making their way from the dormitory to the workshops. It is tempting to describe the boys' time as inmates of this institution with a certain amount of melodrama: to cast them as innocent waifs thrown into a maelstrom of adolescent politicking; to watch them struggle to find seats at the long table while enduring abuse, both mental and physical, from the wily and ruthless gang leader. It would be delicious to share their anguish at being forced to do twice the normal amount of labor in the workshop to cover the gap left by the lazy elite of the leader's circle, to feel the little thrills of triumph as Cordage finally asserts his natural superiority and gathers the weaker boys about him in solidarity, to dab at a tear when observing Robert's kind ministrations to the golden-haired consumptive who speaks his prophetic last words on New Year's Eve as the boys lie shivering in the dark. And who could resist loathing the cruel and sadistic overseer, whose hatred of the boys is matched only by his fear of the headmaster?

However, tempting though it is, we shall refrain. In the first place, although it is entirely likely that much of that is mostly true, none of it can be substantiated, and I haven't the stomach at present for another slander case. And secondly, the only purpose served by describing their tenure at St. Jasper's at all is to carry them from the beginning of winter through to the following spring.

Except for one item that shall be related shortly, the details of their stay with the good headmaster were forgotten as soon as they left the place and left no lasting imprint on their respective futures. (Two items, actually. I shall relate those in due course. Patience.) All you need to know is that the boys were six months at the home; they received some schooling in the mornings and labored in the workshops in the afternoons making all manner of cheap handicrafts for the domestic market; they were fed well enough, if very simply; the winter was bitterly cold but they were as warm as anyone has a right to expect in this climate; and the duck was allowed to ransom itself from the stewpot at the price of an egg every other day or so.

Each boy wore a paper tag with his name and provenance. Cordage claimed to have lost his parents, so his read "Cordage Broome, Orphan." Robert steadfastly adhered to Cordage's admonition that he had no last name, and when asked where he was from would only say, "I don't even know where I *am!*" So his tag read only "Robert, Wayward." Months later, when the home was far astern and the boys were questioned about some kerfuffle or other, a constable took the tag to indicate that his full name was Robert *Wayward*—and so it was from that point forward, Wayward being as good a last name as any other, I suppose. In addition to the tubercular angel in the infirmary—who may be a complete fabrication—Robert visited the duck every day in the little hen-house behind the kitchens.

As I said, very little of their experience during this time can be substantiated, but all indications are that Robert was content with his life there, with the daily routine, the plain food, and his narrow bed in the dormitory. However, it should also be noted that Robert was pretty generally contented so long as he was not soaking wet or starving.

Cordage, on the other hand, was as generally discontent as his past behavior would lead one to expect. He grumbled at lessons, grumbled at the workbench, grumbled at supper, and lay at night grumbling in his bed.

"Why can't we leave?" was his constant question to every teacher and workshop foreman and even the headmaster himself.

"My dear boy, where would you *go*?" was the inevitable response. "This is where you *belong*."

He made the best of his internship by practicing the skills to which I had initiated him during our journey, working with cards and spoons and whatnot in exchange for bits of licorice and other boyhood wealth.

I understand he also dabbled in fortune telling, but with poor results. If I had been there, I could have told him to stick with the cards and leave the fortune telling to those with the proper disposition. To look at a boy's palm and tell him, "You ain't never gonna find no real home," or to cast the dice and say, "You'll lose your legs to frostbite," is to end one's fortune-telling career before it's begun.

A seer will see what he or she will see, but it's what he or she says that puts coins in the purse. Mix a little light in with the darkness to keep them coming back, I say. "You'll lose your legs to frostbite *while rescuing your true love from an iceberg*." "You'll never find a real home *because you're destined to be captain of a pirate ship*." It's just as easy as it looks. But some aspiring prognosticators never get the knack. Once a boy has lost his legs to frostbite you can sit there in the dormitory pulling licorice out of his ears for the rest of the night without ever cheering him up.

➤ Four ❦

YOU ARE FAMILIAR, I assume, with the turning of the seasons and the passage of time. Therefore, it will not surprise you that in the City also late autumn froze down into winter and then winter at last melted gently away. The courtyard, which was brown when the boys arrived, became gray, then white, then gray again before awakening one morning astonished by the green fires of spring.

I don't know how it is where you are, but in the City spring brings a certain uneasiness, an air of restlessness and bemused frustration. Schoolchildren squirm on their benches, businessmen loiter at corners, and the very buildings seem to strain at their foundations, everyone stretching to see something just around the corner.

St. Jasper's, the Sisters of Hope and Mercy, and their inhabitants were no exception. The boys, herded out daily into the courtyard for exercise—St. Jasper's being among the more progressive sweatshops—ceased throwing snowballs at one another and began throwing one another into the fountain. The attendants and teachers and overseers dealt with the boys brusquely or ignored them completely.

On the other side of the iron fence that divided the courtyards, the inmates shuffled or mumbled or howled with greater enthusiasm in the warm sunlight. The older Sisters, like gentle, exasperated brooms, swept their wards from place to places, while the younger Sisters—the betrothed or betrothable—ignored their duties in favor of gazing out the windows or writing Mrs. So-and-So over and over again.

It was the perfect sort of season to leave the management of the place to the foremen and study the maps on one's office walls. The ideal weather to excuse all the sisters and spend the afternoon reading travelogues by the open window in one's boudoir.

One day in, oh, let's call it April, on just such an afternoon, with all the boys and staff out enjoying the bright afternoon, the headmaster wandered down into the dormitory in search of . . . what? Solitude? He had that aplenty. A change of scene? A bit of quietude? Or was he simply wandering the halls at random, one big loose end with no prospects for change in sight? Should he begin muttering to himself and go join the poor wretches on the sisters' side? Burble and toddle around in circles until his whole world was nothing but a noisy gray paste?

A fine captain he was, with a ship that sailed itself and went nowhere. All winter he and the imperatrix had drifted past one another, and though he had flown every flag from every yardarm, there hadn't been so much as an answering shot across his bow. Every Wednesday, weather permitting, after their friendly chat he remained at the gabled window and looked out to the harbor. Time and again the sight of a bright flag on a mast-top would send his heart straining against his waistcoat buttons.

Whither bound, O foreign flag! Take me with you, me and all my boys! You can have us all for the price of hardtack and salt pork!

A clattering sound startled the headmaster from his reverie. He looked up to see a boy sitting alone on his bunk, hunched over something scattered on the floor.

"What are you doing? Why aren't you out with the other boys?"

The boy waved him to silence with such authority that the headmaster involuntarily obeyed. He sat down on the bunk opposite the boy and looked at the scattered objects with him, five dice of different colors. The boy was evidently practicing the well-known secret dormitory game that had relieved many a green youth of all his licorice. No longer startled, the headmaster was quietly amused by the boy's serious expression.

"You know, that game is not allowed. I could confiscate those."

The boy didn't respond but kept gazing at the dice with consternation. "I ain't playin no game," he said. "I'm tellin my fortune."

"I see," said the Headmaster. "Well, how does it look?"

"Can't tell." The boy gathered up the dice and shook them together in his hands. "It's hard to tell your own fortune cuz it confuses the *spheres*."

"I see."

Another scattering, another fruitless pondering.

"Now you're here the spheres don't know which fortune to tell."

"Well, tell my fortune, then."

"Sure, for a knuckle."

"Whatever would you do with a knuckle?"

"Nothing's free."

"How about you tell my fortune and if I like it I won't confiscate your dice."

"Ain't up to me if you like your fortune. It comes from the *spheres*."

He shook the dice with a grandiose flourish and let them spill on the floor. In my professional opinion, his studious gaze was a little affected, but the headmaster seemed pleased by it.

"You ain't—" the boy said. "You ain't never gonna be happy."

This was utterly typical of the type of future young Cordage Broome, Orphan, was prone to see when casting with the dice. He told me once—years later; I don't recall the circumstances—that he didn't see the point in elaborating on the simple messages he received from the *spheres*.

"Let them figger it out themselves," he said. "It's *their* fortune. I'm just the interdromedary."

I suppose that's why old women are more in demand as fortune tellers than young boys.

Nevertheless, there in the dormitory, he must have noticed a slight exhalation from the man or perceived an imperceptible slump in his posture, for he quickly fell back and regrouped.

"You ain't never gonna be happy," he said, *"until your ship finds its way into port."*

The headmaster sat up. "That's not much of a fortune, my man," he said. "What does it mean?"

"I dunno," said the boy. "Take it up with the *spheres*." He scooped up his dice and darted out of the dormitory.

Out in the courtyard, Cordage found Robert climbing out of the fountain for what looked like the fourth time. "We gotta get out of here," he said.

"Cordage!" said a voice through the iron fence. "My little lump!"

"How can we leave?" Robert asked. "It's all locked up."

"We gotta find a way."

"The older boys leave when they grow up. Why don't we just wait?"

"Cordage! My only son!"

"I can't wait that long. I'll go crazy."

"Maybe you're already crazy."

"Cordage!"

"Let me tell your fortune."

"No, your fortunes are mean."

"It's the *spheres*."

"Cordage!"

That very Wednesday, as it happened, the headmaster tacked against the wind up the winding stairs with a secreted bottle of raspberry cordial only to find the imperatrix already there, waiting with a platter of butter cookies. He shut the door behind him, sensing green hills on the horizon. He produced the bottle with a flourish and her eyes sparkled. The shining white shore of his island beckoned, with heaven knew what wonders hidden in the jungle beyond.

"Those look wonderful," he said.

"It's a new recipe," she said. "I made them just for you."

—⊰ FIVE ⊱—

BY A CURIOUS COINCIDENCE, that was the very day of the Great Escape. The boys were busy in the workshop at St. Jasper's and the mentally infirm in the workshop at the Sisters' when without warning a section of the shared back wall collapsed into a heap of rubble, providing a gap in both workshops that allowed an ecstatic crowd of boys and a confused tumble of madmen to pour into the narrow lane behind the building.

It was like the last day of school and the first day of the end of the world all at once. As the inmates flowed into the streets the bewildered staffs of both institutions ran up and down stairs. Where was the headmaster? Wherever was the imperatrix?

When the headmaster and imperatrix finally appeared—satchels in hand—they both seemed rather calmer than the situation warranted, a testament, no doubt, to their superior leadership qualities. Go and call the constables, for mercy's sake, and have them all rounded up, advised the headmaster. Engage masons and carpenters at once to begin repairs, suggested the imperatrix. Whereupon they both headed out their respective front doors. If you'd excuse them, they had appointments to keep in town. Manage as best you can.

They were never seen in the City again.

Although there is no way to verify that Cordage was the first boy to bolt through the gap in the wall, neither is there any reason to suspect otherwise. According to his own account, he was the first one out, and if he hadn't had to go back for stupid Robert then everything woulda been different. As it was, when the wall fell, Cordage was through the gap and gone, along with one or two other boys with similar flighty instincts. Then, after a short pause, the rest of the boys understood the opportunity at hand and surged out the gap into the street.

A very few boys for whom obedience was both first and second nature remained at their benches, waiting for permission to flee. Robert would undoubtedly have been among these last few, but he was caught in the rush and found himself in the middle of a most peculiar gathering. The boys, once the initial escape had been made, stood in the middle of the street and wondered what to do. Lacking proper training, they failed to follow Cordage's example and dash into the nearest alleyway, then dodge through random left and right turns like a panicked hare.

Scattered among them were escapees from the Sisters' side, exhibiting a wide array of responses to their new situation. Some gibbered, some curled up into balls, some tried to claw their way back in while others were still clambering out. Not a few began dancing. So much happened so fast that Robert hadn't had time to work out a response yet when he was grabbed at the elbow by his furiously irritated cousin.

"Cord! I think we're excaping!"

"I know that, you idiot! I come back for you!"

"Cordage! Cordage! My little lump!"

"Oh no, no you don't," said Cordage. He dragged Robert through the crowd into the nearest alley. They rushed down one narrow passage after another, the voice behind them sometimes growing quieter but never disappearing completely.

"Cordage! My boy!"

"No, I ain't."

"But what if you are?" said Robert.

"I ain't. Ain't no crazy man is *my* father."

They hit a blind alley and had to double back. At a conjunction of three alleys, with a dead end at their back, they saw the lunatic appear at the end of one alley; the other led out onto a busy and crowded street.

"Cordage! I found you! You found me!"

"Cheesy biscuits," swore Cordage. "Let's go."

He dragged Robert to the busy street, where they were immediately confronted by a constable.

"Where you boys off to?" he asked. "Not fled from St. Jasper's, by chance?"

"No, Off'cer," said Cordage. "We're on our way to—"

"What's this? 'Robert, Wayward?' That's your name, is it?"

"Yes?" said Robert uncertainly.

"And you," the officer said to Cordage, "you're an orphan like it says here?"

"No," said Cordage. "I'm not an orphan, I—"

"Cordage! My boy!"

The genial lunatic rushed up to them, breathless and ecstatic.

"Is this your father, then?"

Cordage froze, staring his father, unable to do anything but squeak.

"Oh, yes," said his father. "I am Nicolas Broome, stringer, and this little lump is my boy Cordage, returned to me at last after all these years of cruel separation by the mischances of fate!" He sank to his knees and held Cordage at arm's length, gazing at him rapturously. "My boy, my boy," he whispered. "My little lump at last!"

"That's all very well," said the Constable, "but appearances are you all three need to come with me back to the Sisters and St. Jasper."

It should be noted he was not an unfeeling man, nor was he unmoved by the tender scene before him. A father himself, he was loathe to pry Cordage—still rigid with horror—from his father's loving grasp.

"It hurt my heart," he would later say about it, "but everyone's got a job to do."

"Quite right, I think," said Mr. Broome. "Safety in numbers, you know."

He rose and started back the way they had come, back into the dark labyrinth of alleys and side streets that riddled that quarter of the city.

"Here now," said the officer. "We can't go that way."

"I think it's quicker," said Cordage.

"The street's the long way," said Robert.

So the constable followed the retreating form of Mr. Broome, who waited kindly for them to catch up.

"Officer," he said earnestly as they passed through the darkest part of the maze, "have you given any thought to the role string plays in your life?"

The constable considered the question briefly and was about to answer when he found himself flat on his back with his ankles bound in a cunning noose and his detainees fleeing rapidly away.

"Here now!" he cried. "Here now, here now!"

Have I neglected up to this point to describe Mr. Broome to you? Well, a pox upon me, then. Remind me to flagellate myself later. Mr. Nicolas Broome was quite tall and very narrow, even gaunt, with long, stringy hair and a beard to match. He was dressed in a peculiar robe of his own device, made from the blankets of his bed at the

Sisters of Hope and Mercy. Around his waist, binding the robes shut, was a slender cord, thicker than twine but thinner than a hempen rope, spun surreptitiously a strand at a time from his own hair and from threads he picked out of his bed linens. It was this very cord that had ensnared the constable and enabled their escape—and, incidentally, raised Mr. Broome somewhat in Cordage's estimation. Not that Cordage was ready to acknowledge him as a kindred spirit or anything like that. But the man clearly knew a thing or two about string.

They wandered for a while, trying to remain out of sight.

"Where do we go?" asked Robert.

"I don't know," said Mr. Broome. "I've never escaped for this long before."

Eventually, through a series of minor adventures that need no relation here, they ended up under Wood Bridge at dusk, joining a raggedy camp of shapeless, nameless souls.

"Welcome, as likely as not," said a man who introduced himself as the mayor of that camp. "Who are you and what do you do? There's no fires allowed under Wood Bridge, as you might guess. So if you're cold, you'd best find other quarters. Second Bridge, say. But if it's darkness you're looking for, well, you've come to the right place.

"I'm Cord," said Cordage. "Pick a card."

"I'm hungry," said Robert.

"Nicolas Broome, lunatic stringer," said Mr. Broome. "And I think darkness suits us fine tonight."

Supplemental architectural note: Subsequent investigation by an expert, appointed by the mayor, has provided the following explanation for the Great Escape. The immediate cause for the collapse of the back wall of the workshops was the use of substandard mortar for repairs of that wall following the Battle of Fifehill two centuries previously. The collapse itself was triggered when a crucial stone in the repaired wall was struck by a finial that fell from a buttress on a higher level. The finial was dislocated by the head of a gargoyle that fell from still higher up. The gargoyle appeared to have been injured by a stone that fell from very near the peak of the highest level, dislodged perhaps by some unusual activity taking place in the attic. Further investigation was inconclusive, the investigating officer finding nothing noteworthy in the attic.

"The usual rubbish," he said. "An empty cordial bottle and a broken chaise. That sort of thing."

Intermissiary note: This is shaping up to be the longest chapter in the story. By rights, based on length, it should probably be two chapters, but the subject matter suggests it should remain as one. Which do you prefer: one chapter that is just slightly too long or two chapters that are much, much too short?

Well, I thought as much, but what's done is done. If you feel the need for a break, go and clean something, or find something broken and fix it. Take all the time you need.

→ Six ←

WHILE WE WAIT FOR THE OTHERS we may as well refresh ourselves as to the general layout and geography of the City and its constituent parts. You will recall that the City is on an island in the river, and that seven bridges connect the island with what the citizens call "the Other Sides." The bridges were constructed at various times throughout the City's history—

No. I've changed my mind. We will not talk about the bridges here but rather about the varied and variable communities that reside under them: for my money, the most interesting aspect of the City.

So. Seven bridges, each with one foot on the island and one on an Other Side, and little communities huddled like mice under either end, making fourteen *en todum*. (That's Latin.)

Things may have changed now, but at that time the city hadn't spread much beyond the confines of the island, so there was hardly any habitation on the Other Side, save little knots of inns and shops at the mouths of each bridge. That being the case, it makes sense that the communities under the bridges on the island were comparatively more settled and established than those over-water.

For example, under New Bridge, a sturdy, narrow bridge near the best part of the City, the denizens are mostly day laborers who stay only a few months before finding better lodging. On the Other Side, however, the bridge shelters indigent travelers for no more than a day or two at a time. And at East Bridge, where the City side is habited by artists who failed to pay the rent one too many times, the Other Side is generally vacant except for Old Gorm, who has lived there since time immemorial and makes it his business to "keep the flies away," as he says.

Wood Bridge—being somewhat transient itself, burning down or falling over or washing away in a flood every ten years or so— is home to the most mobile of the city's vagrants, those who, for inscrutable reasons of their own, are always on their way someplace else. The camp on the other side is peopled entirely by travelers who wanted to get to the City but arrived after the gates had closed for the night.

And so on around the City, a seven-pointed crown, with Old Bridge being the diadem.

Old Bridge is the oldest, largest, widest, and longest bridge by far, still standing on its original Roman piers and expanded from there in both breadth and width. It is a veritable village unto itself, lined on both sides with shops and houses and even boasting a small chapel. Underneath it dwells the most established and settled community of any bridge in the City, and of any bridge in any city, I'll warrant. The population under the bridge nears a thousand in the stormy months and is never less than several hundreds. There are many actual houses and shanties, with well-established lanes between them, and some families have occupied the same sites for generations untold. Invariably, whenever anyone in the City says he is going "under the bridge," he means he intends to visit the world below Old Bridge, undoubtedly to engage in the shadier sort of commerce that thrives there.

The community on the Other Side of Old Bridge is no less well established, being positioned directly beneath the garrison that is stationed there to stop smuggled goods from entering the city, or at least to profit from their passage. People have even built homes on the broad feet of the piers, all the way across the river, so the twin communities on the shores are connected by a conduit of slat bridges, catwalks, taut-lines, and rickety pontoon buoys.

The community is lively and the economy is vigorous, as you might expect. Do you want to buy something you probably shouldn't buy, do you want to eat something you really shouldn't eat, or do you thirst for questionable drink or long for anonymous company? It's all waiting for you under the bridge. Or perhaps you seek something different? A place to almost call your own? If you are weary of the ramshackle sanitation practices under New Bridge, or find that the people under North Bridge are too devoted to drink for your comfort, you may wish to look for succor under Old Bridge. If you find the disaffected artists under East Bridge and the failed merchants under Second Bridge to be entirely too tedious, you may travel to the other side of the City and make your petition to stay under the only bridge worthy of the name.

Say, for example, that you are a young woman from some foreign place, turned out of the town you had come to call home. You've surrendered your child and made your way to the City, only to discover that the letter you carry directs you to a house that is vacant, and the money provided for your passage home is only enough for a week's lodging at the cheapest inn. What's a poor lost serving girl to do? Go to Old Bridge, talk to the mayor beneath, and make your claim. It turns out there is a tavern so old it claims to predate the bridge itself. You might be installed there, provided you can adhere to the code of conduct. (The mayor runs his hotbed of iniquity according to a strict ethical code so permutated and serpentine it cannot be unraveled even by so complex a thinker as Slogoyban— who visits yearly, nonetheless, though he always leaves before any real trouble starts.)

Or suppose, just for a moment, you are an enterprising merchant who has come into possession of the sole cask of schkoltsch outside Bergerton, only to discover that the sale of this delicacy within the City is not only illegal but felonious. Mightn't you consider setting up shop discreetly under Old Bridge and letting quiet word of mouth spread among a few aficionados to build up a clientele?

What if your great-great-grandfather was the careless prison guard who let a notorious villain escape at a most politically inopportune time? Mightn't his name have been so thoroughly blackened that his descendants remain under the bridge to this day?

Imagine yourself an escaped lunatic stringer. Rag picking is simple enough anywhere in the City, but where to set up shop to unravel the threads and twist them again into good twine, two knuckles the skein? Mayor Underbridge has just the spot, provided you don't let the giggling get out of control. People who live under bridges need string, too, you know, and a whole year may pass in a flash: picking, raveling, twining, hardly able to keep up with demand, while the boys come and go as boys will.

→ Seven ←

AS YOU MIGHT HAVE GUESSED, I am not unknown under Old Bridge. Never an established resident, mind you, but I make my way through from time to time. I meet people and hear stories, and I have a standing welcome at the Black Hearth, the aforementioned ancient tavern.

The Hearth has a passable ale and excellent sausages in season. (Sausage season occurs when the proprietor is able to engage a small, swift boy as a sausage snatcher "up there," and so is determined more by the vigilance of the constables than the caprices of the weather. I suspect Cordage was for a short time so employed, but he would never admit to it.)

Sadly, at my most recent visit sausage was out of season, so I consoled myself with a double measure of cider and eyed the crowd. As I finished my drink I felt a fortune telling coming on and had only to determine whose. The crowd was mostly Underers, but there were enough Uppers to ensure a profitable evening.

I had just settled on a middle-aged man with a stained satin waistcoat and a pretty little parasite on his arm when four loaves of bread came through the door, followed by none other than little

Robert Wayward, looking just as he had when I last saw him but a
shade taller and two or three shades plumper.

"Just four today, Mr. Kolloper," he said, placing the loaves on
the bar.

"Not to worry, lad," said the man. "It's four more than we had
this morning."

Robert was obviously an industrious young man, bent on his
tasks, well on his way to all manner of worldly success. He could
hardly profit from being distracted from his work and drawn into
idle conversation with long-lost acquaintances. Therefore, it was
with the boy's best interests at heart that I endeavored to hide behind
my empty cider mug while he exchanged pleasantries with the man
behind the bar.

But to no avail, alas. I have—I may as well tell you, so as not
to be unduly circumspect or falsely modest—a certain presence, an
aura of character that people find both memorable and pugnacious.
For better or worse, I get under people's eyelids like a rogue lash.

Therefore, I was not surprised and only a little chagrined when
he spied me out.

"Auntie Bones!" he cried.

Kolloper cocked an eyebrow at me. "'Auntie Bones,' is it?" he
said. "So after all these years I have to change the name on your
account?"

"A technicality," I said. "A figure of speech. The boy's simple as
the day is long. Pay no attention to anything he says." I turned to the
boy with my best affectation of joyful surprise. "Why, if it isn't little
Robert from wherever it is! You haven't a spare knuckle for your old
friend, have you?"

He laughed. "No, I don't have any money at all."

"Alas," I said.

Some sort of tumult erupted and quickly subsided behind us. I turned to see that my middle-aged waistcoat had misplaced his parasite and was stumbling out the door in search of her. I felt the fortune-telling feeling evaporate as he carried both his fortunes and mine out into the murky evening.

"Alas," I said again. "We have little in common, young Robert, but we appear at the moment to be equally wealthy."

"Come have supper with us," said Robert. "It's not much, but it's enough."

"Indeed," I said, "and more than I am likely to find here, so long as you keep turning up to meddle with my fortune-telling energy. Never have the prognosticatory vibrations been so disrupted as when I encounter you."

He laughed again. "That's what Cord says, too. He says I irritate the *spheres*."

Does he, now.

We followed the tangled lanes and grubby paths that threaded through the ramshackle community. Never mind how far as the crow flies. In the first place, you are not a crow and neither am I, so the information is irrelevant. And in the second place, there was never a crow to be seen under the bridge except for Percival, a ratty old creature kept by Kolloper at the Black Hearth. And Percival was never seen to fly; he insisted on being carried everywhere he went.

So, feeble earthbound creatures that we were, we picked our way from the tavern to the stringer's lodging. Whether it was a furlong or two or barely a dozen yards away, it took us twenty minutes, which I thought was pretty good time, considering the hour of the night.

Anyone who tells you he knows his way about under the bridge, if his information is more than a day old, is not to be believed. There are landmarks, to be sure—chiefly the stone piers of the bridge itself—and some permanent structures—such as the tavern and a tiny chapel on the far side—but the ways between them are as fluid as the river, which from time to time washes it all away.

Old Bridge was built at the location of an ancient ford. The river is shallow there, with broad, sloping banks backed by steeper, higher banks on either side. The bridge spans these high banks, presumably to allow an invading army the easiest possible access to the City. "Under the Bridge," then, includes not only the land under the bridge proper but the whole area of the shallow banks around the bridge, a quarter mile or more on either side. The entire place might cover barely a half a dozen acres, but you may take my word that there are untold miles of paths to be trod there without ever seeing the same shanty twice.

Nicolas Broome had secured a location under the bridge itself, which would serve him well when the rains came, but quite close to the water, which would serve him ill when the rains came. His home was a blanket and his furniture was a bag of rags. By day he spread the blanket out and sat upon it to pick rags and spin skein after skein of twine, which he sold or gave away or jealously hoarded, depending on his mood. By night he wrapped himself in the blanket, laid his head on the bag, and slept the dreamless sleep that is the blessing of all lunatics. (Spending their days in a tortured dream, they are free when sleeping to simply sleep.)

He greeted Robert warmly and offered me a friendly, vacant smile. We had never met, of course, so I didn't expect him to recognize me, although I thought he should have known me by reputation. But no matter. The duck did recognize me, and we regarded one another with guarded suspicion throughout the evening.

"Hi, Mr. Broome! Hi, Clarence!" said Robert. "I brought some bread. Is Cord here?"

"No, I was about to ask if you'd seen the lump," said Mr. Broome. "He'll be here soon, I guess."

"That boy," said Mr. Broome. "What a trailblazer he is! What a go-getter! He'll amount to something, mark my words! And here he is!" He stood up, dusted off his trousers, and smoothed his hair. "Sit here, my boy. Sit, sit, sit."

Cordage threw his bundle down at the base of the stone pillar that formed Mr. Broome's back wall. Then he sat down heavily and took a pack of cards from his pocket. He shuffled them and began turning them over one at a time, sneering at each one in turn and paying no attention to any of us whatever.

"I have some bread," Robert said again. "Mr. Baker gave it to me for supper 'cause they made more than they needed at the house and Mrs. Mayor only wants fresh bread every day."

"Did you take some to Kolloper?" asked Mr. Broome.

"Oh, sure. He said thanks."

"Good, good," said Mr. Broome. "That's part of the arrangement," he explained to me.

"What arrangement is that?" I asked.

"I'm not sure," said Mr. Broome, "but we try to keep up our end, I think."

Cordage snorted. "Old Klodhopper got Robert apprenticed to the mayor's baker. He only lets you stay here if we bring him stuff cuz you never sell any string."

"I sell some string. I sell lots of string!"

"And then you lose your money or give it away or throw it in the river."

"True. That's very true."

Mr. Broome started to giggle but Cordage poked him with his toe. "Don't do that. Don't laugh now." He looked up at me, then went back to sneering at one card after another. "What are you doing here?" he asked.

"It's good to see you, too," I said. "How's business?"

"I got chased by the constable but I didn't get caught."

"So that's a good day, then."

"I've had worse."

"My Cordage is really moving up in the world," Mr. Broome told me. "He's got his sights on a position at the highest levels!"

"Yeah," said Cordage. "In fact, I have a meeting with His Excellency behind the Slotted Spoon tonight. Is supper ready?"

"No, we need you to start the fire," said Robert. "For the egg."

Cordage rolled his eyes and dug a battered tin box from his bundle.

"Can't none of you start a fire without me?"

I could certainly have started a fire, but I wasn't about to become embroiled in this family imbroglio. Cordage grumbled and grumped and began piling twigs and bits of trash between three smoke-blackened stones.

"I need some tinder," he said. "Do you have any fluff I can use?"

"Certainly," said Mr. Broom. "Do you want jute? Or some hemp?"

"It don't matter."

"The hemp is stronger, you know. But jute is softer and has a nice sheen when it's spun properly."

"It don't *matter*!" Cordage grabbed whatever was in his father's left hand and began striking with his flint.

Keep in mind, all this was happening not in some isolated wasteland but in a crowded milieu of denizens of the deep. We were surrounded on all sides by similar folk in similar states of habitation, some of whom already had fires of their own going.

Why Mr. Broome and Robert relied on this surly boy for their fires was beyond me.

"I don't know why you need me to make your fires, anyways," said Cordage. "If it wasn't for that I wouldn't even come down here no more."

"That's mean," said Robert.

"It's true," said Cordage, blowing the smoking pile of twigs into bright flames.

"I'm doing fine, up in the City. Got everything I need right here." He patted his bundle, a boy after my own heart.

"You should get a real job," said Robert. "Mr. Baker lets me sleep in the kitchen so I can stay warm all winter. Plus I get to eat cookies."

Cordage snorted.

"My boy's going to go far," said Mr. Broom. "He's on his way up, up, up!"

Cordage pulled a battered skillet from his bundle and balanced it over the flames.

"Gimme that egg." He cracked the egg and broke it into the pan, where it fell with a clink.

A clink?

"What?" said Cordage. He pulled something from the pan, slimy with egg.

"It's a knuckle," said Robert. "So what? You pulled it out like you pull things from people's ears."

Cordage looked genuinely bewildered.

"No, it was in the egg, I swear."

"Lemme see," said Robert. He wiped the coin on his jacket. Then his eyes widened.

"It's mine!" he said.

"Is not," said Cordage. "I found it!"

"No I mean it's *mine*! It's my lucky knuckle! I mean, it would be mine anyway, because it was in my duck, but look!" He pointed to the coin. "It's got a R scratched in it. R for *Robert*. It's the one I had in my pocket when we left, the one I found when Uncle Jon was digging by the front door." He pointed at me. "The one *you* took!"

I looked as wide-eyed and innocent as possible. Cordage lunged to grab the coin, but Robert dodged away, nearly upsetting the egg into the fire.

"Phah!" said Cordage. "Keep it, then, I don't care. It's just a stupid knuckle. That looks more like a B than an R anyways." He steadied the skillet. "Stupid knuckle never caused anything but trouble."

"Don't blame the knuckle," said Robert. "If you hadn't tried to grab it from me at the feast."

"Well if you weren't so clumsy and fell over!"

"If you hadn't *shoved* me so I fell on the sausage man's brazier and knocked it over!"

"No, I didn't! I wasn't my fault! He shouldn't have had it that close to his shop, anyways!"

"You didn't have to shove me," said Robert.

"Shut up! It wasn't my fault! It's that stupid knuckle. Why do you care so much about it?" Amid the babble of anonymous voices we were in a little bubble of silence. Cordage poked the fire with a stick. "It wasn't my fault. It was an accident. Stupid knuckle. You shoulda never found it."

"It was just sitting on the steps at the house," said Robert. "*Someone* was gonna find it."

"Well, better someone else than you," Cordage snapped. "Better anyone else living down here in the mud."

I felt a peculiar tingling sensation somewhere in the back of my head.

"What did you say?" I asked.

"I said better anyone else than him find that coin so it would be anyone else but me living down here in this stupid mud," he kicked the ground, "under this stupid bridge." He slapped the stone pillar and then folded his arms on his knees and buried his face in them.

I will pause for a moment to let you consider the significance of the moment. Are you able to string all the pieces together? Do you see what has occurred? Little Robert Baker, formerly Wayward, formerly Berger, has informed us he is both working and sleeping in the kitchen of the mayor, therefore, *living in New House*. Then, Cordage Broome, as tall as his father but better looking, admitted in a moment of despair that he indeed *lives under a bridge*. There, in the space it takes to fry an egg, we have the resolution to the fortune I cast for them so long ago and so very far away. Moments such as these are few and far between, even in a life as long as mine. Savor it while you can.

Half a fortune, rather. You will recall I was interrupted at the time, and that revelation of the second part was contingent upon transpiration of the first part. Well, I am as good as my word, more or less, and within seconds the tingling in my scalp blossomed into the familiar warm rush of visionary energy. I happily informed the boys of this and further promised to provide the remainder of their future upon delivery of adequate remuneration.

Cordage said "Bald—" but both Robert and I stopped him with a hiss before it was too late.

Mr. Broome found our hissing to be most humorous and began hissing himself with great enthusiasm. So much so that Cordage was compelled to put the empty rag bag over his head.

"You can't have my knuckle," said Robert, once the hissing had subsided. "You already took it once and spent it."

I would have liked to discuss the matter at greater length, but a frying egg waits for no witch, so I settled for a fourth of a stale loaf and a mouthful or two of the egg. I! I who has cast fortunes for earls and dukes and been rewarded with hard coin and justifiable fame, forced by circumstance to grovel in the mud for crusts! The ignominy! But it couldn't be helped, I suppose.

"Very well," I said, once supper was concluded. "I have the balance of your futures at hand. Are you prepared for the responsibility of knowing what fate awaits you?"

Robert nodded raptly. Cordage muttered something and Mr. Broome hissed quietly inside his bag.

"Very well," I said. Our little bubble of silence had grown and a circle of ragged onlookers helped to create the proper mood, what with the bated breath and the flickering firelight and whatnot. As with so many things, successful prognostication is all about ambiance.

"There will be," I said finally, hardly daring to interrupt the tension, "a flood."

I felt that the stunned silence that greeted me was appropriate, if a trifle strained.

"Is that it?" asked Robert. "It's not much."

"That's what the vibrations have brought me," I said. "I do not question the vibrations."

"What about the *spheres*?" asked Cordage.

"I don't work with spheres," I said. "Strictly vibrations at this latitude."

"Fair enough," said Cordage.

"But," said Robert.

"Don't worry about it," said Cordage. "I'll consult the *spheres* later."

"All right," said Robert. "But I still say the spheres are mean."

Later that evening we parted ways, Mr. Broome into his blankets and Robert to the kitchens at New House. And I, of course, headed out on my own course as always. But not before joining Cordage at his meeting with His Excellency behind the Slotted Spoon, an event which turned out most profitably for all, but is another story for another time.

A Fourth Expository Interlude

WELL, WHAT OF THE KNUCKLE, THEN? Was it really Robert's "lucky" knuckle, come back to haunt us? One knuckle is much the same as another to me—worth a round bun in the City or a mug of cider in a country inn, the forty-eighth part of a Caspian scruple, and so on—so I really can't say with any certainty that it was *the* knuckle. Robert seemed terribly certain that it was indeed the same coin but could produce no documentation to support his claim. I understand that through the rest of their adventure together it was his practice to keep it close upon his person in a little bag worn around the neck, and that it was Cordage's practice to attempt to relieve him of it at every opportunity, with varying degrees of geniality, I imagine.

But how came the knuckle to the City? It is difficult enough to trace one's own path back through time, let alone the path of an insignificant bronze token of the full faith and credit of the nation. Nevertheless, here in my sunset years, with little else about which to concern myself and hip-deep in materials for this tale, I have been able to give the matter some thought and have arrived at what I hope you will find a satisfactory explanation.

So.

We bypass Robert's unsubstantiated story of its acquisition and begin with the first concrete documentation of its existence: the knuckle was paid to me for most of a dual fortune-telling (still a bargain, by any reasonable assessment) and then spent for a mug of cider in the inn at Wat's Hump. As the proprietor of that establishment is a graspy and miserly man who never makes change for a customer if he can help it, the knuckle might well have remained in his coffers forever, even up to the present day.

However, in those extraordinary days following the fire, the influx of refugees from Bergerton filled all his rooms and drained all his barrels. Thus, he was forced to purchase kegs of cider and ale from whomever he could—local farmers, mostly. Since it was his practice to spend the oldest and shabbiest coins first, I believe this is when Our Knuckle rejoined general circulation, after only a few days.

From that point it knocked around Wat's Hump and environs for a season, purchasing a gill of vinegar here, a measure of barley there; paying a ploughman in the spring or a reaper in the autumn. Eventually, after some months, it wound up in the collection basket or the poor box at St. Travertine, the little chapel in Feeblee Hollow, just over the hill from Wat's Hump. It is noted separately in the ledger there because, due to its age and ill use, it was shaped differently than all the other knuckles and wouldn't sit in a well-behaved stack with them. The entry reads:

14 Otb:
Dixit 27
Knuckle 5, Grip ½
Foreign coin (Voldish?) 1
Knuckle (oblong) 1
Gratias agens pro minuta.

Was it then given to Friar Bowlingreen, the wandering mendicant priest who traveled the country lanes and ministered to those beyond the reach of the churches of stone and slab? Was it then mislaid by him during one of his not infrequent convivial visits to this or that band of Hooligans in the north? And was it not then found in the middle of the path by an exhausted and bedraggled soldier returning in good, wholesome disgrace from a foreign war?

Certainly it reentered the economy of Bergerton around this time and knocked about the tills of the merchants who were still conducting business as the town struggled to recover from the fire. Hard currency was scarce in those weeks, you know—much of the town's metal wealth having been melted together into shapeless lumps. (A word of advice: if you live in a cottage with a thatched roof, consider carefully before following the Bergerton practice and keeping your gold and silver in the attic.)

When he could be roused to some sort of work, one of the matters to which the Burgermeister turned his attention was issuing paper for the metal and trying to work out an arrangement with the mint to have the coins recast. The particular knuckle of our concern narrowly escaped this fate, in fact, only by virtue of slipping through the bartender's fingers at the Yellow Beetle and becoming wedged between the floorboards. It was later discovered by one of the serving girls during sweeping-up and given to her betrothed, a ploughman from Spoodle's Farm, for his journey to the City, the purpose of which was vague in her mind—but somehow, as he continued to explain, inextricably linked to their coming nuptials.

Whether he truly intended to return, I cannot say. Whether or not he actually *did* return, for that you will have to ask her.

Once in the City, the knuckle followed his tortured path: up this lane and down that, from one missed opportunity to another, drawing nearer and nearer to the docks and the magnificent tall ships each day, and deeper and deeper into the back rooms at the taverns each night. More than once it was lost in a game of chance, only to be won back later that night or the next. I don't know the details of the game, but gamblers are a superstitious lot and were always eager to lose the dirty and misshapen coin.

At last, weary with dissipation, the young man sat on a wooden box in front of a small tavern in the middle of Old Bridge. It was midday and warm—unseasonably so, for summer was past and in fact the morning had seen the first scattered snowflakes fall. He should have found the autumn warmth invigorating, he supposed, but it was simply oppressive.

It was Saturday, or Market Day, or something. The bridge was a busy place, with a bustling and a hustling that irritated him and made him both lethargic and restless. A girl was singing and clapping while another girl danced in front of the tavern for a small crowd. He fingered the knuckle with one eye to the left and one to the right. He flipped the coin high in the air. It didn't sparkle; it was too old and tarnished. He caught it and held his breath while he peeked between his hands.

What did he see? Does it matter? He smiled, let all the air out of his lungs at once and stood up as if the earth could hardly hold him down anymore. He kissed the coin, threw it at the feet of the dancing girl, and strode offr, as purposeful and penniless a young man as ever you would care to see.

The singing girl collected the knuckle and later gave it, with some others, after an earnest conversation, to a small, dark woman in exchange for a hand-woven shawl. Against the coming chill, I imagine.

This woman then wandered the world following paths of her own. But who among us does not? At that time, the woman's world consisted of Old Bridge. Mostly the warren below, with its impenetrable snarl of byways, its dark odors and turbulent vapors, its loves gained and lives lost—all the heady, musky, violent joys of human creatures doing their level best to survive against all odds. But also the deck, up in the light, with its shops and tiny cottages— infrequently, when the need for a fresh breeze or the whisper of a forgotten song overpowered her desire to remain hidden.

Before finding the rough stairs that led down to her home, she stopped at the low wall that kept most onlookers from falling into the river below. The sunset flickered on the water and the evening breeze rose, just a little. The knuckle was very old. And green, a peculiar green, that specific green that only bronze can turn. Gray-green like an olive tree at dusk or the color of the sky just before a cyclone strikes. I knew a girl once with eyes of just such a green. She is gone now, years and years gone. She is hardly worth remembering. The memory is not worth the trouble.

The woman on the bridge held the coin and wished a wish. She wished with all her might, wished desperately, wished with all the combined strength of every particle of her being, then tossed the coin into the water.

A fish—one of those large, unpalatable river fish that no one in his right mind would eat—tried to swallow the coin, but the duck got it first.

Part XII

The Darlings of the North End

→ Oпe ←

SLOGOYBAN THE VAGABOND KING certainly knew the City, and he knew it well, as well as anyone could. After all, he brought his little band every year to its gates and encamped them at the foot of Wood Bridge for two weeks in the middle of spring without fail. He knew the poor of the Low Quarter who came to enjoy the sights and the food, their only excursion off the island in all the long, dreary year. He knew the artists who came to mingle and jabber and congratulate themselves on their worldliness. He knew the wealthy, especially, and cultivated their taste for the exotic and expensive. He knew the headmaster of St. Jasper's personally, being the chief purchaser of the products of the workshop, and looked forward each year to their heated and acrimonious exchanges. He even knew the mayor and had known three other mayors before him, and counted them all among his dearest friends. Such friendships as one was able to maintain from the lofty peaks of power, of course.

And the mayor, as you must assume, also knew the City inside and out—every important family, every significant commercial enterprise, each charitable organization and educational institution, all the varied neighborhoods and the different problems they posed for law enforcement. He pictured himself as the master of the world's largest patisserie, with his finger in every pie.

And yet, the city one man knew was not the same as the other's. If you were to drop one man in the city of the other you might as well drop him in the silver gardens of the moon. A flea may travel from one ear to the other and claim to know the dog, while a flea at the tail may know the same dog but have a decidedly different view. Perhaps it is more accurate to say that each man knew the face the City chose to turn to him, and that everyone who knows a place really only knows whatever small slice they have been graced with, whichever narrow alley or bright plaza, which stone tower or shanty or workhouse dormitory.

For Lexi and the Princess, newly come to the city, it presented no face at all save that created by their expectations and imaginations. And what were those? For Lexi, was the City the prize at the end of a long search or the monster at the heart of the labyrinth? Or was it the labyrinth itself, with some secret at the center drawing her in? For the Princess, was it simply more adventure? Did she connect it at all with her grandfather's annual trips, for which he left in discouragement and from which he returned exhausted?

After a short time in the City, the Princess would become just as enraptured with the new sights and sounds and smells as she had been with the Vagabond's ragtag entourage. At first, though, it did not seem so different from any other place they'd traveled through. Larger, to be sure, and Old Bridge was longer and narrower than any town square they had seen, but aside from that it was exactly the same collection of shops and stalls, along with the familiar crowds of strangers who had become both backdrop and foreground to her whole life.

Distractedly, as if by habit, Lexi found a tiny tavern partway across the bridge. She clapped and sang as Princess Something from Somewhere began to dance. Ho hum. Admiring looks from the crowd, the tinkle of coins underfoot—after bluffing her way past the sentries, the Princess had expected something more from this place. Must they revert immediately to performing for the copper and bronze of passersby? They had plenty of money, after all, so much that it was something of a burden in their bundles. Lexi had promised that when they got to the City they would find a money-changer and trade it all for silver filletes and gold kornigs.

And yet here they were, not even in the City proper, still scraping battered little coins from the stones as if it were stardust from the skies. The crowd seemed less than enthusiastic. A few people were watching intently—a young man with dark circles under his eyes, an old man with ragged teeth—but for the most part they looked as bored as she was. They should have known that in a sophisticated place like the City their little act from the country taverns would be old news.

And she was so hungry! Couldn't Lexi smell? The meat pies across the way? And, somewhere, bread baking?

At the end of the song Lexi thanked the good people and gave the Princess half a grip—yes, for heaven's sake, go and find some bread if you must. The Princess learned to her dismay that half a grip didn't go as far as it used to. She returned with a rather small loaf and only one meat pie to find Lexi holding a shawl and watching a strange little woman walk away into the crowd.

"What's that?"

"I bought it from her."

It was very light, with a loose, open weave, made from an uneven sort of homespun thread.

327

"It's very odd. The colors are funny."

"It's foreign." Lexi draped it over her shoulders.

"Is it a scarf or a shawl? It doesn't go with that frock."

"It's comfortable."

"It looks old. Who was she?"

"She liked the song."

"Which one? The one about the maiden?"

"No, the old one. About the birds."

They walked slowly, sharing the pie, attracting no more notice than a pair of birds themselves.

"How do you know it's about birds? The words aren't even in a real language."

"You like that song."

"I've always liked it. But that doesn't mean I know what it's about."

"It's about birds. The man in the song is sad because all his little birds have flown away."

"But how do you know?"

"I just know."

⇀ TWO ↼

OLD BRIDGE DEPOSITS YOU at the foot of the Old Fort, which, being a prison, is the bleakest of all possible destinations. However, from that point, good streets radiate out in all directions and will take you to any point in the City that you like. If your feet are tired, eager men with push-carriages are happy to tote you and your baggage anywhere you please. The push-carriages are unique to the City (since no livestock larger than goats are allowed over

the bridges) and their operators charge too much, but many visitors
feel that such a ride is required, or their experience of the City is
incomplete. I encourage you, if ever you find yourself there, to take
a turn around the west side of the City, stopping for luncheon at the
Gosling. Buy your carriage-pusher a pint and you'll have a friend for
life.

Lexi stood at the center of the plaza in front of the fort and
glanced alternately up at the high wall of the façade and down along
any of the busy streets that led to heaven knew where. There were no
market stalls here, but the place rang with the shouts of the carriage-
pushers and the cries of people calling messages up into the dark,
barred windows that dotted the otherwise blank face of the building.

"How dazzling!" said the Princess.

"Don't be giddy," said Lexi. "It's unbecoming."

"But, the *City*!" said the Princess. "We're here in the *City*!"

"Yes, yes," said Lexi. "Just a moment."

The building before her was more than twice as high as any she
had ever seen, and she found it oppressive. Anything at all could be
going on behind that forbidding pile of nameless stone.

"Lexi? What now? One of those men is coming with a wagon."

"What? We don't know where we're going."

The man pushed the carriage up in front of them. It was a gaudy
thing, a little two-seat open box with two large wheels at the back
and two small wheels in front. It was painted and gilded and covered
with designs and trinkets and flags and little religious icons and all
manner of baubles and frou-frou and bric-a-brac. The man doffed
his cap.

"Young ladies, in need of a carriage ride, are we?"

"No, thank you, we—"

"Yes, of course," the Princess interrupted. "This is Princess Buttercream of Upswitch. She is due at the theater and we have become separated from our party."

"Indeed?" said the man. "That'd be the Grande Theatre, then, would it?"

"If you please," said the Princess. "They will be waiting for us."

She offered Lexi a hand into the carriage and climbed in herself without waiting for an invitation.

"Here now, here now," the man said. "Payment in advance, if you please!"

The Princess gave her best impression of Aunt Maggie's put-out sigh, complete with compressed eyelids. "If you would be so kind as to hand us our baggage."

Eyeing the girls' travel-worn frocks and noting the disreputable state of their shoes, the man experienced a noticeable change of countenance.

"Certainly, your graces," he said, handing them their bundles. "To the theater, then."

He cast off, diving into the crowd. He was a small man, with a crooked leg, but he made his way nimbly as a goat over the cobblestones and between the little knots of people that crowded the way.

Lexi leaned in and murmured to the Princess. "Buttercream? Are you trying to tell me something?"

"You could *use* a little buttercream," said the Princess. "You're thin as a rail."

"What's that you say, then?" the man asked as their giggling subsided.

"She wonders," the Princess answered, "about the ornamentation on the carriages."

"Oh, yes," the man said. "Did it all myself. Each one's different, you know. Each driver does his own, and mine's one of the finest, if you don't mind me saying."

"Not at all," said the Princess.

"Been working on it steady, going on three years now," the man continued. "That there—" he pointed to a bronze medallion nailed to the front dashboard "—that's my father's guild medal, from his days in the trade. A wheelwright he was. And that there crimson ribbon is from my own little girl's wedding tresses. She's in the capital now, bless her. Married a barrister, she did. And if you'll look here on the side . . ."

A quarter of an hour later, having crossed the middle of the City and explored barely a third of the man's carriage, they arrived at the theater district.

"Well, here we are, misses," the man said. "The Grande here on the left, and the Prometheus on the right. It's quiet now, but it'll be scampering quick tonight, no doubt."

"Thank you very kindly," said the Princess. "What is the charge, please?"

"Oh, no, I couldn't," the man said, falsely.

"Nonsense," said the Princess. "Do you take us for wandering waifs, lost in the City, hoping against all reasonable hope for success in the theater and love and happiness, relying only on our fair faces and earnest determination?"

Thunderstruck, the man blinked and offered them a hand down from the carriage.

"Well, the going rate's a knuckle," he said, "but—"

"Then you shall have two," said the Princess, pulling the coins from her purse. "And this besides," she added, pulling an ice-blue ribbon from her hair.

"Why, thankye, miss, thankye kindly. I've just the place for this, tied onto the gaffle pole. Now, I expect, if your party was waiting for you, they'd be waiting 'round the back. Eh? 'Round the back?"

"Yes, of course," said the Princess. "Thank you, sir, you have been most helpful."

She gave a gracious curtsey, and Lexi gave a small nod as befitted her station at the moment.

"Why did you do that?" she asked, after the man had left. "Pay him double?"

"I don't know," said the Princess. "It seemed like the right thing at the time."

"He didn't believe you. About the princess and the theater and all that."

"Of course not," said the Princess. "No one ever believes us, but they always play along, so it amounts to the same thing."

"You shouldn't have paid him so much, though."

"Oh, it doesn't matter. We can afford it. And maybe he'll give us a free ride when we need it, or he'll help someone else because he got an extra knuckle from us today."

You should know that neither of those things ever happened. The man simply spent the extra knuckle on a pastry to share with his wife in the humble room they kept in an attic in one of the older neighborhoods. However, some years later, a young lady of no other consequence took a fancy to the ribbon, and when he allowed her to take it, she thanked him with a kiss on the cheek, the memory of which warmed his heart all through the next winter, which was to be, as fate would have it, his last.

* * *

→ Three ←

NOW, LEXI AND THE PRINCESS did indeed find success and some small fame in the theater world of the City, but their actual career there is not the most interesting part of the tale, serving merely as a vehicle between one adventure and the next. So I will tell you what transpired as briefly as possible.

After their carriage-pushing friend delivered them to the Grande, they made their way to the stage door in search of someone important. The person they found was the stage manager, busy sweeping out the back stage. He had, as does everyone in that business, better things to do than listen to the appeals of young hopefuls. But Lexi had quite recovered her bearings, and something in her demeanor struck him.Why not chance it? he thought. After all, they would not be his problem, whether things went well or ill. He summoned the theater manager.

The theater manager, a stout pint if ever there was one, had seen more than his share of ingénues hoping to understudy or entr'acte their way into the hearts of the public. He was about to dismiss them out of hand when he too was arrested by Lexi's clear-eyed poise. She informed him quite plainly that they were here to perform after delighting all the crowned heads within a hundred leagues.

Allow her to introduce Princess Anyone-you-like from Anywhere-you-please, who learned to dance to save her life as a captive among the cruel Vashtars of Vilishstan. Without waiting for him to catch his breath, she began singing, and Princess Heliotrope of Burgoyne began dancing.

His practiced eye knew a crowd pleaser when he saw it. Interesting. Rustic, definitely, but somewhat exotic by current standards. And the girl's voice had a certain clear, unpolished charm. So "Be gone!" turned into "When can you start?" and the girls found themselves contracted for eight shows a week for a fortnight, as a trial run, at a grip apiece plus tips.

To say they were an overnight sensation would be untrue. But after the first fortnight their contract was extended another two weeks. After that it was extended a month and their pay increased to ward off an offer from the Prometheus. By the time Yule preparations were underway they were not only performing between acts but in the mezzanine before the curtain rose.

In all, Lexi sang and the Princess danced three or four times a day (five or six when there were matinees)—less than half as much as they had worked in the taverns. They were bringing in nearly a fillette apiece each week and had their pick of last season's costumes to boot. They took rooms behind the theater, two tiny attic garrets in a house that was filled with other menial girls from the theater world—chorus members, seamstresses, little flocks from the corps de ballet—and presided over by a house mother of Olympian proportions.

It was the first time in more than a year that they had slept apart—indeed, practically the first time they had been more than arm's length from one another. Lexi, who had always had a predilection for solitude and had been known to grow rather brittle with the Princess during their sojourn, reveled in the clarity of empty space that surrounded her in her room. She would stand perfectly still in the center, with her eyes closed, arms spread, and fingers splayed, as if hoping to absorb the silence into her very skin.

The Princess, however, took to this new community as she had taken to the Vagabonds. Everyone she met was her new best friend, every food she tried was her new favorite dish. She had learned enough of Lexi's grace and style that she could affect a passable degree of refinement, with just enough of her small-town country mannerisms to befriend the girls and charm the boys. She was full of witticisms and happy prattle. Her rustic features glowed most appealingly. If ever she felt uncertain or ill at ease, an inscrutable smile and a tiny nod from Lexi was all it took to restore her confidence.

For her part, Lexi could still command attention by simply remaining still and radiating that peculiar magnetism of hers—how did she do that, I wonder? It was as though her straight spine and narrow carriage was a lightning rod for some mysterious aurora, a kind of St. Elmo's fire of the soul—but increasingly she seemed content to let the Princess be the brighter light in the room. If she was bothered by diminishing to "that girl who sings for the Princess," she did not show it.

When the Princess would join a group to go buy pastries and coffee, Lexi would accompany her but depart early and alone. When some of the chorus members invited them to the Artists' Quarter to watch the painters drink and fight over compositional theory, the Princess would leap to brush her hair while Lexi would feel the need to rest after the evening's performance. When some young men from the Prometheus offered to take some young ladies from the Grande under East Bridge to be alarmed and amused by the scandalous etchings produced by the most disreputable scoundrels, the Princess could hardly get out the door quickly enough, while Lexi protested she had some work to attend to and saw the Princess on her way with admonitions no less stern than the house mother's.

And work she did, mending her own frocks and those of the Princess, and turning her attention back to The Letter after letting it languish for many months. But she also, as it was later discovered, ventured out on her own to explore the City in her own way and to her own ends. Disguised in the shawl she had bought from the woman on the bridge, she trod the streets and alleys unnoticed in the half-light or near-darkness.

What wondrous properties did that shawl possess, that it could so veil her from notice? Pretty or not, St. Elmo's fire or no, Lexi was always striking, with her reserved poise, her ivory skin and black hair and those dark, mutable eyes. But wrapped in plain, faded homespun, she was invisible and anonymous, attracting no attention whatever—passing through all quarters of the City as silently and secretly as a cat.

She came to know the City as well as anyone can, in particular the odd corners where the quieter folk gathered to escape notice, the alleys passed over by the constable's circuit, the nooks and crevices where the mice conduct their business under the very noses of the cats. Through all of this Lexi passed unnoticed, humming quietly and listening intently, as if feeling her way through the dark.

Yes, and one night when winter had truly settled in, she found her way under Old Bridge, down between the piers: another solitary, forgettable waif, hardly leaving a footprint in the damp silt. She looked in at the Black Hearth, waited to be sure, then clutched the shawl about her throat and slipped away around the back. A rough door opened into what passed for a kitchen, and she waited until a large stump of a man, the proprietor, came out to dump a pail of refuse.

"Pardon, please."

She startled him, speaking from the shadows as she did. He cleared his throat to regain his composure.

"Nothing for free," he said. "And no work, neither."

"You have a woman here, serving."

"There's no work here. She's more help than I need."

"May I see her?"

"What for?"

"May I see her, please?"

The man turned back inside and Lexi waited. She kept perfectly still, absorbing the silence into her skin, until the woman appeared at the door.

"What is it you want?"

"Hello."

"Who are you?"

Lexi showed her the shawl. "From the bridge."

"I know, I remember you. Who are you?"

"You knew the song I sang."

"Yes, it is an old song. Everyone knows that song."

"No. When I sing it, no one has ever heard it before."

"From my home, that song—everyone knows it. It is a child's song."

"Where is your home?"

"Who are you?"

"I'm no one. Just the girl who travels with the Princess."

"I don't know any princess. How do you know the song?"

"I don't know. I've always known it."

"It's a song for babies. We sing it to our babies."

"What is your name? Are you always here?"

"Yes, always I am here. I never leave. Where is it I would go? Who are you?"

"I have to go. The Princess will need me."

"Who are you?"

Lexi clutched the shawl about her shoulders against the chill and the damp under the bridge. "I'm Lexi."

"Hello, Lexi." The woman's eyes were darker than Lexi's, darker than the bottom of a well. "I am called Lily. It's short for something."

→ FOUR ←

WINTER IN THE CITY is different from winter in the countryside, or in a small town. In the country, when the cover of winter comes, the land sleeps. The people remain indoors, curled up against the cold. The fields freeze solid, locking the roots and the mice away against the hope of spring. In a small town, the markets close and the shops keep smaller hours. The townsfolk go out briskly and return swiftly. The windows of the houses are bright against the winter darkness.

But in the city, nothing stops, not even for the seasons or the sun. Winter is simply pushed aside to make way for the business of the day. The streets are piled with frozen slush and rotten snow and paths are carved for the people who trudge through on foot and the people who ride through on carriages. In the north end, windows are bright in the high houses and the doors ring with firelight and laughter. In Eastbridge and in the Low Quarter, candles are scarce and windows are dark, but the people come and go as they must despite the chill. All the markets and shops are open, even if customers are few. Everything, even money, shrinks in the cold.

In the Low Quarter, at least, the people can walk dry shod for a time. It is the low, boggy south end of the island, where the working poor build their homes on posts driven into the silt and where, in wet weather, the streets flow with a slurry of mud and waste. The earth there is damp on the driest of summer days. But in the deep of winter, the mud freezes with the rest of the river and those who care to brave the cold—or have no choice—can skip easily over ground frozen hard as stone.

The people of this quarter work on the docks, or in the homes of the rich, or in the stables the rich keep across the river. The young women go to work in the shops, hoping to secure passage uphill out of the bottom. The young men cross Wood Bridge or Second Bridge in search of work, or run away to sea. They are easily replaced with new young men who wash up on the shores of the City or drift down from higher neighborhoods, blown by this or that wind of fortune.

A small community of Vagabonds, exiled from their tribes, clings to one edge of the quarter and tries to make sense of the mystery of inertia. Those born to the quarter mingle with those who climbed up from under the bridges, as Lily surely hoped to do, and those stumbling down from above, as so many surely will—large families in small houses, old urban hermits in single cluttered rooms, bands of urchins evading the long arm of St. Jasper. It is a community forged by necessity: the most fragile society in the city and yet the most resilient, yielding like water at every blow and flowing back together like water afterward. If winter is a desperate time anywhere in the city, it is here, in the frozen Low Quarter where work is scarce but the rent doesn't change, and where the Yule is kept meagerly if it is kept at all.

Lexi and the Princess were warm enough that winter, the house mother realizing wisely that warm girls pay the rent more reliably than frozen ones. Their performances continued as before, with the novelty gradually wearing away, so that a week before Yuletide the theater manager began to consider whether they were still useful. Then, as luck would have it, the oldest son of the mayor was convinced by his friends against all his better judgment to spend an evening at the theater.

The play was *The Indominon*, the great tragedy by Eufrastes. The mayor's son arrived late, understood barely a word, and was ready to leave at intermission—when his attention was violently arrested by the entr'acte performance. He was riveted. He hardly breathed through the songs. Then he sat through the rest of the play just so he could try to find the girls afterward.

Alas, he was told, they were unavailable, but he should feel free to come again the following evening. At the first opportunity he told his father about his newfound appreciation for the theater and insisted that he attend with him the next night.

His Excellency the Mayor was uncomfortable with the play itself (being a tragedy, it was all about men of great power and the fickle ways of fate), but seeing his son interested in anything other than the gaming tables was worth more than a little discomfort, so attend they did.

At the end of the first half, the mayor was in a sullen mood. It wasn't at all clear to him why the king's insatiable grasping for power should bring him such misfortune. But then his son tugged on his sleeve and gestured toward the stage, and the miseries of the first three acts were forgotten. Lexi had stepped onto the stage. She waited with her inimitable poise for the audience to quiet.

Her costume was an illuminated version of a simple peasant girl's dress and her hair was tied back in the country style.

"Masters and mistresses," she said, "Her Royal Highness, Princess Aphasia."

The Princess then stepped out from behind the curtains to great applause. She was dressed in a theatrical rendition of a style the costume mistress called "rustic flambé": a mishmash of varicolored items pulled from the costume closets at the last minute, ornamented with feathers and silk flowers. (We don't know whether the Princess resented being used as an outlet for the costumer's creative whims, but she did seem to enjoy wearing the creations out on the town after the show.)

Before the applause had died away completely, Lexi began to clap and sing as she had done so many times before. Her voice, although no match for the principal soprano, was clear and pure, and lent an authentic air to the complex Vagabond melodies. The prima ballerina was likewise in no danger of having her place usurped, but the Princess's command of the intricate swirling moves was evident.

What is more, during their long months of performance, she had become so comfortable with the dances that she was able to make them her own in a way no Vagabond girl could. She added playful flips of the head and coy flicks of the wrists, little scampering runs, whimsical leaps, and an affected clumsiness to which Lexi responded with feigned disdain. The overall effect was quite charming and the audience ate it up, including the mayor and his heir apparent, up there in their box, goggle-eyed and slack-jawed.

After the play (the king dies at the end, you know), the mayor and his son sought out the theater manager to ask him to find the girls. The manager was completely flummoxed, not having known His Excellency was in the house that night, and rounded up as much of the company as he could muster, including the Princess as well as the major leads and the orchestra master. Lexi, however, was nowhere to be found.

Undaunted, the Princess proceeded to dazzle the current and future mayors. As with her dancing, she allowed affected bits of country charm to bubble up through her affected stylish poise.

"Where on earth are you from?" the son asked.

"Why, I came from Bottle Street just this evening!" she said, then laughed too loudly.

The reciprocal admiration in the room caused quite a glow in all the participants and made the place well-nigh unbearable for any onlookers.

Lexi, meanwhile, was in her room, pouring tea for herself and Lily, the kettle and the two cups being the whole of her kitchen.

"I cannot keep coming here," said Lily. "It is too far in the cold."

"And yet you come," said Lexi. "I'm sorry I don't have any bread."

"I have. Kolloper will not miss it. Me he misses, but not yesterday's bread."

"Why do you stay with him?"

"I am not 'with' him. I only work."

"But why do you stay?"

"Where would I go?"

"Would you go to your own country? Your old home? Back to there?"

"No. I don't know how. I have no money."

"But if you had the money, would you? Could you go?"

"I don't know. It is fool's pride to wish for the impossible."

"It's not impossible."

"Possible for you it may be, but not for me. Besides, why would *you* go? You belong to this country, this City."

"I don't." Lexi shook her head. "I don't even know where I came from. Where the Vagabonds got me, whether they found me or stole me—I don't know." She cleared her throat. Her eyes brightened in a way she had never allowed anyone else to see. "The song of the birds. Where is it from?"

Lily said nothing.

"I belong nowhere, so I can go anywhere." Lexi put down her cup and took the woman's hands in her own. "Where is it from?"

* * *

→ Five ←

A S YOU MIGHT EXPECT, no sooner had the City learned that His Excellency and His Future Excellency had bestowed their admiration and favor on "those girls that do the Vagabond act at the Grande" than Lexi and the Princess were swept up into the highest levels of society. They were *the* sensation of the winter. People came simply to see them at intermission and called loudly for encores. The theater manager was obliged to give them a show of their own between the matinee and the evening show and to not only double but triple their wages to keep them from the Prometheus.

They were the darlings of the north end. A party could hardly be considered complete without the girls there to enliven the crowd. The Princess, in particular, delighted one and all with her tales of their days on the road with the Vagabonds, some of which were partly true. And Lexi played her role as the stolid supporter and guiding hand with aplomb.

When the Princess would wax particularly outrageous—"With bandits on one side and crocodiles on the other, I didn't know what we were to do!"—Lexi would feign an attempt to restrain her—"Now, Highness, you mustn't exaggerate. There were only a few crocodiles, and rather small." Then the Princess, stung, would raise the stakes even higher—"I was too busy fending off the vultures to concern myself with counting crocodiles!"—and Lexi would lapse into exasperated silence, with folded arms and compressed lips, which the assembly found delightful.

They dressed more finely than they ever had before, ate more scrumptious meals, enjoyed more benevolent company, and

343

traveled more comfortably, with a push-carriage waiting for them wherever they went. At Lexi's insistence, though, they kept the same rooms.

"But why?" the Princess asked. "We have enough now to take rooms on the north end, where our friends are."

"But how long will that last? We have friends here, too, and enough money to keep these rooms for six months if the work dries up."

"But these rooms are so small. If we moved, then we could entertain!"

"Entertain? All we do is entertain, day and night. The only thing I want to do in my own room is sleep, and I can do that here as well as in the most expensive room in the city."

"Very well, Mother Hen," said the Princess with a smile. "I will defer to your wisdom in this matter."

And indeed, as the days grew longer and the winter party season wound down, the invitations slowed and the girls supped more and more often in their rooms or with the junior members of the cast. But then, as spring was about to break loose in the city—the ice on the river had already broken up and the cherry trees on Wilburt Place were budding out—the mayor announced one last winter fête, a final diversion before the elite completed preparations to remove to the country for the summer.

And of course, one couldn't cap the winter without an appearance by those darlings of the theater, our very own You Know Who. They had, of course, been guests at New House before, but this was by far the largest and most sumptuous gathering they had attended. As the mayor's special guests they were seated near the head of the table and engaged in conversation with His

Excellency himself, to the consternation of certain ministers of propriety.

"So, Princess Bumblebee," he said. "I understand that horrible Slogoyban and his band are camped out at Wood Bridge again. Are they known to you?"

The Princess started to answer but Lexi preempted her.

"No, Excellency, we know him only by reputation. The tribe we traveled with have all dispersed to the south in search of the fabled pearl fisheries of Shavaaz."

"Just as well, I suppose. I'd hate to wake up tomorrow and learn you had run away with him! I don't really care for the man, if truth be told. But I'll warrant you two could teach his girls a thing or two about dancing, am I right?"

"I really couldn't say. Princess, haven't you had quite enough bread? You'll turn into a loaf yourself."

"I can't help it," said the Princess. "It's the best bread in the city!"

"Yes, we have a boy in the kitchen who has quite a good touch. But save room for dessert! We've got tarts made with the last of the apples. What with Vagabonds all over the highways the produce doesn't come in like it used to, but we've managed to squirrel enough away for tonight, anyway."

"Wonderful," said the Princess.

"Oh, yes," said the mayor. "And with the river broken up now, we'll have barge traffic from Feasley-on-Lobbe and ships sailing up from the sea with all manner of deliciousness on board." He drained his glass and motioned for a refill. "Yes, indeed, we've survived another winter by the skin of our teeth!"

* * *

345

⇥ Six ⇤

AFTER DINNER, LEXI BECAME QUIET and withdrawn, watching the goings-on without moving to be included. Instruments were brought out and music was played. The Princess and the other young ladies danced with the mayor's son and the other young men. The old men remained at the table and plotted and schemed their way through another bottle, while the older ladies retired to the drawing room. The Princess danced and danced and danced, and then someone asked Lexi to sing.

"No, I really couldn't," she said.

But they insisted and she relented at last.

"What a peculiar song," one of the girls said when she finished. "It's very pretty."

"It's a children's song," said Lexi. "It's about birds."

She remained quiet after that, sitting by the fire and even wandering into the drawing room with the ladies from time to time. The Princess found her there a scant hour later.

"We're all going to the Plover for hot cider! Come with us!"

"No, thank you, I'm too tired."

"Please?"

Lexi smiled. "No, Princess Truffle, you go ahead without me. I'm sure you can manage on your own for one evening."

"Never. I'm a wreck without you! And who will protect me from the mayor's son?"

"I suppose you'll just have to protect yourself."

"Well, I suppose I will. But then who will protect *him* from *me*?"

The Princess scampered off to join the others. Shortly afterward

Lexi, unseen by anyone, slipped out through the side door, avoided the queue of waiting push-carriages, and walked alone down the cobbled lanes toward her room.

The Princess arrived at the house after midnight, ferried by the mayor's son's in his personal carriage. She was considerate enough to invite him in to warm up at her fire, and he was gracious enough to accept, but the house mother—who apparently never slept—put an abrupt end to their exchange, and he was forced to be content with a frosty kiss on the cheek.

This was just as well, in the end, for when the Princess had floated upstairs, she discovered Lexi's room with the door ajar, dark and cold inside as a tomb. The bed was undisturbed, and all of Lexi's lovely new gowns were laid out neatly upon it. Her Vagabond rags and her traveling cloak were gone, as well as her few personal items and the bag that held all their money.

How could she? How *could* she! Took all of the money? What could she mean by that?

The Princess passed a fitful night and in the morning went on foot across Wood Bridge to the Vagabond camp. The morning was foggy and gray, balmy and clammy with sticky spring mud underfoot. She sought out Slogoyban, who hardly recognized her at first.

Yes, Lexi had been there, late last night. "She said you would come, but wait for you she could not."

But what did she say? And where did she go?

"Only she said you would come. And this she left for you."

He handed the Princess a parcel that contained what she assumed was her share of the money, along with a letter.

Dear Princess Handbag Magnolia Hardtack
Dear Insufferable Lump
Dear Princess Twinkletoes
It is time—the time has come—it pains saddens pains pains
saddens me—I am sad—it makes me sad
I must now say goodbey goodbye. Don't ask I can't say I can't
tell you I can't explain I am so happy to have been be your frind
friend for so long. I wish it was a I hope you can I whish wish you
happy and well all your days. Please understand There is nothing to
understand. Do not be afraid. I will always, always remember I am
always thinking of you and smiling. And also crying. Only smiling.
Your friend,
Annalexa

The Princess read the letter and then tried to read it again before she looked up, bewildered. "Slobbygon?"

For all his legendary faults, Slogoyban knew a lost soul when he saw one. "Of course, child. It will be as if you never left us."

The mayor's son called at the theater that afternoon, only to learn the girl had paid her rent, packed her gowns, and left hours before in the company of a Vagabond woman. There was no sign of the other girl at all.

The boy, for still a boy he was, despite the whiskers on his chin, raced to Wood Bridge to find the tribe departed. He returned as disheartened as it is possible for a boy to be, the lowering clouds and shifting fog only serving to darken his mood further.

And what a convenient fog it was, too, covering as it did the westward course of the tribe, enabling them to roll their donkey carts through the mud with the proper somber mood. The Princess rode again in the wagon of the scarf-and-shawl woman, and they again shared a few unintelligible words before the gentle rocking of the wagon lulled them into silence.

Princess who? she wondered. And who would do the singing? She looked back, but the City was already disappearing in the mist, and now it was completely gone, with nothing but fog behind and ahead, and she was nowhere. Princess Nobody from Nowhere. Lost in the fog, alone with these familiar strangers, she didn't know what to do. Even whether or not to weep, or even how.

A most convenient fog covering the docks, shrouding two figures boarding a ship: shrouding them as closely as their shawls, ensuring just the same anonymity as if they were two blank pages at the end of a long book.

As far as the purser knew, they were two sisters who'd bought passage to the coast to look after the family property. They stood at the rail and watched the harbor slip backward into the fog. Broad, mist-veiled shores slid past. It had seemed like a natural explanation at the moment, Lexi thought; they could certainly pass for sisters more easily than she and the Princess had. Of course, all that had been half a joke, and all the innkeepers and theater people had been playing along. She glanced at Lily, who was impassive, watching rills of mist flow over the water. Lily was older than Lexi—scarcely old enough to be her mother, more likely a young aunt—but the sister story had felt more like the truth, and that made it easier to convince the purser.

Lexi felt an icy wave of excitement and held her breath to calm her heart. Why not tell the real story? That they were merely two wandering souls, trying after long lifetimes of exile to find their way home, one with the knowledge and one with the money, finally taking a chance and stepping off the edge of the world? Because Lexi had learned one lesson in her life and knew that Lily knew the same thing, something all who travel alone should know: never tell the real story. Let the fog hide their names and cover them all the way to the coast, and then the next thing would present itself, as it always did. Let the fog cover it all.

A most terribly convenient fog, to settle over the City and over the whole countryside, maybe the whole world—as if to say *Yes, yes, spring is on its way, but wait, just wait a little and consider what the winter has been, and what the end of such a winter might mean.*

Part XIII

Exiles in the North

→ Languishing in Prison— A Meditation. ←

T O LANGUISH IN PRISON is not a skill that comes naturally to all. It might seem simple enough, but in fact it takes a special kind of l fortitude to abandon all hope and become inert, to allow each day with its stale bread and tepid water and stone bed to pass without notice: just one more in an infinite string of identical days. For men who can do this, time flows neither quickly nor slowly, for there is no time. They simply exist, like a held breath that will never be exhaled. When they are released—if they are released—these men wake as if from a deep sleep, hardly aged at all in their minds, despite the length and whiteness of their beards.

Another kind of man fails entirely at languishing. He languishes so poorly he can hardly be said to languish at all. To languish properly requires a certain lassitude, a propensity for stillness, and this man is instead agitated and tumultuous. He might be said to fester in prison, or ulcerate, or even inflammate, but never to languish. He looks upon his languishing brethren with a certain disdainful envy. His head is filled with thoughts from waking until sleep, and

355

with dreams all night—thoughts of home, of freedom, of escape, of the structural nature of his prison, the weather, the seasons, and a thousand other things in an unending flood.

Pity the thoughtful man in prison, for whom the stone cell is merely an extension of his own skull, its barred windows the hollow sockets of his eyes.

⇾ One ⇽

S O. THE BERGERTON BOYS variously languished, festered, suppurated, or stewed in the goat caves of Lesser Spleen. The caves were cold but not unbearably so. The women of the village brought them blankets and bundles of straw and sometimes a hot meal in a tin pail. No news reached them, either from Bergerton or from the northern wars. They were unable to communicate with one another, although they were unguarded except by the elderly goat farmer and his wife. The caves were far enough apart that they could only shout to each other, and then the echoes from the stones made their words unintelligible. They would call back and forth to one another, but all their plans for escape were garbled beyond recognition and their voices rolled out over the fields in the dark until the farmer finally bellowed: "Oy! Keep it down, you lot! You're as bad as the goats!"

Incidentally, the boys' great-great-grandfather, Jonathan Berger the Elder, had been a soldier, or so he claimed, during an earlier edition of the northern wars. The details varied from one telling to the next, but in the main he was supposed to have served with no small degree of distinction and to have been perhaps gravely injured, or at least suffered considerable hardship. In one version, he was taken captive and barely escaped with his life. In another, generally related at large, holiday dinners, he was returning from this very adventure when he capsized his donkey cart at Sullivan's Bend. His wife, the lovely Sophia Berger (née Swarpoltz), would then hotly dispute the story, reminding him that she and at least some of the children had accompanied him to this desolate wasteland when the wars were already a distant memory. It was she who had saved his sorry neck, if he would be so kind as to recall.

Peace would be restored only when dessert was served.

War—the wars of my experience, in any case—are vulgar, untidy affairs. The General, bless his heart, loves to go on about this or that engagement as if everything always went according to plan—as if every detail were controlled by his august self, simple as plucking out a tune on an enormous lute. A lute, moreover, for which he himself had hewn the timber, planed the boards, turned the pegs, and tied each fret. A different story is told, of course, by the actual soldiers on the march, and by the fields and villages the armies pass over. They know, as we know, that wars are less like an evening's entertainment and more like a concentration of terrible accidents and poor decisions. They come and go like storms, with inscrutable wills of their own, and rain falls on the just and the unjust alike.

The good women of Lesser Spleen, with their men off in the north, spent the winter waiting for news and dutifully attending their charges in the prison. By the time spring approached they were understandably weary of the task, not to mention anxious about the ploughing and planting that needed to be done. How were they to manage the farm along with feeding the magistrate's goats?

The solution was obvious, to a certain way of thinking. First this prisoner, then that one was discreetly released for a day or more at a time to perform the various and sundry tasks required around a country farm in springtime. As the season wore on, less and less discretion was necessary—it is likely that the owner of the caves had completely forgotten about the prisoners—and the men from Bergerton would simply unlatch their own gates in the morning and walk cheerfully to whichever farmsteads they had become attached to.

The women put them to good use: the fields and pastures around the village had not looked so well-tended for years. Many a fence was mended and many a hedgerow trimmed, many a stile straightened and even a barn or two raised. Then it was summer, with the hoeing and weeding, and then autumn with the harvest of course, and as the days shortened the prisoners protested that another winter in the drafty caves would certainly be their undoing.

Couldn't the bars be boarded up against the wind? Couldn't a stove and a lamp be provided? Well, certainly, so long as they remained well behaved, which of course they did, and no prisoners had ever looked forward to a cozier, snugger, friendlier winter.

And so it was, for all but the officers—that is, Captain and Corporal Berger, respectively. When the LaPierre cousins— Lobelia and Minerva, daughters of Mertick LaPierre and his step-brother Houvard, respectively (Lobelia being the taller, quieter of the two, and Minerva being the shorter, feistier, more comfortably upholstered)—when these ladies, as I say, approached the boys about certain domestic duties they might perform, Captain Berger informed them that, to his great regret, he was honor-bound by the necessities of his office. If he were to be released for any reason it would be his immediate duty to attempt escape at any cost.

But surely the gentlemen saw the benefits of conditional work release, as it were—the fresh air? The beguiling company? Not to mention real food cooked in a real kitchen?

Alas, no, their solemn oaths of office strictly forbade any such conciliation. Was the Corporal heard to tell the Captain to speak for himself? The echoes in the caves made his contribution indistinct. But in the end, no amount of cajoling or pleading by either cousin to either brother bore any fruit whatever, so the Burgermeister's boys, not being the languishing type, spent the summer festering in their cells, the same summer their fellows spent laboring under the sweet auspices of their fair jailors.

It was simply too much injustice to be endured, one cousin was heard to remark to the other on more than one occasion. All the other girls had prisoners; why shouldn't they? More than once they toyed with the idea of forcing open the doors of the cells and compelling the officers to comply with the well-known conventions of servitude at the point of a musket. But their fathers had taken the muskets north, so that plan was scrapped, and they contented themselves with delivering the daily bread and water with a pointed brusqueness that was sure to cut the boys to the quick.

By the end of the summer, the situation at the prison had progressed to the point that the Bergers were the only remaining internees of any consistency. After a day in the fields, it was much easier to curl up in a hayloft or similar space than to trudge all the way back to one's cell and lock oneself in. And besides, that made getting to work all the easier the next day.

Now, keep in mind that the Bergerton Boys were mostly townsmen, to whom manual farm labor was a rare enough thing, or Marshals and Hooligans, to whom it was a complete novelty. But compared with being lost in the wilderness or rattling about in a prison cell, it was like a voyage to the land of pies, all expenses paid. And doubtless the sincere, chaste gratitude shown by the good women of Lesser Spleen was all the reward these stalwart, upright young men needed. Pride in a job well done, you know. Helping those less fortunate and all that.

Whatever it was, it warmed the hearts of the Bergerton Boys right down to their very cockles, and they worked the fields with gusto, staying down in the farms for days on end and returning to their cells only when they "needed a little space." All of which left just the officers in the goat pens and just the LaPierre cousins to tote bread and water.

Which arrangement, by the way, was to enable their eventual escape and flight. But more about that in its proper place.

→ TWO ←

WHAT OF THE MEN of the village? What of Gormer Poltsch and the magistrate and their sturdy company of Lesser Spleen's finest? What became of all the backbone and grit and gumption and whatnot? Alas, I can tell you no more than the women back home heard—vague rumors of battles and such, hints that, against all expectations, the party had seen real action, had been impressed into one of His Eminence's regiments and embarked on an extended campaign far over the northern border. After that there was no news.

In other words, the storm of war had swept them away and heaven only knew which of them, if any, might be blown home again. There was no shortage of wailing and gnashing of teeth when such hearsay found its way into the village. A whole generation of women found themselves in limbo at the gates of widowhood. But at least there was the comfort the prisoners provided: they had plenty of strong young men to tend the fields and plough a furrow or plant a seed as the need arose.

Or perhaps I paint the women of that place with too broad a brush. Certainly not all of them were so feeble as to need such assistance. Many of them surely waited until the dust of their husbands' departures had settled before inviting such felonious vagrant foxes into the henhouse. In fact, fully a score of women—those unable to procure or retain prisoners of their own—openly continued to hope for the men's return and to proclaim woe—woe, I tell you—upon she who entrusted the care of her garden to just anyone who could wield a spade.

After all, there were only nine prisoners to go around (not counting the officers), so when you consider there was a whole village full of temporary widows, well, that's a lot fields for even the most industrious ploughman. But I can assure you (again, proper details in their proper place) that those men from the village who did eventually return found most everything to their liking, fields and wives and children and all.

→＞ Three ＜←

LOBELIA AND MINERVA LAPIERRE were a good many years away from being spinsters in the strictest sense, but they were also a number of years past what narrow minds think of as a woman's prime. They were cousins, as you know, and closer in age than any sisters, their fathers having been engaged in a sort of competition to produce the first grandchild in the family. Those same fathers had long since moved into the village with their wives, leaving the cousins as heiresses apparent to a neat stone cottage with a tumbledown barn and ten acres of boggy pasture.

They were bakers of some note and made a small living trading and selling loaves among their neighbors. With the men all gone to war, they even prospered somewhat. They excelled at a peculiar knotted loaf of sweet dark bread native to the region. The exact recipe is a mystery to me, but I believe it to be a whole wheat and rye base, sweetened with both honey and malted barley. The dough is rolled into ropes and then worked into twisted knots that pull apart easily after baking. The top is sometimes sprinkled with toasted oatmeal. It is made throughout the area, with slight variations from one household to the next, and the bakers are always on the lookout for innovative knot designs. If I ever come across the recipe I shall certainly pass it along.

It was this bread that they provided (along with good, clean well water) to the unfortunate officers in their forlorn confinement, and this selfsame bread that ultimately offered the means of liberation. It happened like this: Each day, the LaPierre cousins would each bake a loaf for a prisoner, besides the other loaves for the day. If one of them were feeling pleasant, she would braid the loaf into a pleasing, enticing shape with the hope of softening the officers' resolve against release. If, however, she were feeling bitter and spiteful, she wound the bread into a wretched snarl and hoped he would choke on it. (It should be noted that the subtlety of the girls' communication *per panem* was completely lost on the boys.)

As each girl was generally upset with one brother or the other in turns, the cousins traded officers frequently. Each Berger received his daily bread, but rarely from the same LaPierre two days in a row. Thus, the cold shoulders were distributed equitably. Eventually, one of the men noticed that two baskets, each labeled "Berger" but slightly different from one another, appeared in his cell on alternate days. He hit upon the idea of leaving a note for his compatriot under the cloth that wrapped the bread. He scrounged around his cell and at last found a scrap of paper and a bit of charcoal. He scratched a quick note and lifted the cloth only to discover the basket already contained a scrap of paper with a message scrawled in charcoal.

Brother, reply when you receive this.
Please reply. Immediately.
Reply, for pity's sake.
Good Lord, are you that dull?
It's been a fortnight!

He removed the note and replaced it with his own, wondering rather uncomfortably if he was really cut out for this sort of military subterfuge business.

This was in midsummer and there followed a protracted and rambling conversation that does not bear repeating here. I shall summarize. The first month, they agreed that they should find some means of escape. The second month, they agreed that neither of them had any good ideas about how to accomplish said escape. The third month, one brother was discouraged while the other suggested that the bread ladies seemed nice enough, and what about that? The fourth month, the first brother agreed about the bread ladies, but by then the other brother was more deeply discouraged than the first. During the fifth and sixth months, which were the coldest, they chiefly complained about the cold despite the snug walls and the small stoves with which they had been provided.

By the seventh month, the first brother had had more than his fill of the whole matter and again proposed bringing the bread ladies into their machinations. The other brother hesitated but was swiftly informed that, stone walls or no, he would comply with his brother's wishes or be torn limb from limb and fed to the Vagabonds' donkeys. All of which led to both of the brothers on the same late winter day saying to their respective Miss LaPierre, "So. You said something once about doing some little work around your farm?"

→ FOUR ←

AT ABOUT THIS SAME TIME, Lesser Spleen's long-lost company of militiamen began their weary journey home from the tumultuous north. They had not really been soldiers when they departed, and one could hardly call them soldiers even now, but they had seen battles, to be sure—more battles than all previous expeditions from Lesser Spleen combined.

They were led now by the magistrate, who upon finding himself in command of the group had immediately negotiated their release from His Eminence's regiment on the grounds that if they stayed they would certainly do more harm than good. Organized into a loose column and treading a muddy track, they drifted south with the last of winter at their back.

The magistrate spent a considerable amount of time brooding, both while marching and while sitting by the fire at night. They had lost their tents almost immediately. They had lost men, nearly a dozen—some in action, some merely misplaced. They had lost limbs and eyes, and so were returning burdened with invalids. That fool of a blacksmith had gotten his hand crushed trying to retrieve that fool hammer from under a laden wagon. He could now no more wield a hammer than he could juggle live sparrows. What was the town to do without a blacksmith?

And without a wheelwright, to boot? How could any commerce be effected without good wagons rolling on good wheels? Assuming anything was left of the village when they returned, how could they expect to build up the economy with no wagons and half the men lamed? The magistrate had made contacts in the north and with the military, and was sure he could find markets for Lesser Spleen's fine produce—wheat and goat cheese and coarse wool suitable for common folk—but the difficulties of transporting freight with no wagons alarmed him.

His son (Strommond Stovepipe, whom you have already met), a bright, strapping lad of nineteen who would far outstrip his father's accomplishments once he got the chance, was of the opinion that no one would ever buy anything from a place called Lesser Spleen anyway and that they should change the name or move to a new town, if not both.

Geographical note: There is no record anywhere of a "Greater Spleen," or for that matter another Spleen of any kind within five hundred leagues of Lesser Spleen, so the meaning of the name is a mystery. My personal theory is that the name is a corruption of the original name in some lost aboriginal tongue, but formal scholarship has been slow to take up the thesis.

And so it came to pass that the men of Lesser Spleen, maimed and exhausted, returned near the spring equinox to find the ploughing half done and the peas and carrots already sown.

"Merciful heavens!" said the magistrate. "Are they still here?"

He had forgotten all about the wayward tramps from Bergerton; if he *had* thought about them, he would have assumed they had long since made their way hence. They were just goat pens, for mercy's sake. Any fool could have—! Only a fool would have—!

But no matter. All's well, as they say. He granted them all immediate parole (after checking on the state of his own property) and bade them quit the village that instant or be dragged away feet first.

He was very proud of that little speech, impromptu as it was, and so was somewhat perplexed when it met a response that was ambivalent to say the least. Some of the women, it seemed, having discovered they were in fact actually widowed, wished to keep the new men they had acquired. Spoils of war, so to speak. And some of the men from Bergerton wished to return home but take their jailors with them. To help oversee their integration back into productive society, as it were.

The magistrate felt they could bloody well do what they pleased and was baffled that they seemed to be asking his permission.

"Well, very well then," he said,. "But you can't take any wagons or carts with you!"

Now, while this was happening, the Burgermeister's boys and the LaPierre cousins were hunkered down at their revolutionary headquarters around the kitchen table, making final preparations for their daring escape. Their plan was to rush into the village, round up as many of the men as they could find within the hour, and then head cross-country, avoiding roads or paths in order to make their escape with not only flair and bravado but also discretion.

The cousins, it emerged, intended to join them in their flight, having become disenchanted with the farming life after their barn collapsed and the heavy winter rains turned their pasture into a hog wallow (without any hogs).

No, the Captain insisted—alas, dear lasses, the way would be much too rough and unpredictable for two such delicate creatures to thrive. The Captain had become somewhat fond of the reserved and almost demure Lobelia but vowed silently to himself not to let such affections sway his purpose.

But wait, the Corporal countered, why shouldn't they come along at least part of the way? It was their bread they were taking, after all.

Nay, nay, the Captain insisted. The danger, the peril, et cetera. But he vowed they would keep the ladies always in their hearts, of course, and cherish their memories and all that.

Hang on, the Corporal sputtered. (The sprightly Minerva had taken rather a liking to the quiet and thoughtful man, by the way.) He proposed instead that they take the ladies with them and keep them, instead, in their house. At home. Back home in Bergerton.

What a pickle for the Captain! Oh, the trials of leadership! Insubordination and traitorliness before the venture had even begun! Fortunately, he was saved from further frustration by a shout from outside.

Fearing at first that it was the forces of law come to imprison them again, the officers crouched beneath the windowsills and told the women to save themselves. However, when they peered out, they beheld not the cavalry but the Bergerton Boys who had chosen to return home, along with an assortment of bonny lasses and fetching damsels and comely widows and so on. After being apprised of the situation, viz., immediate parole without conditions, the officers quickly reformulated their plan. They would remain through the afternoon to ensure all was ready. The LaPierre cousins would bake another dozen loaves for the road, and then they would all fourteen of them escape the next morning after a good night's sleep. This plan delighted the entire company and everyone got a kiss on the cheek out of it, even the officers and their respective bread ladies.

⟶ Fɪᴠᴇ ⟵

THE NEXT MORNING was a bittersweet affair, full of happy couples setting out, happy couples staying behind, old comrades parting ways, and friends since childhood bidding each other farewell, not to mention the tide of joyful reunions mixed with inconsolable losses that had attended the return of the militia to the village. It was altogether too sentimental to endure, so they wrapped it up as quickly as possible, with a short, deliberate speech by the magistrate, who had, as you know, a way with words.

"Be gone, already," he said, "and leave us in peace for pity's sake!"

So the remnant of the Bergerton Boys set off for home, laden with bread and fair company, with a light wind at their back, leaving the rest of their brethren-in-arms behind to fare how they would in their new homes.

(They fared about as well as you might expect, with no great distinction or calamity. One in particular—the youngest son of the keeper of the Yellow Beetle—eventually bought the prison and turned it into a hostelry, which eked out a meager profit for many years and finally flourished under *his* son, during the tourist boom that followed the liberation of the Busselplatz. It was a fad for a time among newlyweds from the capital to honeymoon in the former prison, which they no doubt felt was a delicious irony.)

And now, seeing them on their way, we can spare them a tender thought or two. They seem so young, don't they? For all their road-weary days, and for all the troubles of the bitter winter, they are charmingly innocent as they stroll through the countryside under the chalk-blue sky. You have doubtless been on cross-country adventures of your own, and so I hardly need remind you that nothing makes quite so sweet a bed as new grass in early spring. And if the night is chilly and one can share one's blankets with amiable company, well, so much the better. Let us leave them to it, then. Let us take no thought—as they themselves certainly took no thought—of the travails of the road ahead or the terrible black storm beginning to brew hundreds of leagues away, far out over the sea.

Part XIV
The Flood

→ Oпᴇ ←

ONCE UPON A TIME, there was a city on an island in a river. Seven bridges connected the city to the mainland, and highways great and small connected these to the rest of the country. Ships traveled up to the city from the sea and barges traveled down from Feasley-on-Lobbe and beyond. The city sat perched on its island with tentacles finagled into every crevice of the surrounding district and considered itself the center of the world, from which all things flowed and to which all things were drawn.

But really, the river was the heart of things, and the long limbs and the breathing lungs. The river held the city suspended in its palm and viewed it with indifference. It gave nourishment, and the city prospered. It lay sullen and turgid in late summer doldrums, and the city sweltered. It rolled on its great back like a stallion and the city clung to the banks, straining not to be washed away.

The river was simply the river and no more regarded the city than the sky regards the flight of an arrow. It wound its way from the mountains to the sea across a vast, hilly plain, joined from time to time by smaller rivers and streams. You can look at a map, if you

373

like. A map of any river will do, really. Rivers all behave the same and always will until the seas are full.

The river flowed in a more or less southeasterly direction but looped so wildly that at any given point one might be going any direction at all. Lush greenery carpeted the shores on either side; beyond that rose the banks that in most places were as high as a man of average height. The wider riverbed flooded every spring. Residents of the lower, greener places—wildcats and hedgehogs and such—took it as a matter of course and climbed the banks to wait it out.

Further from the water, as much as a quarter-mile in places, a higher bank of ten or fifteen yards sloped up from the river valley to the plains proper. This bank contained the floods that came once a decade or once in a generation. The poor farmers who tilled the fertile, shifting soils of the valley gambled with the luck of thieves, trading cheap land and good harvests for the occasional deluge.

The bridges to the city spanned the higher banks where they drew in close to the river's edge. The island was a huge, rocky outcrop that had weathered innumerable storms and stood fast through countless floods. Its people wisely clung to their stony home and trusted that their city, with its roots sunk so deep in the earth, would see them through anything. In other words, they didn't give the river a thought as they went about their business, keeping not a single eye on the sky or the horizon.

⇢ two ⇠

SPRING AT THESE LATITUDES means mud, and Vagabonds are no strangers to mud. Muddy roads and muddy fields, muddy lanes and muddy camps. You might say a Vagabond lives his life just one step beyond the mud from which he came. The Vagabonds say so themselves, after all, so why wouldn't we?

From living so close and so daily with mud, most Vagabonds have become especially skilled at staying clean. Even in the brightest clothes that would show any spot, it is rare to see a Vagabond, man or woman, soiled at all above the ankles. That spring, however, was especially muddy, and there wasn't a person in the country, Vagabond or otherwise, who didn't go about spattered to the knees or higher.

Before the snow was entirely gone, the rains started. Not the refreshing, steady rain of late spring or the cleansing cloudbursts of summer but scanty, spitting rain, the kind that fades in and out without ever really starting or stopping. A feeble spritzing that serves only to moisten the already waterlogged countryside and maintain the goopy slurry of mud that coats everything from foundation stones to peaked gables and boot-soles to hatbands.

Slogoyban the Vagabond King, whom no man can destroy, who has lived forever and seen all things, looked to the drooling sky with his eyes half-lidded and spoke under his breath.

"Sorry?" said the Princess, who trudged beside him. "I didn't catch that."

Her command of the Vagabond tongue was no stronger than it had ever been, and the muddy road before and behind them had put her in a brittle humor.

"Apology, Princess. The sky, she holds her breath, but not for long."

"What does that mean?"

"I mean the rain, she will come more before she is less."

"Do you mean a storm is coming?"

"Always a storm is coming, no?"

"But you mean soon?"

"It is easy to be successful to foretell a storm in the springtime."

"You don't make any sense. Do we need to find shelter?"

"We are Vagabonds, Princess. The storm *is* our shelter."

Despite his reluctance to say anything that might actually be construed as meaningful (you have met the Vagabond King before, correct?), Slogoyban passed word among the caravans that they should keep to higher ground when topography permitted.

"The hills, they will be our friends, I think."

→ THREE ←

FAR AWAY FROM THE VAGABONDS—how far I cannot say, but near enough to sleep under the same stars (which were hidden behind the same clouds)—the Burgermeister's boys and their retinue of hangers-on were making their way home. Just as they had reached Lesser Spleen by traveling approximately north, so they planned to find their way back to Bergerton by going generally in a direction they hoped was of a mostly southerly persuasion.

The brief thaw that had accompanied their departure passed. They found no more soft beds of new grass and as often as not had to make do with damp drifts of last autumn's leaves. The bread was long gone, so they breakfasted on porridge and dined on gruel. At night they bundled up as well as they could and in the morning brushed the frost from their blankets before rolling them up.

When, after nearly a fortnight of wandering, they came upon the very beech grove from which they had launched their assault on Wensbrook Meadow and realized they had traveled barely a day's journey for all their trudging, black clouds of mutiny began to gather on the officers' horizon.

Some of the company were inclined to return to Lesser Spleen, if anyone knew the way. Others suggested they colonize this uninhabited country and found a new town on the very spot.

The women, for their part, thought the whole thing was absurd. Hadn't they a compass? Not a single compass among all of them? Or a map?

The Captain protested that any shortcoming of their equipage was the fault of the government, and to take any complaints to the capital.

Someone suggested again that Beech Grove was a very appealing name for a little village.

Absurd!

And besides, in the absence of sun or stars, who could navigate? These clouds! These constant clouds!

The Captain was again admonished to shut his absurd mouth and be quiet for just a moment and let a body think.

Half the group lapsed into uncomfortable silence while the other half continued making plans for the glorious township of Beech Grove. This state of affairs continued for some time until the township discussions broke down over disagreements on civic bylaws, and Minerva LaPierre decided that, since Wensbrook Meadow lay just over that hill, they could hardly do worse than put that hill to their backs and travel cross-country in as straight a line as possible for as long as possible. After all, the wilderness couldn't go on forever, right?

In fact, wildernesses can go on forever, as any experienced wanderer will tell you. That is, one can wander in the wilderness for the rest of one's days, which is as close to forever as anyone is likely to get. And the number of one's days in the wilderness may turn out to be rather few, if proper precautions aren't taken. I don't know whether I am making myself clear. Do you get my point? Don't get lost in the wilderness. You might die.

But fear not: the Burgermeister's sons, the remaining Bergerton Boys, and their companions do not die in the wilderness at this time. Whether by dumb luck or woman's intuition, their time in the wilderness lasted only another day and a half, whereupon they emerged into a pleasantly thawing, rather muddy, slightly greening country of small farms and hamlets.

They passed by an inn and were directed to the proper road. They spent the snuggest night they could remember in a nearby hayloft. Frosty nights gave way to days of heavy mist that beaded their cloaks with moisture and gave them the feeling of walking along the bottom of the sea. The road rounded some hills and climbed others, and occasionally passed someplace with a name someone thought he might recognize.

Was the mist lifting? Were they drawing closer to Bergerton?

Only time will tell, I suppose.

→ FOUR ←

SLOGOYBAN HAD LED HIS BAND into some hilly country west of the City. In a wild stretch between two villages he took them off the road. The hills there were bare on the windward side, with clumps of woods nestled in the sheltered leeward crevices. He took them past several such stands of trees before he found one to his liking—chestnut and oak, mostly, just beginning to bud out.

He had the wagons and caravans drawn up close together and unhitched the donkeys.

"Do not hobble them tonight," he said. "If they wander away, they will wander back. They know who has the oats."

He had the goats tethered, however, much to their dismay.

"Goats, they don't care about oats," he said.

A breeze had blown the mists away, but the sky was glowering, as if after so many weeks it had finally made up its mind what kind of sky to be. Slogoyban installed the Princess with the scarf-and-shawl woman. Since neither could understand a word the other said they got along very well, each carrying on her own one-sided conversation.

He made his rounds through the camp, ensuring each caravan was tight and snug, that there was enough wood for the little stoves they carried, that all the children were accounted for, and that all the old people were looked after. Soon soups and stews were bubbling in the kettles and he climbed to the crest of the hill to taste the strengthening breeze. The top of the hill was bare and provided a view for uninterrupted miles across the land.

The sky to the west was a sickly yellow and, as he watched, the sun dropped into the wafer-thin gap between the clouds and the horizon, the first sun to be seen in weeks. It blazed briefly, yellow, orange, red, and violet, and then was gone, leaving a sudden chill in the breeze. To the south, the clouds grew darker, almost black, rolling up over the land.

Occasional fingers of lightning flicked down to brush the ground below, like oars sending the great boats of the clouds scudding forward. Too far away to hear yet. No, there it was, just below the noise of the wind: the low thump and tumble of thunder across the hills.

What sort of a life is this, Slogoyban? Running from one storm to another, through mud and frost and snow, always with the wind in your face. How long can a people live in a land and still be strangers? How many generations travel this same track, camp in these same woods, and still not call it home?

The people behind him in the caravans, the families and the children, the brassy young men and the frothy girls, the oldest of the old, guarding their last teeth while night falls, where did they belong? Where could he take them? Around and around the same roads forever, one town after another, north and south, east and west, winter after summer after winter, chased by the moon and the stars. What was to be done for them, after all? Bring them stumbling into the promised land? Shield them from the storm here on this hilltop with just his will and stubbornness?

He was rather a striking sight, if anyone had cared to see, wind-whipped as he was in the semi-darkness, the approaching lightning flashing in his black eyes. A bit grandiose for my taste, but he was a man of action, after all. He may be forgiven a moment of private posturing, I suppose.

But no. You are a foolish old man, Slogoyban. Go back to your caravan before you freeze to death. Not so old as all that, really, but older in the winter. Heaven preserve you until the summer, old man, and let the youth creep back into your bones. He closed the door to his caravan and tied it shut just as the rain began and the wind whipped up in earnest.

→ FIVE ←

WANDERING HOPEFULLY HOMEWARD through the wide and hilly country, the Burgermeister's boys and their retinue passed one farm and then the next before anyone said anything. It was probably one or perhaps both of the LaPierre cousins, and she or they were probably suggesting the party find shelter for the night. The suggestion may have been rather pointed, and, in fact, may have been the third or fourth such suggestion in the past couple of miles.

But the breeze had cleared the mists away, and the Captain wanted to make as much progress as possible before darkness, which seemed quite the most sensible course.

The Captain's attention was then drawn to the fact that, with the mists gone, one could plainly see the sky growing alarmingly dark and thundery, with the wind picking up as well. In short, all the makings of a springtime gale were at hand.

But there was at least an hour of daylight remaining, such as it was—more than enough time to reach the next farmstead.

The discussion continued over another hill and into a little dale, whereupon the Corporal spoke up in tentative favor of the ladies' proposal that shelter be sought with all possible expediency. His exact words were lost in the rising wind but were something along the lines of "We'd better get our [indistinct] out of the storm before we get them frozen off!"

The rest of the company made a great show of looking huddled and miserable as the first drops began to fall. But what was there to do? They were more than a mile past the last farm. The next farm was probably just over the next hill, so over the next hill they went, only find a rocky, scrubby little valley with no sign of habitation except a tiny, forlorn, perhaps even abandoned stone cottage no bigger than my grandmother's chicken house, backed by the sway-backed skeleton of a former barn.

At the sight, the LaPierre cousins turned back immediately and had to be physically restrained. The Captain was sure a substantial farm waited just over the next hill, over there where lightning was striking with surprising regularity.

The Corporal meekly favored trying the chicken house, just to see if anyone was home.

The Captain was opposed to that strategy, but the whipping of the wind, not to mention the clamoring of the company, made reasonable conversation difficult, so the officers withdrew to a little grove off the side of the road. Shortly, after what was apparently a spirited discussion, they re-emerged, slightly disheveled.

When asked what next, the disgruntled Corporal gestured sarcastically at the Captain.

The Captain adjusted his hat and announced that he would personally approach the cottage and try to secure some measure of shelter for them. It was the closest sure thing, he said, and furthermore he was encouraged by the small light twinkling in the one window, which was almost certainly not the ghost of the ancient tenant waiting to terrorize them unto madness. So the bedraggled group followed him down into the valley.

Inside the tiny cottage, Rolfo Peake had felt the storm coming in his bones for two days and would have closed the shutters on the window but had been forced to wait for his cat, that rascal. Things were certainly picking up out there now, no mistake. Soon he would have no choice, and the cat would have to weather the weather out there on his own, fleas and all.

The wind whistled through the chinks in the stone walls so fiercely that he hardly heard the knock at his door. That wasn't the cat, surely. It must be the ghost, since no travelers would be out in such a gale. But at a second knock he opened the door a crack.

"What do you want? It's a terrible night!"

"Yes, please. Traveling. Shelter." The man seemed not in possession of his full faculties. The wind, no doubt.

"Well, come in, then, come in, come in. Mind you, it's been a good while since I had any company. A good while. I'll have to find my other spoon!"

"Yes, well, about that."

Rolfo peered out into the gloom and saw that the man was accompanied by, oh, mercy, more than a dozen men and women, all creeping toward his doorsill.

"Well. Well, well, well. I'll just put another kettle on, then, shall I? Another kettle?"

"We have our own spoons, if that helps."

"It does indeed, it does indeed. Come in, come in, come in." He wondered briefly if people still said everything two and three times or if he should try to tone it down a little.

"I don't think we should impose," said the man. "Couldn't we just stay in the barn?"

"In the cow barn? Heavens no! I wouldn't make my cows sleep in that barn, let alone travelers."

"Where do you keep your cows, then?"

"Well, fortunately, I don't have any cows at this time, so I haven't troubled to think about it. Come in, come in, come in."

With everyone inside, the little cottage was filled to bursting. Rolfo welcomed them in, bade them all sit on whatever empty surface or floorboard they could find, and proceeded to forget their names as soon as he heard them.

"I'll just make some soup, then, shall I? Just the thing for a blustery night, I think."

He shook a spider out of a large kettle, poured in a pail of water, and swung it over the fire.

"It's my mother's recipe, you know, for storm soup."

"What goes in it?" someone asked.

"Anything," he said. "Everything you can find. Everything except the spiders. You've all met, have you?"

He added bits of this and that to the pot, along with whatever bits of this and that his visitors could provide. While the soup cooked he forgot all their names again, welcomed the cat back with glee, and shut the shutters. He lamented the lack of anything other than water to drink.

"To get us through the night, you know. Here's the soup then. I've not enough bowls, I'm afraid."

He set the kettle in the middle of the floor and they all had at it with their spoons, right from the pot, happy as a flock of chickens on threshing day. The storm did all the typical stormy things you would expect, with wind that howled and rain that slashed, and they all cuddled up together to sleep through it, with heads in laps and arms around shoulders, all in one great pile with the cat purring loudly on top.

⇢ Six ⇠

STORMS SEEM TO COME AND GO by caprice, but in fact they travel with a purpose and follow a definite path. Anyone with time to gather the records and stomach to review them may plot the general courses on a map: the winter blasts that come down from the north; the summer squalls that sweep up from the west, smelling of spices. Storms in the spring blow in off the sea. They smell of salt and tar, for those who care to notice. They roll across the river plain, drenching it utterly, the wettest of all storms. Then they roll up to the Furrows and the mountains, where they are checked until spent.

The Furrows is a terrible and remote country, far to the west and north of everything, packed up against the base of the mountains: mile after mile of craggy hills of gravel and shale with hardly a green thing growing anywhere. At this time, and in this tale, if any traveler had been out that way searching for rare medicinal plants or avoiding legal entanglements, she would have seen the storm move in rather more slowly than usual, lower and darker, dropping more and more rain on the bald land.

Water simply runs off the stony earth in that place, down the long channels for miles. It stirs up the mud, it moves the rocks around, and perhaps some of it seeps into the hard soil, but for the most part it simply flows, tumbling along until the channels become streams and the streams become brooks and the brooks empty one by one into the headwaters of the river. The river then winds through a canyon, somewhat north of anyplace anyone in his right mind would choose to live. The torrents of rain wash dead trees off the slopes and into the river. The last of the ice is just breaking up here. At narrow places in the canyon ice and logs jam up and block the flow, creating temporary lakes of muddy, swirling water that swell and then burst to great dramatic effect.

And each little lake that bursts cascades down into the next, all the way down the canyon until at last the whole thing is washed out onto the plain. The river at this point is so excited about its robust new contents it can barely contain itself. Just look at its tangles of logs and floes of ice! What a lovely, murky brown it has become! Just wait until they see this down in the valley!

* * *

→ SEVEN ←

AND LO, THE PEOPLE OF THE CITY woke the day after the storm to find they had survived to see the bright blue sky again. They found the river somewhat swollen and the streets washed utterly clean. They congratulated themselves on their tenacity and brimming cisterns. Such a gale and such rain! The air had seemed half water! Those who could afford glass windows congratulated themselves on their ability to afford replacements.

The markets were a trifle slow to open, as one might expect, but by noonish things were back to normal. A bit crowded, even, as people rushed to get the day's produce in the house before the next showers came, as they surely would. And what a strange lot of people there were milling around: wastrels from under the bridges, complaining that the rising river had flushed them out of their so-called homes.

Well, that was bound to happen from time to time, wasn't it? It couldn't be helped—no, it couldn't really be helped at all; it must be lived with. Although it certainly made for cluttered, untidy market-places. Hadn't those people someplace else to go?

Just past noon Wood Bridge was closed to cart traffic by the captain of the guard at that post. This edition of the bridge was fifteen years old and bulging most alarmingly before the swollen river. Farmers with their produce, already delayed by the muddy roads, were compelled to truck their goods up to Old Bridge or turn for home. Unhappy with either choice (the tolls at Old Bridge were somewhat higher than Wood Bridge, but no one would sell any peas and new carrots back home, would they?), some stayed to set up an impromptu market catering to the trickle of foot traffic that still crossed Wood Bridge from the City side.

Water began to lap at the highest piers of the bridges, up to the very doorsill of the Black Hearth and the little chapel on the other side. Kolloper Underbridge remained to watch the residents of his kingdom pack up their belongings into rude bundles and head off in search of any ground not under water.

"This ain't bad," he said. "The Hearth's stood here since before the bridge was built and she'll be standing when it's long gone."

Across the river, between the piers he watched Father Whatever-His-Name-Is wading through the water with a bundle and a pewter candelabra.

By midafternoon, the rain had returned. But now it was only a misty, spitting rain, as in the weeks before the storm—just enough to keep things damp. Tiny rivulets flowed down the stone sides of the buildings and between the cobbles of the streets. In a million places water dribbled into the river, which rose steadily. Kolloper retrieved a bottle or two and climbed up onto the roof of the Black Hearth and watched Father Whoever make one last trip from the chapel.

"See you on the other side, Father," he said. "You think this is bad? This ain't no flood."

The water rose above the docks at the harbor and all the ocean-going ships headed downstream as a precaution against being run aground or cast adrift. Second Bridge was overtopped. Wood Bridge collapsed an hour before dark, carrying some small, unfortunate number of citizens with it. And just as darkness fell—just as the sky was almost black—the richest of the rich were the first to see an extraordinary sight that would be part of the lore of the City for years to come.

From their houses on the northern point of the island, they saw through the gloom what appeared to be a tumbling wall of water and trees and timbers. As it drew closer, it became clear that, in fact, that is exactly what it was, with some admixture of wrecked houses, broken river barges, waterlogged furniture, and the occasional screaming person in need of immediate rescue. All this debris rushed past the high people in their high houses and collected against the bridges. Two spans of North Bridge collapsed almost immediately. High Bridge, being a single span and the highest in the city, was spared. East Bridge withstood the assault but was overtopped and became a very effective dam. New Bridge crumbled to rubble almost at the first touch.

But Old Bridge, the venerable right arm of the city, remained resolute and simply collected whatever flotsam happened to wash against its piers. As the water rose, it lifted the most interesting collection of detritus almost level with the deck of the bridge, including the front half of a very fine river barge containing Billet Holdfast, the executor of Feasley-on-Lobbe.

Some good-hearted citizens helped him from the rubble onto the bridge. Whatever happened to your town? they wanted to know. What has become of your empire?

Holdfast gestured vacantly at the growing heap of rubble washing up against the bridge.

"You're looking at it, I think," he said.

As they spoke, Kolloper clambered out from under the bridge onto the top of the remains of Feasley-on-Lobbe and was likewise helped up onto the bridge.

"Thank you kindly," he said. "Very considerate of you to bring your town down here to give an old man a lift."

* * *

→ Eight ←

FOR THE NEXT WEEK things were very dicey in the city. The Low Quarter was completely submerged. Eastbridge was under three feet of water. (East Bridge is the bridge, Eastbridge is the neighborhood. Do you see?) Water reached the very lip of the Old Fort. The remaining dry parts of the city were thronged with people. Nothing and no one could get in or out. Of all the bridges, only two were passable. High Bridge still stood, but the bank on the other side had washed out and few had the fortitude to attempt the leap from the end of the bridge to the ragged edge of the roadway. Old Bridge stood as strong as ever, but one had to cross a flooded plain on the opposite side to get to its foot.

So anyone on the island who hadn't been washed away found his options somewhat limited, to say the least. Waterlogged and famished crowds wandered the streets or collected at the feet of buildings. Those whose homes remained intact found their larders emptying with alarming speed. Emergency rules against profiteering were swiftly invoked and largely ignored. The bakers at New House gave away as many loaves as they sold. Some good-hearted rich people brought as many of the newly homeless as they could support into their vast homes. Other good-hearted rich people, by virtue of their absence, allowed their kitchens and pantries to be ransacked by the desperate and the starving.

As the water receded, some things became apparent that would change the character of the City forever. Fully half the Low Quarter was completely washed away, never to be recovered. The harbor and the docks were completely destroyed. Virtually all the tenements and boarding houses in Eastbridge were uninhabitable. Where would the ships dock, assuming they ever returned? Where would the working poor live? Without the working poor, who would unload the ships and polish the silver? And where would the artists live?

These questions reverberated through the economic length and breadth of the island. (Actually, only the artists asked the question about the artists. But the questions about ships and the poor had quite a wide discussion.)

As it happens, I can tell you the answers to all these questions, but none of them has as much bearing on this tale as the one over-riding question on everyone's mind: What under heaven are all these people going to eat?

The simple answer to that is "porridge and turnips." And the complex answer behind that answer is this: After the storm, the farmers in the area learned that Feasley-on-Lobbe had been washed away and they returned to the longer but surer route along the old road to Old Bridge. A small army of carts gathered at the edge of the water and waited as the flood slowly retreated. Every day, and then every hour, more of the road emerged and the carts crept forward until they could splash through the last few yards and gain the bridge, at which point a steady stream of grain and root vegetables began flowing into the city.

By this the people of the City learned there was food to the west, and perhaps work, and perhaps homes. Couldn't life in the country perhaps compare favorably with city life in the boggy Low Quarter or under a bridge? Or maybe a fairer question is, couldn't it have taken something less than a catastrophic flood to spark that idea in some heads? Well, that's neither here nor there. The upshot is that once Old Bridge was opened up, the carts that came in loaded with turnips left loaded with the belongings of refugees, all trundling over the bridge to whatever fate awaited them in the new, green lands to the west.

As for the other questions raised a moment ago, as I said, they have no real bearing on this tale. I will tell you, however, that under Old Bridge at that same time, Kolloper found the Black Hearth still standing, just as he had expected. Father Whatever found that the chapel had collapsed, just as he had feared.

"If I can get over there, I'll give you a hand," Kolloper called. "And if you can get over here, I'll give you a drink."

→> NINE <←

OH, VERY WELL, you've been patient enough, I suppose. The other issues the city faced were resolved thusly:

The docks were rebuilt, largely with timbers collected from the wreckage of Feasley-on-Lobbe. Executor Holdfast oversaw the project and became the new harbormaster. What was left of the Low Quarter was rebuilt with warehouses that support the harbor, and boarding houses and inns that cater to sailors. No one lives there permanently now. New Bridge was rebuilt and improved, and a new settlement developed on the other side, called New Town. In time, it became a replacement for the Low Quarter. That is, the working poor live there, but—being outside the city—it has its own jurisdiction and is much more pleasant and safe, if a bit less colorful, than the Low Quarter ever was.

And the artists? The artists occupied the Old Fort, evicting the two prisoners they found there and refusing to give it up. They remain there to this day, emitting manifestos and other such nonsense and running something they call the *Academie Collectif* or some such ghastly thing.

Part XV

Back Where We Started

→ Oпe ←

Y ES, AND THREE DAYS' JOURNEY to the west of the City (by the straightest route) lay the smoldering wreckage of a town presided over by a forlorn nincompoop in a cockeyed house as empty as Yorick's skull. Perhaps that is too harsh a description. But the year and a half since the fire had not seen much in the way of improvements. The population was still a fraction of what it had been, the marketplace still struggling, the roads but lightly traveled.

However, the town did have a few things going for it. It was not under water. It was not flotsam washed up on the rocky shores of the island. The spring produce was coming in nicely, certainly more than anyone could sell or eat, since there were so few people left in the town.

All that did little to console the Burgermeister. A year and more had passed since calamity befell the town, yet still he moped around his empty house, sat by a cold fire in his study, ate his tasteless meals with Cook and the Harpies in the kitchen. The dining room was simply too vast.

The town councilmen—the few that remained—brought papers now and again, and he approved them all. What difference could it make? The town was a shell. The Tapping of the Keg had been forgone last fall for the first time since the beginning of time. The world had clearly spun free from its axis. What possible harm could come from approving this or that petty resolution?

And then the storm blew the rest of the roof off the Beetle and he was entreated by the proprietor for a grant to have it re-thatched. Why couldn't the Beetle pay for the job itself, for mercy's sake? Heaven knew they charged enough for their watery ale.

That cut the proprietor to the quick, it did, for—begging your pardon, but His Municipality well knew that business hadn't been what it should these past months. It would be a shame, it would, to have to close up and leave the town with only the Spotted Dog.

"Oh, very well," the Burgermeister sighed. "Call over the thatcher and see what he says."

As it turned out, the thatcher was more than willing to take the job, and at a substantial discount from his normal rate.

"Work's been scarce, you might say, what with half the town gone away."

Indeed, the roofless stone walls of a hundred cottages stood like empty husks, open to the sky. The town should have been a thatcher's dream, and the thatcher had indeed spent the whole past year laying up bales of cane and straw. But with so many people gone, if someone who remained found his roof in disrepair, he simply moved to a vacant house with its roof intact. So the thatcher was willing not just to repair but to replace the whole roof of the Beetle for half price plus a quart of ale at each day's end, simply to demonstrate his craft and remind everyone what a good, tight roof looked like.

Thus a small number of improvement projects began, the first for many months. The marketplace was finally cleared of the last scorched timbers. People began inquiring about plaster and whitewash. A most annoying pothole in High Street that had been diverting foot traffic and cartwheels alike for over a year was filled in and paved over with new cobbles.

The Burgermeister even indulged himself so far as to go to the muddy place in the square and gaze at it with visions of a fountain in his mind. Was that a spark of optimism he felt? He hardly dared consider it. Optimism had, for so long, seemed impossible and offensive, if not downright profane. Still, one couldn't stew in one's own juices forever. Silver linings, and all.

⇢ two ⇠

WHEN NEWS OF THE FLOOD reached the town and people learned the city had been cut off, the Burgermeister's first thought was for the well-being of the city's larders. Surely some use could be made of the surplus produce that had been piling up. He sent word around that a relief caravan, organized by himself, would depart with all haste, the levies reduced to a very reasonable amount in light of the present difficulties.

The next day, when he learned that Feasley-on-Lobbe had been washed out to sea, he paused a moment to lament the fate of those who had lost their livelihood, railed briefly against heaven's injustice, pontificated for a bit on the value of competition in a thriving marketplace, then raised the levies right back up to where they had been.

Lack of flexibility, that had been their downfall. Shortsightedness. Water transport had its place, he supposed, but consider: A highway, no matter how ill behaved, will never swell up and swallow your town whole, now, will it? Wagons are cheaper than barges to build, and if they leak they don't sink out of sight in the roadway. He congratulated himself repeatedly on being the great-grandson of a visionary landsman and not some upstart river rat.

He particularly enjoyed the phrase "upstart river rat" and muttered it to himself as he worked to guard against flagging spirits. His enthusiasm felt thin and fragile, laid over his habitual despondency in a brittle film that might crack at any moment. His glassy fervor was maintained by a careful balance of restless activity and grandiose planning.

When, after another week or so, the first refugees arrived, his initial anxiety was checked by a stroke of genius. He realized that the huddled bundles of rags wheeling themselves into the square were not simply vagrants or beggars with designs on his well-known charitable feelings. No, they were men and women with families and goods and skills who only needed a home and a place to work. And what had Bergerton in abundance but empty homes and shops?

He offered a roofless cottage to any family that needed a place to live and an empty shop to any craftsman. If they thatched it before the next winter, it was theirs. If the original occupants returned and complained, well, he would deal with that later. For my part, I can't say whether a roofless house in the town is any better than a tenement flat in the Low Quarter, but any walls are better than no walls, I suppose, and the thatcher soon had more work than he could manage and was looking forward to a most prosperous summer.

Of course, one shouldn't be too reckless with one's resources, the Burgermeister mused, and in his quieter moments he admitted that some unsavory characters might slip into the town under cover of his good graces. Generosity was a magnet for fraud, he opined, as he had the locks changed in the house. Civil disruption is an invitation to the unscrupulous and opportunistic, he informed several newly-minted Marshals. Those people had better not meddle with this now, he muttered to the world at large. "This" was the rosebush, and the Burgermeister was not prepared to take any chances. He added more pulleys and wires to his alarm device, and issued a decree that prohibited the unauthorized cutting of any plant material and posted it on his own doorstep.

"That should do it," he muttered with some satisfaction.

The rose, just beginning to bud out, declined to comment.

The Burgermeister had his hands more than full, managing it all. He met each arrival and considered each applicant himself. He walked the town with each bedraggled family to help them find a suitable place and provided them with a license of occupancy (conditional on certain fine points of legal nonsense) signed by his own hand. He toured the square with each prospective merchant and haggled over locations. He doled out craftsmen to the available workshops and ordered additional pews for both churches, to be paid for from his own coffers.

Magnanimity suited him, he reflected one afternoon as he sat in his study wondering whether it was too early for a small brandy. Certainly, Bergerton had more to offer in the way of stable housing and employment than any upstart river town that let itself be washed away so easily. He said it again to himself as he poured. *Upstart river rats.*

And then a most ungodly racket of shrill female screaming pandemonium issued from the kitchen and caused him to douse himself all down the front and fling his third-favorite brandy glass up nearly to the ceiling.

"Great heaven!" he shouted. "Great heaven!"

He bolted toward the kitchen as well as he was able, having become somewhat more unwieldy in recent months.

"Great heaven, what is it?" He had a momentary vision of giant river rats running about the room with the severed limbs of their victims hanging from their mouths.

What met him instead, thankfully, was a simple domestic kitchen scene, with the dominoes scattered and the teakettle upset, and Cook and the Harpies shrieking and waving their arms, crowding around a disreputable-looking, bearded madman and two youths, one stout and one gangly to the point of famine, begrimed and besmirched and to all appearances frightened out of their wits by the attentions of the women.

"Oh Nick! Oh Cord!" Lucy wailed.

"Mercy! Mercy!" Maggie shrilled.

Sylvia sobbed wordlessly and Cook turned from one to the next, pointing with her spoon.

"Some nerve! The state of you! Some nerve! To think!"

"Great heaven," the Burgermeister whispered. "Can it be?"

Indeed it could, and if you are as surprised as he was, well, you haven't been paying attention. With the Low Quarter flooded, the bridges washed out, the city in turmoil, and to all appearances a riot brewing, Mr. Broome and Cordage had found Robert hiding from the mob that surrounded New House on the sixth day, made a quick assessment of their fortunes, and joined the throng leaving the city.

"But what about—?" Robert had asked.

"Never mind about that," Cordage had said, and that was that. Back to Bergerton they went.

The Burgermeister pawed his way through the throng and grasped each boy lovingly by the collar.

"How in heaven's name?" he said. "Look at the state of you!"

"We come in by the kitchen," said Cordage.

"The front door was locked," said Robert.

"Well of course it's locked," said the Burgermeister. "With all this riff-raff about, you can't be too careful. We can't have just anyone wandering in!"

"Riff-raff," giggled Mr. Broome. "Riff-raff. Oh, Lucy! I've made so much string!"

→ THREE ←

WHEN COOK HAD RECOVERED enough to form complete sentences she scolded the boys for not informing her in advance that they were coming. Three more for dinner! The nerve! Well, she supposed she could find something to make do. The rest of the company retired to the study so the Burgermeister might retrieve his glass and try again to pour a drink before his nerves gave out completely.

But no sooner had he sat down, and no sooner had blankets been thrown over the settee for those grimy boys, and no sooner had he asked for more details—any details at all, really—than there was a knocking at the door, and voices in the hallway, and Tall Butler entered to announce, "Some young men to see you, sir."

"Are they riff-raff or reprobates?"

"I really couldn't say, sir."

"Well, then, are they malcontents or unwarranted?"

"I can ask."

"Oh, just show them in, for goodness' sake."

Tall Butler bowed diffidently and turned to go. He had been working on diffidence lately and thought he had managed it rather well. The Burgermeister wasn't as impressed and thought his manner merely timorous. But no matter. Brandy in hand, feet upon the hearth, boys on the settee, he was about to—

Great heavens! Soldiers! Are we under attack? But no, of course not.

"Great heaven," he whispered as his glass slipped to the floor. "My boys?"

As indeed it was, the officers of the Bergerton Boys themselves, Captain and Corporal Berger, respectively, flanked by a full contingent of future Mrs. Officers, in all their threadbare, road-weary, footsore, glimmering glory.

The scene was everything you might expect. The young men, as handsome as ever, scruffy and well-traveled as they were, probably saluted their father or some such nonsense, while the Burgermeister likely became misty and drew his sons to him in an awkward embrace. And there were introductions all around, and how lovely, and couldn't you have written, and how terrible, and then the Burgermeister sent Henders down to the cellar for a bottle. A bottle of what?

"It doesn't matter. Anything! Everything! And glasses, all the glasses!"

Cook came in and threw up her hands.

"Four more for dinner, then? And how am I to manage that, I wonder?"

→ FOUR ←

WELL, BEING COOK, she managed robustly, if simply, with a large kettle of stewed miscellany, a brick of cheese, and all the bread she could scrape together. The dining room, which had been doubling for Town Halln, was in no state for dining—nor, she reasoned, were the new arrivals in any state for such a refined space—so she cleared off the kitchen table and began laying out.

But what an uncooperative bunch these new arrivals were! It was just as she remembered, bodies in and out the doors, up and down the stairs, snatches of everyone's stories flying about and colliding in the air. Maggie was a whirlwind, trying desperately to know everything that had happened to everyone all at once. Sylvia and Lucy oscillated between doting on their sons (and husband, let us not forget) and helping the LaPierre cousins with rooms and baths and clothes and whatnot. Cheese and bread and new berries seemed to fly off the table faster than she put them out. At this rate dinner would be over before it had begun!

And in the middle of it all, the Burgermeister sat in his study, trying to have a manly drink with his prodigal sons, misty with pride and unable to make head or tail of anything they told him, so far did it stray from the exploits he had imagined for them. He searched their meandering tales in vain for the glorious battles, the midnight raids, the comrades dying in their arms. Still, they were magnificent. Magnificent men, his sons had become. It was almost painful to see.

And with such a ruckus in the house now, the knock at the door was hardly heard, except by Tall Butler, who was in the hallway practicing his diffidence. But when the door was opened the Burgermeister could hear, even from as far away as his study, a voice—a man's voice with an unmistakable foreign lilt.

"Thunderation!" he cried. "Conflagration! How dare he? Does he mock me? Did he not understand a year ago that he was banished forever? I'll have him quartermained! Banished from this town, forbidden from this house, forever banned from this place!"

All this bluster was affected in part to buy time while the Burgermeister tried to rise from his deep chair. Being somewhat out of breath and, as I mentioned, somewhat more cumbersome than in the past, it took some doing.

"Henders!" he bellowed, lurching finally to his feet.

Tall Butler returned to the room, feeling that diffidence wasn't really called for. He considered switching to obsequiousness, although that wasn't scheduled until next month, and he was scarcely confident in his abilities in that regard. Nevertheless, he was prepared to give it a try. He took a deep breath, but before he could begin the Burgermeister erupted again.

"No! Why does he torment me? There is nothing here for him. Does he not see? Is it not enough to see the scorched stones and the bleached bones of this town? Must he still come to visit our wounds with salt? Does—Should—"

The Burgermeister paused for breath, and in that small space, in the little silence between the Burgermeister's dark thoughts, a mild voice was heard.

"Meister? If you please. The Princess."

Slogoyban, standing in the doorway as obsequious as you please with hat in hand, inclined his head. The Burgermeister stared.

"You!" he sputtered.

Slogoyban gestured, looking askance into the hallway, gently coaxing.

Whereupon, after some hesitation, the Princess stepped into the room and curtseyed gracefully and pertly, all her spunk and Lexi's poise rolled into one. The Burgermeister stared.

"You," he whispered.

"Grandfather," she said. Then she started to tremble. "Hello, Grandfather."

* * *

→∂ FIVE ←

SUCH A SCENE! You would have thought all the missing children had come home at once. Cook came in to announce supper and was pulled into such a jumble of embraces and tears that by the time she had extricated herself she was quite done with the matter of cooking.

She handed the ladle to the Corporal.

"The kettle's on the stove, if anyone cares."

The Corporal's solution was to bring the kettle into the study, along with an assortment of bowls and mugs, while Henders gathered the last of the bread and cheese. The study was by far the coziest room in the house, and now it was filled to the brim with the most lively, exhausted chattering anyone could remember. Seated on the chairs, or on the floor, or on the Burgermeister's desk, or on the hearth, people filled every corner of the room, each trying to hear and be heard, trying to put the whole thing together and not miss a drop.

With all the clamor in the room, it's a wonder the Burgermeister heard the bell at all. But hear it he did, jangling like a wild thing above the window, stirred to life by his bizarre contraption of wires and pulleys.

"Aha!" he cried, lurching from his seat yet again. "The scoundrels! They're at my rose! Away from my rose!"

He huffed through the crowded room, pulled aside the drape, and heaved open the window, the very window through which he had first observed Slogoyban and Lexi, the very drapes he had drawn against his boys' glorious departure. There was, as he had expected, someone at his rose. It was a woman, apparently, hooded and cloaked, smallish and somewhat scrawny—probably oldish, too; he couldn't tell. She was up to her elbows in the sprawling bush, evidently caught by the sleeves of her cloak. She glanced up with small, hard eyes and a look of defiant chagrin.

Then the Burgermeister's glass slipped from his fingers. The third time was too much to ask of the poor thing and it shattered.

"Bonita?" he whispered. "My Bonny?"

"Of course it is, you ridiculous man," I said. "Of course it's me."

→ Six ←

N O ONE ELSE had taken any notice. They continued jabbering away as if what they had to say was the most important thing in the world. But between the Burgermeister and the woman in the rosebush—that is, between Jon and myself—you could have heard a pin drop. Even a very small pin. The most minuscule pin in your sewing kit dropped onto, I don't know, something very soft, like a baby bunny or a bowl of whipped cream. A pin dropped there would have reverberated like a gong in the gulf of silence between us.

Jon seemed intent, for a moment, on pressing thirty-odd years of lost thoughts into that silence, but I hadn't time.

"I'm caught," I said. "My sleeves are caught. Why on earth have you never pruned this monster?"

And with that, the spell was broken. All the years dropped away like the wrappings of a parcel. He was once again that handsome oaf with visions of greatness in his eyes. I was the winsome, willowy creature who once dazzled him right down to the soles of his outlandish shoes. No one else could see it, of course, but that's the way the spell works. It's one of the benefits of being a part-time witch. You can see anyone else in any way you please. I can show you how it works sometime, if you like.

I continued working to extricate my sleeves while Jon stood looking like his heart might explode. I thought, all things considered, that I had really best be on my way, and nearly had myself loose when—

"Auntie Bones!"

Little Robert squeezed into the window beside Jon. His greeting was much more enthusiastic than I felt the situation warranted.

"How did you find us?" he asked. "This is my Uncle Jon's house. We thought you got lost after we excaped the flood."

He climbed out the window and handed me the heel of a loaf.

"Have some bread. This is Uncle Jon."

Yes, yes, I know this is Uncle Jon. *Everybody* has an Uncle Jon. I myself have two.

I had worked out early on who the boys were, despite their childish attempts to conceal their identities. Of course I had. If I seemed surprised to see Robert and Cordage now, well, that was only to perpetuate the illusion out of concern for their feelings. Yes, certainly, at some point in our journey, it must have dawned on me that my young traveling companions were in fact my very own nephews. The family resemblance alone should have been enough. Nothing so plainly obvious could possibly have for so long evaded my acute observational faculties.

Robert tugged on one sleeve but was unable to disengage it from the thorns.

"Cord!" he called. "Come help me get Auntie Bones unstuck!"

Cordage climbed out over the sill and observed us with an infuriating smirk.

"You again," he said. "I should have known. I should have seen it in the *spheres*."

"You and me both," I said.

They were finally able to get me loose, but before I was able to dart into the shadows they bundled me over the sill into the Burgermeister's study and practically into the arms of the Burgermeister himself. I felt *singularly* awkward. I am not accustomed to feeling awkward in any way whatever, so to feel singularly awkward was both disconcerting and infuriating. Disconcerted, furious, and awkward. A most complicated stew of adjectives, to be sure.

"Hello, Uncle Jon," I said.

The Burgermeister, however, simply seemed amused, if somewhat bitterly.

"Hello, Auntie Bones," he said. "Won't you come in and have a drink with me?"

You may, from where you sit, wonder why I had come back to Bergerton at all, and to the house in particular. I can only reply that, once one is caught up in a tide of refugees from a terrible disaster, and once one is swept along in the wake like so much flotsam, one must, to a certain extent, accept the shores onto which one is washed. Oh, I could complain to the sky for leaving only one passable road in the whole country, I could blame my old bones for rattling only so far and no farther. I could curse the rose itself for having only buds—dozens of fat buds all over every cane—and hundreds of treacherous thorns, but not a single bloom. But what would be the point? Circumstances have coalesced around us all in such and such a way, and we might as well see what comes of it.

And it wasn't too late, even still. I could bolt at any moment. The window was at street level—if worse came to worst I could dive through and escape with only minor cuts and bruises.

(I have since learned, by the way, that there is a word for that. For exiting a room through the window. The word is "defenestration." I could *defenestrate* myself from Jon's study, just as Cordage and Robert were *defenestrated* from the inn at Wat's Hump. I suppose I could go back to the beginning and add the word there, but why dwell on the past? Best foot forward, I say.)

"One drink, I suppose," I said. "But I really couldn't stay."

"No," said Jon. "You couldn't."

He set down his favorite pair of brandy glasses—a gift from me, if I recall—and unstoppered the decanter. But his hands were shaking, poor thing, so I reached out and steadied them as best I could. It wouldn't do for any more liquor to be spilled that evening, you know.

→⟩ SEVEN ⟨←

WHILE HE WAS POURING, word seemed to have gotten around the room that something of great portent had happened, so we found ourselves at the center of a silent circle of attention, more wide expectant eyes than I had ever seen in one place before. Among them were my boys—my own boys!—all grown and as handsome as anything, looking as if they were trying to find something in me to recognize. And Maggie, who I supposed I hadn't really the right to call my daughter, looking blank, as if she hadn't a way to categorize me.

And the others: Little Robert and Cordage and Mr. Broome, and Lucy Broome, don't forget, whom I knew from a girl, and Cook and

Old Robert who had wandered downstairs at last, and the butlers and the LaPierre girls and Sylvia and the Princess, all looking as if they expected something from the situation, as if some great question floated overhead that required an answer.

What could they want from me? I had become once again just a doubtful young girl, remember, but they couldn't see that. They only saw the same transient old woman bent over like a shepherd's crook who had stepped in a few moments before.

"Well," I said finally. "The first thing you need to understand is—"

"No," said the Burgermeister. "Not tonight. No questions and no answers. No one is to explain anything to anyone for the rest of the night." He raised his glass. "We will have a toast, and then we will tell stories. Everything will make sense in the morning."

Or so we can hope.

"A toast then," he called out. "Anyone?"

There was a pause, and then someone, one of the butlers, I think, said, "Health and long life?"

"Heaven help us," said the Burgermeister. "Anything but that."

"Anything but that!" shouted Mr. Broome, raising his glass high.

"Here, here!" said Old Butler.

So we drank to "anything but that" and then the Burgermeister told a story.

"When I was a boy," he said, "my father sat me down in this very room and said, 'Son . . .'"

I tried with all my might to find a salient point in it, some hidden depth that would illuminate the magnitude of the evening's events, but to no avail. Like all his stories, it wandered from one point to another like a ball of yarn batted about by a kitten.

After he finished, Mr. Broome told a tale from his days with the Sisters. Then the Captain, with assistance from the Corporal, told a humorous story about a rabbit hunt that occurred while the regiment was lost in the north. I watched for a chance to sneak away, but Jon kept refilling my glass and I didn't want to be rude. I had intended to be on my way, you know, but with the late hour I thought I might as well inquire about sleeping in the stables before I departed in the morning.

And then I was awakened, alone in the study, by a most unpleasant commotion streaming in the window with the morning light. I sat up on the settee—where apparently I had been cocooned with a blanket and pillow by one or another of the butlers—and tried to find my shoes. Outside, a swirl of voices continued to ebb and flow with tones of wonder and consternation, punctuated with such nonsensical expressions as "Golly!" and "My word!" and "Well, I'll be!" I gave up on the shoes, made my way to the window, and pushed it open. The crowd fell silent.

There was an impractically excessive amount of light outside, but squinting I was able to see the family—Jon and Little Robert and Cordage, the Captain and the Corporal with their new ladies, the aunts and the Princess and half the staff—along with a growing number of neighbors and passers-by, all gathered around the front of the house staring at the rosebush, wide-eyed and incredulous.

The bush was covered in blossoms. Absolutely covered, as if every closed bud from the night before had burst at once, in every color from morning until dusk—pale pinks, fierce reds, plump yellows, musky auburns, demure purples, peaches, plums, and everything in between: no two blooms alike, all glittering exultantly in the brilliant newborn sunlight. It shimmered. It practically vibrated. The colors flowed and coalesced, as if even more new buds were bursting open as we watched, more and more flowers crowding in front of one another. The crowd was rapt, caught up in the same swirl of color and light, looking at the rose and looking at me as though they expected something. Still half asleep, still squinting against the light, I couldn't tell whether their faces were reflected in the flowers or the other way 'round.

"Good morning," I said.

"Good morning," said everyone.

Coda

ONE THING LED TO ANOTHER, and I did not depart that morning, nor the next. The house was all a-tumble, with so many people returning after so long and some new people besides. It was all the ladies of the house could do to maintain some kind of order. Fortunately, there was so much to do that there was relatively little friction between them. The ladies of the house, I mean. But I imagined that in time the normal tug-of-war over tea cozies and hand washing would resume. I had not, at that point, asserted claim to any authority, although there was no shortage of opportunities for my opinion to be of great value. All things in good time.

I am working actively to distance myself from that "Auntie Bones" appellation, which serves no purpose in the present circumstance. Never mind that in the depths of my heart I know I will be Auntie Bones until the very end. I also deny that I have ever told a fortune to any of them in their various travels, ever passed any of them along any road or lane, been anywhere near a battlefield or prison of any kind, or rubbed shoulders with the theatrical elite in the City. As far as anyone knows—as far as you know, and I will hold you to it—I am simply Bonita W Berger, lately returned after a lengthy absence and gradually resuming whatever place may be found for me.

I no longer cast fortunes. It is doubtful, really, that I ever did, and rumors to that effect are to be treated with utmost skepticism. In any case I certainly won't be casting any fortunes in the future, for all the trouble they cause me.

No, it's the quiet life from now on. I've forsworn cabbage farming and all the rest. No more the vagrant life for me. No sir, no madam—all those many acquaintances of mine scattered through the district, amassed through all those carefree years of travel, they'll just have to make do with the insides of their skulls where memories of me are concerned. If they need me you can tell them where to find me, residing quietly behind these sturdy walls or enjoying a peaceful cider at the Beetle.

Oh, very well, just one more fortune. For old time's sake, as it were.

Let's see.

Robert Berger the Elder, who doesn't recognize me or anyone else (although he sometimes calls Little Robert "Johnny"), will linger for a year or so before he finally passes on, to the mixed grief and relief of the whole household.

Sylvia and Little Robert will open a bakery in The Shop, which will be the most successful concern at that location in anyone's memory. The LaPierre cousins will help out at first but will then open a competing bakery across the square. The ensuing conflict (which will come to be known as the Great Bread War) will divide the town and result in several fairly strained holiday dinners. Little Robert will one day find himself married to a charming, plain girl from town and end up the happiest Berger of any generation before or since.

The Burgermeister's boys will marry their Lesser Spleen girls (the name of Lesser Spleen will never change) and devote their adult years to the maintenance and promotion of the local militia, which will never be called to active duty again. They will live together with their families in the big house, and no one except perhaps their wives will be able to tell them apart when they are not in uniform.

The Broomes will endeavor to establish another rope and string emporium and will continue to be hampered by Mr. Broome's tenuous grasp on reality. Cordage will leave for the City, ostensibly to attend university, but will run away to sea at the first opportunity and return a few years later with a tattoo of a treasure map on one arm and a girl—an actual girl, not a tattoo—named Louise on the other. Louise will be from someplace called "California," which until that moment will have been thought by the residents of Bergerton to be a place no less fabulous than Atlantis.

Margarita, my dear Maggie, will stun the known world one day by announcing her engagement to Mindulus Bunnister, the assistant choirmaster at Our Lady. They will be married in June of that year, with the service presided over by both priests so as not to cause a schism.

The Burgermeister will manage the town well enough for a few more years and then will retire to focus on designs for the fountain, which will never be built. His sons (our sons!) will not take over rule of the town, their military duties taking up all their time. But the Princess, to the surprise of all except her grandfather, will turn out to be the ablest administrator anyone could ask for.

She will be serene and poised, unflappable in negotiations. She will be reasonable and prudent with the coffers but will have a fine sense of those things that add color to a town's life. Under her leadership, Bergerton will build its first theater and establish a public library. She will maintain a long and cordial association with His Junior Excellency, mayor of the City, traveling there at least twice a year for the rest of her life.

But she will never marry, and she will be the last Berger to rule Bergerton. Her final grand projects will be the establishment of an elected mayoral office and the surveying of the right-of-way for a rail line to the City, which will forever remove any economic threat from Feasley-on-Lobbe or any other upstart river town.

I, for my part, will grow smaller and wiser and more indispensable until I am finally installed in a niche in the wall of the kitchen, where I can keep an eye on Cook.

And you, my darlings, if you choose to believe it—if you care to take these words into your heart and let them guide you all your days—you will continue on as you have to this point, turning sometimes left and sometimes right, making this choice or that, attaching great weight and value to one thing while ignoring or even actively avoiding another thing, working to get closer to you-know-who, trying to stay away from that other awful person, juggling heartbreak and boredom—and hopefully enjoying a nice cup of something from time to time—forever after, until the end.

→ Acknowledgments ←

TK

⟿ About the Author ⬿

K ENNETH HUNTER GORDON ANSWERS TO "Kenny" in real life. He's reasonably handy with tools and can probably fix it if he can find the right glue. His favorite punctuation mark is the ellipsis. He lives in Salt Lake City with his family; prior to that he lived in Los Angeles, where he played in a reggae band and almost met Tracey Ullman. He's been publishing poetry and short fiction in literary magazines for many years. This is his first novel

Seriously, the ellipsis . . . Is it a pregnant pause? A raised eyebrow? A wistful trailing off? It has such character, yet it's so ambiguous. Like arugula . . .

CPSIA information can be obtained
at www.ICGtesting.com
Printed in the USA
BVHW070432081118
532490BV00001B/1/P